A DELICATE
MARRIAGE

A DELICATE MARRIAGE

MARGARITA BARRESI

atmosphere press

For Andrew, for everything.

PROLOGUE

The Hurricane 1928
- Marco -

Marco Rios spotted the red flag fluttering above the police station and sprinted home, giddy with anticipation. *A hurricane! Finally!* Weaned on legendary tales of "The Big One," the San Ciríaco hurricane of 1899, he yearned to experience nature's full power, a typical fourteen-year-old living for forbidden adventure. But when he burst into his wooden house and registered Papá and Mamá's somber faces, he tamped down his enthusiasm. They'd been busy securing their belongings and moving things off the floor in case of flooding.

"Susana, take the children to the church," Papá said, grabbing his straw hat. "I'm going to get my mother."

Mamá paled. "Have you gone completely loco, Diego? Tell me you're joking." She grabbed a basket of sewing notions, stuffed it onto an already crowded shelf, and shook her head at Papá. "It'll take you hours. You won't make it there and back in time."

"Ay, mi amor, she's my mother. I have to get her," Papá said. He pointed out the window. "It's not even raining yet."

"I'll go with you, Papá," Marco said.

"Absolutely not!" Mamá clutched Marco's arm. "You're staying right here. One loco in the family is enough."

"Marco, I need you here to take care of your mother and sister." Papá addressed him as an equal. "Can you do that?"

Marco's chest expanded. "Sí, Papá. I'll protect them with my life." He held eye contact with his father for several seconds. Papá nodded, quickly kissed each of them, and headed out. Mamá clenched her fists and released a grunt of frustration. She fired a few choice words under her breath before bolting back into action. She grabbed three blankets, a handful of guavas, and her rosary before shepherding Marco and Julia toward the town plaza, where the church bells clanged a warning.

San Felipe crashed into the shores of Yabucoa before Marco's father could return. As the storm pummeled the church's cement building, those who'd taken refuge inside blocked their ears against the high-pitched howling of the brutal wind. Lips moved in silent prayer while the humid air intensified the weighty tang of incense. Marco, Mamá, and Julia huddled on a wooden pew near the white marble altar, their bones vibrating with each violent gust. Electricity crackled around them. Their arm hairs stood at attention.

When the building began to shake violently, Padre Palacios ordered the windows opened just an inch to relieve the pressure. The storm's cacophony was more present with the windows ajar, and the lashing rain began to leak inside. Time stood still while the wind hummed, whistled, and howled a deafening song of destruction.

Marco, fully cowed, was deeply ashamed of his earlier excitement and naiveté. How could Papá and Abuela survive this storm's fury without a strong shelter? San Felipe was a beast from Hell.

The storm raged overnight, and though Marco fought to keep his eyes open, he eventually surrendered to sleep. He woke to the smell of burnt candle wax and the sound of weeping and pulled himself upright to see Padre Palacios holding his mother's hand, offering the usual platitude, "If he's gone, my dear, it's God's will."

Marco trembled uncontrollably, his mind refusing to accept the unthinkable. He sprang to his feet, darted to the back of the church, and pounded up the bell tower stairs to the town's highest vantage point. He scanned the devastated valley for a trace of his father. The countryside, just yesterday a hundred shades of green, appeared denuded as if a giant's hand had ripped out its flora. Ancient trees lay tortured on the ground, and few houses, including his own, remained standing. The vast detritus of humanity lay scattered: a black cauldron, a doll's torso, a twisted bicycle. Smashed avocados, plantains, papayas, and guavas littered the ground alongside pig, chicken, horse, and cow carcasses. The destruction was incomprehensible. Yet the sky shone an incongruous bright blue, as if denying culpability.

Papá, where are you? Marco's steely grip on the steeple's railing turned his knuckles white. He stayed there all day, pacing back and forth in the turret, holding vigil for his father.

In the four long, frantic weeks that followed, neither Papá's nor Abuela's body surfaced. Marco had examined every inch of Guayanés Beach, where coconut palms that once grew along the shore in majestic rows lay crisscrossed in the sand like scattered pencils. He'd scoured the flattened and flooded sugarcane fields, combed the banks of the swollen Guayanés River, and sorted through endless heaps of felled branches, boulders, pieces of homes, and panels of corrugated zinc. Within days, the heavy, repugnant stench of death had saturated the air. Mosquitoes, rats, and cockroaches abounded while the coquí tree frog's evening melody sounded muted.

After another day of fruitless searching, Marco approached the khaki tent he shared with Mamá and Julia, one of a sea of canvas shelters the National Guard had set up for survivors. The ground, pure mud in the days after the hurricane, had dried into a landscape of ditches he traversed via a network of wooden planks. He wore black wool pants, some American's idea of what was needed on the island, and the scratchy fabric irritated his skin and made him sweat.

He studied what was left of his family. Julia sat stiffly on a wooden crate outside their tent and shrieked as Mamá stabbed a comb through her hair, attacking a particularly unruly tangle. Marco's heart ached at how thin they were. How long would they have to live like this? Without Papá's earnings, they had no funds to build a new home nor promise of an income large enough to afford a mortgage.

Would they be reduced to living in a mountain shack like destitute jíbaros? His throat closed, and his eyes pooled. He shook his head. No! He wouldn't succumb to his grief. He was the man of the family now, and he'd be strong for Mamá and Julia. He'd promised Papá he'd take care of them. It was up to him to improve their circumstances, to protect his family from ever again having to endure such a crisis. Marco made a vow. He'd dedicate his life to improving the circumstances of his people. Next time, his family would have a solid and modern home. Next time, Puerto Rico would be prepared.

PART
ONE

CHAPTER 1

- Isabela -
September 1935

Isabela Soto, astounded at the man in the front row's resemblance to Carlos Gardel, had trouble concentrating. Gardel, the Argentinian King of Tango, had tragically perished in an airplane accident last June. Could this be his ghost? The man's liquid brown eyes had locked in on her from the moment she took to the makeshift stage in the tropical courtyard replete with clove-scented alelí flowers. His stare unnerved her. One more poem, and she'd be done declaiming for these University of Puerto Rico students, could leave the spotlight, not something she usually relished. *Focus Isa.* Gardel's doppelganger sure was focusing on *her.*

Aware the twilight turned her hazel eyes dark green and showed her aquiline nose and high cheekbones to their best advantage, Isabela inhaled deeply before projecting the first lines of the Manuel Fernández Juncos poem, "La Serenata,"

"Eran las diez de la noche,
y la hermosa luna llena—
como un globo de alabastro
que en las olas de luz navega—
daba claridad al cielo,
penumbra dulce á la tierra,
y ese misterioso encuentro,
esa majestad serena
con que impresionan el alma
las noches puertorriqueñas."

Isa loved the rhyming story of Fernando, a scoundrel who roams the countryside enjoying "that mysterious enchantment, that serene majesty with which Puerto Rican nights stamp the soul." He's looking for naive girls to seduce with his song but must instead deal with Juana's savvy father. More than twenty stanzas later, she finished to enthusiastic applause. She'd delivered Fernández Juncos's words with humor and feeling and basked in the crowd's adoration as she curtsied, left the stage, and made her way to Dr. Chardón, the University chancellor. As always after a performance, she felt whole, a void inside her filled to overflowing.

Dr. Chardón congratulated Isabela with a kiss on the cheek. After hearing her declaim many times at the Casino de Puerto Rico, the exclusive social club they both belonged to, he'd asked her to provide the entertainment this evening. She'd jumped at the chance, always eager for an opportunity to perform. Dr. Chardón steered her indoors toward the refreshments, and she sensed rather than saw Gardel's twin rise and follow. The three arrived simultaneously at a table laden with Spanish cured meats and cheeses.

"Ah, Señorita Soto, let me introduce you to one of our top students, Marco Rios," the chancellor said, welcoming her admirer with an enthusiastic pat on the back.

Isabela blinked rapidly to clear her vision. Part of her had really believed this young man was Gardel's spirit. But no. He was merely a flesh-and-blood someone else. She'd met the real thing when Gardel had visited Puerto Rico that spring, just before his death. No, Marco Soto wasn't Gardel, but he was the singer's double with dark hair brilliantined off the forehead, soulful eyes, and a charming smile.

She offered her hand, and Marco took it gently, bent his head, and feigned a kiss over it as was proper.

"Encantado, Señorita Soto. Thank you for those renditions."

"It was my pleasure." Isa beamed a high wattage smile.

"Ah, so you enjoyed my little attempt at cultural enrichment?" Dr. Chardón shook his finger at Marco. "You business majors need to care about more than numbers."

"I absolutely agree," Marco answered before addressing Isa again with reproach. "If only you'd included my favorite poem."

"And what, pray tell, is your favorite poem?" she said, amused. Was it some sort of nursery rhyme?

Marco took a deep breath and, with considerably more intensity than was warranted, recited,

> *"Cultivo una rosa blanca*
> *En junio como en enero*
> *Para el amigo sincero*
> *Que me da su mano franca.*
> *Y para el cruel que me arranca*
> *El corazón con que vivo,*
> *Cardo ni ortiga cultivo;*
> *Cultivo una rosa blanca."*

"¡Qué dramatico!" Dr. Chardón laughed after Marco raised one arm in the air and swept it downward, bowing to the floor. Isabela took delight in this boy's goofy gusto. He'd delivered the poem as if it were a tragic Shakespearean piece.

"Ah, José Martí. One of Cuba's best," she said before adopting a teasing tone. "But Dr. Chardón tells me you business students are practically savages."

"Cultural heathens," Dr. Chardón said, shaking his head.

"With some exceptions!" Marco raised his right index finger. "I read poems to Mamá in the evenings while she sewed." He addressed Isabela directly. "But where are my manners? You must be thirsty. Would you like a glass of punch?" Marco offered his arm, and Isa allowed herself to be led toward the punch bowl and away from Dr. Chardón, who moved on to greet other guests.

Isabela considered this appealing young man and imagined him reading poetry to his genteel mother as she embroidered a handkerchief in their sitting room. He had impeccable manners, but his suit jacket looked worn, his shirt collar a bit threadbare. Perhaps his family had lost its money in the stock market crash, like so many others. Isabela accepted the glass cup of punch by the handle and took another sideways look at Marco. He sure was attractive! And tall. Taller than Gardel. A bit on the bony side, though.

"Señorita Soto, what do you do when you're not reciting poetry? A girl like you must stay busy batting admirers away," Marco said with a smile.

"You must think I'm very frivolous, Señor Rios," Isa said with a slight frown. Why didn't men ever take her seriously? "I'll have you know I'm preparing for an acting career. I'm going to study in Mexico and be in films." Surely her modernity would impress him.

"Ah. Puerto Rico will be poorer for your absence." Marco's voice was tinged with disappointment. "I don't have much time for movies, but they're great fun. Sometimes I find the acting overly theatrical, though, almost silly." He shook his head.

"As overly theatrical as your poetic delivery just now? As with most things, there's good acting and bad acting." Isabela raised her eyebrows, cocked her head toward one shoulder and then the other, and took a demure sip of her punch.

"Well," Marco said, eyes twinkling, "Clearly, I need lessons. Would you see a movie with me before you leave for Mexico? You can teach me all about the nuances of acting." Marco placed his palm on his heart. "Consider it an ongoing part of Dr. Chardón's cultural enrichment efforts."

Isabela mulled over the offer. This Marco Rios was better looking than any of her beaus and offered entertaining conversation. Dr. Chardón certainly admired him. Marco didn't appear to have much means, so Papi would disapprove of him. Papi had been pushing the insipid Serrallés boy on her lately, making noises about marriage. A shiver of delight scooted up her spine at the thought of bringing Marco Rios home and creating a bit of drama in her life.

"I'd be pleased to contribute to your education, Señor Rios. Shall we say next Saturday at one? And, please, call me Isabela."

"Very well, Isabela. I'll be counting the minutes until Saturday afternoon."

What a quirky young man, thought Isa as Mariano, the family chauffeur, drove her home. So eager to please, yet confident. She'd never dated anyone without knowing his entire pedigree: the son of so-and-so who is the cousin of this one and related to that one by marriage. Marco Rios had to be respectable enough, or Dr. Chardón wouldn't have introduced him to her. But how exciting, maybe dangerous, to not know anything else about him. This would annoy Papi, who practically required a dossier on any of her admirers. Ironic, given her own background.

Papi conveniently forgot her mother had been a jíbara, the poorest of the poor on the island. What would her suitors think if they knew the true circumstances of her birth? What would Marco Rios think? Not that it mattered, really; she'd no interest in marriage. She wanted an acting career and thirsted for the tonic of applause and adoration like she'd received tonight. Her destiny awaited in Mexico, where directors like Miguel Contreras Torres and Fernando de Fuentes made important films. Nothing mattered more than getting there.

If only she could convince Papi to let her go. Lately, her Mexico hopes had started to fade like the tropical sun setting on the pink horizon. It was looking more and more like she'd be stuck on this island forever. Isa sighed. Her thoughts turned to Marco Rios again, and she stopped breathing as a bold idea crystallized in her mind. ¡Dios mío! What if there was a way to force Papi's hand? Her pulse raced. All Papi cared about was marrying her off respectably. But what if Papi thought she'd fallen in love and wanted to marry someone he deemed unsuitable—could she convince him to let her go to Mexico as an alternative? Yes, yes... The plan was ingenious! Papi would never see it coming. A giddy joy tickled her heart. She'd make Mexico happen.

Isa checked the time as Mariano dropped her off the following Thursday at Teté's house, her high school friend who'd married one of the Banco Popular boys. Gladys, who'd just returned from her honeymoon in Argentina, would also be there. Isa had less and less in common with these old friends who'd begun to drop like flies into the morass of marriage. She'd been avoiding them, and her visit was overdue. But would an hour be sufficient time? She'd have to play it by ear.

Gladys had already arrived and was seated beside Teté on the ivory Art Deco sofa straight out of a Carole Lombard movie that Teté had ordered from New York. They sipped coffee from Teté's prized Limoges cups—ecru with a green striped border and golden mock-bamboo handles. That Limoges coffee service set was Teté's baby. Isa pitied the actual baby who broke the first piece.

Isa greeted both friends with a peck on the cheek, sat on the upholstered chair perpendicular to the couch, and crossed her legs. She helped herself to a cup of coffee from the Limoges pot arranged on the scalloped brass and glass coffee table.

"Look, chicas! It's Laurita." Teté held up that week's *Puerto Rico Ilustrado*.

Every issue featured a full-page photo of one of San Juan's debutantes with an always-flattering caption, such as "beautiful and charming" or "gentle and gracious." This week's selection, Laura Reyes, gifted with beady eyes and a bulbous nose, was "distinguished and intelligent."

Gladys leaned in to take a closer look at the photo. "Ay, pobrecita. 'Distinguished and intelligent' won't help her find a husband."

"Don't be mean. She's very sweet," Isa said, and took a sip of her coffee.

Gladys shrugged. "La mona, aunque se vista de seda, mona se queda."

Isa secretly agreed no amount of silk could make Laura attractive, the poor thing. Isa remembered her own caption: "Isabela Soto. Enchanting flower of society's garden." She'd rather be "distinguished and intelligent."

Teté closed the magazine and addressed Gladys. "Did I tell you Almacenes Rodríguez is selling the most exquisite hand-embroidered sheets?"

"De veras?" Gladys said, setting her coffee cup down. "Do they have tablecloths? Can you believe I didn't get a single one for a wedding gift?"

"Huh." Teté turned to Isa. "When are you going to start buying linens? God knows you don't lack suitors!"

"Who? Javier?" Isa leaned in toward her friends and mock whispered, "He keeps declaring his undying love for me, but have you seen how he looks at men?"

"What! Really?" Gladys's face registered disbelief, followed by understanding and then acceptance. "Hmmm." She nodded her head, eyes squinted.

"That does make sense," Teté said, also nodding.

"And what about Papi's favorite, Pedro Serrallés? He might be heir to his family's rum fortune, but I've had more interesting conversations with my hairbrush." Isa threw her hands up in despair.

"Well, there must be someone you like," Gladys said.

Isa shrugged. "You know I want to be an actress, not a wife."

"You're going to stay jamona?" Teté's tone was stern. "Isa, you need to stop dreaming. You know your father will never let you be an actress. And what's so terrible about marriage? Gladys and I couldn't be happier."

"I want to be independent. Not some man's property."

"Is that how you see us?" Gladys said, eyes brimming with hurt.

Isa was at a loss. She'd offended her friends, but she couldn't help how she felt. No man had aroused her like her ability to move an audience fired her soul. She lived to elicit surprise, merriment, desire, even love. What a thrill it was to have, if for a few moments, complete control over her public's emotions. Their applause, tears, and laughter were as sweet and nourishing as honey, almost as if her mother were beaming love down from heaven. But Gladys and Teté wouldn't understand.

"No, no, of course not," Isa stammered, then recovered and added, "but you know how some men are, a bunch of macho roosters who want to keep their wives pregnant at home while they run around with all sorts. You managed to find the last two good ones."

Isa sensed her friends relax and was pleased to have diffused the situation. They spent the next half-hour discussing Gladys's desire to become pregnant immediately and Teté's ongoing décor plans. When Isa finally excused herself, she felt like she'd broken out of jail. God, she needed new friends.

The next day, Isa stepped onto the wide veranda through her home's thick wooden front door. Her two half-sisters, five-year-old Matilde and four-year-old Rosario, played quietly in a corner. Mati's head was covered in twisted strips of rags, another of her stepmother's fruitless efforts to get the girl's stick-straight hair to curl. Meanwhile, a frizzy halo of auburn ringlets framed Rosie's freckled face. No one knew where her coloring came from.

The two girls were so engrossed in their dolls that they paid Isa no mind as she plopped herself on the verdigris metal glider and stared through one of the Moorish arches into the lush garden and the quiet street beyond.

She thought about yesterday's visit with Teté and Gladys. Everyone's fascination with marriage perplexed her even more when she considered her family's example. When Connie married Papi on a ship back home from Spain after only knowing him for two weeks, she'd been a vivacious, free-wheeling spirit. Isa was fourteen, and

Connie was a balm who'd soothed the pain of her grandmother's death in the aftermath of Hurricane San Felipe. But with the birth of each baby, her stepmother had become increasingly focused on the tedious minutiae of running a household. Even with servants to cook, clean, and help with Isa's two half-sisters, Connie was constantly frazzled. While still elegant and fashionable when adorning Papi's arm at social events, her joie de vivre had diminished. Sometimes, Connie's pluck was still evident, like when she banded with Isa against Papi's notions of what was appropriate. But overall, her spirited stepmother had gone from flapper to faded. Isa's friends had embarked on the same path, and it deeply saddened her.

Meanwhile, Papi did whatever he wanted, coming and going at all hours. On several occasions, Isabela had greeted her father with a kiss only to smell cheap perfume overpowering the citrusy 4711 cologne that permeated his suits. Surely Connie smelled it, too. But her stepmother suffered these affronts silently, her once brilliant inner light growing dimmer by the day. Isa refused to live like that.

But, at twenty-one, she'd become a nuisance for Papi to marry off. She'd managed to keep him at bay during the three years since her debut, but he was losing patience. Soon she'd be too old to parade around with other single girls at social events, bait for the most eligible bachelors.

"No! It's my turn to be the mami!" Mati whined to her younger sister, interrupting Isa's reverie. Rosie made a face but handed the infant doll over to Mati. Mati swaddled it, smiling fondly at her "baby" as she rocked it.

Isa rolled her eyes and shook her head. Her young sisters were already being indoctrinated, the poor things. Groomed to be good little wives and mothers. As the oldest, she felt a duty to pave the way for them, to give them the option of living a different future. They, too, could be actresses. Architects. Nurses. Why not doctors?

Yes, she'd stay strong and win the Mexico battle, if not for herself, for her sisters. She was ready to put her exciting new plan into motion. Step one would be easy: charm Marco tomorrow. Tiny teeth of remorse gnawed at her heart at the thought of turning the endearing young man into a bargaining chip. Yet getting to Mexico was imperative. Marco's bruised ego would recover.

Isa rose and stepped inside, intent on fetching crayons and drawing paper to distract her sisters from their dolls.

CHAPTER 2

– Marco –
September 1935

Marco woke on the morning of his date with Isabela and stretched his long body head-to-toe under the mosquito netting covering his bed. He took a few more minutes to loll. So rare for him. Highly skilled with numbers, he'd been accepted to La Upi, as everyone called the University of Puerto Rico in the Rio Piedras sector of San Juan. As a senior, he earned a modest income teaching freshman accounting, enough to afford the relatively low tuition and room and board at the widow Doña Teresa's house, but not much else.

Desperate to make a good impression on Isabela's family, Marco had asked to borrow a quality suit jacket from his friend Sammy's vast collection. Sammy, a scion of the Lopez Aceveda insurance family, had been in all of Marco's classes, and they'd forged a tight bond despite their economic differences. A knock on the door announced his arrival, and Marco smiled in greeting as Sammy entered the room, holding up two jackets on hangers.

"Hola, Marco. Doña Teresa let me in," Sammy said, folding the jackets over the back of Marco's desk chair. "What are you still doing in bed? I thought you'd be up already, what with your exciting date today." Sammy wiggled his eyebrows.

Marco yawned in response.

"God, I wish I hadn't skipped that cultural enrichment session so I could have met this woman of your dreams."

"You must have come across her at parties, Sammy," Marco said, sitting up in bed. He leaned toward the nightstand and lifted the etiquette guide he'd been studying last night, uncovering a newspaper clipping. He silently read the caption for the fiftieth time: "The gracious Señorita Isabela Soto charms tango singer Carlos Gardel at a Condado Vanderbilt Hotel breakfast in his honor." The woman, chin lifted, beamed at Gardel with adoring eyes and coquettishly brandished a Spanish fan in her right hand. She was the same beauty he'd met at Dr. Chardón's house last night, the one whose fingertips sparked against his when he took her hand in greeting.

Marco got out of bed, handing the photo to Sammy. "Here, see for yourself."

Sammy feigned confusion. "She looks like Carlos Gardel?"

"No, pendejo." Marco punched him in the arm. "The woman in the picture. That's Isabela."

Sammy squinted to take a closer look. "Sí, I've seen her before, but I don't know her. Anyway, they're all the same, these flighty debutantes. Ten minutes of her vapid conversation, and you'll wish you were alone in the library with one of those art books you love to devour."

"Dr. Chardón is right, you know. Leaders should be well-rounded and cultured," Marco said. "Besides, Isabela held my interest for much longer than ten minutes. I'm not worried about that. But I have a feeling her father's going to be another story." Marco mock-shivered and made a frightened face. "What did you find out about him?"

"My father says the family is originally from Ponce. He's in the import business—mostly luxury goods—and very rich. You know that car that Carlos Gardel rode around in when he visited Puerto Rico? It was Don Gabriel's."

"No wonder Isa met Gardel. What about his politics?" Marco paced the floor.

"No idea whether he favors independence or statehood. Best avoid that whole chaotic topic. Stay neutral, but don't be mundane or boring. Put all that cultural knowledge to use. Talk about the Hindenburg or the latest motorcar technology," Sammy said.

Marco nodded, thinking up additional topics as he continued to pace the room. Sammy picked up the jackets he'd brought and held them up, a double-breasted cream linen jacket in one hand and a two-button marine blue sport coat in the other.

"I brought you two, although I think the sleeves might be a bit short on you."

Marco pulled the blue jacket off the hanger and shrugged it on. He considered the sleeve length. "What do you think?"

"Not too bad at all," Sammy answered. "You can keep these, by the way."

Marco's face flushed pink as he nodded a silent thank you to his friend. He told himself this situation was different from when he was forced to wear those awful charity clothes after Hurricane San Felipe. Sammy was doing him a favor, friend to friend. Still, asking for help cost his pride dearly.

After a late breakfast of café con leche and toasted pan de agua slathered in butter, Marco bathed, shaved, and dressed with meticulous care. He wore light gray trousers, a white shirt, striped tie, and Sammy's blue jacket, even though the sleeves were definitely too short.

Before leaving the house, he patted his breast pocket to confirm he had his wallet. He was bringing extra money, wanting to afford whatever refreshments Isabela desired. He'd been given the ultimate opportunity—a chance at wooing his ideal woman—and he would not squander it.

During the breezy but warm trolley ride from Rio Piedras to Miramar, Marco held his arms slightly away from his torso to aerate his armpits. If only he could will his body to stop perspiring. Why did men wear so many layers in the tropics? He glanced around the car's interior, envying those who seemed unbothered by the heat. An older woman, weary in her simple dress, brought to mind his mother. What would Mamá think of him dating a fancy rich girl? Would she approve or accuse him of putting on airs?

After the hurricane, Tío Ernesto had built a modest three-room cement house for Marco's family next to his fancy homestead and successful bakery business. Mamá refused to let him splurge on indoor plumbing, wouldn't take any more of her brother-in-law's charity, so they made do with an open-air kitchen and outhouse. But when the stock market crashed the following year, Marco and his family, like many others, fell deeper into austerity.

During high school, Marco dutifully rose at the rooster's crow each morning to make deliveries for Tío's bakery. Mamá would already be hunched over her black Singer sewing machine, pumping away with her feet under a watercolor cardboard print of Jesus with the bleeding heart. Mamá, a fast sewer, earned almost a dollar on a good week. Marco's delivery job and the needlework Julia fit in around school brought in a few more pennies. Together they eked out a living while Marco bided his time until he could free Mamá from her drudgery and his family from poverty.

They had plenty of bread, thanks to Tío's bakery, and Marco foraged for fruits on the weekends with his friends. But Mamá mostly cooked root vegetable stews—yucca, potatoes, yautía, and yams seasoned with cilantro, onions, garlic, and peppers. Every day a variation on the same meal, sometimes with bits of bacalao when they could afford the dried cod.

After his weekend deliveries, Marco embarked on adventures with his cousin Nando. They'd roam Barrio Aguacate and eat mangoes until their stomachs were so distended, they were forced to lie on the ground, arms spread out like Jesus on the cross, moaning in pain. Bananas, pomegranates, guavas, sweet limes, and oranges abounded, but mangoes were their favorite. They swam in the ocean, fished in the Guayanés River—hooking worms on bent sewing pins for bait—and collected fireflies in jars. During the harvest, la zafra, they nagged the sugarcane macheteros for pieces of cane they'd suck dry. They flew homemade kites, tying bits of glass to the strings and staged vicious duels where they tried to cut each other's creations down.

Life had been harsher but freer in Yabucoa. Certainly more verdant and peaceful, he thought, as the brassy honk of a car's klaxon startled him. He'd been so engrossed in his memories that he almost missed his stop.

Feeling calmer after his reverie, Marco stepped off the trolley at Stop 12 and strolled into the Miramar neighborhood off Ponce de León Avenue. He marveled at the quiet enclave of grand homes and luscious gardens, each more impressive than the next. Number 650 Calle La Paz was no exception. Blue and yellow Spanish tiles framed each of the white cement home's windows. An elegant scrolled cartouche crowned the second story, and ocher terracotta tiles edged the roof. Arched openings and two peaked roof towers contributed to the Spanish Revivalist design. A driveway and carport on the left side of the house led to a separate building he assumed served as a garage and servants' quarters.

A wrought-iron fence with mosaic-adorned white cement pillars fronted the Soto house. It enclosed a manicured garden teeming with pink amapolas, yellow bell flowers, and red jungle geraniums. Marco opened the walkway gate just as a sprightly grey lizard skittered across the stone path. A bougainvillea vine laden with a riot of purple blooms scaled the right side of the house, and the heady scent of gardenias saturated the air. Marco smiled when a yellow-chested warbler shook its feathers in the marble birdbath at the garden's center. It was wondrous, as if a microcosm of the countryside he loved had sprouted in San Juan.

Despite the bucolic surroundings, Marco's sweat glands awakened in full force. His shirt stuck to his body as if he'd just run a race against Nando through the hills of Yabucoa. But this was not Yabucoa; this was a tony suburb of San Juan where sweat was likely prohibited. He inhaled a deep garden-scented breath and asked Papá for help and guidance. *Papá, ayúdame y dáme fuerza.* As he neared the veranda steps, he imagined a comforting warm pressure on his lower back, Papá's hand gently guiding him toward his destiny. It was enough to give him the courage to lift and firmly lower the iron doorknocker at the stroke of one.

"¿Sí?" A lean middle-aged woman with an apron tied around her waist opened the door.

"Buenas tardes. Soy Marco Rios, here for Isabela Soto."

"Buenas tardes. Entre, entre. Isabela needs a few more minutes, but Don Gabriel is in the sitting room. Follow me."

Marco gawked at the home's splendor. Sunlight streaming through the French windows set agleam intricately carved wooden beams and bounced off crystal chandeliers to create a mosaic of dots on the walls and painted tile floors. Chinese vases, stained glass lamps, gilded mirrors, paintings, and art objects abounded without appearing cluttered.

How much had all this cost? Marco felt like an intruder and, conscious of making a lumbering sound on the tiles, tried to lighten his step. By the time they entered the sitting room, he'd twisted himself into a knot of self-doubt. *Marco, pull yourself together.*

"Don Gabriel, Marco Rios is here," the woman said to Isabela's father, who sat on an upholstered club chair reading the newspaper. Don Gabriel looked up, folded *El Imparcial*, set it on a side table, and rose to greet Marco. His light brown hair, grey at the temples, was combed neatly to one side. Like Marco, he was clean-shaven, a rarity these days when most men sported thin mustaches. His lightweight cream suit appeared fresh and unwrinkled.

"A pleasure to meet you, Marco," Don Gabriel extended his hand. Marco, who towered over the older man, surreptitiously wiped his palm on the side of his trousers.

"It's an honor to meet one of San Juan's business leaders." Marco offered Don Gabriel a firm handshake. "We students have much to learn from your generation." It pained him to register the man's disapproval at seeing Marco's frayed shirt cuff peeking out of his too-short jacket sleeve.

Don Gabriel gestured for Marco to sit on the wood and cane settee, a traditional piece of Spanish furniture not known for its comfort, before sitting back down in his plush chair. "Everything I learned, I learned on the job from my father. He was a master of the import trade. Now everyone goes to school to learn business from books. Ha!" Don Gabriel shook his head. He crossed his legs and leaned back in his chair.

"You were fortunate to be born into a family that could afford you such an advantage." Marco felt it safe to reference Don Gabriel's heritage.

"And you?" Don Gabriel raised an eyebrow and crossed his arms in front of his chest. The question was a challenge.

Marco, taken aback, took a moment to ponder his response. He didn't want to appear disrespectful, but he refused to allow this man to believe he was Marco's better simply because of family lineage. Rivulets of sweat coursed down his torso, tickling and daring him to fidget.

"I was born into a wonderful but humble family. I learned about business from my Tío, who runs a bakery."

"You want to be a baker?" Don Gabriel said. His caustic tone belied his amused look.

Ignoring the jibe, Marco leaned forward earnestly. "No, sir. I aspire to propel Puerto Rico into modernity. I've studied hard so I can do my part."

"Ah, an ambitious young man. That can be good or bad, depending on your intentions." Don Gabriel's eyes bored into Marco's.

Marco understood the inference, met the man's stare, and affirmed, "I assure you my intentions are completely honorable."

Don Gabriel smiled. "Yes, well, everyone's intentions are honorable, aren't they? Until they're tested. Believe me, you have not yet been tested."

Sweat dripped down the back of Marco's head onto his shirt collar, but he resisted the urge to wipe it with his handkerchief. He would not give Don Gabriel the satisfaction of seeing him intimidated or flustered. Before he could think of a response, Don Gabriel veered the conversation toward a new topic.

"Tell me. How do you feel we should move forward politically?"

Careful, Marco. Stay in the safe zone.

"We're a divided island torn between pushing for statehood or independence," Marco answered. "Wherever we end up, I hope it's peaceful. Albizu is calling for a violent revolution, but force is not the answer to our problems." Surely Don Gabriel would agree. Since losing the 1932 election and declaring it rigged, Nationalist leader Pedro Albizu Campos had preached violence as the only way to attain independence. His disciples called the slight, dark-skinned prodigy who'd earned a scholarship to Harvard El Maestro, the teacher.

"I dislike that Albizu. How can a Harvard valedictorian, a lawyer, be so irrational? We need independence, but not by force."

So Don Gabriel favored independence, like Papá. Marco took a risk because, like many of Papá's generation, Don Gabriel probably hated los Yanquis.

"Independence has always been a worthy goal, but I agree with Senator Muñoz Marín. We need help from the Americans to get on our feet first." Marco's body heat had reached feverish proportions.

Don Gabriel scowled and batted away Marco's opinion as if waving off a fly. "We can fix our own problems. We don't need the U.S. We were a damn country an entire century before the Pilgrims even thought about crossing the Atlantic. Yet they come here to suppress our traditions and change our language. Who the hell are they to tell us what to do?"

So much for staying in the safe zone. Marco was livid at himself for riling up the old man and at a complete loss for how to proceed without further fueling Don Gabriel's anger. Thankfully, the clicking sound of approaching heels broke through the tension. Marco's relief at seeing Isa enter the room was so great he would have collapsed had he been standing.

"Ah, here she is, my lovely daughter," Don Gabriel said, smiling at Isabela.

She was a vision, bright and stylish in a lavender dress with a white sailor collar. A slim navy belt, white gloves, and a brown felt hat adorned with a quill feather enhanced her refined look.

"Marco, welcome to our home. I hope Papi hasn't been too much of an ogre." Isabela extended her hand toward him while shooting Don Gabriel a suspicious look.

Marco leaned over the proffered hand and caught a whiff of her perfume: jasmine, roses, and sunshine. Isa smelled like a joyous day in the countryside.

"It's been a pleasure chatting with your father," Marco said.

"We've had a lovely conversation, Isa. And why wouldn't we?" Don Gabriel asked, all innocence and purity. "I'm harmless."

"As harmless as a snake," Isabela countered and turned to Marco. "We should go. The film begins at 1:40, and it's a ten-minute walk."

Don Gabriel called out, "Carmen! Are you ready?"

"Here I am!" The woman who'd shown Marco in rushed through the sitting room's arched entrance pinning a black straw hat onto her hair. "A volar, que el sol cambia."

"True. But we have enough time for you to take that off first," Isa grinned, pointing to the apron still tied around the woman's waist. Carmen untied herself, chuckling, and headed toward the front door.

"Enjoy the movie, you three." Don Gabriel waved them off, looking satisfied with himself.

Marco thanked him, offered Isabela his arm, and followed Carmen outside. *¡Dios mío! We're being chaperoned!* Sammy hadn't mentioned anything about chaperones. He'd never been on a chaperoned date. Granted, most of Marco's encounters with women had occurred in public, either at the Yabucoa Plaza, with more people present than at a Vatican Mass, or going out in groups of students from La Upi. Besides, he was a gentleman and an adult. Girls who dated him did not need a chaperone for crying out loud!

Marco struggled to find something to say, his carefully curated list of conversational topics forgotten.

"Isabela, ah—*Mutiny on the Bounty* is supposed to be fantastic," he finally uttered. "Although I wish we didn't have to wait so long for movies to arrive on the island."

"I know! I try not to read anything in advance. I'm excited for

Clark Gable, though. Here, let Carmen get a little ahead of us." Isabela held him back lightly by the arm. "So we can speak more privately."

"Does she always accompany you on dates?" Marco asked.

"No, no! I usually go where everyone knows me, so believe me, I have a hundred chaperones on every date. Consider yourself lucky to just have one." Isabela smiled ruefully while giving his arm a quick squeeze. Marco's heart skipped a beat.

"I don't mind, but I'm surprised. Doesn't your father trust you?"

"Oh, he trusts *me*. It's men he has no confidence in. If someone Papi doesn't know wants to sit in the dark next to me for a couple of hours, you better believe he's sending Carmen along!"

"Rest assured, I will be on my best behavior, as always," Marco said, trying to shake off the meaning he'd gleaned from Isabela's words: he was not of Isa's ilk, and Don Gabriel would never trust him.

As they walked past the storefronts and apartment buildings lining Ponce de León Avenue, a new concern troubled Marco. Was he to pay for Carmen's movie ticket? What about refreshments afterward? Dear Lord, did he have enough money? This time he did wipe the sweat off his face and neck with his handkerchief.

His first question was answered when they reached the elegant Fox Theater, and Carmen and Isabela stepped to the side of the box office window, obviously waiting for him to buy their tickets. He completed the purchase with fumbling fingers, grateful he had enough for all three tickets and even for a Coca-Cola afterward. He guided both women into the theater's blessedly cool Art Deco lobby.

Isabela exhaled contentedly. "If air conditioning isn't the most glorious invention ever, I don't know what is."

"It almost feels too cold." Carmen wrapped her arms around herself. Marco silently agreed and shivered as the frigid air hit his sweat-dampened skin.

"Shush, Carmen! There's no such thing. This is heavenly!" Isa twirled in appreciation.

"You would love the natural air conditioning in the Yabucoa mountains. The nights are sometimes even cooler than this," Marco said.

"Yes, but then I'd have to live in the mountains," Isabela said, laughing. Marco bristled, but then thought this city girl didn't know what she was missing.

Isabela sat between him and Carmen, and for three endless hours, he was acutely aware of the warmth emanating from his date's skin. He longed to take her delicate hand in his but did not dare. When Captain Bligh, the film's brutal tyrant, ordered a man thrown overboard for complaining of thirst, Isabela gasped and squeezed his forearm, generating an electric shock that traveled straight to his groin.

When the delicious torture finally ended, Isabela turned to him. "Now that was great acting, Marco. Don't you agree?"

"Nothing too melodramatic, true. Although Captain Bligh was a bit sadistic. It's hard to believe people can be that cruel," Marco said as they stood to exit the theater.

"It's supposed to be a true story," Carmen said. "But I would have risked Bligh's wrath to be with Clark Gable. Bah, listen to me. Perro flaco soñando con longaniza."

Just a skinny dog dreaming of sausage. Marco smiled, grateful for the humor.

"Carmen!" Isabela exclaimed.

"What?" Carmen looked from Isabela to Marco. "Just because I'm not married doesn't mean I can't appreciate a handsome man."

"Some chaperone," Isabela said, shaking her head.

The three erupted in laughter. As they exited the building, Marco pointed to the right.

"Come. There's a café on the corner. Let's sit and have a drink."

"Are you sure you can spare the time from your studies?" Unease shadowed Isabela's face. Was she worried about his financial capability to buy them a Coca-Cola? Not that she was wrong to worry. He flashed a confident smile before shame could bring him down.

"Today, I have all the time in the world," Marco said.

They sat at a table and ordered their refreshments while Marco said a silent prayer of thanks that he'd had the foresight to scrape together extra cash. After paying for the drinks, he'd have nothing left over, not even trolley fare. The walk back to Doña Teresa's house would be long, but he didn't care about that now.

"You know, I was glad there wasn't a storm scene," Isabela said. "A movie could never capture the horror of a real hurricane."

"And why would you want to?" Marco asked, more bitterly than he meant to sound. "I lost my father to San Felipe. That's not an experience I'd like to relive." He lowered his eyes and looked away. Would the pain of losing Papá always feel this raw?

"Oh, I'm so sorry, Marco." Isabela placed her hand on his arm. "I lost my grandmother to San Felipe, too. Well, she died of pneumonia afterward, but it was San Felipe's fault."

"My condolences, Isabela." Marco looked back at Isa. "Were you close?"

"Abuela raised me because my mother died in childbirth, and Papi was traveling the globe for his business back then. San Felipe plucked me from a peaceful existence in Ponce and dropped me in San Juan to live with my father and brand-new stepmother. They were both strangers, really. My head's still whirling from it all." Isabela bobbled her head, googly-eyed.

"I bet it is! And did we really need San Ciprián just four years later? I'd just started at La Upi and wasn't able to contact my family for a week," Marco said.

"You must have been frantic," Isabela said.

"Yes. It was a relief to finally get through on the phone. At least fewer died than during San Felipe, but the coffee plantations will never be the same." Marco shook his head.

"Hurricanes change lives," Carmen said.

"San Felipe certainly changed mine," Isabela said.

"Mine, too." Marco looked at Isabela, feeling a genuine kinship with this girl from another world who smiled at him with such compassion.

Back at the house, Isabela invited him to sit in one of the wrought-iron chairs that matched the verdigris glider on the veranda, a small round table between them. Carmen brought them lemonade and went back inside, to Marco's surprise.

"I've really enjoyed our afternoon together," he said, taking advantage of this alone time with Isa. "Will you remember me when you're in Mexico?" He couldn't believe he'd just found this creature, only to have to let her go.

"Oh, Marco. I have a confession to make." Isabela slumped backward. "Mexico is just a dream. My father won't let me go. He thinks acting is immoral. I'm afraid I'm stuck on this island for eternity."

A bolt of glee burst from Marco's heart, causing a tingle in his extremities.

"But that's wonderful!" *Stop smiling, Marco.* He understood Isa's dream was crushed, even as his was becoming a reality. "I mean, not that you can't be an actress, but that you're staying here."

"Is it? What good is life if you can't do what you most enjoy?"

"Well, we'll have to find new things for you to enjoy."

She sighed. "Such as?"

"I can think of twenty outings sure to delight you."

"Twenty?" Skepticism knotted her delicate eyebrows together.

"Give me twenty Saturdays, and I'll show you." He was shocked at his boldness.

"Twenty Saturdays! That's almost half a year. You're crazy." Isabela frowned in disbelief and swatted his arm, though a slight smile pulled at the edges of her mouth.

Marco ducked away from her. "Okay, okay. No need to get vicious. Let's start with just one."

"What do you have in mind?" She narrowed her eyes.

"It's a surprise. Be ready next Saturday at one." Marco held his breath. *Please, please, please say yes!*

Isabela pursed her lips and nodded slowly. "Sure, why not?"

Marco's delight caught in his chest, causing a coughing fit. Isa pounded on his back and handed him his lemonade. He took a sip and cleared his throat before apologizing. He quickly confirmed the details of their next meeting and bowed to her hand before leaving, allowing no time for Isabela to change her mind.

The seven-mile walk home, with just the coquís and their melody to keep him company, passed in a blur while his brain concocted twenty perfect experiences to share with this extraordinary woman. This girl was a delight, beautiful and charming, but not empty-headed, as Sammy had warned. He arrived at Doña Teresa's at nine, more energized than when he'd woken up that morning.

CHAPTER 3

- Isabela -
October 1935

Isabela stood on her tippy toes in her pajamas, body straight, arms up by her ears. She bent her knees and leaned back as far as she could before straightening up again, then repeated the motion. Rosie stood by her side, mimicking Isa's every move.

"Thirteen... fourteen... fifteen!" Mati counted out, proud to know her numbers. The rag curls covering her head shook with each count.

Muscles spent, Isa collapsed on the floor, glad to be done with her exercise routine for "maintaining your figure," as prescribed in *El Imparcial*. Rosie fell beside her, laughing, and not one to be left out, Mati joined in.

"Thanks for your help, girls. Come on. Let's see what Carmen has for breakfast." Isa took a sister's hand in each of hers.

"But where are you going de paseo today?" Mati asked.

"None of your business, nosy," Rosie answered, clearly feeling superior to her older sister.

"That's right, Rosie," Isa laughed. "Besides, it's a secret."

She and Carmen were spending their fifth consecutive Saturday with Marco, and as usual, she had no idea what adventure he'd planned. The Saturday following their *Mutiny on the Bounty* date, they'd taken the trolley to the beach in Condado near the old Borinquen Park. She'd always thought the Taíno word for the island, "Borinquen," so much more romantic than the businesslike "Puerto Rico," rich port. They admired the stately homes built on what used to be a boardwalk and set a blanket on the sand under the shade of two palm trees. They talked, enjoyed the ocean breeze, and hunted for seashells while sand pooled uncomfortably inside her white oxfords, rubbing against her stockinged toes. Marco bought them piraguas, shaved ice in delicious flavors. She picked raspberry, he anise, and Carmen tamarind. Except for her blistered feet, a most enjoyable day.

Isabela had never considered what her escorts spent on her, but Marco was of modest means and having him splurge his hard-earned money on her—not to mention on Carmen—felt wrong. He'd seemed so nervous on their first date when it was time to pay; obviously, he hadn't expected to cover the cost of three people. At the café that day, Isabela had given Carmen a warning look not to order a second soda. All their dates since had been frugal, but she had to also admit inventive and, well, fun. An afternoon at Muñoz Rivera Park, a walk on Paseo La Princesa along the periphery of Old San Juan's fortress walls, a tour of La Upi's lush campus. Who knew there were so many amusing things to do outside the sphere of the Casino de Puerto Rico? The endless string of té danzants, formal dinners, and balls felt suffocating compared to her carefree Saturdays with the handsome and charismatic Marco.

Best of all, Papi absolutely hated her new beau. Yesterday, on her way to fetch a glass of water from the kitchen, she'd overheard Papi and Connie talking in the living room and stopped to listen, hiding in the hallway shadows.

"I don't like that Marco," Papi said, his voice an angry whisper. "Who does he think he is sniffing around Isa like a dog?"

"Don't be crass, Gabriel," Connie said. "I find him very sweet. He's a gentleman, not some sinvergüenza set out to compromise Isa's virtue."

"He's smarter than that. He wants her money. Her virtue can wait."

"Where is your sense of romance? It could be true love." Isa wondered how Connie could still believe in true love after enduring Papi's rampant womanizing. She must be a real romantic at heart. "And wouldn't that be priceless?"

"Priceless, maybe, but certainly costly. He's unsuitable. We can't introduce him to our friends."

"Dr. Chardón vouches for the boy."

"So, he's smart. That's not in question. I just want Isa to be happy, and how can she be happy with someone like Marco?"

"Why not? Because he's poor?"

"Look, Connie. I've spent twenty-one years feeling guilty for bringing a bastard into the world, trying to make Isa's life one of luxury and ease. Now, this Marco wants to undo it all."

Papi's words pierced Isa's heart like a dagger. Is that how he really thought of her, as his bastard child? Not that the words surprised her, really, but they hurt nevertheless. She questioned whether his efforts to "ease her life" were really for her benefit or to keep up appearances.

"Well, go ahead and tell her she can't see him. She'll like him even more. She'll probably want to marry him." Connie laughed.

"God forbid! I need to put an end to this soon."

Isa had set her hurt aside, put it in a little box and stored it in the deep recesses of her heart. At least her master plan was unfolding perfectly, she thought, leading her sisters into the dining room to join Papi and Connie at the table for breakfast.

"You going out with the jíbaro again, Isa?" Papi asked. "Why are you wasting your time on that upstart?" He slurped from his daily glass of fresh-squeezed orange juice and glared across the table at her.

"Is Marco a jíbaro?" Mati asked with a confused expression.

Isa sat down, unfolded her napkin on her lap and carefully said, "No, Mati. He's a student. We have fascinating conversations, which is more than I can say for most men I know." She tucked into the plate of fried eggs and ham Carmen placed before her.

"He's a poor country boy with stars in his eyes." Papi's stare smoldered.

Like my mother, who you took advantage of? She lifted her chin and said, "Carmen likes him."

"Let Carmen date him, then." Papi huffed.

Carmen raised both hands palms up, clearly not wanting any part in the argument, and scurried back to the kitchen.

"Ay, Papi." Isabela rolled her eyes. Her sisters laughed, and Connie placed her hand over Papi's on the table as if to placate him.

"Bah!" Papi said, finally looking away from Isa. He slurped his café con leche.

"You know, if I was in Mexico, I'd focus on my acting studies instead of dating anyone at all." Isa threw the thought out, hoping it sounded like a casual aside.

"Look, Isa," Papi stared down his fleshy nose at her. "It's one thing to recite poetry and be in those little Casino plays. But traipsing around a stage or on screen like a lunatic is out of the question. Acting is not an appropriate pursuit for a girl of your breeding." He waved a hand dismissively. "Actors have loose morals and dirty habits. You know I forbid it."

Isa bristled at Papi's protestations and glanced at Connie surreptitiously, who shrugged at her. Her father's hypocritical protestations were even more infuriating since both she and Connie, unbeknownst to Papi, were aware of the bootlegging business he'd run during Prohibition. The lucrative side enterprise was the only way his luxury goods import business survived after Black Tuesday. Papi broke the law and regularly put his family in danger during those days. That he should speak of loose morals was laughable.

"What are loose morals?" Rosie asked Connie, her cherubic red hair and freckles accentuating her innocence. Connie placed an index finger on her lips to shush the girl.

Papi frowned at Rosie, then focused back on Isa. "It's time you settled down, got married. What about that nice Serrallés boy?"

Again with the Serrallés boy. "He's an idiot," Isa scoffed, throwing her head back and sighing. "All I ask is for a few months there, Papi. To study with María Tereza Montoya."

"Absolutely not. This Montoya person comes from a family of actors, right? She's probably a complete degenerate." Papi waved off the request.

"She's been honored all over South America, Papi. Besides, I doubt the King of Spain would invite a degenerate to perform for him." Isabela struggled to keep the sass out of her tone.

"What does he know? Not enough to keep his throne," Papi scoffed.

The conversation had become a ping-pong match, with Connie and her sisters quietly alternating their gaze back and forth from Papi to Isa.

"If you let me go, I'll come back and marry whoever you want." She pressed her hands in prayer.

"If I let you go, you won't come back," Papi said and flashed her his "I wasn't born yesterday" look.

Throwing caution to the wind, Isa tried a new tack. "I'm a grown woman. I don't need your permission."

Connie gasped, and Mati and Rosie stared at Isa in shock.

But Papi didn't take Isa's bait. "Really? Who's going to pay for the trip and lessons?" He wiped his mouth with his napkin.

"But Papi, don't you want me to be happy?" Hadn't he said as much when he complained to Connie about Marco?

"I'm sorry, Isabela, truly I am, but my decision is final." Papi wadded his napkin, threw it on the table, and rose to start his day. Connie squeezed Isa's shoulder in solidarity as she followed Papi out of the dining room with the girls.

But Isa had spotted a brief flicker of doubt behind Papi's eyes. Was she starting to wear him down? Could he be considering Mexico as preferable to Marco? A flutter of hope spread across her chest, and she shored herself up. This battle was not over. She'd continue to bide her time until Papi succumbed to her demand: she'd give up Marco, but only in exchange for Mexico.

Poor Marco. She regretted having to use him as a pawn in her stand-off with Papi. Isa enjoyed his company and didn't need to pretend to like him. The heat that emanated between them certainly didn't come from the Puerto Rican sun. No, Marco made her squirm, tingle, and sweat. She wished he'd kiss her already. It was driving her mad, but with Carmen always present, finding a secluded moment for a stolen kiss proved impossible. Maybe he'd be a terrible kisser, and she'd have no trouble giving him up. Isa promised herself to let Marco down gently when the time came. In the meantime, she looked forward to their date.

Isa checked her make-up in her bathroom mirror, for once in peace, because her sisters were at the park with Connie. She never wore much, just a hint of blush, mascara and, of course, lipstick.

Marco had hinted that today's activity would take place outdoors, so she chose a light rayon crepe dress in powder blue and a wide-brimmed white hat decorated with silk violets. Her chin-length hair was arranged away from her face in bouncy curls thanks to a post-breakfast beauty parlor visit. Her Tangee raspberry lipstick matched her Cutex nail polish, which the manicurist applied leaving a small half-moon of bare nail at the base, as was the fashion. She liked that Marco was tall, so she could wear heels, giving her the confidence to carry herself with regal posture.

"Isa, Marco's here!" Carmen called up. Isa's stomach flipped. She admired herself one last time in the mirror and hurried downstairs, heart pounding.

Marco beamed at her from the bottom of the stairs, holding what looked like a kite. *How fun!*

"I've never flown a kite." Isa clasped her hands in delight.

"You're in for a treat!" Marco answered, and they headed out with Carmen in tow.

They made an attractive couple, and Isa loved how they turned heads sitting hip-to-hip on the trolley to Old San Juan, the warmth of his thigh pressed exquisitely against hers. Her arm exploded in goosebumps each time she brushed her gloved hand against his during the steep walk to the hilltop cemetery, which Marco insisted was the best kite flying site in the city. By the time they arrived, every piece of her hungered for his touch.

They entered through a tunnel that led to the main gate and began walking to the left toward the twenty-foot-thick wall separating the cemetery from El Morro fortress. Gravestones and ornate marble angel sculptures shone blindingly white against the brilliant blue, cloudless sky. Here rested some of Puerto Rico's greatest statesmen and artists, men of significant accomplishments, for whom avenues and schools were named.

While beautiful, the place was somber, and Isa vowed to keep her desire in check.

"Look. José de Diego." Isa placed her hand on a bust atop a tall pedestal. "Leader of the independence movement against Spain. One of Papi's heroes."

"If only he'd been successful." Marco briefly covered her hand with his. His skin's heat burned through her glove, taking her breath away and sending a shiver down her back. So much for her vow.

She quickly recovered, wondering whether Marco had sensed her reaction. "He was a great poet, too. I have all his books." Isa paused for a moment and cocked her head. "Come to think of it, many of the esteemed statesmen buried here were also poets." She counted on her fingers as they continued their walk, "Manuel Fernández Juncos, Salvador Brau, José Gautier Benítez, Alejandro Tapia y Rivera. All the greats."

"Real Renaissance men."

Isa nodded distractedly. Where, she wondered, were the women? Isa imagined attaining such renown as an actress that she'd be laid to rest with these men on a cliff overlooking the Atlantic Ocean, enjoying the trade winds for eternity. Goosebumps of a different kind than those Marco elicited sprouted on her arms at the thought, and she hugged herself, rubbing them.

At the end of their stroll, Carmen claimed exhaustion and made herself comfortable on one of the above-ground graves, her back resting on its tombstone. She held an umbrella to shield herself from the sun and watched while Isa and Marco flew the diamond-shaped kite he'd fashioned out of newspaper and sticks. Marco showed Isabela how to catch the wind and then let the string out to keep the kite afloat, his body close behind hers. She leaned her torso against his, lips parted and breath quickening.

A loud cough from Carmen's direction brought Isa back to her senses, and she jumped away from Marco.

"Let me see you fly it now, Marco. Do some tricks!"

Marco expertly guided the kite through impressive acrobatic maneuvers. Not that Isa was paying much attention to the kite. Marco danced a graceful ballet with his bony frame. He'd shed his jacket, and his lean muscles strained against his shirt. Her fingers itched to caress them, his hair, his lips. He took her breath away.

A small audience of children appeared out of nowhere and tittered at the opposite end of the cemetery. They were dirty, skinny, shoeless, and half-dressed—some in just shirts, some solely in diapers, and a few in raggedy pants or dresses. They clapped at Marco's tricks and clamored for more. Marco happily obliged, further bewitching Isa with his kindness.

When he let the kite fall back to earth, the children ran toward him, eager to examine it up close. Marco explained how he'd made it and showed one of the boys how to get it up in the air. The children jostled to be next, and one by one, Marco gave them all a turn. While the kids flew the kite, Marco offered Isabela his arm and walked her to the edge of the cemetery so she could see where the children lived in the slums of La Perla.

Isabela knew La Perla existed, had driven past it many times, but she'd never seen it up close. The slum sat between the ancient San Juan city wall and the rocky coast of the Atlantic and stretched from the cemetery to the San Cristobal fort at the lower end of Old San Juan. Marco had placed her hand on the crook of his arm, and the electric feel of his fingers over hers disconcerted her. How could she feel joy at his touch while witnessing such horrific conditions?

"See those little wooden shacks with the tin roofs?" Marco asked. "That's more or less what I lived in after San Felipe destroyed my home and killed my father."

Isabela took in the shacks, some with tarpaper walls, precariously situated on the rocks. She was astounded that people lived like this. Marco had, too. Had her mother?

"Oh, Marco. These conditions are wretched. Why do they live here?"

"There's no work for them in the countryside, so they come to the city. But neither the factory wages nor the few coins they get to clean houses are enough to afford a real home in San Juan." Marco's jaw was taut, his eyes hard.

"At least they're on a hill, so when it rains, the water flows down," he continued. "In El Fanguito, the new slum near your house, they build their houses on stilts over a lake of mud. People walk on planks to get around. They don't have clean water or a sewer and have no choice but to throw their waste where the kids play. Disease is everywhere."

Isa's stomach roiled. "I know. I hold my breath every time we drive by. I can't imagine what's it like in there," she said, thinking about the clean water that came out of the taps at home and realizing she took its cleanliness for granted.

"May you never find out," Marco said, eyebrows pulled together. "Poverty's rampant all over the island, but it doesn't have to be this way. Our generation can change things."

"But how?"

"¡Señor, señor!" Before Marco could answer, one of the boys ran toward them, interrupting their conversation. "Thank you for letting us use your kite." He handed it back to Marco.

"No, no." Marco pushed the kite back. "If you promise to share it, you can keep it. And make some more, now that you know how."

The children thanked him effusively and went back to flying their new toy.

"Marco, that was very sweet," Isabela said, moved again by his kindness.

"Look how excited they are at having some newspaper glued to a couple of sticks. I had few toys growing up, but at least I had a clean home and the countryside as my playground. They really have nothing." Marco shook his head.

They watched the children for a few moments. Marco's vulnerability and eagerness to improve these children's lives fueled Isa's desire. She looked at him and then over her shoulder at Carmen, snoring loudly with her mouth wide open under the umbrella. As Isa turned back, Marco pulled her to him. His eyes questioned her for only a second before he leaned down slowly to kiss her. *Yes, yes, yes!* Isa's knees buckled.

His lips were soft but explosive on hers, his tongue tender but ardent as it explored her mouth. She placed a trembling hand on his cheek and kissed him back, every cell in her body dancing with desire.

They broke apart quickly when the children started whistling and making fun of them, afraid Carmen would waken. But that kiss! Her heart beat a flamenco in her chest. She'd undoubtedly miss that in Mexico while she earned herself a spot in this burial ground.

CHAPTER 4

- Marco -
October 1935

The day after kite flying with Isa, Sammy convinced Marco to take a much-needed study break and go out for beers and a game of dominoes, Sammy's treat. He may as well go, Marco thought, since all he could think about was that perfect kiss with Isabela. He kept reliving it in his mind, each time becoming fully aroused. Yes, he needed a beer. They met at La Tertulia, the fritters-and-drinks spot the students liked to frequent. They ordered two Coronas, a basket of cornmeal and cheese surullitos, and scoped the women scattered among the tables. None could hold a candle to Isabela.

"Oof, dire pickings here today," Marco said. His stomach grumbled in response to the aroma of frying deliciousness wafting from the kitchen.

"What about that blonde over there? She has tetas to feed an army!" Sammy said.

"She's obviously not a real blonde. Anyway, she looks cheap. Would you marry that girl, bring her home to meet your mother?"

"Whoa! Who said anything about marriage? Cálmate, amigo." Sammy laughed. "I'm just looking for a good time."

"I'm tired of just having a good time." Marco shook his head. "I want to marry a girl like Isa, someone I'll be proud to have on my arm when I'm successful. Think with the head on your shoulders, hombre, not the one between your legs."

"Things are going that well with her? You want to get *married?*" Sammy's disbelief was comical.

"She's my dream girl." Marco shrugged.

"Too bad you're not her father's dream man." Sammy chuckled and sipped his beer. Marco gave him a sideways look and leaned back in his chair. Maybe not yet, but he'd win Don Gabriel over eventually.

"Let's play." Sammy upended a box of dominoes onto the wooden table with a loud clatter, momentarily drowning out the slow and sultry bolero playing on the café's radio. They flipped the tiles face down and shuffled them in circles with their palms. Each selected seven tiles and expertly tilted them up with curled fingers to examine their hand. Sammy took the first turn.

"Have you been listening to Albizu? He's getting more and more incendiary." Sammy placed the first domino on the table face up as he brought up the latest hot topic, the same Marco had briefly discussed with Don Gabriel while waiting for Isa before their first date.

"Who has time to listen to those endless speeches of his?" Marco scowled and played his tile. "I hate that Nationalist mierda. Violence is not the way to independence. Besides, we must rebuild our economy before we can think about autonomy."

"True, true," Sammy said, pondering his next move.

"Where are those surullitos? I'm starving." Marco glanced toward the kitchen and took a swig of his beer.

While he waited for Sammy to decide his next play, Marco thought about the Liberal Party, which he and most of his fellow students backed. Its leader, Luis Muñoz Marín, supported Roosevelt's New Deal policies. The eternally rumpled, sad-eyed Muñoz Marín had spent most of the 1920s drinking and writing poetry in Greenwich Village, and was known as El Vato, the poet. Yet as the son of Luis Muñoz Rivera, the greatly respected island statesman who'd tried to broker independence from Spain back in the day, Muñoz Marín was granted instant credibility the moment he'd jumped into the island's political arena. Marco thought Muñoz was doing stellar work in the insular senate.

Marco agreed with Muñoz's insistence that Puerto Rico needed help from the Americans until it could get back on its feet. Dr.

Chardón had even developed a national reconstruction plan based on the New Deal. With that kind of progress in the works, now was not the time to rock the American boat.

Marco's father, like Don Gabriel, had been adamant about attaining independence for Puerto Rico. But Marco was certain he'd want it done peacefully, not as Albizu preached. Papá would have also understood the need to have a healthy economy first. Yes, reconstruction before independence was the correct path. It was also a direction that would afford him opportunities to make a difference, better his circumstances, and impress a girl like Isabela Soto.

Sammy finally took his turn as the piping hot, golden surullitos arrived. Marco popped one of the mini cigar-shaped fritters in his mouth and instantly regretted it.

"Oh, oh—so hot!" He spit out the steaming surullito and chugged his beer.

"Hermano, you have no patience." Sammy shook his head. "And one thing Puerto Ricans need is patience."

"Yes, a less determined people would have given up long ago." Marco's next move strategically blocked the game in one direction.

"Why couldn't Spain have won the war?" Sammy banged his next domino on the table. "We were so close! Almost our own country." He took a surullito, blew on it, and gingerly took a bite.

"A tragedy. From Spanish colony to American. My father could pontificate for hours on that topic," Marco said, smiling at the memory. He pondered his next move.

"Mine, too! Our fathers were right on many levels, though. How do we live on this ridiculously fertile land but grow only sugarcane for export? Then los Yanquis charge us a fortune to import all our food." Sammy held up a surullito to illustrate his point.

"Sí, but it's been thirty-seven years. It's time to stop dwelling on the past. The New Deal reforms will help us make real progress." Marco played his domino, preventing Sammy from laying tiles in yet another direction. "Albizu's followers must understand that we still need the Americans and their money."

"Yes, it's time to propel this island into the future," agreed Sammy, slamming a double five on the table. "Let's go to the future now, so I don't have to live through the rest of this trouncing." He shook his head in disgust.

Marco chuckled at Sammy's frustration.

Just then, a student rushed into the café, arms flailing, and yelled, "Put Albizu on!" He jumped over La Tertulia's serving counter and spun the radio's dial to change the station. "Listen!" he yelled as the sound of Albizu's gruff voice filled the air. Marco, Sammy, and the other students gathered around and quietly listened to Albizu decry the Americans and Chardón's reconstruction plan.

Marco and Sammy looked at each other, eyes weary and dark.

"Why are people listening to him?" Marco spoke loudly, his thoughts spinning as he absorbed Albizu's affronts. "Sure, Chardón's plan is contingent upon New Deal funding, but how else will we pull this island out of the mire?" He threw his arms up in frustration.

Albizu continued in angry bursts over the airwaves, "I denounce Chardón and his deans! They are trying to convert the University into an institution of American propaganda with the help of Muñoz and the Liberal Party. Any students who support Dr. Chardón and his plan are faggots, whores, traitors, and cowards!"

The huddled students protested loudly at the brutal rhetoric.

"Who the hell does he think he is?" Marco's blood was on fire. He separated himself from the group of students to pace and fan himself with his hat, nervous energy getting the best of him.

"How dare he insult us?" Sixto, a fellow student, expressed his outrage.

"He's not just insulting us; he's declaring war!" Sammy added, frowning and shaking his head.

"Albizu is Enemy Number One! Enemy Number One!" Sixto started a chant, clapping his hands to accentuate each word. The crowd immediately joined in.

"Enemy Number One! Enemy Number One!" The students cried in unison.

Sammy climbed on a chair and, with his index finger extended high in the air, shouted, "We must defend our honor!"

The students erupted into a chorus of *sís* and other assertions. Sixto ripped a piece of paper out of his notebook and sat down to write. "I'm starting a petition. We're declaring Albizu persona non grata at La Upi!"

The crowd cheered, and everyone got in line to lend their signatures to the cause.

Over the next two days, Marco and his friends collected almost three thousand signatures and decided to hold an assembly to formalize the proclamation. With Chancellor Chardón's blessing, the students scheduled their event for eleven on Thursday morning. However, worried the Nationalists might try to cause trouble, Dr. Chardón arranged for police presence.

On his way to the student assembly that Thursday, Marco passed yet another heavily armed policeman and questioned Dr. Chardón's and the police chief's wisdom. They'd placed officers on every street corner in Rio Piedras *and* all over campus! This would only taunt the Nationalists. Dressed in a jacket and tie, he started to sweat, both from the sun's prickly heat and the tension in the air.

As he approached the Escuela Normal building, the palm trees in front rustled in the warm mid-morning breeze. The structure, with its classical Greek facade, tall white columns, green wooden shutters, and terra cotta tile roof, was one of his favorites on campus. He climbed the wide entrance steps, waving at Sammy, who spoke to a group of students by the open front doors.

"Marco, help me round up these stragglers," Sammy greeted Marco. "We've got a crowd of several hundred inside, and it's almost eleven."

Marco nodded, glad to hear they had a good turnout, and ushered the remaining students indoors. The building's floor-to-ceiling shutters were closed, and the absence of sun felt almost as refreshing as a cool breeze on his hot skin. As he followed the last of the students into the theater-style assembly hall immediately to the right of the front entrance, the loud screech of a car's tires pierced the air and sent a shiver up his spine.

"What was that?" one of the students in front of him turned to ask, eyes alert.

Without responding, Marco darted the short distance back to the building's entrance, arriving in time to see a grey sedan barreling down Braumbaugh Street aimed directly at them. His blood froze when a suited man tumbled from the still- moving car. He was loading a pistol!

"Get back!" Marco yelled to several students who followed him. He ducked behind one of the heavy wooden doors and managed to push it shut and then the other just as the earsplitting cracking of gunshots assaulted his eardrums. Students spilled out of the assembly hall into the corridor, fear and questions on their faces. The sour smell of dread infused the space.

"Stay in! Stay in!" Marco shouted, pushing the crowd back, his face streaked with sweat. "There's a tiroteo outside!" Marco spotted Sammy in the crowd and motioned to him. "Sammy, help me keep these people away from the windows and doors."

Marco and Sammy had difficulty making themselves heard over the racket of frightened students, but they managed to get most of the crowd back into the assembly hall. The popping of shots continued, along with the rapid hammering of machine guns, followed by a deafening BOOM that shook the building and left their ears ringing.

"Jesus, what the hell was that?" Sammy asked. The students quieted down and looked at each other helplessly. Another scattering of shots sounded, and then silence.

Marco's heart pounded in his chest like a captured rabbit's. The only time he'd felt this helpless, the world had swirled outside the church where he'd weathered San Felipe with his family. He struggled to breathe in the air so thick with tension. Time stood still.

Finally, Marco heard men shouting orders outside and a loud banging on the building's doors.

"Is anyone hurt?" a gravelly voice called from outside.

Marco and Sammy glanced at each other with relief and quickly pulled open the doors. "Nobody's hurt," Marco said to two policemen holding machine guns. "But what's happening?"

"It's the Nationalists. They shot several people and threw a bomb at the police chief's car. It's a bloodbath. Nobody leaves this building." Students gasped and cried behind Marco. Some shouted in anger. Others prayed. Marco shook. He tried to prop himself up against the wall, but his legs gave way, and he slid down to the floor.

"Those fucking bastards," Sammy said, joining Marco on the ground.

Marco put his head in his hands and shook his head in disbelief. Was this what the future held for his island?

After calling his mother and Isa and assuring them he was unharmed, Marco spent a sleepless night only to relive the traumatic experience the following morning as he read the newspaper in Doña Teresa's living room. Four Nationalists and one poor innocent bystander, on his way to buy a lottery ticket, were dead in what the newspaper christened, "The Rio Piedras Massacre." Another four people were injured, one critically. Dr. Chardón had canceled classes until Monday, and Albizu vowed vengeance.

The son-of-a-bitch who instigated the killings of his own followers and murdered innocent people wanted vengeance? Who would listen to such mierda? Marco, enraged, paced back and forth, gripping the newspaper in his fist. *What do these animals hope to accomplish with senseless violence? We have enough suffering on this island. Do we have to kill each other, too?* He sat down and raked his fingers through his hair. He ached for peace, for progress, for the Puerto Rico his father had envisioned.

Marco contemplated the disturbing front-page photo: a dead Nationalist lying in a pool of blood on the pavement. He carefully ripped it out and put it in his wallet alongside the clipping of Isabela and Gardel, a new totem to guide his actions.

CHAPTER 5

- Isabela -
November 1935

Isa noticed a marked change in Papi's attitude toward Marco after the Rio Piedras Massacre, and not for the better. Even though Marco and the students had been innocent bystanders to the violence, Papi believed he'd purposely put himself in danger. Marco could do as he pleased, but putting Isa in peril was unacceptable. Yet Connie had warned Papi against forbidding Isa to see Marco.

Instead, her father launched a campaign to keep her so busy she wouldn't have time for Marco. Of course, Isa had free moments here and there, but coordinating her availability with Marco's schedule and Carmen's time was daunting. And, as much as she ached to see Marco, Isa couldn't risk doing so on the sly. Oh, how tongues would wag if someone saw her gallivanting with a man unchaperoned. Papi would kill her—his efforts to keep her respectable erased in a second.

Isa had no choice but to let Papi and Connie drag her to the Casino's Discovery Ball celebrating November nineteenth, the date Columbus landed on the island. The ball's entertainment committee had requested she recite a poem, but as Isa approached the microphone at center stage, she felt detached from the glamorous crowd assembled in the glowing white marble ballroom. Gardenias abounded, exuding a sickly-sweet odor that turned her stomach. She fixed her gaze on the massive crystal chandelier glittering above her audience, trying to curb her aversion. Isa waved an enormous mosquito away from the orchid pinned to the shoulder of her seafoam-green tulle dress, took a breath, and launched into Luis

Lloréns Torres's poem, "Canción de las Antillas." She knew most of the long ode by heart and didn't need to refer too often to the typed text in her hand. Isa finally finished to raucous applause and shouts of "Brava, Isabela!"

The rest of the evening should have sped by in a blur as she glided among the guests with the confidence of the adored. Instead, she felt as if her soul was floating above her, watching her woodenly go through the motions of attending a party. Neither the sumptuous surroundings, her attentive admirers, nor the orchestra's sweet danzas could shake her indifference. Isa turned inward, where images of Marco cluttered her head. The way the skin by his eyes crinkled when he grinned. The cowlick he was constantly pushing off his forehead. His highly shined shoes. His joy at introducing her to new places. The sparks she felt every time he touched her. That kiss! Her heart did a little flip at each memory, confirming her suspicions. She was falling in love with this man. But what about Mexico?

As the Christmas holidays approached, Isa managed to schedule a quick date with Marco before he left for Yabucoa for his school break. On a rainy Saturday morning in early December, Mariano drove Isa and Carmen to meet Marco for breakfast at La Bombonera in Old San Juan. Marco splurged on mallorca pastries topped with powdered sugar, while Carmen opted to afford them some privacy by sitting at the counter with a cafecito, her back to them. They nursed their coffees and chatted gayly about inconsequential matters, happy to be in each other's company again, the desire between them palpable.

Marco suddenly reached for Isa's hands and said, "Tell me, Isa. Why does a girl like you care even a little about a guy like me?"

Isa's heart raced, and her breath caught in her throat. Good God, they were finally going to talk about their feelings. Did Marco have feelings for her? Did they mirror her feelings for him? She squeezed Marco's hand to keep hers from trembling. "I care more than a little." *Had she really said that?* Her face must be as fiery red as a flamboyán tree in full bloom.

"But why? You must have your choice of wealthy suitors, men from your world. I can't compete with them." Marco's eyes were downcast.

Isa was stunned to witness this uncertain Marco. Yet his vulnerability was endearing and calmed her nerves. "Men from my world," she said with a dismissive chuckle that got Marco to look up, "are conceited idiots who only care about money and status and not a bit about a woman's opinions or dreams. They bore me to death."

"But I don't?" Marco, seemingly recovered, gave her a hopeful look.

That was more like it! Isa shook her head, eyes merry. "With you, I experience life! Every time we're together, I learn something new. You make me feel alive!" She squeezed his hands.

"But I'm just a jíbaro with big dreams."

Again, Isa was taken aback. He really thought he was inferior to her, this seemingly self-possessed man. Surely, he'd feel differently if he knew her real story. Isa made up her mind on the spot. If this relationship was to have any kind of future, she needed to summon all her courage and tell him right then. She extracted her hands from his and clenched them on her lap as beads of sweat erupted on her hairline and upper lip.

"You might think you're not good enough for me, but I need to tell you a secret that may change your mind." Isa held Marco's gaze, but her voice wavered. "Something I've never told another soul."

"What can that possibly be? Tell me." Marco appeared bemused. Would he still feel that way after he heard? Was she really going to tell him?

Isa spoke quickly before she could change her mind. "I'm the illegitimate child of a jíbara." She held her breath but kept eye contact with him. Every nerve in her body was on high alert. Her skin felt like it was crawling with red ants.

Marco's face scrunched in confusion, and his voice became a whisper. "What do you mean?"

"Her name was María," Isa continued more slowly. "Growing up, I didn't know much about her." She saw the news beginning to take hold behind Marco's eyes and sensed him fighting to keep his features neutral. His Adam's apple bobbed up and down. *Had he just gulped in shock? Oh, God!* He had but nodded for her to continue. And so, she did. It was too late to turn back now.

"Carmen was the one who told me the story. María was a laundress at our house, only seventeen, and Papi was a year older. Supposedly they fell in love, and he got her pregnant, but she went back to the mountains before Abuela found out. Abuela would have never allowed a marriage between them. When María died giving birth, her mother decided to make me Papi's problem and dropped me like an unwanted package at Abuela's house."

"What did your abuela do?" Marco's eyes were saucers. Was he reacting to the story or to what it revealed?

"She told everyone I was Papi's daughter and that my mother died in childbirth."

"Didn't people wonder where you'd come from? Your father wasn't even married, was he?" Marco asked.

"If your family is prominent enough, people look the other way and don't ask questions. And when I moved to San Juan after Abuela died, I had a fresh start."

"Huh," Marco grunted.

"My whole life, I've felt an emptiness deep in my core. I don't know anything about my maternal roots or who I really am. Am I a socialite or a jíbara? Can I be both?" Isa brushed a tear from her cheek. Exhausted and drained, she looked at him with openness and trust, waiting for his reaction. *Say something, Marco.*

"You're far from a jíbara," Marco finally responded, his eyes kind. "Jíbaros are uneducated, and that's why they're poor. You take a jíbaro out of the mountains, provide an education and a way to make a living, and he becomes an asset to society. Like you."

A rush of love overwhelmed her and literally took her breath away. "You really don't think less of me?" Isa asked once she could speak again. She brushed away the tears now flowing freely.

"Never." Marco reached for her hands again.

"Thank you, Marco. I'm humbled. I listen to you talk about how you want to improve conditions for the poor and the jíbaros, and it feeds my soul. I'd also like to help my mother's people, my people. I can't bear that Rafael Hernández song 'Lamento Borincano' about the jibarito who goes to the market with great hopes and returns to his family having sold nothing. It guts me."

"That's because you're a compassionate woman." Marco pulled Isa's hands to his mouth and kissed them.

Isa's heart swelled. He accepted her, jíbara roots and all.

The next day Isabela gathered all her *Cinelandia* magazines, intent on throwing them away. Who cared what movie stars wore or did when people in the poorest parts of her city were dying of tuberculosis, malaria, and measles? Who was she to have so much while others lived in misery? How rewarding could a life full of applause possibly be when some can't think beyond their next meal? If her mother had lived, would Isa be one of the suffering poor? These questions weighed heavily on Isabela's mind, and her acting ambitions, which she'd relegated to the back burner during the past two months, felt selfish and vapid.

She was relieved and grateful that Marco accepted her as she was. All her life, she'd felt less than, even in comparison to her half-sisters, as much as she loved them. Perhaps that's why she'd thirsted for applause. On stage, she received unconditional love. Nobody cared where actors came from, which was probably why Papi didn't want her to move in those circles. It would put her on the level of the masses, deny all his efforts to elevate her status, perhaps diminishing his own in the process. This was becoming all too clear to her, yet unimportant.

Isabela threw herself on her embroidered bedspread and stared at the ceiling. She'd learned so much from Marco. For the first time in her life, she'd begun forming her own political opinions, which neither centered around independence nor statehood. The only viable side to be on was the side of the people. She was anti-suffering. It was as simple and as critical as that. Forget Mexico! Instead, she'd join Marco in the fight for a modern Puerto Rico, their passion forging a formidable team. They would change lives for the better! Isabela imagined working side by side with Marco, emptying the slums, having intellectual conversations with the island's brightest minds, and lobbying for policy changes. She'd be the Puerto Rican Eleanor Roosevelt. At Senator Muñoz Marín's invitation, the American First Lady had toured several slums during a visit to the island two years ago. Her input was instrumental in ensuring FDR's New Deal benefits included Puerto Rico. Isa would follow in Mrs. Roosevelt's steps. She, too, would visit a slum and see first-hand how she could help.

She'd been curious about slum living conditions since her peek at La Perla the day Marco took her kite flying. He'd said El Fanguito, a slum in a mangrove mere blocks from her sumptuous home, was even worse than La Perla. She knew one of the young housemaids, Elena, had family there. They'd come from Jayuya after Hurricane San Ciprián had leveled that town's coffee plantations four years ago. Isa got up to ask Elena to take her to El Fanguito tomorrow.

"¿Pero cuantos tornillos les faltan a ustedes?" Carmen turned away from the kitchen sink to face Isa and Elena, eyes stern and voice raised. "You're completely crazy. El Fanguito's no place for sightseeing, Isa. You'll catch tuberculosis and die unless your father kills you first."

"Shhh! Papi will only find out if you tell him. I need to go, Carmen. I want to see how I can help."

"Métete a mono y pierde el rabo." Carmen waved a dish rag at Isa in warning.

"Nothing's going to happen," Isa countered.

"¡Dios santo!" Carmen wiped her brow. "And you, Elena, how can you be partial to this insanity?"

"I'm only taking her to my aunt's house. It's in the driest part. We won't go any further."

"See? I'll be perfectly safe, Carmen."

Carmen raised her eyes to the sky and crossed herself.

As Isa and Elena approached the Martin Peña mangrove, the fetid stench became excruciating, practically solid in its stifling burden. It gripped Isa like a vise. She took shallow breaths, refusing to insult the residents of El Fanguito by plugging her nose. These were her mother's people, country jíbaros, who'd moved to San Juan with high hopes for a better life. The first squatters had built shacks on stilts at the mangrove's edge, but as more and more families poured in, the slum began to spread over the swamp toward the lagoon. Today, they'd stay on the dry part.

Isa eyed the haphazard landscape of small huts. Each was eight or ten feet long, perhaps slightly wider, with walls patched together from cardboard and wood scraps. Corrugated zinc and flattened tin cans passed for roofing material. Naked children, many with distended bellies, played in front of the houses and stopped to stare as the young women passed. Isa tried not to stare back. These conditions were more than deplorable; they were inhuman. How desperate things must be for jíbaros to trade the clean air of the mountains for this nightmare existence. Isa struggled to process this reality, so diametrically opposed to her own. Her fight or flight instinct kicked in, but she forced herself to keep following Elena, adrenalin coursing through her veins.

"Watch your step," Elena said as she led Isa over a network of planks raised two or so feet above the muddy ground. A sad dog with protruding ribs approached them, hopefully, but Elena shooed him away. Isa concentrated on navigating the narrow planks, placing one tentative foot in front of the other, breathing as little as possible. They passed a man digging a hole to bury his garbage next to several snorting pigs rooting in the mud. A rooster crowed over the humming din of daily human life.

"What if someone comes from the opposite direction?" Isa asked.

Elena chuckled. "You hug, do a little dance to get by each other, and pray nobody falls in."

Isa shuddered at the thought of falling into this mire full of garbage and human waste. "I thought you said your aunt lives in the dry part."

"This *is* the dry part." Elena took a left off the main path and followed a long plank to one of the shacks. Its wooden door hung wide open, revealing a naked toddler behind a small gate designed to keep him inside. Isa imagined one of her sisters tumbling into this mud and shuddered. No wonder disease ran rampant in the slums.

"Wait here," Elena told Isa. Elena ruffled the child's head and called out to her aunt before stepping inside.

Isa rested one hand on the house to steady herself. By breathing as shallowly as possible, she'd made herself lightheaded. Her hat offered protection from the biting sun, but the heat was still powerful, and she'd sweated through her dress. Her belly felt queasy, and her head pounded. She needed to sit down, but would there even be a chair?

"Señorita Isa," Elena stood at the doorway. "Please meet my Titi Gloria."

A haggard woman wearing a faded calico dress welcomed Isa inside with a shy smile and offered her a glass of water, which she poured out of a large tin can. Isa thanked her and drank gratefully while taking in her surroundings. In addition to the door, two windows with open shutters let in light and anything else that desired entry, evidenced by the numerous mosquitoes and flies buzzing around. A contained cooking area for a wood fire lay dormant in a corner beside a raised plank used to prepare food. Above it, a shelf held rice, dried beans, and a tin of saltine crackers. Several old cans full of water dotted the floor. A handmade table with four rough-hewn chairs completed the furnishings, and stacks of empty burlap sacks along the perimeters looked like they served as bedding. A few pieces of clothing hung on hooks while a freshly laundered dress and two pairs of work pants dried on a clothesline strung across the hut. She didn't want to imagine how they went to the bathroom. Profound sadness squeezed her heart and threatened to make her cry, but Isa swallowed her tears.

"Titi, we brought you some things," Elena said, handing her aunt a paper bag that held canned sardines and pears, a pound of coffee, and two pounds of dried cod.

"Gracias, mija. Gracias, Señorita Isabela." Gloria kissed her niece and bowed her head to Isa, inviting them both to sit. She set about placing crackers on a plate.

"Thank you, Doña Gloria, for welcoming me to your home," Isa said. "Don't worry about feeding us. We just had breakfast."

Doña Gloria ignored Isa's protestations, placed the plate of saltines on the table, and insisted they partake. Because refusing would be rude, Isa nibbled on a cracker, hoping it would help settle her stomach. She asked for another glass of water, pronouncing it the most refreshing she'd had in a while.

"It's just from the government faucet at the entrance," Doña Gloria said. "The kids go in the morning and after school."

I'm drinking the precious water children lug here over those planks! Embarrassed, Isa set the glass down.

"Doña Gloria, thank you for your hospitality, and please forgive me for barging in on you like this." Isa placed a gentle hand over Doña Gloria's cracked fingers. "I see much need here, and I'd like to know how I can help."

"I have six children, but my husband's a mason, so we eat. Many have it much worse because the men can't get work. The Lopez family next door has nine children and no job."

Isa tried to hide her shock at the thought of that many people living in one of these tiny huts. "How do they survive?"

"Sometimes they get food vouchers from the government, and sometimes they buy on credit if the shops let them. The Pentecostals come around with food and clothes, and some girls from La Upi also help. But we also help each other. I'll give them the sardines you brought, if you don't mind."

"Of course, please do." Isa nodded, struck by the woman's generosity. "And your children are in school?"

"Yes, they're learning to read and write. Imagine that. They'll be smarter than their parents and able to get ahead." Doña Gloria smiled widely.

"You never learned to read or write?" Isa asked, not surprised. Most jíbaros were illiterate.

"No, not me." Doña Gloria shook her head and frowned, as if the thought was ludicrous.

"Would you like to learn?" Isa said, horrified at the thought of not having books in one's life.

"Bah! What do I need with reading? Besides, I'm too old."

Before Isa could counter the woman's misconception, they were interrupted by a voice calling, "¡Doña Gloria!" A woman younger than Isa called from the hut's entrance. "You need anything today?"

"No, no. We're fine," Doña Gloria responded before turning to Isa and saying, "This is one of the girls from La Upi."

"Beatriz Ayala, at your service." Beatriz held her hand out to Isa.

Isa shook the hand and took in the broad-faced young woman in the cool, sleeveless cotton dress and practical rubber boots. "Mucho gusto, Beatriz. Soy Isabela Soto. Doña Gloria tells me you and some others help here."

"Sí, we bring food, clothes, help the children with their homework, things like that," Beatriz said. "Right, Doña Gloria?"

Doña Gloria nodded while Isa's wheels turned. People were already helping here. Could she bring herself back to this hellish place and join them?

"Tell me, do you have to be a college student to join your efforts?" Isa half hoped her lack of higher education would exclude her, the question of whether to return to this place quickly settled.

Beatriz's laugh sounded like a chorus of tiny bells. "Don't be silly. We'll take extra hands where we can get them. It's hard work but very rewarding." Beatriz rummaged through her purse, took out a pen and paper, wrote down her phone number, and handed it to Isa. "Please call me. I'll be happy to tell you more and help get you started if you're really interested. We'd love to have you."

"Oh, thank you," Isa said, her voice tentative as she accepted the piece of paper.

"Well, I'm off to complete my rounds." Beatriz waved. "Nice to meet you, Isabela."

Isa and Elena visited with Doña Gloria for a bit longer. The more Isa learned about life in El Fanguito, the more she wanted to bolster these people, and the less she thought she could bring herself to return to this God-forsaken slum. She didn't want to think about what kind of person that made her.

Isa lay awake under her mosquito netting that evening with a new appreciation for Mrs. Roosevelt's character and fortitude. The smells and sights she'd experienced today had shocked and angered her. It wasn't a matter of whether she could bring herself to return to El Fanguito; she had to go back. She'd find the strength to join Beatriz. But how? If only she could discuss what she'd seen with Marco. He'd be so proud of her initiative. But she didn't want to disappoint him by failing to follow through, either. She'd keep today's visit to herself until she had a concrete plan of action she was confident she could implement.

Isa imagined herself and Marco as leaders of the young new set bringing progress to the island, her work to improve El Fanguito conditions lauded, her illegitimacy inconsequential. She'd find the courage to work in the slums. Her physical aversion was a mere roadblock, one not nearly as insurmountable as getting past Papi.

He'd indulged her and let her see Marco for this long because she'd stopped asking to go to Mexico, and he was glad to see her cheerful. But he would soon demand she date someone more appropriate. Papi's need to keep up appearances would far outweigh his desire for her happiness.

Before falling asleep that evening, Isa prayed she wouldn't run out of time before realizing her new dream.

CHAPTER 6

- Marco -
December 1935 to April 1936

Marco thanked God for his height as he navigated through the throngs at the dock, all waiting for loved ones to disembark the *S.S. Coamo*. He was meeting his cousin Nando, home from Columbia University, and together they'd ride to Yabucoa in a car Tío Ernesto had hired. Finally, he spotted Nando following a luggage porter down the gangplank.

"Nando, Nando! Over here!" Marco waved his arms and tried to shout above the hubbub.

"¡Hermano!" Nando waved back.

The cousins, close as brothers, enveloped each other in a firm hug. Marco added his suitcase to the porter's dolly, and the two men followed the porter as he expertly wove through the crowd. They breathed a sigh of relief once safely inside the hired car.

"Boy, am I happy to be home after sixteen days on that ship!"

"How about a little pick-me-up, then?" Marco reached into his jacket pocket and pulled out a half-pint of rum.

"Cousin, you never disappoint. Hand that caneca over." Nando opened the bottle and took a long swig. "Ahhhhh. Nectar of the gods." Marco laughed and grabbed the bottle back.

"¡Dios mío! I can't wait to eat real food," Nando said. "Americans don't know how to season *anything*. And forget that brown water they call coffee." He made a face, shaking his head. Marco passed him the bottle back, and Nando took another swig of rum. They emptied it quickly, and soon Nando snored, leaving Marco to ponder his last conversation with Isa.

He couldn't have fathomed Isa's secret in a million years. When she revealed her illegitimacy, he'd been dumfounded, ears ringing as if a bomb had exploded near his head. What a tale! Her grandmother must have been a formidable woman to demand the entire city of Ponce overlook Isa's origins and welcome her with open arms. Once again, proof of the power of money. God forgive him; he couldn't help but look at Isa in a new, slightly dimmer light. But was it because of her illegitimacy or because she'd conveniently escaped its consequences?

He'd meant what he said about jíbaros being made, not born. Jíbaros were the only trace left of the Taíno Indians after the Spaniards forced them into slavery and worked them to death. The few Taínos who escaped into the mountains intermarried with humble Spanish farmers and later African slaves, creating the jíbaro. City folks thought they were lazy, but he knew jíbaros worked hard and had hearts of gold. The Puerto Rican literary canon was replete with novels, songs, and poems elegizing the unassuming jíbaro. But if being a descendant of a jíbaro was nothing to be ashamed of, why did so many Puerto Ricans tout their European heritage over their indigenous roots? Papá had boasted he could trace his ancestors to Spain, Italy, and Corsica, that they might be related to Napoleon.

Who knew where Isa's maternal roots led? But was that important? Her character, beauty, and grace more than made up for her questionable, albeit secret, background. And secrecy was the key. If nobody knew Isa was a bastard and a jíbara, what did it matter?

Pursuing Isa had been an aspirational fantasy. He'd had zero expectations of success. Part of him had presumed she'd be a wearying, self-centered, spoiled woman. Yet she was vivacious, kind, intelligent, and cultured. He'd been surprised at her eagerness to understand the plight of the Puerto Rican people, her refusal to remain one more of the oblivious rich. Yes, of course, she'd be an asset at his side. By the time Marco reached Yabucoa, he'd made up his mind. He'd overlook Isa's illegitimacy. They need not discuss the issue ever again.

That evening, Marco, Nando, Mamá, Julia, Tío, Tía, and Marco's six cousins gathered around Tío's extra-long dining table for a joyful, chaotic dinner of carne frita, tostones, and arroz con habichuelas.

Sated, Marco, Julia and Mamá said their goodbyes and walked next door to the tiny cement home Tío had helped them build after San Felipe. Two months into their ordeal, when they were still living in a tent, a solemn Mamá had sat Julia and him down and said, "Mis hijos, you've been courageous throughout this terrible time, and I'm proud of you. Your father would be proud, too." Her words sounded strangled. She glanced down, paused for a moment, then raised her eyes and continued, "Obviously, we can't live in a tent for the rest of our lives. But we're going to have to make sacrifices."

"Sacrifices?" Marco asked. What, he'd wondered, did they have left to sacrifice?

"We can't afford to build a new house unless we sell our land." Mamá's tone was unfaltering.

Marco's jaw dropped.

"Sell the land?"

"It's the only way." Mamá's eyes were kind, but her words cut him to his core.

"No. Absolutely not. Papá broke his back to buy that little plot of land and build our house, to give us security. Selling it would dishonor his memory," Marco couldn't control his shaky voice. How could his mother even think of betraying Papá's legacy this way?

"Be reasonable, amor. What good is the land without any money to build on it? Tío Ernesto has offered us a small piece of the property behind where he's putting his new bakery and home. We can use his leftover materials and buy whatever else we need with the money we get for the land."

Marco's stomach had roiled as the tent spun around him. He couldn't look at Mamá, couldn't stay inside the airless tent for one more second. He'd sprinted toward the river and, once near its banks, collapsed under a decimated mango tree before allowing wrenching sobs to consume his body. He wept until his anger finally abated, and exhausted, rested there with a pounding head, overcome with grief and resignation. Mamá was right. What else could they do?

He'd vowed to be strong for Mamá and Julia and pledged to buy Mamá the kind of house she deserved one day. That day was approaching; he was certain.

As soon as they entered their humble home, Julia begged exhaustion and retired to her room, leaving Marco and Mamá to chat in the living area. They sat on simple wooden chairs with a small round table between them. Marco caught her up on his studies, eager to get the update out of the way so he could tell Mamá about Isabela.

"Mamá, I've been seeing a special girl." Marco's eyes twinkled.

"¿De veras, Marquito? Tell me about her!" Mama broke into a smile, and Marco could almost see the little grandchildren he knew his mother envisioned.

"Her name is Isabela, and she's beautiful, kind, and lots of fun." Marco pulled the newspaper clipping of Isa and Gardel from his wallet and proudly handed it to Mamá, pointing at Isabela. "Look, that's her."

"Pero Marco, why is she in the newspaper?" Mama frowned in confusion. "And with Gardel! Who is this girl?" She handed the photo back to Marco.

Marco eagerly filled Mamá in on Isa's details. "Her father is a bear, though. He doesn't think I'm good enough for his daughter, but I will prove him wrong." At least, Marco hoped so.

"Marco, mijo, I thank God every day for all the blessings he's sent you," Mamá said, placing her hand over his on the table between them.

"And I thank God for your love and support." Marco took his mother's hand, gently kissed it, and released it.

"I've always encouraged you to follow your dreams." Mamá wrung her hands and looked pained.

"I sense a 'but,' Mamá."

"It's just... do you really think a girl like that will be happy for long going on your little inexpensive outings? She was raised to live a different life than you can offer her."

"I do think about that, Mamá." Marco nodded in agreement. "I'm not so naive as to believe love can overcome all obstacles. It's all an adventure for her right now, and maybe she'll grow weary, but I won't let it get to that point."

"And how will you manage that?" Mamá looked dubious.

Why would Mamá doubt him? Hadn't he accomplished everything he'd set out to do? Disquieted, he answered, "By making money. Hard work and wise investments, Mamá. I have a plan. No need for you to worry."

Mamá crossed herself and murmured a prayer. "May God continue to watch over you, Marco. I will pray for you and Isabela both."

Marco could still see the unease in her eyes and wondered whether his mother's concern was valid.

Marco wrote to Isa the next day, letting her know of his safe arrival home and telling her he missed her. A few days later, he received a letter from her, so their missives must have crossed in the mail. He took the letter outside and sat under an acerola tree to read it, hands trembling.

> *Querido Marco,*
>
> *I hope you're enjoying your time in Yabucoa with your family, but I miss you so! Why must the Christmas season be this long? We just celebrated the birth of baby Jesus and still have New Year's, Three Kings Day and Las Octavitas for eight days after! Meanwhile, Papi's forcing me to attend every party we're invited to.*
>
> *I've drawn the line at the Casino's Three Kings Day fiesta. They're asking everyone to dress like jíbaros—the privileged*

playing at being poor. Can you believe it? It's reprehensible, and I've made my opinion known to Papi, Connie, and the powers that be at the Casino. Alas, my protestations have fallen on deaf ears, as I suspected they would. I'll stay home and play with Mati and Rosie instead. If it wasn't for my sisters' excitement, these would be bleak days indeed.

I wish you un próspero año nuevo, Marco, with many wonderful things coming your way in 1936.

Con mucho cariño,

Isa

Marco reflexively crumbled the letter in his fist as a heat wave overtook him. He was proud of Isa's refusal to participate in the Casino farce but raged at the Casino and its members. How dare they demean these humble people! The jíbaros traditionally came down from the mountains every Epiphany to sing agüinaldos to the townspeople. The gift of song was all they had to give, and they gave it gladly. These San Juaneros could learn a thing or two about generosity and grace.

He thought about Miguel Pou's painting titled *Our Daily Bread* of a barefoot jíbaro dressed in the customary tan pants, long-sleeved white shirt, and broad-brimmed straw pava hat with the ends left unwoven. Resigned and tired, he lugged a massive bunch of plantains. Painted in 1902, it could be any jíbaro today. They'd made such little progress in the last thirty-four years.

Casino comemierdas! He strode into the house and threw the crumbled letter in the trash.

On the eve of Three Kings Day, Marco helped his two youngest cousins gather bits of grass to put by their beds, a snack for the Three Kings' camels. Gaspar, Melchior, and Balthazar would leave them flower-shaped cookies, tops, and a small flute this year.

The next day, while the entire family walked home from church, the jíbaros began to arrive from their mountain homes, some on foot and others on horseback. They congregated in small groups holding cuatro guitars, güiros for scratching out rhythms, drums, tambourines, and maracas. All wore their best pants, clean white shirts, and pava hats.

Marco knew they'd stop at Tío's house and play for a while, and in return, they'd enjoy plenty of food and drink. He chuckled, thinking he wouldn't want to be a jíbaro the day after Reyes.

An hour later, the party was in full swing behind Tío's bakery, and Marco rubbed his hands together at the sight. A wood plank supported by cinderblocks served as a bar with rum, beers, the deadly pitorro moonshine, and plenty of coquito, creamy coconut eggnog with lots of cinnamon, on hand. A large woman wearing a fancy flowered dress fried blood sausage morcillas and alcapurrias of taro root and meat in a giant black cauldron over a wood fire. A whole pig roasted on a spit, the fire tended to by a jíbaro who turned the lechón periodically, ensuring evenly crisped skin. It smelled of burning wood, frying food, and dripping pork fat.

A bevy of boisterous kids played games with their new toys, and everyone was dressed in their finest outfits. A long table was laden with pasteles, arroz con gandules, marinated green bananas, and countless sweets, including arroz con dulce, coconut kisses, almond cookies, flans, and cakes from Tío's bakery. Pasteles, made of taro root and plantain masa stuffed with seasoned pork and wrapped in plantain leaves, were his favorite.

Marco's stomach growled.

"Marco!" Mamá laughed. "We better feed that monster."

"Sorry! But I can't help it. Doña Teresa doesn't cook like this, you know. Yabucoa knows how to celebrate." Marco rubbed his hands together and made a beeline for the pasteles.

He licked his fingers as he devoured delicacy after delicacy. Food had always been abundant during holiday celebrations, thanks to Tío. Nobody starved in his town during the holidays, no matter how poor.

A quartet of jíbaros playing instruments entered the party, and the crowd joined them in song.

"Hacia Belén se encamina
María con su amante esposo,
Llevando en su compañia
A todo un Dios poderoso.
Alegría, alegría, alegría,
Alegría, alegría, y placer,
Que la Virgen va de paso
Con su esposo hacia Belén."

Marco's heart swelled with pride at his culture. Maybe it was the coquito, but his eyes teared at this beautiful Reyes celebration, heavenly food, lush green mountains, clean air, and his family's delighted faces. He felt sorry for the stiff people at the Casino de Puerto Rico, pretending to be jíbaros and eating food half as delicious as this. Actually, no. He didn't feel sorry for them. It was precisely what they deserved.

Upon his return to San Juan, Marco ached to see Isa, to take her in his arms again and kiss her sweet lips. They'd been able to schedule a date between all the social commitments Don Gabriel continued to thrust upon his daughter. Marco couldn't wait to get her out of the house and away from Don Gabriel. They'd go to the movies, where Carmen might fall asleep again if they were lucky. At the very least, he'd sit next to Isa and feel her warmth fuel his desire.

Isa sat waiting for him on the veranda, a vision in pink and more beautiful than Marco remembered. His legs grew weak, and his heart beat an erratic rhythm that pounded in his ears. Upon seeing him, Isa jumped up, ran down the stone path, and wrapped her arms around Marco in a tight hug. He reciprocated, taking in her garden-fresh scent, but reluctantly broke the embrace, trying to hide his arousal.

"Welcome back, Marco!" Isa said.

"Christmas was long, wasn't it?" Marco, eyes soft and liquid, took Isa in.

A pointed "Harrumph!" coming from the house interrupted their reunion. Marco glanced behind Isa to see Don Gabriel's face clouded with disapproval. His erection shriveled like a grape drying in the sun. He was back, alright!

"Feliz año nuevo, Don Gabriel," Marco greeted the sour-faced man.

"Same to you, of course," Don Gabriel answered, manners trumping his dislike.

"Marco, let's get going," Isa said. She was as eager as he to get away from Don Gabriel! "I'll get Carmen."

"No," Don Gabriel held his arm out, palm up. "Carmen's busy. *I* will be your chaperone today. Let me get my hat."

Panicked, Marco searched Isa's face for an explanation, but she looked dumbfounded. Before they could speak, Don Gabriel returned and guided them toward Mariano, who held the passenger car door open in the driveway. Don Gabriel motioned for Marco to get in the front, then sat in the rear with Isa.

Marco's head spun. There'd be no chance of a kiss now, maybe no touching at all. And what would they talk about with Don Gabriel hanging on their every word? Marco took several deep breaths, trying not to explode.

"Papi, remember when you used to take me to the movies in Ponce behind Abuela's back?" He heard Isa address her father in the back. "Marco, Abuela thought movies were indecent, so Papi would sneak me out whenever he was home from his travels. Remember that, Papi? That's when you used to be fun."

"What are you talking about? I'm still fun! We'll have a great time today, the three of us."

Isa sighed, and they rode the rest of the short way in silence.

Marco bought their tickets with a feeling of déjà vu back to their first date. It pained him to purchase Don Gabriel a ticket when the man could afford to buy the entire theater. Look at him, grinning with satisfaction. Of course, Don Gabriel sat between Marco and Isa, commenting loudly throughout the movie and blowing his nose into an already sodden handkerchief several times. Marco leaned away from the insufferable man and seethed, ignoring the action on the screen. Instead, he accessed his knowledge of the Spanish Inquisition and plotted ways to torture Don Gabriel. This man had been fun once? Ha!

The date finally ended without a moment for Marco and Isa to speak privately. Isa said goodbye with tears in her eyes, leaving him frustrated, sad, angry, and more determined than ever to beat her father.

Moving forward, Don Gabriel insisted on chaperoning Isa and Marco. That was: when he made himself available. The man feigned sickness on two occasions, forcing the cancellation of both dates. Then he banned them from canoeing at Isla Verde Beach because such an outing would involve revealing bathing suits.

Though enraged, Marco was determined to stay cool and bide his time. After all, Don Gabriel was a busy man. He couldn't keep this farce up forever. *Patience, Marco, patience.*

Marco took a break from his studies one April afternoon to visit with Isa on her veranda. Don Gabriel sat on the glider next to her, reading work papers, Marco across from them. Thrilled to be in each other's company, Isa and Marco chatted about inconsequential matters and fell into a companionable silence. She perused a poetry book while he read the latest news.

"Things have been quiet since Albizu was jailed," Marco remarked. The Nationalist leader was captured in February after his men assassinated the island's American police chief in retaliation for the Rio Piedras Massacre.

"Yes, it's good to have that lunatic behind bars," Don Gabriel said, looking up from his papers. The two men agreed on that much.

"Now we can concentrate on moving forward without all his shenanigans and distractions. There's work to do with the Americans," Marco said.

Don Gabriel trained steely eyes on Marco. Marco's blood ran cold, and he berated himself for making a mistake of such epic proportions.

"You still want to stay under the American's thumb?" Don Gabriel's harsh tone prickled Marco's skin.

Marco leaned back with a sigh and addressed Don Gabriel. "We can't go backward, Don Gabriel. If the Americans leave, more of the poor will flood San Juan."

Don Gabriel shrugged. The man's callousness was inconceivable. Marco was at a loss for words.

Isa's head shot back. "Papi, half the population is already unemployed! We can't have more people end up in the infernal slums. We need to get the children out of those horrible places. They play in the foul mud amid garbage as if it's normal."

Isa spoke with such conviction that if Marco didn't know better, he'd think she had first-hand knowledge of the conditions she described.

"You speak with the soft heart of a woman. Don't worry about such things." Don Gabriel patted Isa's leg.

Marco gathered his wits and forced himself to adopt a conversational, not confrontational, tone. "If the island is in economic misery, who'll buy your fancy imports? You'll be ruined, like everyone else."

"A few years of schooling, and you think you know everything about commerce, don't you?" Don Gabriel raised an eyebrow and shook his head as if pitying Marco.

"Papi can survive anything," Isa rolled her eyes. "Believe me; he's very resourceful. Someday, I'll tell you exactly how resourceful."

Don Gabriel did a double take, seemingly confused at Isa's comment, and stayed quiet.

Marco's heart did a little flip. Was there going to be a "someday" for them? He forced his brain to return to the discussion at hand. "We need jobs like the ones the Puerto Rico Reconstruction Agency can create with American dollars."

"Bah!" Don Gabriel appeared tired of the conversation. Had Isa's comment taken the wind out of his sails?

Isa addressed her father. "Why can't you see that food is more important than political status right now?"

"¡Don't tell me what to think, niña malcriada! And, you—" Don Gabriel pointed at Marco, "Stop filling my daughter's head with nonsense."

"Don Gabriel, none of us likes being a colony, but we have other problems to solve first. PRRA's work is critical. In fact, I hope to join the agency." Marco tried to turn the conversation to a lighter topic, perhaps one that might impress Don Gabriel, who sat back, arms crossed, smoldering.

"Oh, Marco! You could do so much good!" Isa intertwined her hands, a brilliant smile lighting up her face.

"Lucky for me, Dr. Chardón was tapped to run the agency."

"Yes, lucky for you," Don Gabriel's words dripped sarcasm, and he turned his attention back to his work.

Was there no pleasing this man?

"Will he offer you a position?" Isa looked hopeful.

"Let's just say my prospects are excellent," Marco said. He was fairly certain Dr. Chardón would offer him a job at PRRA but didn't want to count his chickens just yet. PRRA, like many New Deal agencies, was shifting its focus from short-term relief efforts to long-term economic reconstruction. Marco ached to play a part in the agency's monumental plans: building an island-wide hurricane-proof infrastructure, creating decent public housing, and fostering manufacturing capabilities, among other initiatives.

"I will pray to San Antonio and put him upside down in a pot of beans," Isa announced.

"No! No!" Marco said in mock horror. "That's to get a boyfriend!

You need to pray to San Cayetano for a job." He didn't need Isa attracting any new suitors! Don Gabriel's sabotage efforts were more than enough.

"What do I know about superstitions?" Isa waved him off, cheeks crimson. "I just want you to get that job."

Marco grinned and winked at her. He enjoyed influencing Isa's political opinions and had been impressed by her passion today. Marco had years of Don Gabriel's influence to counteract, but he'd made excellent progress. Like him, Isa wanted to make a difference. With a bit more molding, she could become his perfect supporter. He envisioned attending important government galas with an elegant Isa on his arm, coming home to her after a long day of breaking barriers, and watching her bring up their children, the first generation to populate a genuinely modern Puerto Rico. What a team they'd make!

Certainly, their chemistry was undeniable. He'd fallen under Isa's spell instantly, and when they first started seeing each other, Marco had dared, once or twice, to imagine she might be falling for him. Was his wishful thinking becoming a reality? But even if she did want him, how long was she willing to wait for him to become a success? He was about to graduate with excellent job prospects, but earning money would take time. Would she be patient?

And what about Don Gabriel?

CHAPTER 7

- Isabela -
May 1936

Doña Susana, Julia, and Tío Ernesto traveled to San Juan to attend Marco's graduation and inspect potential lodgings for Julia, who'd start teacher's college in September. Julia had received a scholarship as part of an effort to train more Puerto Rican teachers and decrease the need to import Americans for these jobs.

The night before graduation Isabela was joining the family for dinner at La Mallorquina, an Old San Juan mainstay since the days of Spanish rule. Marco had told her how hard his mother worked after his father's death, all the sacrifices she'd made for him and Julia. He worshipped his uncle and adored his sister. She was eager to meet them all.

"Do you think they'll like me?" she asked Marco with a coquettish but nervous smile as Mariano drove them to the restaurant. Tired of chaperoning, Papi had allowed Isa to attend on her own since they'd be with Marco's family at the restaurant or with Mariano in the car.

"They will love you. Your beauty and grace will stun them."

"¡Ay, Marco!" Isa pretended to dismiss the compliment, but she hoped he was right.

Isabela loved La Mallorquina's Spanish ambiance, the tall ceilings, black and white tiled floors, white-washed walls, and dark wood furniture. The tantalizing aroma of garlic sautéing in olive oil enveloped them when they stepped inside. As the maître d' showed them to their table, she quickly spotted Marco's relatives. Smartly dressed and coiffed, they sat straight as palm trees, best manners on show. Even though Doña Susana exuded a general air of exhaustion, Isa saw that Marco got some of his good looks from her. Tío Ernesto, white-haired, stocky, and wearing eyeglasses with thick black frames, stood to welcome them and poured them glasses of red wine from the bottle already on the table. Isabela sensed Julia carefully inspecting her like a specimen under a microscope. Unsmiling and with arms crossed under her ample bosom, she looked like a grumpy old judge about to pass a harsh sentence. She was a pretty girl, but she didn't seem very happy. Isa squirmed in her seat.

"I hope you don't mind, but we ordered a paella. It's the house specialty," Tío said.

"I love paella!" Isabela said, trying to ignore Julia's continued big-eyed stare.

"Paella sounds great." Marco smacked his lips.

"Julia, what a beautiful dress. It looks like the latest from New York," Isabela said, trying to engage the girl.

"Ha! It's a Mamá original. Not everyone can shop at Gonzalez Padín, you know." The bite in Julia's tone was unmistakable, and Isabela sat in stunned silence. She caught Marco giving his sister a puzzled look while Doña Susana quickly changed the topic.

"Isabela, Marquito tells us you went kite flying," Doña Susana said.

"Yes, she was a quick study," Marco said, glancing fondly at Isabela and placing his hand over hers.

"I enjoy learning from you, Marco. That day you opened my eyes to the plight of the poor on this island." Isa placed her hand over her heart. "My heart breaks at what those people endure."

"*Those people*'?" Julia shot daggers of contempt at her. "You know Marco doesn't come from much, right?"

Isa was taken aback. She'd meant no offense, but Marco's family had surely had it better than the people of El Fanguito. She'd been back twice with Beatriz but hadn't yet committed to making regular visits. She was tempted to give Julia an eyewitness account of what poverty really looked like, but without thinking, she responded, "Yes, of course. And if it hadn't been for my mo—"

Marco was quick to step on her words. "We all come from some-where, Julia. There's no shame in where one starts."

Isa swallowed hard. She'd almost divulged her secret, informa-tion Marco obviously did not want his family to know. Her insides twisted, the thought of paella suddenly repulsive.

"Just as long as she realizes we don't live in palm huts and sleep in hammocks." Julia's tone dripped with sarcasm, her eyes as hard and sharp as flint. This was the girl Marco said was sweeter than sugarcane syrup?

Isabela's cheeks burned. She wasn't sure which was worse or infuriated her more: that Julia hated her for no reason, or that her background embarrassed Marco.

"Of course, Isa knows that, Julia," Marco said, his tone a tad too gentle in Isa's opinion. This Julia deserved a spanking. So did Marco, come to think of it. "She also knows it will take an enormous amount of work to eradicate hunger and misery on this island. We need all hands on deck. In fact, I have an announcement."

All eyes fell expectantly on Marco. Isabela took a deep breath and attempted to relax her pursed lips.

"You know how I told you Dr. Chardón now oversees the Puerto Rico Reconstruction Administration?" Marco waited for his family to nod in response. "Well, he offered me a job yesterday. You're look-ing at the newest accountant in PRRA's Finance Division." Marco clutched his lapels and thrust out his chest.

Everyone erupted in cries of congratulations, and Isa felt some of her tension dissipate. She couldn't stay angry in the face of such fantastic news. Marco already had a job! A good job! At PRRA, he'd have a hand in many of the government's improvement projects. He was on his way! She smiled so widely it hurt.

"What will you be doing exactly?" asked Tío after hugging Mar-co and patting him on the back more times than was necessary.

"I'll develop budgets for more than sixty public works projects, including the new cement plant and all the housing that'll replace the slums."

"¡Ave María purísima! ¡Qué bueno!" Doña Susana said, eyes moist. "Your father would be beside himself."

"He'd place an announcement in the newspaper!" Tío said. "But don't worry, I'll make sure everyone in Yabucoa knows Marco Rios is going places."

Isabela watched as Marco's family continued to lavish praise upon him. He was their pride and joy, and she couldn't blame him for wanting to put his best foot forward in their presence. Best not to introduce herself as the bastard child of a jíbara. She didn't know what she'd been thinking. Julia's hostility, however, remained a mystery. The girl hadn't given Isabela a chance, but Isa would win Julia over, earn her esteem, and prove herself worthy of Marco.

"That's not all." Marco continued. "My professors have asked me to continue teaching at La Upi. I'll hold classes two nights a week, starting in September."

Everyone burst out in cheers again.

"A toast to Marco!" Tío said, raising his wine glass.

"To Marco!" everyone responded and clinked glasses. *Marco deserves this celebration and much more*, thought Isabela as she continued to beam her broad smile. But she sensed that Doña Susana's cheer was forced. Her sad eyes belied her. Marco must have seen it, too.

"¿Mamá, qué the pasa? ¿Poqué tan triste?"

Doña Susana waved him away. "Ay, ignore me, Marco. I'm just an old lady who's going to miss her son. It's clear you've left Yabucoa for good." Susana smiled sadly and dabbed at the corners of her eyes with her napkin.

"That's probably true, Mamá. The work I need to do is here in San Juan, but Yabucoa will always be in my heart. But don't worry. I'll buy a car and visit you whenever I want." Marco smiled. Isabela looked at him in surprise.

"You know how to drive?" she asked.

Marco laughed. "No, but like anything else, I'll learn."

Isa nodded. Of course he would.

"I'll look forward to your visits, mijo," Susana said.

"What about you, Julia?" Isabela asked, desperately trying to make some sort of connection with this reticent girl. "Will you go back home after getting your teaching degree?"

"They need teachers out on the island. So I suppose that's where I'll go," Julia said with resignation. "Unless my brother wants me here permanently." She smiled wickedly at Isa.

"Marco will be glad to send you home after watching you for four years," Doña Susana said. "He's going to make sure you're on your best behavior. Right, Marco?"

"Of course, Mamá. We will watch her like hawks."

"We?" Julia said, her left eyebrow raised.

"You know what I mean," Marco said, waving his hand as if dismissing Julia, which only made her glower at Isa more intensely. "Ah, here comes our food. It smells divine." They sat in silence while the waiter served everyone from the sizzling pan of saffron rice topped with langostinos, mussels, chicken, chorizo, red peppers, and peas.

Isabela's appetite returned. So, Marco thought of them as a couple. She savored this news as much as she enjoyed the first delicious bite of paella. Her heart did a little somersault. But her hands clenched when she looked down the table at Julia, whose face was now turned away. *Can I win this girl over?*

The next evening, Connie chaperoned them at Marco's graduation ball because Papi was indisposed. Isa said a little prayer of thanks for small miracles because if Papi had come, he'd have stuck to Marco and her like a barnacle. Instead, Connie sat with Dr. Chardón's wife, catching up on gossip and flicking her Spanish fan to cool herself. What a treat to be alone with Marco at a table.

The Escambrón Beach Club boasted arched windows facing the Atlantic Ocean, a dance floor tiled in large black and white squares, an outdoor terrace, and a boardwalk leading to the beach. The club hosted popular events, such as dances when U.S. Navy ships were docked in San Juan. Isabela had never been there and was eager to partake in these festivities "of the people," as Papi called them.

When the Carmelo Diaz Orchestra started up, Isa's excitement escalated. She'd finally get to dance with Marco. But the first song passed, and then three more, and Marco didn't make a move. He seemed content to chat with the steady stream of friends who stopped by their table with congratulations and to discuss future career plans. When the orchestra led into one of her favorite songs, Isabela tapped her foot, swayed with evident enthusiasm, and sang the lyrics softly. But Marco seemed oblivious. Finally, frustration won out, and she took matters into her own hands.

"Marco, this music is fabulous. Won't you take me for a spin on the dance floor?"

"Ah, Isa." Marco's cheeks flamed, and he looked down to avoid her gaze. "I'm afraid I've been keeping a secret. I can't dance."

Isabela was astounded. How could he not know how to dance? Determined to show sensitivity, she recovered her composure and generated a smile. "What do you mean you can't dance? You're a math genius. If you can count, you can dance. Come with me." She stood up and playfully pulled Marco by the arm.

"No, Isa." Marco looked terrified.

"Marco, don't be ridiculous. I asked you last night if you knew how to drive, and you said, 'No, but like everything, I'll learn.' How is this any different?" Isabela inched them onto the dance floor. "Follow my lead on this waltz, and I'll count aloud. We'll keep it simple. You can do this." She put her left hand on his shoulder and placed his right on her waist, their other arms clasped and extended.

"Stand up nice and straight. We're going to move in a square. Step back with your right foot. Now, out to the side with your left. No, don't look at your feet. Look at me. Now feet together."

"Again. Right foot back, side, together. Now we do the same with the left. Left foot back, side, together." Marco was doing a decent job, but his look of concentration was so intense Isa almost burst out laughing. She forced herself to remain serious.

"Good, Marco, good. Right-two-three, left-two-three, right-two-three, left-two-three. See? You're doing it!"

"Ha! We're dancing, Isa. We're dancing!" He looked like a little boy who'd just mastered tying his shoes. "But look at those other couples. The girls are spinning and turning." He stopped, hesitant once again.

"Patience, Marco," laughed Isa. "We'll get there. Just keep counting for now."

Isabela taught him the danza and even the fox trot, but Marco enjoyed waltzing the most because he danced it best. Connie smiled at them fondly whenever they glided past her table. After a particularly vigorous stint on the dance floor, Isabela and Marco pushed their way through the throng of sweaty bodies, desperate for fresh air. They told Connie they were headed to the outdoor terrace, and she waved them away, making no effort to follow. Outside, the salty ocean wind was blustery, and Isabela shivered as it hit her damp skin. Marco draped his suit jacket on her shoulders, and as she thanked him, he pulled her gently toward him and placed his lips on hers. An ardent flutter traveled from the pit of her stomach through every cell in her body before settling firmly in that special place between her legs, leaving it throbbing. *What deliciousness. Mother of God, please don't stop.* They kissed and kissed until she felt a hardness in his pants pressing against her.

Isabela shook in Marco's embrace while he looked intently into her eyes and breathlessly whispered, "Isabela Soto, most beautiful of women, I love you."

"And I love you," she whispered back. She was the luckiest girl on earth, and all that mattered was this moment. After Marco kissed her again, they stood side-by-side facing the water, Isa's head resting on his shoulder.

Isa reached into her satin clutch and handed Marco a slim leather case tied with a blue satin bow. "I almost forgot! I have something for you. So you can begin your new job in style," she said, excited to give him the black and gold Montblanc pen she'd carefully selected, the distinctive number "4810" engraved on its nib.

"This is too much! This pen costs more than everything I own put together," Marco said, his voice filled with such wonder it sounded fearful.

"Nonsense. This pen will play a part in Puerto Rican history," Isabela said, full of optimism. "¡Así que adelante! Let your illustrious career begin!"

"I love it," Marco assured her with a smile. "And I'll put it to excellent use."

They beamed at each other.

"I have something for you, too." Marco reached inside his jacket, pulled out a small cardboard folio, and handed it to her.

Isa loved a surprise, and pleased, she opened the folio to a photo of Marco dressed in a stylish white tie tuxedo. *He probably borrowed it from the photographer's studio.* But so what? He'd had his photo taken for her, and her joyful heart was ready to burst.

"You look so handsome!"

"Read the back." Marco removed the photo from the folio and turned it over in her palm.

"To the best of girlfriends." Isa read aloud. "With love, Marco."

Isabela was overjoyed. This was no spur-of-the-moment declaration of love. He'd planned to give her this, planned to profess his love for her tonight.

"I love it, and I love you, and I will treasure this forever," Isa whispered. "I must give you a photo of me, Marco."

Marco smiled as he reached into his pants pocket and pulled out his wallet. He opened it and pulled out a worn newspaper picture of her and Carlos Gardel. Isa gasped.

"I've carried your portrait for more than a year, Isabela. And that is how long I've loved you."

Isabela stood stock still, utterly speechless.

"Isa, I hope you don't think I'm a lunatic," Marco said with a concerned expression.

"Oh, you're definitely a lunatic," Isabela composed herself. He'd loved her even before they'd met! "But this lunatic needs a better photo of me. Maybe one without another man in it." Isa laughed.

"Yes, please!" Marco nodded with a smile, his features relaxed once again. He offered Isabela his arm and escorted her back inside.

They danced until the early morning hours, and Isa floated home in a cloud of delight. *He loves me!* She relived the evening's events as she struggled to fall asleep. Marco had gotten the hang of dancing so quickly! He'd held her thrillingly close during the *boleros*. And those kisses! She never wanted to kiss anyone else. But that newspaper photo he carried around. How strange that he'd clipped it long before they'd met. If Papi found out, he'd accuse Marco of stalking her, of being a social climber.

And what if he'd started with such intentions? Who was she to throw stones when her initial motives for going out with Marco had been less than pure? Yet she'd failed to persuade Papi to let her study acting in Mexico. Instead, she'd unexpectedly fallen in love, and unexpectedly or not, Marco had, too. But was love enough, she wondered, to smooth over their differences and bridge their two vastly different worlds?

CHAPTER 8

- Marco -
July 1936

Marco had always believed in himself, but even he was surprised at how quickly the life he'd envisioned began to fall into place. His job thrilled him, and his perfect woman loved him as much as he loved her. She'd even charmed Mamá and Tío, even though all bets were still off with Julia.

"Marco, that girl is a comemierda. Ay bendito, I'm so glad she feels sorry for the poor," Julia had said to him after that dinner.

"She's not a snob. She didn't mean it that way, and you know it."

"Yes, she did, Marco. I read that letter she wrote you at Christmas that you threw away. Her family went to a party pretending to be jíbaros!"

"Julia! You had no right to do that!" Marco couldn't believe his sister's gall. "Besides, her family went, not her. She was offended by the party's theme."

"Marco, a spoiled girl like her is used to getting what she wants. What are you, her new toy? She must be blinded by your looks."

"I would hope, Julia, that I have more to offer her than looks. If you can't be nice, then be quiet." Marco's tone turned sharp.

"Qué locura. This is madness, and you will only get your heart broken." Julia always liked to have the last word.

Marco huffed. Tío and Mamá liked Isa; he wouldn't worry about Julia's opinion.

Marco was proud to have moved past Isa's illegitimacy; in fact, he now considered it an asset. How could Don Gabriel oppose a marriage between Isa, an illegitimate child of a jíbara, and Marco, an educated and mannered man who, although poor for the moment, could trace his lineage straight back to Europe? Who from Isa's set would marry her if he knew she was a bastard?

Yet he hesitated to show Isa his beloved Yabucoa, even though she kept asking him to take her for a visit. Rather than be satisfied with how far he'd come, Marco was embarrassed for Isa to see how poor he'd been and how humble Mamá's life remained. He sent Mamá a small sum each month, but she still sewed her fingers off to make ends meet. And, honestly, he doubted Isa would think less of him when she saw where he came from. It was he who hesitated to show her his origins while they were still so plainly modest, perhaps pitiable. Marco would much rather wait, buy his mother a lovely house and then bring Isabela to visit, allowing his poverty to take on a romantic tinge, something from the past, roots safely buried.

He felt the wait would be short. Even though he'd just graduated, his job at the Puerto Rico Reconstruction Agency came with copious responsibility. He managed the $580,000 budget for the Agency's first public housing project, El Falansterio, where more than two hundred families from San Juan's Miranda slum would soon relocate. The three-story apartment buildings featured indoor plumbing and a contemporary Art Deco design with rounded corners and geometric details. It would be a model urban community, a beautiful example of what was to come.

PRRA's plans also included building the island's first cement plant, replacing other urban slums and rural wooden shacks with cement homes, and creating a sanitation infrastructure that would reduce disease significantly and improve the standard of living for thousands. They'd construct new schools, medical centers and hospitals, hydroelectric plants to bring electricity to the mountainous areas, and a connecting road infrastructure. Puerto Rico would finally join the modern world. His head spun at the possibilities, and his chest swelled with pride at being in the thick of it all.

Work had consumed him since starting his job, and he'd only managed to visit Isa twice briefly. She'd been surprisingly understanding of his absence, encouraging his efforts to make a strong initial mark at PRRA. Marco knew most other women would have turned petulant and demanding at this lack of attention, and tonight he'd planned a show of appreciation for her support. He told Isa he needed to spend all weekend at the office putting the final touches on a budget. She'd been disappointed but accepting, lending all the more sweetness to his surprise. When they'd met at Dr. Chardón's house eight months ago, she'd recited a funny poem about a boy with ulterior motives who serenades a country girl. Tonight, *he* would serenade Isa, but with romantic intention, to demonstrate his love for her.

He'd enlisted Hector, a guitar-playing sophomore student of his, and planned to begin with Irving Berlin's hit, "Cheek to Cheek," a nod to his recently acquired dance skills.

Marco made himself wait until nine o'clock before tiptoeing in the dark across Don Gabriel's lawn with Hector. They stopped next to the blooming azalea bush below Isa's second-floor bedroom window, and with clammy hands, Marco cued Hector to begin. Hector played the brief introductory notes, and Marco broke out in song,

"Heaven. I'm in heaven.
And my heart beats so that I can hardly speak."

He flashed a gleaming smile as Isa stepped onto the wrought-iron Juliet balcony, hands clasped in delight, and continued,

"And I seem to find the happiness I seek,
When we're out together dancing, cheek to cheek."

"Marco!" Isabela waved to him, face bright and joyful, and threw a handkerchief for him to catch. His heart leaped to see her so excited.

Marco continued singing with zest but had barely reached the end of the third stanza when Isa suddenly disappeared from the window sideways, as if someone had pulled her by the arm. He glimpsed Don Gabriel tipping a metal bucket over the balcony railing, and barely registered the splash of water headed his way before it hit him. Suddenly he was drenched, cold, and silenced.

"Papi!" He heard Isabela's shout of horror before she appeared again at the window.

She was immediately pulled back into the room, and Marco could hear Don Gabriel shouting at her, "Did you tell that descarado he could come here at all hours of the night? Has he no respect?" Marco's pulse quickened at the insult.

An exasperated-sounding Isa answered her father, "Dios mío, Papi, it's a serenata! It's *supposed* to happen at night."

Marco's fingernails bit half-moons into his palms. Isa shouldn't have to defend him to her pigheaded father. Marco wasn't a violent man, but he desperately wanted to clock Don Gabriel on the head.

"Night or day, I don't care. This boy needs to stay away," Don Gabriel said.

Marco, eyes narrowed, pressed his lips together and shook his head. He took several deep breaths, trying to manage his fury and humiliation. A future with Isa better be worth this kind of belittling.

"Isa!" Marco called up in an attempt to interrupt the argument.

"Are you nuts? Aren't you wet enough?" Hector, dry as a bone, asked with a wry smile. Marco shot him a look that erased Hector's smile and silenced him.

"Stay there! I'm coming," Isa yelled down.

Marco tried to compose himself in the short time it took Isa to come outside. He didn't want her to see him so shaken. By the time she reached him, he'd forced his mouth into an amused grin, held his arms wide at his sides, and said, "Good thing I'm waterproof."

"Marco, it's not funny! I'm so, so sorry. My father is a crazy tyrant." She made to hug him, but he pulled away.

"No, you'll get wet," he said, holding her at bay.

"I don't care! Are you alright?"

"Of course. Very refreshed." He took off his jacket and twisted water out of it.

Carmen joined them outside and handed Marco the thickest towel he'd ever seen. "¡Dios e salve, lirio!" she said, shaking her head as she returned to the kitchen.

He took the towel and rubbed his hair. Carmen was right. Maybe only God could save him from Don Gabriel.

"Papi's a monster. He had no right to do that to you." Isa's voice quivered.

"Ah, he's just protecting you. I'd do the same for Julia." Marco pounded the side of his head, trying to shake water out of his ear.

"No, it's more than that, Marco. He doesn't like me dating you. I'm afraid he's going to forbid me from seeing you." Isabela wrung her hands.

The hair on the back of Marco's neck stood on end, and his body launched into full fighting mode. Nobody got the best of Marco!

"Don't worry, Isa. I'll prove my worth before it comes to that," Marco said, his determination stoked by the idea of beating Don Gabriel. "I *will* gain your father's respect."

"You have your work cut out for you."

Why was Isa skeptical? She should believe in him by now. Marco opted to lighten the mood. "I'm ready," he said, pounding his chest like a gorilla. "Let 'Operation Win Don Gabriel Over' begin!"

Isabela laughed. "God help us!"

"Oh, He will," Marco said. Not caring whether Don Gabriel was watching from upstairs, he kissed Isa deeply before leaving with Hector. The sweetness of her mouth lingered on Marco's tongue as the two men walked to the trolley stop in silence. When he envisioned his future, Isabela was by his side. He needed her to become the man he was determined to be. He couldn't let Don Gabriel, or anyone else, get in the way of making this woman his.

July Fourth fell on a Saturday, and Marco looked forward to watching the annual parade travel down Fernández Juncos Avenue. He enjoyed the pageantry of its colorful floats, marching dignitaries, and soldiers dressed in military regalia, though the commemoration of America's independence meant nothing to him. Like most Puerto Ricans, Marco loved a celebration, even of a borrowed holiday. He brought it up one afternoon as he and Isabela sat side by side on the Soto's wooden settee, listening to the radio while Don Gabriel pretended to read the newspaper in his cushy armchair.

"Isa, let's go to the July Fourth parade next weekend. I think there might be fireworks that night, too."

"That sounds like fun," Isa said. "Let's!"

Don Gabriel's newspaper crinkled loudly as he thrust it aside and interrupted their conversation. "I'm afraid Isa will be busy that day getting ready for the July Fourth ball at the Condado Vanderbilt Hotel. The Sotos will be making a family appearance." Don Gabriel offered Marco an insincere smile as if Marco needed reminding he wasn't part of the family and wouldn't be included.

Isabela shook her head at her father, clearly disgusted. "What are you talking about, Papi? You always spend July Fourth at home with the shutters closed. It's a day of mourning for you. Since when do we go to that ball?" She rolled her eyes at Marco.

"Since now. I already have the tickets." Don Gabriel, who'd folded the newspaper into thirds, thwacked it against his palm.

"I can't believe this. What about Marco?"

"What about him?" Don Gabriel looked Marco up and down and shrugged. "He can buy a ticket, too. It's a free country."

Marco's heart dropped. He could imagine what a ticket to this ball cost. But Don Gabriel had thrown down the gauntlet, and Marco needed to rise to the occasion.

"Of course, I'll get a ticket and join you, Isa," Marco said in his most charming tone.

"Marco," Isabela whispered with concern.

Marco winked at her as a signal not to worry. Isabela smiled, and he saw her shoulders relax. She was in. They'd figure out a plan together.

The following week passed in a flurry of preparation. Marco dedicated every moment outside of work to getting ready for the ball. First, he tallied his expenses:

Ball Ticket	$ 2.50
Tuxedo	$25.00
Shirt	$ 1.50
Shoes	$ 4.00
Corsage	$ 1.00
Refreshments	$ 5.00
Total	$39.00

The total was more than his monthly rent at Doña Teresa's house. He made $125 monthly and would have to spend thirty percent of it in one night. The thought of doling out such an amount made his breath catch. A family could eat for months on that money. But he had to fight for Isa; she was worth it. She *was*, right? Yes, of course she was! He'd consider it an investment.

Marco got paid on Friday, but that was too late to order a tuxedo and have it tailored, so hat in hand, he went to Sammy to ask for a loan. Sammy's father provided his son with a very generous allowance, and now that Sammy worked at the family insurance company, he also earned a salary. He wouldn't mind lending Marco a few dollars for a good cause.

"You don't deserve this shit treatment," Sammy said after he heard Marco's woeful tale. "Doesn't this Don Gabriel know he's dealing with one of the finest minds on this island? Who does he think he is?"

"He's Isabela's father. He's in control, and I have to beat him at his own game."

"Then you shall," Sammy said grandly, taking out his wallet. "I want you to take this hijo de puta down."

"Ah, Sammy! I can always count on you!" Marco briefly closed his eyes, relishing a new-found lightness.

"You're also going to need cufflinks. I'll loan you a pair."

"Anything else?"

"No, I think you'll be just fine, Cinderella." Sammy slapped Marco on the back. "As long as your carriage doesn't turn back into a pumpkin."

Marco groaned, then said a little prayer.

CHAPTER 9

- Isabela -
July 1936

At the top of a sweeping Imperial staircase, through several grand archways, the ballroom at the Condado Vanderbilt Hotel shimmered. Glowing chandeliers, flickering candles, and women's bright jewels were reflected in the imposing gilt-framed mirrors adorning the walls. An exotic mélange of perfumes filled the air with floral and citrus notes and the occasional hint of bay rum, tobacco, and sandalwood. Groups of guests, including Isabela and her family, sat around small tables draped in white linen while others danced to the lively tunes of The Mario Dumont Orchestra.

"There he is!" Isabela exclaimed when she spotted Marco entering the ballroom. He cut a dashing figure in his long-tailed black tuxedo with a white waistcoat and black tie, hair slicked back and staying off his forehead for once. Isabela waved to catch his attention, and he beamed when he saw her. "Here he comes." She wondered whether the butterflies in her stomach were due to pleasure or trepidation.

"Qué bueno. I'm looking forward to this evening with Marco," Papi said, hands on his lap. That his tone held no sarcasm worried Isabela more than if Papi had been overtly hostile.

"Gabriel, please be nice," Connie warned before taking a sip of her gin and tonic.

"Por supuesto. Why wouldn't I?" Papi's countenance exuded innocence as he stood to greet Marco. "Bienvenido, Marco. Join us, por favor."

Marco bowed to Papi, kissed Connie's hand, and presented Isabela with an orchid corsage. The precious white flower was so sweetly delicate that even Papi gave a small grunt of approval. "Oh, it's beautiful, Marco. Would you pin it on me, please?"

"It would be my pleasure." Isabela could smell Marco's brilliantine as he leaned close to pin the corsage on the shoulder of her dress. Immediately, her inner core tingled, and her face burned. Her body had a mind of its own whenever Marco touched her.

"Come, sit down," Papi said. He grabbed the empty chair next to Isabela and moved it between him and Connie. Isabela let out an irritated sigh as Marco sat down where Papi instructed.

"Ladies, you both look enchanting tonight," Marco said.

"How gallant of you to notice," Connie said with an encouraging smile as she flipped open a crimson lace Spanish fan with her white-gloved hand. Her dress was ephemeral, made of white chiffon with three long red, white, and blue scarves trailing from her shoulders to the floor. Isabela wore a fitted satin dress in a deep scarlet, her lipstick a perfect match.

"Marco, may I offer you a drink?" Papi asked.

"Certainly. But the next round is on me."

Papi waved a waiter over, and Marco ordered a scotch. Isa wondered how he could drink that putrid concoction. Like Connie, she much preferred gin. At least Marco didn't smoke like so many of her past suitors. He really didn't have any bad habits.

"Isn't that Orlando Santiago Velez?" Papi asked, jutting his chin toward a young man approaching their table.

"Yes. But my goodness, he's gotten handsome!" Connie said.

Papi stood to welcome their visitor. "¡Orlando, muchacho! How was Princeton? Are you back for good?" Papi shook Orlando's hand and slapped him on the back.

"¡Sí! No more winters for me!" Orlando laughed. "It's so good to see you all. Doña Connie, Isabela." He kissed them on the cheek.

"Welcome home, Orly," Isabela said, and introduced her friend to Marco.

Papi pulled an unoccupied chair from the nearest table and put it next to Isabela. "Join us for a drink, Orlando."

"Gracias, Don Gabriel, but I already have one." Orlando lifted the glass he was holding.

"To your health, then," Papi said as he clinked glasses with Orlando. "What are your plans now that you're back?"

"Well, it's a good time to be an architect here," Orlando said. "PRRA's reconstruction projects have created many opportunities."

"Marco works at PRRA," Isabela said proudly.

"¡Qué bien! I admire the Agency's efforts," Orlando said.

"We're moving in the right direction, but we have more catching up to do before we become a modern nation," Marco said.

"Every step forward counts," Orlando said.

"As long as it's a step away from the blasted Americans," Papi said. Orlando and Marco shared a conspiratorial smile, and Orlando turned to Isabela.

"I've been away from the island for too long, and this danza is tugging at my heart," he said. "Would you do me the honor?" He held his hand out to Isabela.

"Ay, Orly. You were always a flirt. But the song is almost over, and I promised Marco the next dance." Isabela smiled ruefully at Orlando, who glanced at Papi with raised eyebrows and a question in his eyes.

"By all means, please dance with your friend," Marco said, nodding to Isabela, his tone clipped.

Orlando raised his hands, palms up. "No, no. I didn't mean to intrude on your evening. Please, enjoy." He bowed slightly at the waist before taking his leave.

"Would it have killed you to dance with the boy?" Papi said.

"Ay, Gabriel, por Dios. She's here with Marco." Connie's fanning grew agitated.

"Woman, you are going to fan that thing into pieces," Papi said. Connie did not deign to answer or even look at her husband.

The waiter delivered Marco's scotch. Isabela watched as he took a significant swig, almost finishing the drink. *Dear Lord, I hope he doesn't overdo it because of Papi*, she thought.

"Isabela, let's show them how it's done." Marco stood and offered Isabela his hand, leading her to the dance floor. Good gracious, the self-assurance! He'd just learned to dance a few weeks ago. Isabela hoped he remembered how. But as Marco led her in a waltz, she was transported by the rhythm, the music, his body heat, and his skin's clean, soapy smell. Even though he tripped over her feet twice, the spell remained unbroken. They laughed and twirled for three more songs before returning to the table.

"Those are two left feet you were born with, son!" Papi laughed. Isa thought she heard Connie mumble words that shouldn't come out of a proper señora's mouth.

"Papi! Don't be mean. Marco is a quick learner and is on his way to becoming a great dancer. Maybe even better than you." She gave Papi a snarky look.

"Isabela has been an excellent teacher," Marco said, trying to make peace.

"Some things can't be learned," Papi said, waving his hand dismissively.

"I've yet to encounter any such thing," Marco answered with a confident smile. He finished his drink with a flourish. Isabela was proud of how he was handling himself with her father.

Papi grumbled and waited for several beats before saying, "We need more drinks."

"Caballero," Marco said, waving the waiter over. "Don Gabriel, what would you like?"

"A bottle of champagne for the table," Papi addressed the waiter. "And please make sure the glasses are chilled." Isabela's face went slack. Connie stared at Papi in horror. What was Papi doing? Marco couldn't afford a bottle of champagne! But before she could intervene, Marco calmly and firmly addressed the waiter.

"Sí, por favor. The finest in the house." *What is he doing?* She tried to catch his eye, but Marco stared straight ahead at the dancing couples. Papi glanced around the room, smiling and waving to friends as if he didn't have a care in the world. Connie continued her furious fanning.

Isabela clenched her teeth. *This is it*, she thought. *There is only so much abuse a man can take, and this will be Marco's breaking point.* Her armpits created sickle moons of anxiety on her beautiful red satin dress. Marco continued to watch the dancers. Why wouldn't he look at her? When Papi left the table to greet some friends sitting nearby, Isabela grabbed Marco's arm.

"Marco," Isabela whispered.

"Shhh, Isabela. Don't worry."

"But..."

"Isa, I will take care of it." She'd never heard him so resolute.

Papi returned with Tadeo Quesada, the son of an old friend of his from Ponce. "Look who I found, Isa. Remember little Tadeo? He's been in New York studying to be a dentist."

"Congratulations, Tadeo. It's great to see you! May I present my escort, Marco Rios? Marco, this is Tadeo Quesada." The two men shook hands as Isabela smiled sweetly. Tadeo looked at Papi in confusion, much like Orlando had, and made a hasty exit as the waiter arrived with the champagne.

Every muscle in Isabela's body tensed as she watched the waiter distribute the champagne coupes and pour the bubbly drink. She was living a nightmare, a nightmare that would end with Marco leaving her. As the waiter filled her glass, she caught sight of a shiny object in Marco's hand, a money clip holding a small wad of cash. He discreetly asked the waiter how much he owed, peeled off several bills, told the server to keep the change, and raised his glass.

"A toast to the Soto family," he said. "May you always enjoy good health and happiness. ¡Salud!"

Stunned, the Sotos raised their glasses and automatically responded, "¡Salud!" Papi choked on the champagne and fell into a coughing fit while Connie pounded him on the back rather spiritedly. Isabela's adrenaline rush abated, leaving behind aching arms and legs. Her mind raced. Where did Marco get that money? Had

Connie passed it to him? He had enough to feed several El Fanguito families for weeks!

Connie was the first to recover.

"And to *your* health, Marco." She raised her glass to Marco, winked, and gave him a conspiratorial grin.

"Don Gabriel," called a voice from behind their table. "How good to see you!"

Papi turned toward the voice. "César, old friend! I didn't know rascals were invited to this fancy ball." The two of them laughed as if recalling a private joke.

"Connie, remember César Cintrón? He's been trying to get the senate to behave."

"A pleasure to see you, César," Connie said.

"This is my daughter, Isabela, and her friend Marco Rios."

Isa blinked at her father in confusion. Had Papi really been gracious and introduced Marco as her friend? Could he be thawing a tiny bit?

"¡Ave María, Marco! I didn't know they ever let you out of the PRRA office," César looked delighted to see Marco and shook his hand.

"It's good to see you, Don César."

"Gabriel, it's wise of you to befriend one of the rising stars of the new generation. This young gentleman is doing fantastic work." Papi, once again, looked at a loss. Isa was gleeful. Could it be her father was finally getting his comeuppance?

"Don César, I'm humbled by your praise," Marco said. "I do what I can because I believe in a bright future for Puerto Rico. We're all working hard toward that goal, eh?"

"Your generation is turning this island into something to be proud of, right, Gabriel?" César winked at Papi, who nodded silently, seemingly in a catatonic state. With the tables now turned, Isabela's concern shifted to her father; she wondered how much torture *he* could endure and hoped he didn't have a heart attack.

"Ladies and gentlemen," the orchestra leader announced, "Please make your way to the terrace. The fireworks are about to begin!" A drum roll accentuated the announcement.

"Oh, let's go outside," César said, leading the way as the others followed. Marco and Isabela secured a spot at the white balustrade overlooking the ocean. Marco put his arm around Isa and pulled her to him. She looked up at his handsome profile and wished they were alone so they could kiss.

The whistle and pop of the first firework sounded, and the sky glowed red. As the spectators murmured their appreciation, Isabela looked around and spotted Papi and Connie behind them in the crowd. Papi's stare scorched her, his eyes hotter than the pyrotechnics exploding in the sky. She shivered and quickly faced away.

Papi thinks I'm betraying him, but why can't he see how wonderful Marco is? With the thunderous boom of each firework, Isabela's heart sank further and further. She loved Papi, and she loved Marco. She could never choose between them.

CHAPTER 10

- Marco -
July 1936

"You should've seen his face, Sammy, when I took out all that cash you made me bring," Marco said the next day when he stopped by Sammy's house to return the borrowed cufflinks. "I'm sure he thought I'd robbed a bank or made a pact with the devil! Which I'll probably have to do to pay you back."

Sammy waved him away. "Bah, take as long as you need. It serves him right for being such a pompous ass. Aren't you tired of his insults?"

"Sí. I've had enough. I can't wait until Isa and I marry and are free of his iron rule once and for all." Marco raked his fingers through his hair.

Sammy laughed but abruptly stopped when he saw Marco's determined face. "What, you're serious? Don Gabriel will kill you before he lets that happen."

"We're adults and don't need his permission." Marco crossed his arms in front of his chest.

"You're going behind his back? That's a lot to ask of Isabela. Will she disobey her father?"

"I'll find out this afternoon. This needs to be resolved before I lose my mind."

"You're proposing?" Sammy's eyes were wide.

"She'll either say yes or no. Either way, I'll have an answer, and we can all get on with our lives."

"I've seen the way that woman looks at you. There's no chance she'll refuse you."

"Pray for me, Sammy."

"I will pray to San Judas, saint of lost causes. And if she says yes, consider your debt to me erased. It'll be your wedding gift!"

"Ay, Sammy. I can't wait to have money to throw around like you. One day I'll pay you back in spades."

Marco phoned the Soto house and was thankful Isabela answered. "Isa, my love. I need to see you."

"Ay, Marco," Isabela whispered over the line. "I'm not sure that's such a good idea. You got the best of Papi last night. I really think he needs some time to calm down."

"It's very important. Please. Sit outside and wait for me."

Isabela sighed. "And if Papi sees you? You know that won't go well."

"It's a risk I'll take. I'll be there in less than an hour." Marco hung up before Isa could protest again.

The day was sweltering, and Marco was already sweating when he donned his best jacket and caught the trolley to Miramar. He sat by an open window and held his hat in his lap, imagining life with an adoring Isabela. Running a household would come easily to a bright and capable girl like her. He pictured himself at the head of a dining table while Isa served a succulent pernil she'd roasted until the meat fell off the bone. Several tidy, impeccably dressed children would wait patiently for their portions. What would they be like, these children? Beautiful, of course, but also whip-smart. After all, they'd have his genes. And like thousands of Puerto Rican women before her, Isabela would make a devoted mother. What a family they'd have. They didn't need Don Gabriel. They'd do things on their own, their way.

By the time the trolley reached his stop in Miramar, the breeze had dried his sweat, and the daydreaming had calmed his nerves significantly. He walked the short distance to the Soto house, full of grit and purpose. Isabela waited for him on the veranda, sitting in one of the wrought-iron chairs, legs crossed at the knee, her dangling foot shaking like a maraca. When Marco opened the gate and rushed toward her, she stood, her index finger on her lips.

"Shhhh. Papi is napping," she spoke softly as Marco reached her and took her trembling hands in his. "Let's not wake the tormenter."

But Marco had come on a mission. He stood before Isa and rushed his first question, afraid to lose his nerve. "Isa, do you love me?"

"My God, Marco. Yes! With all my heart, I love you."

"Then, will you marry me, Isa? Let's make a life together."

"Marco!" Isabela looked thrilled, then frightened. "What about Papi?"

"I am proposing to you, not him," Marco said firmly. "We'll stand united and ask for his blessing." He tried to hide his aggravation. He'd had enough of Don Gabriel imposing himself on his happiness.

"I know, but—." Isa bit her lip, eyes downcast.

"I'm a poor man, Isa, but not for long. With you at my side, I'll conquer the world. I can't give you a diamond ring, but will you have me, anyway?" Marco went down on one knee and looked up at Isabela, who focused on him again, her eyes glistening with tears. He held his breath and prayed Isabela would be brave. *Follow your heart, Isa. Please.*

Marco detected a shift in Isa, a new steely determination. "I would be honored to stand beside you for the rest of our lives, Marco," she said before turning serious and pointing her right index finger at his face. "But you must promise me one thing."

"Anything, my love." He would have promised her the world and beyond.

"Promise I will always be your one and only. I couldn't bear to be married to a cheating man like Papi. It would kill me."

Marco wasn't surprised to learn Don Gabriel was a cheater. Most men of his station and ilk had dalliances and even long-term mistresses. But Marco never would. Not if he had Isa. "I solemnly swear there will never be another woman for me," he said, holding up his palm. What an easy promise! Who in the world could compare to Isa?

Isa held his gaze for a second, broke into a grin and threw her arms up in the air with abandon. "Then let's get married!"

Marco picked her up by the waist, spun her around, and shouted, "You've made my wildest dream come true!"

"Oh, my God! Are we really doing this?" Isabela squealed. Marco continued to spin them until they fell on the metal glider with a clatter, dizzy and laughing.

"¡Qué alboroto! What's going on out here?" Connie appeared at the front door. "You're going to wake your father."

"We're getting married!" Isabela exclaimed.

"Dios mío, please save us," Connie made the sign of the cross. She broke out in a huge smile and hugged the couple, saying her congratulations, but then blanched. "When are you going to tell your father?"

"Now is as good a time as any," Marco said, taking Isabela's hand and heading inside.

"I'm not sure there will ever be a good time," muttered Connie.

"What is this escándalo?" A grumpy Don Gabriel descended the stairs, hair tousled and shirt untucked.

Isabela looked at Marco, who nodded and squeezed her hand in reassurance. "Marco and I are getting married," she said stoically, her posture erect as she stood her ground.

Take that, Don Gabriel! Marco couldn't hide his elation.

Don Gabriel, now in front of them, gave them a long, hard look. He addressed Marco very quietly, with great disdain. "Wipe that smile off your face. You've had the audacity to come into my house and charm my daughter with your fanciful talk of the future, and I put up with it because I know she's capricious. I figured she'd tire of you soon enough. But you're very clever, aren't you? Somehow you managed to weasel your way into her heart."

Don Gabriel's face was crimson, and the veins in his temple throbbed. Marco resisted an urge to step back. "She's blinded, but I see you for what you are. You want her social standing, her contacts, her money. And now you have proposed to her without having the decency to ask me for her hand in marriage first? Go back to the mountains, you jíbaro. Leave my daughter alone."

Every word of Don Gabriel's vitriol landed like a punch in Marco's gut. His brain was on fire, but his muscles were frozen. How dare he speak to Marco that way when Isa was the daughter of a jíbara?

Isabela swept between him and her father, her voice sounding far away to Marco's searing ears. "Marco and I are in love. We're going to make a life together."

"You're willing to give up this life to live in a hut?" Papi scoffed. "What about your dream of becoming an actress?"

Marco's adrenaline kicked in, and his shock turned to fury. Who the hell did Don Gabriel think he was? He took a step forward, ready to tear him to shreds, until Isa pulled hard on his arm.

"He doesn't live in a hut, Papi. And there are more important things in life than being an actress. What about love? Think about you and Connie. You were married within days of meeting. Marco and I are in love, too. Can't you understand?"

A grim silence settled upon the room as Papi squinted his eyes, lifted his chin, and moved so close to Isa they stood nose to nose.

"Fine. I'll make a deal with you," Papi said. "I'll send you to Mexico for six months to study with that actress person. If, when you return, you still want to marry this boy, you'll have my blessing." He crossed his arms, smugly certain that he'd played the winning hand. Marco wished he could take Isa's place in the showdown but knew better than to interfere at such a critical juncture.

"I could never be away from Marco for that long, Papi," Isabela said firmly. "I don't want to go to Mexico. I'm staying here with him." Don Gabriel jerked his head back, and Marco reveled in the man's shock.

"Over my dead body!" Don Gabriel exploded, white spittle collecting at the corners of his mouth. "Get out of my house! Get out!" he howled, lunging at Marco, who deftly evaded him.

Connie, running interference, grabbed Marco's arm and quickly led him to the door. "Marco, go. Give them time to hash it out. He'll come around," she tried to reassure him as she pushed him out of the house.

His self-esteem in tatters, Marco struggled to hold back tears during the trolley ride home and kept his hat low on his forehead, shielding his eyes from curious glances. He was overwhelmed by a tsunami of emotions. Not since his father's death had he felt so hopeless and diminished. Don Gabriel's words had brought back to life every slight and insult Marco had ever endured for being poor. He'd worked exceedingly hard to better himself, get an education, be at the top of his class, and win Isabela's love. But in Don Gabriel's eyes, he would always be a jíbaro. Is that how the rest of the world would always see him, too? But, no. Isabela loved him. Of this, he was sure. How could Marco convince Don Gabriel he was worthy of his daughter? He *was* worthy of his daughter, carajo. She'd barely escaped being a jíbara herself!

As he labored to fall asleep that night, doubts swirled in his head, interrupted by the occasional hopeful thought. He was riding a roller coaster of optimism and despair. Where it would stop was completely beyond his control.

CHAPTER 11

- Isabela -
July 1936

Isabela pushed past her father and rushed upstairs to her bedroom. She slammed and locked her door, so enraged she thought she'd burst into flames. She let out an agonized groan and threw herself on her bed as violent sobs shook her body. How could Papi be so cruel? What a hypocrite he was! She would not give Marco up. She wouldn't! She cried intermittently for hours, despair coursing through her veins, and refused dinner when Connie knocked on her door. Finally exhausted, she fell into a dreamless sleep.

Connie and Carmen tried coaxing her out the next day to no avail. Even Carmen's picadillo, Isa's favorite dish, didn't tempt her. She felt no hunger, only shards of pain in her heart. Isa resolved to stay in her room until she withered away. She only left the bed to use her bathroom.

Late that afternoon, when the coquís were starting their serenade, she was startled when a pebble shot through her window and landed loudly on the tile floor. Her sisters must be playing outside. Isa forced her body off the bed to close her shutters and was surprised to spot Carmen below, holding a basket of food.

Isa whispered down, "No! I'm not eating. There's nothing to live for without Marco."

Carmen whispered back, "Eat. But we'll let your father think you're starving. You'll get what you want, mija. Don't underestimate the power of women. Nosotras hacemos de tripa corazones." Carmen smiled at her and winked, confident that women performed miracles.

Isa gently bit her lip and thought Carmen's proposal through. Could they do this? Tears prickled her swollen eyelids as she felt a glimmer of hope. Her heart fluttered. Yes! Together, they'd outsmart Papi.

Isa nodded down at Carmen with enthusiasm.

Carmen mimed for Isa to hang a sheet over the windowsill. Isa tied two sheets together, and Carmen knotted one end around the basket handle. Isa carefully pulled it up. Her stomach rumbled as she took in the thick ham and cheese sandwich, a bowl of hearts of palm and tomato salad, several bags of plantain chips, coconut macaroons, and two magazines. Her resolve to starve herself forgotten, she dug into the hearty feast.

Later that evening, Connie knocked on her door again. "Come on, Isa. You need to eat. I'm leaving a plate of food out here for you. Please, cariño. Eat something."

Regret pricked her conscience when she heard her sisters plead in unison, "Isa, we miss you. Come out, please." They sounded frightened, and for a second, Isa's resolve wavered. No, she was doing this for them as much as for herself. Mati and Rosie would marry whoever they loved, Papi be damned.

Two more days passed, with Carmen feeding her through the window and Connie worrying. She felt terrible for causing Connie distress. None of this was her fault. Besides, Connie was a romantic, and she liked Marco. Isa instructed Carmen to fill Connie in, and Connie took to the plan like a natural, berating Papi and pushing him to apologize.

Isa was engrossed in a novel on the fourth day of her "hunger strike" when a loud knock made her jump.

"Isa!" Papi's shout was muffled by the thick door. "Enough of this drama. Connie says you haven't eaten since Friday. Come out of that room this instant."

"I have nothing to live for without Marco." Isa felt surprisingly calm in the face of Papi's displeasure.

"You have everything in the world and more."

"I don't have love." She didn't care if she sounded melodramatic.

"Don't be ridiculous. Come out and eat." Papi banged on the door.

Isa responded with silence, calmly flipping through the magazine pages.

"Fine. Starve. Have it your way."

She heard his angry footsteps march all the way down the stairs. Well, at least he'd come himself this time. The plan was progressing.

When Carmen brought her food that night, she whispered up with a mischievous grin, "Don Gabriel está color de hormiga brava."

Isa pictured her father as an angry red ant, easily squashed, and the thought cheered her.

"He thinks I'm starving. Some father!"

"Don't worry. Está a punta de caramel. I really think he's almost ready to give in. Stand your ground."

Isa assured herself she could wait Papi out forever. After all, she had nothing to lose.

On Saturday, the seventh day, Papi knocked on Isa's door gently this time. "Isa, amor. I'm sitting out here, and I will not move until you come out. You haven't eaten in a week, querida. Please. You're wasting away in there." His tone was conciliatory.

"You don't care. You've never cared about me!" Isa called out from her bed. How could a father let his child starve for seven days?

"What are you talking about? I love you with all my heart."

"Is that why you left me with Abuela while you traveled all over the world? You know, the girls at school made up stories about me." Isa wrung her hands at the memory. "They said my mother had been a witch, that you'd stolen me from the Amazon jungle, and even that I was really Abuela's daughter."

"I'm sorry, Isa. I didn't know that." Papi was doing a great job of sounding sincere. "But I do know your abuela loved you very much."

"Did she? Or did she just want to disguise your bastarda, make sure I turned out nothing like my jíbara mother? Nobody's ever cared about my happiness!" Tears flowed down her cheeks, a lifetime of hurt in liquid form.

Papi's voice broke as he answered, "All I've ever cared about and everything I've ever done is for your happiness."

"Then let me marry Marco." Isa rose from the bed and leaned against the wall by the door, arms crossed.

"You barely know the man." Papi sounded weary.

"You knew Connie for a *week* before you got married on the ship from Spain. And do you remember what you said to me? You said, 'When you know, you know. Why make love wait?'"

"Yes, but Connie and I come from the same background. Isa, you can't possibly think you'll be content being poor, scrubbing toilets and ironing sheets. You know that, right?"

"Marco and I will have a different type of marriage, Papi. He's going to accomplish great things, and I will be at his side supporting him. We'll work together for a better Puerto Rico."

"You're young and have dreams. I understand that. Not too long ago, you begged me to let you go to Mexico to study acting. So, go! You have my permission."

Isa sighed and threw her arms up in the air. "That was the foolish and selfish desire of a silly girl who longed for applause. I don't need the love of an audience anymore. I have Marco's love."

"What about your family's love?"

"Papi, the absence of a mother's love creates an enormous hole in one's heart. I've been trying to fill it my whole life."

"Oh, my sweet girl." Papi was openly weeping now. "I'm so, so sorry."

How surreal! Papi had never cried in front of her; she didn't even know he could. But did she really have the upper hand now? With a trembling hand, she slowly unlocked the door, turned the knob, and pulled it open. Papi was hunched over in a wooden chair, hands on his head, strangled sobs escaping his chest.

"Ay, Papi." Isa rushed to her father. She couldn't bear to see him so despondent.

Don Gabriel stood, and the two held each other in a tight hug.

"Isa, Isa. I didn't know." His tears dampened her shoulder.

"It's not your fault, Papi." Isa rocked back and forth, attempting to soothe him.

"Yes, it is. I want to make things right, Isa. You deserve to be happy."

"Then let me marry Marco."

Papi pulled away from her, eyes liquid, and nodded.

CHAPTER 12

- Marco -
July 1936

Marco spent an agonizing week trying to concentrate on his work. Carmen had called him several times with updates on the situation at the Soto's house. Isa was fighting Don Gabriel with Carmen and Connie's help. But Don Gabriel wasn't stupid. Surely, he'd figure out they were feeding Isa behind his back. Unless he thought the women in his home incapable of disobeying him. That wouldn't surprise Marco.

How much longer could the man hold out thinking his daughter was starving to death? Part of Marco applauded Isa's grand gesture, but the wait was excruciating; he was ready for the drama to end.

Come Saturday, faced with forty-eight hours without work to distract him, Marco despaired and stayed in bed as long as possible, forcing himself back to sleep each time he awoke. But as the summer heat flared and rendered his small metal fan impotent, he dragged himself out of bed and began his morning ablutions.

He was enjoying a cup of Doña Tomasa's potent café con leche while reading the paper on the balcón when Mariano pulled up to the house in Don Gabriel's fancy car. Marco stood up, every fiber in his being desperate for positive news.

Marco watched silently as Mariano got out of the car, doffed his hat, and addressed him. "Señor Rios, the Sotos have sent me to ask if you'd be so kind as to come with me to their house."

"The Sotos? Does that include Isabela? Is she out of her room?" Marco's words tripped over each other.

Mariano smiled. "She is, indeed. And anxious to see you."

"What about Don Gabriel? What's happened?" Marco followed Mariano to the car.

"I think your prayers have been answered," Mariano said with a kind look as he opened the door to the sedan's back seat and ushered Marco inside.

Marco never failed to notice the leather's luxurious smell and creaminess. Was he a prisoner on his way to the guillotine? Or did he dare believe Mariano and fancy himself a prince awaiting a warm welcome at a foreign embassy?

They arrived quickly at the Soto house. Marco considered how long the trolley, with its numerous stops, took to travel the same distance. He wished he'd had more time to compose himself. What would Papá have done in such a situation? He would have faced it like a man and put forth his best effort. *Papá, how I miss you. Please give me the strength to get through this.*

Carmen ushered him inside, where Connie, Don Gabriel, Isabela, Mati, and Rosie had gathered in the living room waiting for him. He rushed to a seated Isabela, kneeled before her, and held her hands.

"Are you well, amor?"

"Yes, Marco. I am very well." Her smile had never been more luminous.

"Please take a seat, Marco," Don Gabriel addressed him. He sat across from Isabela with slumped shoulders, looking wilted.

"Marco, first, I must apologize for the unkind words I spoke to you," Don Gabriel said, looking Marco in the eye. "I do admire how you've managed to rise from your humble beginnings and I expect you have a fine future ahead of you. But like every father, I've only been watching out for Isa's best interests."

Even when apologizing, Don Gabriel spoke in a condescending tone.

"I'm no stranger to ardent love. As you may know, Connie and I had just met when we got married." He gave Connie a half-hearted wink. "However, you must understand that when a poor man wants to marry a rich woman, that woman's father is obligated to make sure the man is interested in her for the right reasons."

Oh, this was too much. Marco attempted to interrupt Don Gabriel, but the man shook his head and continued.

"Isa has convinced me that your love for each other is real and true. If you're willing to marry without a dowry and without ongoing financial support from me, then you have my blessing."

Marco doubted his ears for a second. He held back a smile and responded with gravity, "I appreciate your position, Don Gabriel. And I assure you I will live my life with one goal: to make Isa happy." He stood, moved to where Isabela sat, clasped her hands in his, and kissed them.

"Very well." Don Gabriel pressed his lips together. "Congratulations." He stood and left the room as the sisters and Connie descended on the newly engaged couple, kissing and hugging them until they all tumbled to the floor in delight. Marco giggled along, but as he glanced around, he couldn't help but wonder whether removing Isa from this privileged life would change her.

PART
TWO

CHAPTER 13

- Isabela -
February 1937

Isabela examined herself in the mirror as Connie pinned the floor-length lace veil to her upswept hair. By day's end, her life would be irrevocably changed. She was no fool. Living on much less than she was used to would be difficult, possibly grueling at times, but two things gave her confidence and fueled her desire to move forward—her love for Marco and their joint commitment to improving the lives of all Puerto Ricans. She had love and a purpose far beyond her old vain desire to be adored by an audience. Her life would matter.

"There you go, querida," Connie said, giving the veil a tug to ensure it held. "You're a beautiful bride. How are your nerves?"

"I'm more excited than nervous, really."

"What about tonight, after the wedding?" asked Connie with a meaningful look. "Are you ready?"

Isabela blushed furiously. "Connie! ¡Dios mío!"

"Well, marital relations are a critical part of a husband and wife's bond."

"I know! I know!" Isabela waved Connie away.

"Good. Do you know not to lie there like a dead fish? Men like to know you're enjoying it."

Isa put both hands up in surrender and whisper-shouted at Connie, "No! Stop."

Connie laughed, leaving Isa with the horrifying image of her father and stepmother naked in bed. She shook her head and replaced that picture with the thought of how Marco's skin would feel next to hers. A frisson of desire sent shivers up her spine. She could transform the heaviness and swelling between her legs into an explosion of pleasure with her hand. Imagine what the real thing would feel like! It was going to be a spectacular night. Isa dabbed Joy perfume on her pulse points, breathing in its luxurious jasmine notes. She'd have to ration it from now on because who knew when she'd be able to afford another bottle.

As Connie pronounced her ready and left to help dress Isa's sisters, Papi knocked on the door.

"May I come in?" he asked, dapper as always in a dark blue suit with a crisp white pocket square.

Isa turned away from the mirror to face her father. "How do I look, Papi?"

"Like the most radiant woman in the world," Papi's voice shook. "Marco is a fortunate man."

"And I'm a fortunate woman," Isabela said, tucking an escaped wisp of hair behind her ear.

"I've come to believe that, mija. I really have." Papi placed his hands on Isa's shoulders and looked at her intently. "Marco is a hardworking, smart man. He'll go places. But most importantly, he loves you. You will forge a good life together, but it will be challenging at first."

"I know it won't be easy, Papi. You never taught me how to be poor!" Isabela gave him a cheeky smile.

"He's already earning a good salary, Isa. Besides, you're very clever and resourceful, so this experience will only make you stronger. Now I know I said I wouldn't help you financially, and I doubt Marco would take my money anyway, but Connie and I have a special wedding gift for you," Papi said slyly.

"Really? What is it?" Isa asked, eyes shining.

"A brand-new top-of-the-line wringer washer!" Papi beamed proudly at her.

Isa screeched, "¿De veras?" Her mouth hung agape in disbelief.

"De veras."

She flung her arms around him and exclaimed, "Thank you, Papi! You are the best Papi in the history of papis!" She didn't let go until she'd had her fill of his comforting scent, a mix of citrusy cologne, oily brilliantine, and sandalwood shaving soap.

Isa felt like a queen walking down the aisle of Perpetuo Socorro church on Papi's arm. Her wedding dress was simple but elegant, a white silk floor-length gown cut on the bias to show off her curves. She loved its cap sleeves edged in the same lace as her veil, its boat neck, and the small train that pooled behind her. As she approached Marco, so handsome, waiting at the altar in his new black suit, she felt love radiate from his entire being and thanked God once again for sending her this unique man. Mati and Rosie were adorable in pink tulle dresses and took their flower girl duties seriously.

The ceremony sped by in a blur. She lost herself in Marco's eyes, the cadence of the nuptial Mass, and the comforting tang of burning candles and incense. When Marco presented her with the traditional thirteen gold arras, coins symbolizing his commitment to supporting her, she teared up. Surely her heart would explode from trying to hold this much joy. She loved this man with her very soul, and he loved her back. Together, they'd be unstoppable.

Isa hadn't minded that Papi insisted on a no-frills wedding. She was happy to avoid another grand society soiree with people who meant little to her. She did invite Gladys and Teté, even though they hadn't stopped crowing about how they *knew* she'd end up married. Their worlds, at least for the moment, would remain miles apart. There would be no Limoges tea service in Isa's home.

After the ceremony, she and Marco accepted congratulations from their small group of guests before heading to Papi's house for a festive lunch. Even though Carmen's food was abundant and delectable, Isa barely ate. Anticipation for the night's activities had canceled her appetite. However, she was glad everyone else celebrated to their heart's content. Even Julia traded her usual sour puss for a smile, lending Isa a glimpse of the Julia Marco loved.

Marco had planned a honeymoon in El Yunque rainforest, much to Isa's delight. Papi generously offered them Mariano's chauffeuring services, and as they climbed into Papi's car, their guests—none more enthusiastically than her sisters—showered them with rice and flower petals. On the way to the romantic mountain spot, Isabela leaned her head on Marco's shoulder and reflected on Carmen's odd send-off. She'd given Isa a long hug and whispered an admonition in her ear, "Today is a happy day, querida, but remember quien bien te quiera te hará llorar." Leave it to Carmen to bring up sorrow on Isa's happiest day. Marco would never hurt her, and it was laughable to think *she'd* ever make her beloved cry. There would be no sadness in her marriage.

As the car ascended El Yunque's tallest mountain, the air grew cooler. Coastal palm trees gave way to tall bamboo plants, lush ferns, deep green foliage, and the occasional roadside waterfall. The narrow and steep mountain road challenged Mariano with sharp bend after bend; he honked the horn at every blind curve to alert any cars coming in the opposite direction. As Isa and Marco swayed in the back seat, she was thankful neither suffered from motion sickness. Now that would be a terrible way to ruin a wedding night!

Marco had reserved one of El Yunque's new overnight cabins by the Pavilion restaurant and swimming pool. After saying goodbye to Mariano, he scooped Isa up and carried her over the small cabin's threshold. But once inside, he froze as if unsure what to do next.

"Mi amor, you can put me down now," she laughed, and Marco lowered her with a light squeeze.

Isa rubbed her upper arms vigorously. "It's freezing in here. How can it be this cold? I was just sweating in San Juan."

"We're in the mountains, querida. But don't worry. I'll warm you up." He wiggled his eyebrows.

"Oh, so you're going to light a fire?" teased Isa, pointing to the large stone fireplace, the focal point of the cabin's living area.

Marco raised his left eyebrow and jokingly responded, "I look forward to lighting a fire in you, my beautiful wife." Turning serious, he pulled Isa to him, and they kissed deeply. Her hands explored his back, traveled to his neck, and landed on his cheeks. She broke the kiss reluctantly, her body ablaze with yearning.

"Wait, Marco. I need to change into my wedding nightgown."

Marco looked pained. "Oh, my love, my love. Why bother? I'll just take it right off, you know." He pulled her toward the bedroom, walking backward. As Marco unbuttoned the front of her traveling dress, Isa readily gave in, all thoughts of wedding night attire wiped from her mind by desire. Their clothes came off in a flurry, each helping the other undress as quickly as possible. He laid her on the bed and gazed at her nude form.

"You're even more luminous than I imagined." His eyes roved her body.

Isabela blushed at being so openly admired. She could feel the taut skin of his erection on her thigh but was too overwhelmed to peek at it. Marco's hands roamed her breasts, cupping them while his mouth found her nipples, soft kisses turning to urgent sucking. The pleasure was overwhelming. She was weak with desire, her breathing quick and shallow. Marco poised himself over her as if doing a pushup and urgently pried her legs open with his own. His erection bounced against her inner thighs repeatedly, and she fought an impulse to laugh, picturing a wooden stick trying to hit a piñata. Why couldn't he find where he was supposed to go? Should she help him? *Hurry up, Marco!*

He finally used his hand to guide himself into her, only to meet with resistance.

"Are you alright, Isa? I don't want to hurt you." His voice was thick with need.

"Just do it quickly, Marco," she gasped. "Hurry!"

Marco plunged into her wetness, and she barely noticed the fleeting pain of losing her virginity. She instinctively moved her hips against his as he thrust in and out of her. Just when she was starting to revel in the rhythm of their rocking bodies, Marco emitted a deep-throated moan, and she felt his entire body tense before going limp. Marco slumped over her, all his weight pressing on her unsatisfied desire. *Is it over?* But she was still shaking with need. Marco lifted his head from where it rested on her shoulder and kissed her tenderly.

"Mi bella Isabela. You are a dream come true." His dark eyes were velvety and hooded, and he looked at her with such love it was almost impossible to look back. "I love you," he whispered.

"And I love you," Isabela said, stroking his face, for she didn't know how else to respond. Maybe the next time would be better, she thought, as she settled under the covers for the night and felt his semen slowly trickle out of her.

When she woke the next morning, Marco was already up. She donned her negligee, a delicate white silk concoction that rivaled her wedding dress and found Marco studying a sheaf of papers before a roaring fire. He smiled and rose to greet her with a kiss.

"Good morning, my love. Aren't you a vision? I thought I'd let you sleep in. Yesterday was a big day, no?"

Isabela stretched her arms above her head luxuriously and yawned. "It sure was! But what time did you get up? What are you doing?"

"Ah, too early, for sure," Marco smiled. "I was just double-checking my math on these Falansterio budgets, but I can finish while you get dressed for breakfast." He glanced back down at the paperwork he'd been poring over, brow furrowed. "The architects underestimated the construction costs, and I'm afraid we'll have to charge higher rents than we expected to make up the difference."

"People will have to stay in the Miranda slum?" Isa asked with concern.

"Some might."

"Well, you need to solve that, of course, but this is our honeymoon. Work can wait a few days." Isa crossed her arms and cocked her head to the right.

"Progress doesn't wait for love." He pulled her to him, eyes pleading. "Once you see the day I've planned, you'll forgive me, I promise."

Isa put a hand on his chest and pushed him away from her. "Huh," she huffed, and pointed her right index finger at him. "I better not see those papers again this weekend." She tried to look as stern as possible.

"I give you my solemn vow." His shame-faced expression convinced her he was serious.

"Well, then. I'll get ready for breakfast." She gave her rear end a little wiggle as she walked back to the bedroom, humming a tune, his laughter echoing behind her.

As she dressed, Isa thought about how pleased Marco would be to hear her news today. After much soul-searching, she'd contacted Beatriz Ayala, determined to regularly make herself useful in El Fanguito. Beatriz welcomed her warmly and gave her valuable pointers, such as telling Isa to dab Vicks VapoRub beneath her nose to help mask the slum's putrid odor.

Isa got herself a pair of rubber boots and began with short trips to distribute food and clothing. She honed her balancing skills while traversing the planks and acclimated to the conditions well enough to visit for longer periods. She made her visits secretly, under the cover of "wedding errands." Lord knows she didn't need Papi on her case, but she also kept her efforts from Marco. She wanted to surprise him with the news as a wedding gift.

Recently, she'd begun to teach a handful of adults to read and write, much to the amusement of their children. Beatriz had been right. The work was exhausting and draining but spiritually uplifting. The more she got to know Beatriz, the more she liked and admired the younger woman. Isa had four years on her, but Beatriz was wise for a nineteen-year-old, and they were becoming fast friends.

She'd tell Marco today and couldn't wait to see his face. He'd be so proud of her!

Isa donned wide-legged navy blue pants, a white blouse, and flat chestnut oxfords for their hike to La Mina Falls. They followed a somewhat treacherous path peppered with slippery moss-covered rocks and arrived at the thundering waterfall, panting from the effort and sweating from the humidity. The air was cool and refreshing at the waterfall's base, where they lingered before carefully climbing onto a couple of rounded grey boulders, where they enjoyed a picnic lunch.

Isa was fascinated by her verdant surroundings. This foliage was so different from the pretty flowers and fruit trees she was used to that it was hard to believe it all grew on the same island. Spanish moss, vines, and clusters of tiny orchids adorned the throngs of towering tabonuco and giant-leafed yagrumo trees that formed the forest's shady canopy. Enormous ferns, spiky birds-of-paradise, wild ginger, and jasmine surrounded them, while green mosses and a wealth of fungi covered the ground. The earthy scent of fertility and abundance thickened the air while wildlife abounded. They'd spotted giant snails, strange and wondrous insects, all types of frogs, and hundreds of colorful birds, including two emerald green parrots they decided were courting.

Relaxed by the sun's warmth, her being replete with happiness, Isa decided the time was perfect for Marco's surprise.

"Amor, you know I admire everything you're doing at PRRA." She lay on her side facing her husband, head propped up in her hand.

"I know. I know. You just don't want me doing it on our honeymoon." Marco smiled wryly, eyes focused on the mesmerizing cloud shapes floating in the deep blue sky above him.

"True." Isa laughed. "But that's not why I brought up the subject. It's just that the people in the slums need more than a decent home. They need to be able to get ahead. But how can they when so many are illiterate?"

Marco turned his head to face Isa. "I think we're making progress in that area, at least in San Juan. Children are going to school."

"Less than half." Isa shook her head and sat up straight. "And what about their parents? They need to learn, too."

"There are literacy programs for adults," Marco pointed out.

"But not where they live."

"Teachers won't go into the slums." Marco raised his eyebrows, clearly thinking the concept ridiculous.

"Not true." Isa shook her head and pointed at herself, her expression giddy. "*I've* been teaching in El Fanguito since Christmas."

Marco shot upright, eyes as big as breadfruits. "*You what?*"

Thrilled at his amazement, Isa clapped her hands, her expression giddy. "It's true. I've been making excellent progress with two young mothers there." She awaited Marco's praise.

"Let me understand this correctly. You, Isabela," he pointed at her chest, "have been inside El Fanguito. You've braved the stench and pestilence to teach people to read?"

Isabela nodded, eyes bright. "Yes! I've made friends with women from La Upi who help there."

"Have you gone completely insane?" Marco exploded.

Isa recoiled, shocked at this reaction. Before she could respond, Marco continued to yell. "You want to catch tuberculosis, and who knows what else? Bring diseases home to your husband and children?"

"We don't have any children, Marco," she spat back at him. He was being ridiculous.

"Yet." Marco emphasized the word.

"Fine. I'll teach until I get pregnant."

"No. Absolutely not. I forbid it." Marco banged his hand on the rock.

Was he serious? Isa didn't know whether to laugh or cry. She stared at him, aghast for several seconds, before finding her voice again. "Did you just forbid me to do something? Are you Papi now?"

"No, but I'm your husband." Marco's face was dead serious. "No wife of mine is going to slosh around the slums, embarrassing me and spreading disease."

Isa raised her left eyebrow. "I wasn't aware that my helping others would embarrass you."

"You know what I mean, Isa," Marco said in a conciliatory tone. "You're too precious to me. I can't let anything happen to you." He reached over to hug her.

Isa, still stunned, succumbed to the embrace. She decided to change the subject, let Marco think she'd given up. For now. Why ruin their honeymoon with disagreements?

When they returned to the cabin for a rest, Isa dozed off lazily on the sofa under a light blanket. She awoke with a start and sat up, confused about where she was but alert enough to notice Marco quickly hiding something behind him. The rustle of papers gave the "something" away.

"You promised!" She popped her eyes at him.

"I know, my love, but I really need to complete this work."

Isa shook her head. "It's our honeymoon, a time to celebrate our love. Your work has no place here." Her tone was sharp. She, too, had the power to forbid things in this marriage.

Marco looked sheepish. "You're right, my wife." Marco gathered the papers and stuffed them into his briefcase. He went to sit by Isa on the couch and took both her hands in his. "Will you forgive me?"

Isa sighed before replying, "Ay, Marco." She got up, pecked him a little too hard on the cheek, and went to dress for dinner.

The restaurant, just a short walk from their cabin, glowed from a mix of candlelight and the fire roaring in its enormous stone hearth. They feasted on goat fricassee, mofongo, and flan. The romantic surroundings and rich food lulled Isa into a better mood. *This is more like it*, she thought. Marco held her hand across the table. They sat in easy silence for a bit, watching other couples on the dance floor. Two songs later, Isa said, "Let's dance, my love." Marco did not respond.

"Hello?" Isa waved her hand in front of his face. "Are you there?"

Marco started. "Oh, sorry." He looked down, sheepish.

"Work again," Isa stated with disbelief and flopped her hands on her lap. This obsession with work was unacceptable, and she'd speak her mind before it got any more out of hand.

"Listen, Marco." Isa waited until he looked back up at her. "I know you need to make your mark at PRRA, and I'm keenly aware it takes long hours, intense focus, and dedication. We've sacrificed time with each other, expecting it will pay off in the long run. But when you're with me, I need you to be with me—heart, mind, and soul. I already share you enough with your job." Isa felt the heat of annoyance flush her cheeks. He was forcing her to act like a child demanding attention.

Marco immediately offered her his hand, eyebrows knit together with concern. Glad he was taking her seriously, she reached across and put her palm in his.

"You're right, my love," he said. "I didn't mean to be neglectful. You're the light that keeps me going, and I pledge right here and now to be one hundred percent yours when we're together."

His eyes searched hers so intently Isa almost felt sorry for him and decided to lighten the mood.

"Good, because you take all this for granted," Isa struck a model's pose. "And you do so at your own peril." She flashed a wicked smile.

"Duly noted," Marco said, glancing toward the dance floor. "Did you want to dance?"

"No, let's call it a day."

"Yes, let's warm up that bed," Marco said.

Isa nodded, hoping the second time would be an improvement.

After making love—if leaving your wife with a fire between her legs qualified as making love—she rested her head on Marco's chest.

She'd expected life with Marco to be challenging, but financially, not because he ignored her or left her wanting in bed. Much less because he forbade her to pursue meaningful work. She tossed and turned until the early morning hours and wondered whether she'd made a terrible mistake.

CHAPTER 14

– Marco –
February to May 1937

The honeymoon was everything Marco had hoped for. The love-making incomparable, being so close to Isa transcendent. And even though Isa expressed displeasure at his preoccupation with work, he knew she understood his drive. He'd been aghast to learn she'd ventured into El Fanguito, and to impress him, no less. But she'd deferred to him quickly when he'd objected, thank God.

They happily set up house in Rio Piedras, in a one-bedroom third-floor walk-up apartment. It was convenient to the trolley that went to his office in Puerta de Tierra and next door to La Upi, where he taught two nights a week in the Business College's Evening Division. He was impressed at the booming metropolis Rio Piedras had become; it had grown alongside La Upi, which now enrolled more than 4,000 students. The mix of scholars and young professionals living in the area was visible evidence of San Juan's growing middle class.

Their bright white apartment building sported touches of Spanish Renaissance architecture: red roof tile and arched openings displaying dark wooden front doors. Marco absolutely refused to purchase cheaply made goods, so their home remained sparsely furnished with just a well-made sofa and a two-chair dinette set. The radio, which Isa had absconded with from her father's house, sat on the living room's tile floor. Thank God Tío had gifted them a bed and bureau. Also, Mamá had embroidered their initials on sheets and towels that Connie had given them behind Don Gabriel's back. And, of course, Isa had been ecstatic at receiving a wringer washing machine from her father, although Marco felt additional living room furniture would have been considerably more practical, since they had nowhere for visitors to sit. After all, how much laundry did two people produce? It should be easy enough to wash it all by hand.

In March, he finally took Isa to Yabucoa and gave her credit for enduring the arduous público trip from Rio Piedras without complaint. They changed cars five times during stops in La Muda, Caguas, Cayey, Guayama, and Arroyo, each time squeezing in with other sweltering folks excited to visit family on the weekend.

Marco asked the público driver to let them out at Yabucoa's town entrance. Chest tight, he guided Isabela to his mother's small home behind Tío's bakery. If Isa was surprised at its simplicity, she hid it expertly. He was certain Mamá had spent the previous day cleaning and making sure their few pieces of furniture were as shiny as possible, that her meager possessions were displayed to their best advantage. He hated to think of his mother working so hard to impress Isabela.

"Bienvenida, Isabela," Mamá said as they entered, moving in to give them each a kiss and a hug. He'd been right; the house smelled of wood oil and ammonia. "Julia! Marco and Isabela are here."

Julia, home from university for a brief visit, emerged from one of the bedrooms wearing a sleeveless teal cotton dress with a coral collar and belt.

"My favorite brother has arrived!" Julia squealed, rushing to give him a hug.

Marco's tension melted at the sight of his sister, who grew prettier each day. Even though she was studying in Rio Piedras, his work responsibilities and her class schedule left them little time to see each other.

"It's wonderful to see you, too, favorite sister." Marco laughed.

"Hola, Julia," Isabela interjected, leaning over to kiss Julia on the cheek.

"Hola, Isabela," Julia responded with a cool nod.

Oh-oh. Julia, who'd been charming at the wedding, was back to her contrary self. When would his sister finally warm up to Isabela?

"Sit down. Sit down," Mamá said. "Julia made a sweet potato cake. It's her specialty. How about a slice with a cafecito?"

"Sounds delicious, Doña Susana," Isabela said.

"Marco, tell me. How's work?" Mamá asked, doling out slices of the still-steaming cake. She poured everyone coffee, replacing the ammonia smell with a sweet and smoky aroma.

"I have calluses from holding a pencil all day." Marco held up his right middle and index fingers. "But I love every minute of it. We're building homes and schools for the people in the slums and soon for the jíbaros, too. All in cement. You won't believe how this island is going to improve."

"Do the jíbaros know this? Because they don't like charity," Julia warned.

"I think once they understand how the improvements will benefit their children, they'll be open to the changes. Who doesn't want healthy and educated sons?"

"Or daughters," Isabela said, throwing Marco a meaningful look.

"Yes, of course!" answered Marco. "Either is a blessing." Although he definitely wanted sons, he kept that thought to himself.

"And, Isabela. You must be busy with the new apartment," Mamá said.

"I never realized housekeeping was so time-consuming," Isa said.

Marco winced, knowing Isa had just unwittingly fanned the flames of Julia's dislike.

"It must be so hard for you. What's your least favorite chore?" Julia asked, sounding sincere to Marco's ears, which put him on high alert.

"Cleaning the toilet is definitely the worst." Isa scrunched her nose.

"I wouldn't know. We don't have a toilet here, so I've never cleaned one," Julia said.

Isa shifted her weight on the chair and scratched her neck, her expression perplexed. Marco could tell she was wondering where they did their business.

"Enough talk about—" Marco hurriedly tried to interrupt, but Isa put a hand on his arm to stop him.

"No, Marco. It's fine. Julia, what do you mean?" Isa asked, frowning and seemingly at a loss.

"See that tiny shack out there?" Julia pointed out the window, her face dark with scorn. "That's our latrine. Just a hole in the ground. Its main advantage is no toilet to clean."

"Oh," Isabela said, clearly taken aback. Marco felt the heat of humiliation seep through his pores. They were just a bunch of peasants who squatted like animals to shit in a hole.

But Isabela quickly recovered. "Well, your legs must be strong from all that squatting, Julia. No wonder they're so shapely."

Marco let out a loud guffaw, half at Isabela's response and half at seeing Julia outmaneuvered.

Upon their return to San Juan, Marco eagerly re-immersed himself in the work that so excited and sustained him. After seeing Mamá's house through Isabela's eyes, he was more motivated than ever to get his mother the modern home she deserved. A shrewd eye for finances and a newly discovered talent for negotiation helped him bring the Falansterio construction costs under control and earned him high praise from new PRRA Director Ernest Gruening. Marco was also assigned to the Eleanor Roosevelt Urbanization project in Hato Rey, a community of homes PRRA planned to build with its own water system, sewage facilities, school, and police station. The scope of this undertaking thrilled him beyond measure, as did the welcome salary increase that came with his new responsibilities.

Between the raise and the teaching earnings he'd squirreled away, Marco had finally saved enough to fulfill his promise and move Mamá to a better house. He asked Tío to look for potential deals back in Yabucoa. By April, Tío had found a cozy two-bedroom house on Muñoz Rivera Street, a few doors down from where Marco's family had lived with Papá before the hurricane. The bank had foreclosed on the house, which initially gave Marco pause. He felt guilty benefiting from the misfortune of others. But he reminded himself that one person's misery during this Depression was another one's gain and that someone might as well be him. He'd arranged an advantageous rent-to-buy deal with the bank and stopped worrying about the fate of the previous owners.

The day had come to surprise Mamá with the news, and Marco was giddy with anticipation as he and Isa arrived in Yabucoa. He knocked on Mamá's door and was delighted to see her surprised face.

"¡Mijo! ¡Isabela! What a surprise!" Elated, Mamá threw her arms around them both. Then, pulling away to arm's length, said, "But what are you doing here?"

"We've come to take you somewhere very special," Marco said, eyes agleam. "Take off that apron and come. Tío's driving."

Mamá gave him a puzzled look and reached behind her back to untie her apron.

"Trust me, Doña Susana, you're going to like where we're going." Isa, who'd been very quiet during the público journey, he'd even say morose, finally showed signs of life and enthusiasm. Marco suspected a tiny bit of her resented the money he was spending on his mother when they still needed things for their apartment. But her generosity of spirit had won out, and he loved her for matching his excitement.

Marco's heart was full as Tío parked his car in front of Mamá's new home. Painted a light aqua blue, the modest house sported a narrow veranda separated from the sidewalk by a low wall.

"We're here," Marco said.

"But who are we seeing? I'm not presentable for a visit." Mamá, flustered, patted down her hair.

Marco got out of the back seat, opened the front passenger door for his mother, offered her the crook of his arm, and led her toward the house. He brandished a set of keys in his other hand. "Welcome, Mamá, to your new home."

"I don't understand," Mamá said, frowning.

"I've rented this house for you, but eventually, you'll own it. Come! Let's go inside!" Marco pulled Mamá, eyes wide and hands covering her mouth, through the front door. Tío, Isa, and Marco commented on the modern amenities, including the tiled kitchen and full bathroom, while Mamá remained speechless.

"Marco, this is too much," Mamá finally whispered. He'd only seen her cry once before, the morning after San Felipe when Papá hadn't returned.

Overcome with love, he embraced Mamá tightly and said, "I only wish it could be more. You deserve the world for all the sacrifices you've made for Julia and me. I hope you'll be very happy and comfortable here."

"How could I not?" Mamá said. "Thank you, thank you, my son! And Isa! Thank you both for your generosity. I am so lucky to have all of you." She threw her arms open to include Isa and Tío in the family hug.

Marco was thrilled at the joy on Mamá's face. Isa's expression, too, was full of love, and he could tell his wife was proud of her husband's ability to offer Mamá this small luxury and bring her such happiness. He hadn't expected to accomplish this goal so soon, only nine years since he'd made himself the promise. After enduring God's tests for so long, perhaps he was finally being rewarded.

Marco relived his triumphant moment the following evening while listening to the radio with Isa. How pleased she'd been! It had been silly of him to think she begrudged the expense of Mamá's house. Sure, they needed furniture, but that would come soon enough. For now, they had all the critical necessities. Yet Isa's mood had again turned gloomy during the trip home, and he didn't think it was due to the heat and discomfort of the crowded público. Something else was bothering her, and if it wasn't the money he'd spent on Mamá's house, he had a hunch what it could be.

Isa assured him their small apartment was easy to keep clean. And while her forays in the kitchen had varying degrees of success, he always lauded her efforts. No, what bothered Isa, what she complained about most, was the inordinate amount of time she spent doing laundry, despite having a washing machine. Her hands, previously soft as rose petals, had become rough and red.

He needed to free her from that drudgery. But how? Their budget was tight, especially now with Mamá's rent to pay. There was no money to send laundry out. But he worried Isa's spirit would soon fracture. Sure, she'd signed up for this life, but he'd promised her it would be temporary. They'd only been married a few months, but for someone brought up with every luxury, it must feel like an eternity. He needed a new source of income, something he could do on the side that didn't require too much of his limited free time. Maybe he could teach an additional class at La Upi.

He turned to Isa on the sofa and said, "Amor mío, I've been thinking of ways to bring in extra money so you can send the laundry out. What if I taught another class?"

He'd expected her to be ecstatic at the prospect of being freed from laundry duty, but her irritated tone surprised him.

"How can you possibly find time for that? You work long hours at PRRA and then teach two nights a week, while the remaining nights you prepare for class or grade assignments. I barely see you as it is. When exactly would you have time to add another responsibility?"

Marco tried to appease her. "I'll make the time. Adding another class won't be that much work, since I already have the lessons planned."

"It still sounds like less Marco for me. Who am I keeping this house for if you're never even home?" She crossed her arms in front of her chest and continued in a clipped tone. "You know what I should be doing? I should be teaching people in the slums to read."

"But the dangers! We talked about this." Marco's body was heating up. He was so tired of this obsession of hers. When would she give it up?

"We didn't talk. You forbade," Isa responded, her tone arch. "Look, I need to feel helpful. At the very least, I should be connecting with friends, uncovering opportunities for you. You know, Teté's husband works at Banco Popular. I could talk to—"

"Absolutely not. My future will be built on merit, not connections." Marco was adamant. Sure, Isa's connections could help his career, but they'd eventually lead back to Don Gabriel. He refused to owe that man anything in any way, even if indirectly. "Besides, you know my work at PRRA is important to me."

"And to me, too." Isa took his hands in hers with an expression so earnest it melted Marco's heart. "But what if you can help move Puerto Rico forward in other ways? Why not see whether you can meet that goal and also earn more? I'm sure there are ways. I can help you figure it out."

Isa was practically begging. Was she really that desperate to escape her housekeeping duties?

"Get ahead because of who I married? What would people say? Especially your father. I'll lose any inkling of respect I've earned from that man."

"But we're a team, Marco."

"Of course," Marco said gently. "You have your duties, and I have mine. And mine are to provide for us." His voice turned firmer. "I don't want you soliciting for me. Just the mere thought makes me cringe." Marco watched as Isa's face fell. He was sorry to disappoint her, but had she really expected to be his agent? She was his wife!

"Well, I don't know what you're going to do then because teaching another class is not an option," Isa said, turning away from him and picking up a book she was in the middle of reading.

Marco let her have the last word. Self-respecting men opened their own doors. Besides, they already had so much more than he'd grown up with. Why couldn't Isa appreciate that? He should have married someone poor, like him. Huh. No use thinking about that now. He'd fallen in love with *this* woman, and the pressure was on to keep her happy.

CHAPTER 15

- Isabela -
May 1937

Isa hurried from the trolley, changed into the rubber boots she carried in a leather-strapped canvas bag, slathered Vicks into her nostrils, and approached El Fanguito. She had a scant two hours before she'd have to head back to take care of her household duties before Marco got home. While she didn't relish sneaking behind her husband's back, he'd left her no choice. Her work in the slum provided a vital and satisfying counterpart to the drudgery of cooking and cleaning, and she refused to give it up because of Marco's cockamamie ideas of what a wife was allowed to do. After endless cajoling, rationalizing, ego stroking, and outright begging—all to no avail—she'd decided that what Marco didn't know wouldn't hurt him.

She smiled as she came upon Beatriz distributing bags of canned goods from the back of a faded red pickup truck. Bea borrowed the truck on occasion from her father, who owned a furniture store. A long line of people stood waiting their turn in the mid-morning heat, relieved to know their families would eat today.

"Hola, Beatriz," Isa greeted her friend. "Do you need help?"

"Buenas, Isabela. No te preocupes." Beatriz waved her away. "I know your students are waiting for their lesson. But come see me when you're done."

"I will!" Isa dashed over the planks, greeting the naked children she knew by sight now, and swooped into the Lopez house to drop off a package of rice and dried beans.

"God bless you, Isa," Doña Martina, the Lopez matriarch, called after her. Isa flashed a bright smile.

"Enjoy it in good health," Isa said.

The skeletal brown dog who loitered on the plank leading to Doña Gloria's house wagged her tail upon seeing Isa. "Here you go, Luna." Isa gave her a beef bone she'd saved from dinner the previous evening. Luna barked twice in appreciation and headed off to enjoy her treat in private.

"¡Hola, Isabela!" Doña Gloria greeted Isa at her hut's entrance and motioned her inside, where three other women waited. A baby napped in a corner, protected by a mosquitero Isa had procured.

"Buenos días, señoras," Isa greeted her students. "¿Como están?"

"Bien, bien, Missy Isabela," they answered almost in unison.

Isa got a kick out of her new name. Schoolchildren called their teachers Missy or Meester, whether or not the teachers were American. She liked being called Missy. It made her feel official.

"Did everyone do their homework?" Happy to see nods all around, Isabela launched into the day's lesson. She was proud of her students' progress these past four months. They could write their letters, sound out simple words, and carry out basic addition and subtraction functions. These women were inspirational. With little time to spare, they doggedly carved out enough minutes each day to make steady progress. Luisa had even been able to help her son with his phonetics. Her delight at being able to do so had filled Isa's heart.

Her students made quick work of the day's lesson, so Isa assigned their homework and made a mental note to bring new books with her next time. Her sisters provided an endless supply and never seemed to miss the ones Isa "borrowed." She said her goodbyes and set out to find Beatriz humming a lively tune.

Isa's friend was where she'd left her, her food supplies depleted, the queued crowd dispersed.

"Hop in. I'll give you a ride to the trolley," Beatriz said, opening the truck's passenger door for Isa. "I'm dying of thirst. Do you mind if we stop at Luli's colmado?"

Isa's mouth watered at the thought of an ice-cold, sweet and fizzy malta. "What are you waiting for, woman? Let's go!"

Beatriz put the truck in gear and asked, "How did it go today?"

"Well, they're almost reading," Isa said. "I think they could get jobs soon and make real money instead of taking in laundry for practically nothing. Doña Gloria could even take the baby with her if she worked in a store or sold lottery tickets."

"Yes, but their husbands want them at home." Beatriz shook her head, lips tight.

Isa knew Bea's family was fairly modern in that her mother worked as a teacher, even though her father owned a profitable store. This wasn't the norm, and certainly not Isa's experience, neither with Papi nor Marco.

"I bet they like eating more than they want their wives at home," Isa said.

"Speaking of wanting the wife at home, how is Mr. Mussolini?"

Isa rolled her eyes. "As fascist as ever. He's lucky I love him."

Bea shook her head. "I don't understand why he's not supportive of your efforts here. From everything you've told me about Marco, you'd think he'd be proud of you."

"It's complicated, Bea," Isa said, staring out the passenger window. "He wants to help the poor, but from afar, so he doesn't have to be reminded he was poor once."

Bea nodded, lips pursed.

Isa turned to face her friend. "Now he's worried about how much I hate laundry. I don't like lying to him, but what choice do I have? I can't tell him I want to send our laundry out so I can spend more time here."

"Would he have a conniption?" Bea grinned mischievously.

"A massive conniption." Isa shuddered, imagining Marco losing his temper like Papi did. She continued as Beatriz pulled over in front of Luli's, "I'm pretty sure he thinks I resent the money he's spending on his mother's rent. As if I would begrudge that poor woman the basic comforts of life."

"He can't possibly think that," Beatriz frowned in disbelief and put the truck in park.

"Who knows?" Isa threw her hands up in the air. "Last night, he talked about teaching more classes to pay for laundry services. Can you imagine? I see him so little as it is. But he's sweet trying to find a solution."

"Too bad his pride won't allow you to make some connections for him."

"I've given up on that notion. But, hmmm," Isa ruminated. "What if I wash the clothes less often? He probably won't even notice they're still dirty."

"Ay, Isa. He might not notice, but everyone around him will. Please save them from that fate!"

The two women burst out laughing before going into the colmado for their drinks.

It was indeed a laundry day, and later that afternoon, after putting a pot of beef stew on the stove to simmer, Isa washed the clothes as Carmen had shown her, step by tedious step. The laundry process was endless. And dangerous! Look at how the machine wanted to suck her fingers into the wringer. Isa winced, imagining the pain. Her shoulders dropped, and she expelled an exasperated sigh as she bailed dirty water out of the machine's washtub and into the kitchen sink. She dripped in sweat as she filled the tub again, getting ready to rinse the clothes and then wring them for the second time.

How had she never realized the amount of work servants did? Her mother among them and without a washing machine to boot. Her mother had hand-scrubbed the Soto family's clothes, squeezed them, hung them, and ironed them over and over in an endless loop of tedium. Isa imagined her mother with muscled arms and rough hands. *Pobrecita*, thought Isa. *My poor, poor mother.* Isa's heart broke a little thinking about the mother's love she'd missed. But if her mother had lived, Isa, too, would be scouring floors or laundering clothes for others.

Carmen had warned her, "Al demonio y a la mujer, nunca les falta que hacer."

"I'd rather be a demon than a woman if neither ever lacks work. At least demons have powers," Isa had said while Carmen crossed herself, horrified at Isa's sacrilege.

Isa chuckled at the memory and hung Marco's undershirts to dry in the bathroom. She heard Marco enter the apartment and hurried to the living room, wiping her sweaty face with a towel.

"Hola, amor," Isa greeted him with a kiss. "I was hanging the last of the laundry."

"You only just finished?" Marco asked. "You must be exhausted, cleaning all day in this heat. I worry about you, Isa." She caught him glancing down at her red hands and her peeling nails.

"I'm perfectly fine, querido. Carmen warned me that a woman's work is never done." Isa went into the kitchen, stirred the stew, and pulled bowls and silverware from the cupboard to set the table. Marco followed her.

"No. This is all too much for you. I'm going to ask Julia to help you in the afternoons," Marco said.

Isa could not believe her ears. How in the world could Marco think that was a good idea? While Julia wanted to emulate Isa's elegance and aspired to a wealthy lifestyle, she resented Isa for being to the manor born. Julia wanted what she disliked Isa for having had. And now that Julia was earning a college degree, something Isa did not have, she'd been putting on absurdly intellectual airs. No, having Julia around could possibly kill her. And God forbid Julia find out about her forays to El Fanguito. She'd tell Marco for sure, and all hell would break loose.

"Don't be silly," Isa gave him a carefree smile. "I'm perfectly capable of running my own home."

"You never cease to amaze me, beautiful Isa," Marco said, sitting down. "And what delicacy did you prepare tonight? Carmen taught you well!"

"Carne guisada with a side of yucca." Isa was pleased with how quickly she'd learned the ins and outs of Puerto Rican cooking. Carmen had taught her to make sofrito, the base of every Puerto Rican dish, by sautéing diced cubanelle peppers, tomatoes, onion, garlic, sweet ají peppers, recao, and cilantro in oil. Once the aromatic mixture was ready, Isa was amazed at how adding beans, chicken, different types of vegetables, or meats created a hearty stew that essentially cooked itself. It was easy! And to think she'd barely known how to slice a mango when Marco proposed.

As Isa served Marco, she registered the sour look on his face. Was something wrong with her stew?

"No yucca for me, Isa. Come to think of it, I don't want yucca at my table again, or any root vegetable," Marco decreed.

For a second, Isa thought he was joking, but his scowl indicated otherwise.

"But why? They're so good, Marco! I love yucca and yautía!"

"You wouldn't like them so much if you'd had them every day growing up. I won't allow viandas in this house. They're common."

"But what about sweet potatoes and yams?" Isa pleaded.

"All viandas, Isa. If it was a root, we're not eating it." Marco's expression brooked no argument.

She gave in because she understood he didn't want to be reminded of his years of hardship. But really, wasn't he being a tad ridiculous? First came his absurd fixation with purchasing goods of only the highest quality, doing without until they could afford the best. Then he refused to use her contacts to help his career. And now he'd developed a sudden abhorrence to viandas. Not even Papi was that inflexible.

Isa started bringing viandas and bacalao to El Fanguito, which Doña Gloria boiled during their lessons and then doused with oil and vinegar for a shared lunch feast. Heaven! Just because Marco wanted to be a vegetable snob and deny himself didn't mean she had to. Besides, it was probably his fault she'd been craving this dish so often. Isn't that what happens with forbidden fruit?

Come June, Isa realized her food cravings had nothing to do with forbidden fruit and everything to do with pregnancy. In May, her breasts had been tender, as they always were before her menses, but the bleeding never came. She hadn't experienced morning sickness or nausea, so she'd thought nothing of it until she missed her menses a second time. After she received the phone call confirming her pregnancy, Isa sat down to let the news sink in. She was going to be a mother, was going to be responsible for a tiny, helpless creature. She should be in a panic. But, no. For the first time in her life, Isa truly understood what it meant to be overjoyed. She gently placed both hands on her still-flat stomach and imagined the life that was developing inside her, a life she and Marco created, a tangible manifestation of their love.

She'd learned to delight in Marco's pleasure during their lovemaking as if she was giving him a gift each time. But she never felt the mad release of orgasm during intercourse like her husband did. She liked the feel of Marco's hands and mouth on her breasts, after which he'd enter her, and she'd move her hips to help him finish quickly so she could enjoy the lovely closeness of post-coital snuggles and caresses. What a wonder that such actions created life. Isa shook her head, smiling. She tried to imagine the look on Marco's face when she told him, but all she could conjure in her mind's eye was an endless stream of brightly-hued celebratory fireworks.

Myriad concerns began to swim around the edges of her happy consciousness. She tried to push them back to no avail. How would they afford to buy the things a baby required, especially if Marco continued his insistence on only having "the best"? A baby needed a crib, a bureau, and a rocking chair, at the very least. Could she continue visiting El Fanguito, and if so, what precautions would she need to take? How would she continue to manage all her chores? There already wasn't enough time in a day.

Stop it, Isa. Surely Papi would help them out with some of the things the baby needed, and maybe Carmen could come by once in a while. She'd also speak with Beatriz about the best course of action in relation to her slum work. They'd figure out a way for her to remain involved. She willed the celebratory fireworks back to the forefront of her mind and forced herself to focus on the positives. They'd made a miracle. She couldn't wait to tell Marco.

CHAPTER 16

- Marco -
June 1937 to August 1938

Marco wished the trolley would speed up. A colony of ants had taken residence in his veins; he was ready to jump out of his skin. Finally, he hopped out two stops early, bolted toward home (leaving the trolley far behind), and burst into the apartment breathlessly, shouting, "Isa! Isa!"

"What is it? Why are you yelling?" Isa stood in the kitchen doorway, wiping her hands on a dish towel, concern etched on her face.

Oh, no! He'd worried her. Marco stood in the middle of the living room, trying to catch his breath. He pulled at his tie to loosen it.

"No, it's good news! I had the most amazing day!"

"Really? I sort of did, too." Isa dropped the towel on the dining table and moved toward Marco. She had a sparkle in her eye, but Marco was sure his news would surpass hers in importance. She could wait.

"What? Did you cook the pork chops without burning them?" Marco teased. He flopped himself on the sofa and pulled her down with him. This was going to be so good.

"Ha. Ha. Ha," Isa responded. "I haven't burned anything in ages, for your information. Nor ruined any clothes in the wash."

"That's true! But, Isa," Marco grabbed her by the shoulders, his entire face smiling at hers. "Gruening told me again today what a great job I'm doing. So much so that..." Marco let the last words of the sentence linger on his tongue, building up the suspense.

"What? What? Tell me, you sinvergüenza," Isa slapped him playfully on the shoulder.

"I'm going to oversee the feasibility studies for the bottle and cardboard factories!" Marco threw his arms overhead triumphantly.

Isabela hugged him and squealed, "Marco! Just what you've wanted, my love! I'm so proud of you!"

"Come, let's go out to dinner and celebrate." He tightened his tie as he rose and moved toward the apartment door, exuberance in his step.

"Can we afford it?" Isa held back, putting a damper on his thrill. He reminded himself that soon she wouldn't need to worry about such things.

"It's a special occasion. Besides, I'll be getting a raise to go with my increased responsibilities." He pulled Isa toward him again. "Come, let's go to El Nido. A celebratory meal is in order!"

"Then yes! Because we're both starting new projects."

"What do you mean?" Marco had forgotten that Isa also had news.

She patted her lower belly. Marco had trouble reading her expression. Excited? Fearful?

What? The news took a moment to register, and then his mouth dropped. A baby! A bevy of mixed emotions—happiness, fear, tenderness, doubt—weakened his knees and forced him to sit again. He was going to be a father! He'd barely processed the news when concern for Isa took over. Marco sprang into solicitous mode. "Are you okay? Do you want to sit down?" His wife was pregnant!

"Ay, Marco. I'm not broken," Isa started to untie the apron she wore around her waist, her cheeks opalescent. Pregnant women did glow! He had to admit that whenever he'd envisioned Isa pregnant, she'd been curled up on the bed sobbing and asking for Carmen. But this tranquil woman seemed pleased, as if she looked forward to this new stage. He and Isa's love would create a perfect tiny human. Marco was ecstatic. His career was on the fast track, and now a baby! He looked toward the ceiling and made the sign of the cross. *Gracias, Papá.* He missed his father, but he liked having a guardian in heaven.

Marco knew babies cost money, and since his children would have the best of everything, his focus on finding new sources of income intensified. As he explored the fiscal feasibility of building bottle and cardboard factories to support the rum industry, he realized that the new Puerto Rico was going to require massive amounts of construction during the next few years. New factories would mean additional housing for the workers. Factory management would also need suitable accommodations. It was a breathtaking business opportunity, ripe fruit ready for picking. Once again, he turned to his trusted friend, Sammy, who continued to toil miserably at his father's insurance firm. They met for beers at a small bar near campus after one of Marco's night classes. The place was dark, and the jukebox played a Mexican mariachi song.

"¡Sammy, hombre!" Marco embraced Sammy, who was already seated at a table, two beer bottles at the ready. "How goes the insurance trade?" Marco put his briefcase down and took a long pull from his beer.

"Profitable, but abysmally boring," Sammy said. "And working with my father is torture. He still thinks I'm three years old and need constant supervision."

"Ouch. That sounds painful."

"Very. I need to get out, hermano, do my own thing. But enough about my sorry life. I drive by the Falansterio every day. Impressive work!"

"Thank you. The families seem happy. Such an improvement over the slums, right?" Marco said, adding, "Even though the rents ended up being higher than anticipated."

"Not as high as they could have been had you not saved the day by reining in the building expenses," Sammy said.

Marco appreciated his friend's propensity to give credit where credit was due, but waved Sammy's praise away and leaned into the table. "Listen, I'm working on something else, Sammy, a business opportunity of unprecedented magnitude." He'd spoken quietly and now held his breath.

Sammy rolled his eyes. "Always with the hyperbole. Although I confess, I'm intrigued. Hold that thought while I get more beers."

"A Corona for me, chico. I can't stand this new India shit," Marco said, breathing again and pointing to the bottle he'd been drinking. His hands were as sweaty as when he'd first met Don Gabriel. He needed to sell Sammy on his vision, get him exhilarated and eager to participate.

Sammy returned to their table and handed Marco his Corona. "Bueno, compay, what fantasy are you chasing now? I thought you'd take a break after getting the PRRA job *and* marrying the debutante. What's next, world domination?"

Marco ignored Sammy's ribbing and pulled a folded map out of his briefcase. He carefully spread it open on the table. "This is Rio Piedras, and here is Hato Rey," he said, pointing. "Look at all the available land. The government is bringing industry to the island, Sammy, and the people who run those companies will need to live somewhere nice. But nobody realizes this yet. This land is up for grabs right now. It's just waiting for someone to buy it, build on it, and make a fortune."

Sammy looked intrigued. Marco could tell he had his friend's full attention and continued with his pitch. "I've just managed the construction budget of more than two hundred apartments in El Falansterio, and I'm on the Roosevelt Urbanization development team, creating what is essentially a small town. I know how to do this. More importantly, I know how to do this really, really well." Marco paused and looked at Sammy. "Remember when you loaned me the money for the July Fourth ball so I could finally wear down Don Gabriel? I promised you that someday I would pay you back in spades. This is it, brother. This is how I'm going to pay you back." Marco pointed at Sammy with his right index finger.

"What exactly are you proposing?" Sammy danced his beer bottle on the table and leaned over the map.

Marco grinned and spread his hands. "If you put up the funds for our first purchase, something small to start, I'll manage the project and ensure it's profitable. We'll use the earnings to buy our next piece of land, and so forth, each time going bigger and bigger."

"I don't have a lot of liquid assets readily available, Marco." Sammy shook his head. "How much are we talking?"

Marco pulled a small bundle of photos and papers from his briefcase and spread them on the map. "Look at this apartment building. It's like the one I live in." Marco handed Sammy the photo.

Sammy grimaced and pulled his head back. "You're joking, right? This dump is ready for demolition. It's falling apart."

"Exactly," Marco said with a satisfied smile. "That's why we can get it for next to nothing and spend most of the money fixing it up. Then we rent the apartments and create a steady income to fund additional projects."

Sammy's face relaxed into a grin. "You think you're King Midas."

"You *know* I have the golden touch." Marco felt it in his bones— he had Sammy. They discussed costs and division of labor and agreed to have a mutual friend handle the legalities of their partnership. They clinked beers to toast their unbeatable collaboration, and Solemar Enterprises, named for their island's sun and sea, was born.

"You're doing what?" Isa's glare clearly communicated her incredulity and annoyance.

"But, Isa." He took a step toward her, and she took a step back, thrusting out her palm.

"No. I'm calling the manicomio right now to come get you."

He knew she was angry, but her little pregnant belly was bouncing so adorably that he couldn't take her seriously. It took all his self-control to hide his amusement. He forced a serious countenance.

"I know you think I'm crazy, but Sammy and I need to take advantage of this opportunity. It's not going to wait until I'm less busy."

"Marco, you aren't just busy. You're consumed with work every single moment of the day and night. I don't think that's healthy. You don't rest!"

"It's temporary, my love. Once the business gets going, I can scale down my other responsibilities."

"I miss being with you, Marco." She finally stepped toward him and placed her hand on his arm.

What did she want from him? He couldn't be in two places at once.

"Spend time with Connie and your sisters. Isn't it cooler at your father's house, anyway?"

"Yes, but I want *you*."

Marco did wish he could spend more time with Isa, of course. But these were their sacrifice years; he needed to pay his dues. Throughout the rest of her pregnancy, he tried to make life as easy as possible for her, beginning with sending their laundry out.

While Isa brought the baby to term, Marco and Sammy resuscitated the old building, giving it a rebirth of its own. He was busier than ever, working a full-time job, teaching two nights a week, and overseeing this new venture. Isa was right. He wouldn't be able to continue this pace for long. He'd been spending sleepless nights lately, his lists of things to do swirling like cyclones in his brain. So much was riding on Solemar. If the venture succeeded, he could quit PRRA and still be dedicated to edging Puerto Rico into modernity. With blazing motivation, Marco called upon his sizable multi-tasking skills and had every apartment rented two weeks before the baby was born. Solemar now had a steady income.

It was time for the next investment.

Marco's son was born on March 8, 1938, and weighed exactly eight pounds. They named him Diego Miguel, Diego after Marco's father, but Miguelito fit him best. Marco could stare at Isa and Miguelito for hours. She glowed when she held him, her sweet voice singing him lullabies. He'd known she'd be a special kind of mother. She'd been in good hands with Connie and Carmen during the pregnancy, but he'd still worried. Pregnancy could be a delicate matter. But all was well, and now Isa's days would be consumed with caring for the baby. They'd each have their own endeavors, and he could worry a little less about her. At least the pregnancy and Miguelito's birth had quieted her ludicrous desire to teach people to read in the slums.

Marco kept an eye on Miguelito in the living room on a Saturday afternoon three weeks after the baby's birth. Miguelito rustled in his bassinet, and Marco hurried to pick him up before he launched into a full-blown protest at not being held. Isa was taking a nap, and he didn't want to wake her.

"Hola, hombrecito. Did you have a nice dream?" Marco picked the tiny pink baby up like Isa had taught him, carefully supporting his head. Miguelito stared at him with wise old man eyes. "What are you thinking in that little head?" Marco rocked his body from side to side, walking the baby around the apartment.

"This is your home, little boy. You'll never have to worry about it blowing away in a storm. You'll never have to wonder where your next meal comes from or whether you can afford shoes. That's right, because your Papi will be here to make sure your life is perfect." Marco gave his son an adoring look. Miguelito gurgled and tried to put both fists in his mouth. Marco was certain the baby was thanking him. "You're welcome, little one. You are most welcome."

On the first Sunday in August, Isabela, Marco, and five-month-old Miguelito joined the Sotos for a family dinner. Once everyone was done admiring Miguelito and commenting on how big he'd gotten, the conversation quickly turned to the biggest news of the moment—the assassination attempt on Governor Winship by the Nationalists.

"They rounded up seven people involved in the shooting," Don Gabriel said after they sat down to eat, continuing the conversation they'd started in the living room. He eyed the platter of tostones Connie passed him and took three of the crispy fried plantain rounds.

"The Rio Piedras Massacre, killing the police chief, and now this," Marco said from the other end of the table. "They're savages! Believe me, I've seen their work up close."

Don Gabriel nodded. "They'll do whatever Albizu wants. The man's in jail, for God's sake, and still leading the crazy masses. It makes Puerto Ricans look like angry animals." Don Gabriel waved a tostón in the air before chomping down on it. "We're cultured, intelligent people. We'll vote for independence, not kill for it."

Isabela, who sat across from Marco, chimed in. "But, Papi, what about the Ponce Massacre last March? The Nationalists were demonstrating peacefully and the police shot at *them* for no reason. How many died? Twenty? And hundreds were injured, even women and children." Isa shook her head sadly.

"You're right, Isa." Marco nodded. "The cycle of violence on both sides needs to stop. People are tired. That's why Muñoz is gathering so much support. His vision of a peaceful social and economic revolution resonates, especially with the poor."

"He wants to turn us all into Yanquis," Don Gabriel scoffed.

"I like Don Luis Muñoz Marín," seven-year-old Mati said. "I learned about him in school."

Marco girded himself for a Don Gabriel tirade.

"¡Nena, no!" exclaimed Carmen, who'd entered the room holding a water pitcher. "Los niños hablan cuando las gallinas méan."

"Ay, Carmen! Children speak only when chickens pee. You used to say that to me." Isa laughed.

"But chickens don't pee," Mati said.

"Exactly." Don Gabriel nodded.

"Don't listen to them, Mati," Connie said. "You talk all you want."

"Not when she doesn't know what she's talking about," Don Gabriel said, giving Mati a pointed look. "Muñoz became a traitor the moment he gave up on independence."

"Muñoz makes a good argument, Don Gabriel. We don't have the resources to be independent. His plan preserves our dignity while propelling the island into modernity."

"Colonies are not modern," scoffed Don Gabriel.

"We wouldn't be a colony. We'd simply get benefits just for playing nice with the Americans," Marco sighed. He knew he'd never change Don Gabriel's mind, was sorry he'd started down the Muñoz path, and sighed with relief when Connie came to the rescue, expertly guiding the conversation to less controversial topics.

After dinner, Don Gabriel offered Marco a brandy, and they sat on the veranda while Isa's sisters took turns holding Miguelito in the living room.

"What did you end up naming your building?" Don Gabriel asked Marco, swirling his glass to warm the liquor.

"El Comienzo."

"Very nice. Commemorating the beginning of your business." Don Gabriel sipped his brandy.

Marco leaned forward, elbows resting on his knees, hands cradling his glass. "And it's fully rented, Don Gabriel. It's all happened much faster than we expected."

"Good management on your part, I'm sure. So, what's next?"

Marco marveled. Don Gabriel's compliments still took him by surprise. "We're going to the bank. We have our eye on a plot of land in Hato Rey perfect for building three homes, but we need the capital to do it," Marco said.

Don Gabriel leaned back. "I'm glad you're fired up, but don't let yourself be seduced by your initial success. Take it slow. You don't want to owe the banks too much. Many have lost it all by overextending themselves."

"But now is the time to strike. Opportunity abounds."

"That may be, but remember that things can change overnight. Look what happened when the stock market crashed."

Marco straightened and placed a hand on his father-in-law's knee. "Don't worry about me, Don Gabriel. I'm comfortable riding the momentum. Soon I'll be able to fulfill my family's every need and desire. Nothing can stop me."

Don Gabriel's tight smile did not go unnoticed.

CHAPTER 17

- Isabela -
April to August 1941

"Sing it again, Mami! Sing it again!" Miguelito, just turned three, clapped his hands next to her in anticipation as Marco drove them to El Morro, the massive Spanish fort at the entrance of Old San Juan Harbor, for kite flying and a picnic. Marco had purchased a burgundy Chrysler sedan the year prior, and Mariano had taught him and Isa how to drive it.

"Very well," Isa said. "But this time, you sing with me. ¿De acuerdo?" Her son nodded, and Isa sang slowly until Miguelito chimed in.

"Pollito, chicken,
Gallina, hen,
Lapiz, pencil y
Pluma, pen.

Ventana, window,
Puerta, door,
Maestra, teacher y
Piso, floor."

"¡Muy bien, Miguelito!" Isa clapped her hands and laughed. She always cracked up when he said "gweendoh" for "window." They had to work on that before he started nursery school in September. Nursery school! It's true what they said about time flying when you had children. *I hope this one is as much fun as Miguelito*, she thought, gently rubbing her protruding stomach. With just two months to go, the new baby would arrive in time to keep her company after Miguelito left her for his days at school.

God, but she reveled in motherhood. She hadn't expected that. Growing up, she'd thought her sisters adorable but annoying and only mildly interesting. Yet her heart was constantly bursting with love for this tiny creature who depended on her fully and loved her unconditionally. They were a team, and she strived to make their time together as memorable as possible. She took great joy in his exuberance and wanted him to relish his carefree time as a little boy instead of feeling ruled as she had growing up in Abuela's house.

Marco made enough money now for them to afford a larger apartment in a building with an elevator and someone to help with the cooking and cleaning. She'd stolen Elena from Papi's household and set her up in a small bedroom off the kitchen. With Elena's help at home, Isa continued her literacy efforts in El Fanguito two days per week until her belly grew too big for her to safely balance on the planks. She'd had a close call with her first pregnancy, had almost fallen into the putrid mud, and would not risk such a horrendous fate again.

Though a loving and supportive father, Marco was largely absent from their day-to-day lives. She missed him but was proud of his endeavors. He'd left PRRA to work full-time at Solemar and still taught one night a week. She wished he'd stop teaching altogether, but he claimed to love it too much. The man never wanted to give anything up. Isa sometimes chuckled when she thought how worried she'd been that Marco might have affairs like Papi. Ha! When would he find the time?

It was a breezy day, perfect for kite flying, but first, they let Miguelito explore the fort to his heart's delight, pretended to die when he shot them with a cannon, and held him up so he could look out the rounded sentry boxes that hovered over the breaking surf. Afterward, Isa spread a blanket on the portion of the great lawn closest to the fortress, away from the noisy military swimming pool near the cemetery. Elena had packed them a light meal of ham and cheese sandwiches on pan de agua, baby bananas, and dulce de coco, Miguelito's favorite sweet. She watched as Marco taught Miguelito the mechanics of flying a kite, a fancy store-bought kite, not homemade like the one Marco had flown with her when they were dating.

Two raggedy boys, around six or seven years old, approached her husband shyly from the cemetery's direction, curious to examine the brightly colored kite up close. She watched, stunned, as Marco ignored the boys, turned his back to them, and steered Miguelito away. Her son craned his neck backward, curious. Having gotten the message loud and clear, the boys retreated toward La Perla, glancing back at her husband and son every few steps with resigned expressions. Marco, unfazed, finally got the kite up and waved to her, calling, "Look, Mami! Look how high the kite is!"

She sat in shock, rooted to the ground. Disbelief and anger churned in her chest. Where was the kind man who'd given his kite to those children the first time they'd come here, the one who'd shown her how hard life was for the poor, especially in the slums? A rush of adrenaline broke through her stupor. She grabbed a sandwich and the baby bananas and sprinted after the boys.

"¡Niños, niños!" She shouted at them, hoping they'd stop before reaching the slum.

They turned around, expressions inquisitive but weary, and waited for Isa to catch up.

"My husband is teaching our son to fly the kite today, but maybe he can teach you next time. Would you like a treat instead?" She held the food out to them.

"Sí, señora. ¡Gracias!" Nodding, the boys gave her a big grin, grabbed the food, and scurried away.

As Isa returned to the blanket, she shot Marco a scathing look, which he ignored. For the past five years, her husband had worked to ensure people no longer had to live like these boys. How could he treat them with such callous disregard? And more importantly, how could he treat people like that in front of Miguelito? The boy would grow up thinking he was better than others. Was this who Marco had become while she'd been busy raising their son and trying to help the very people her husband apparently snubbed now?

She had noticed subtle changes in Marco, true, but hadn't connected them to form a clear picture. Now his collective actions began to make sense. Marco still insisted on buying only the best of everything. He'd rather have two extraordinary suits than six mediocre ones. That's why they'd waited so long to get a car. He refused to own a cheap model and saved for a Chrysler, not top of the line, but close. He seemed to think he could erase his years of poverty by surrounding himself with quality. Viandas, sadly, were still banned from their dinner table. It irked him that Papi bought Miguelito extravagant toys. He hated accepting anything from Papi but forced himself to make exceptions when his son was involved.

A year ago, he'd asked Papi to sponsor them in a quest to join the Casino de Puerto Rico, mostly—she suspected—to discomfit the society he felt had scorned him. But the truth was nobody cared that Marco had been poor, and they were gladly accepted as members. Their generation of men and women had answered a call to arms to work for a better Puerto Rico, and successes were celebrated enthusiastically, regardless of where anyone came from or who "their people" were. Puerto Rico was changing, and they were part of the movement toward modernity. They were supposed to lift the poor up, not lift themselves above the poor.

She understood Marco's desire to put the past behind him, but he'd gone too far and was trying to erase it completely, denying his roots. This was not the man she fell in love with. She needed *that* man, the original Marco. Marco had never even set foot in the slums he was helping to empty and scoffed at any efforts to improve conditions there.

"If you help them, they won't leave," he'd say. "They'll stay in the slums rent-free instead of moving to the housing projects."

Isa knew better. She was proud of the part she played, albeit small, in improving her island. Her work in El Fanguito grounded her, satisfied her thirst to make a difference. Her first pupil, Doña Gloria, was now a supervisor in her children's school cafeteria, and the family had moved into a small house in Barrio Obrero. It pained her to be unable to share these successes with Marco, but he wouldn't understand. He wanted to lift his people up without getting his hands dirty.

Finished with the kite flying, Marco and Miguelito returned to her side, interrupting her irate musings.

"Did you see us, Mami? Did you see how high the kite went?"

"I sure did! I told those boys that you're getting to be an expert and that you and Papi will teach them how to fly it next time. Won't that be fun?" She shot Marco another dirty look.

Marco rolled his eyes at her but didn't respond.

"Sí, Mami. I'll teach my baby brother, too!"

"Or sister..." Isa smiled at her son.

Isa would bring Marco down a few notches whenever necessary; she wouldn't let him forget where he'd come from. If not for Marco, then for her children. He'd made noises about stopping at two, a number the government was promoting for the "modern Puerto Rican family." But she wanted to keep her options open and had no desire to undergo la operacíon that some in her class opted for, and many of the poor were tricked into. She felt the baby kick and smiled.

On a warm night in mid-June, a wrenching pain jerked her out of a sweet dream where she'd been swinging in a hammock and tickling Miguelito.

She gasped as her body reflexively bent into a fetal position. Her lower back muscles contracted and twisted while a spiking pain spread outward from the center of her spine to the front of her belly, where it finally abated. Isa tried to remain calm as the contraction ebbed and wondered how long she'd been in labor while asleep. This was no beginning contraction; she knew that much from giving birth to Miguelito.

"Marco," she called out. He snored a symphony beside her.

She was perspiring, her body so fiery her skin felt oppressive. Slowly and with great effort, she turned toward Marco.

"Marco." He didn't stir. Intent on waking him before the next stab of pain arrived, she shook him while trying to keep her distance from his body heat.

"Marco! Marco!" *Wake up, you miserable man!* "Marco!"

Blast this damn man who could sleep like the dead. She shook him again. Her bottom half was damp, so she assumed her water had broken. She glanced down and, alarmed, shook Marco harder.

Marco mumbled. His eyes reluctantly fluttered open. And then he appeared to become instantly awake. "Isa! What is it, my love? Is it time?"

"Yes," she gasped. "The contractions are strong, and I think I'm bleeding, too."

"Oh, my God!" Marco jumped out of bed and threw on some clothes while another contraction hit Isa. She doubled over as the wave of pain spread from back to front, causing every muscle in its path to clench in agony. She managed to get herself upright, and Marco helped her into her robe. His face was ashen and serious; it frightened her. How bad was the bleeding? Shaking, she kept her tears at bay.

Marco grabbed her pre-packed suitcase and walked Isa to the elevator and then the car. At her urging, he ran back up to let Elena know they were leaving and to call Dr. Gil so he'd meet them at the hospital. She tried not to think about the red stain spreading on her nightgown.

Auxilio Mutuo was only a ten-minute ride away, but it felt like ten hours to Isa, who suffered three more incapacitating contractions during the ride. *Sweet baby, don't be so impatient to come into the world. Dear God, please let this baby be safe*, she silently prayed while maintaining a two-handed, white-knuckled grip on the lip of the car's dashboard.

When they arrived at the hospital's emergency entrance, Isa was quickly wheeled into a delivery room, and Marco was shown to a sitting area. Two nurses in nun habits attended to her while they waited for Dr. Gil to arrive. The contractions continued, and she knew the urge to push was coming. But when Dr. Gil entered the room a few minutes later and examined Isa, his worried expression terrified her. Something was seriously wrong. Oh, God, but the pain! She could barely breathe now through the contractions.

"Isa," Dr. Gil's voice broke through her fog of agony. "The baby is breech, and you're hemorrhaging. I need to operate. We're giving you anesthesia. Do you understand?"

Thoroughly disoriented now by agony, Isa nodded, or at least thought she did before her pain miraculously floated away, and she welcomed the absolute darkness that enveloped her.

When Isa regained consciousness, a nurse sat next to her, stroking her hair. Dread coursing through her veins, she grabbed the nurse's hand, but before she could articulate her fear, the nun smiled and said, "You have a beautiful baby boy."

"Thank God, Sister," Isa said. She relaxed her grip and closed her eyes again.

Later, as she tenderly felt her bandaged abdomen, jiggly like a rubber balloon half-filled with water, Dr. Gil entered her hospital room, and she learned how close she'd come to dying.

"After I delivered the baby, you were still hemorrhaging, and we couldn't stop the bleeding," he told Isa. She sat propped up by pillows, Marco at her side. Dr. Gil exchanged a look with Marco. "I'm sorry, but I had to remove your uterus. It was either the uterus or you, and I couldn't leave that beautiful boy without a mother, now could I?" Dr. Gil smiled paternally.

Isa was confused. She looked at Marco, whose face she couldn't read, and then back at Dr. Gil.

"The baby is okay?" she asked, her brain not making sense of the other news.

"The baby is perfect," Dr. Gil said. "But I'm afraid this one's your last."

Isa looked back at Marco again, who squeezed her hand with a sad smile. No, this couldn't be. She'd wanted at least one more child, ideally a daughter. The mother-son bond was special, but she imagined mothers and daughters had transcending relationships. Now she'd never know. She closed her eyes and willed herself to sleep the devastating news away.

Isa quietly grieved at the prospect of not having any more children. While Marco's lovemaking had not improved one iota since their honeymoon—he took longer now, but still had no idea how to please her—at least each time she submitted to her wifely duty, she'd had a chance at pregnancy. Now he would arouse her but leave her both unfulfilled and childless.

Or maybe he wouldn't find her changed body attractive any longer. Her abdomen had been sliced up like a lechon's, the scar an angry red welt. Isa thought about the government's campaign to get women sterilized after just two children. Was this how they felt after la operación? What a misguided path to population control.

Keenly aware she'd never experience milestone baby moments again, she cherished every second with Luis Gabriel, nicknamed Luisito. Twice, when she'd forgotten to put a cloth over his tiny penis while she changed his diaper, and he'd peed straight up into her face, she'd laughed so hard her stomach hurt. Yet it hadn't been remotely funny when Miguelito had done it.

Miguelito, after a brief period of adjustment to no longer being the sole prince of the castle, became fascinated with the baby. He loved caressing Luisito's head, which, unlike his own, had come out bald and remained that way, while Isa cautioned him to "be gentle."

He was protective of his baby brother and proud to be the "big boy" in the family. And so Luisito joined the Miguelito-Mami team almost seamlessly, and the three of them carried on with the business of being a family while Marco continued to focus on his work.

One August afternoon, while Isa played with Miguelito and the baby napped, the downstairs buzzer rang.

"Titi Julia!" shouted Miguelito upon seeing Elena leading Julia into the apartment. He adored his aunt and swiftly rendered her immobile by wrapping his arms around her legs in a hearty embrace. After finishing her course of study at La Upi, Julia had adamantly refused to return to Yabucoa, "that backwater town." Much like her brother, she'd reinvented herself into an urban sophisticate and taught history at San Juan's most prestigious public high school, La Central. The only thing she hadn't left behind was her antipathy toward Isa, although she'd kept it somewhat in check since her nephews were born.

Julia bent over to tickle Miguelito so he'd release his grip on her. "Who's the best sobrino in the world?" she asked him, laughing.

"Me!" he replied and dissolved into a puddle of giggles while she continued to tickle him mercilessly.

"Stop it, you two. You'll wake the baby," Isa said. "Hola, Julia." She kissed her sister-in-law on the cheek and wondered what she wanted. Isa wasn't in the mood for Julia's jabs today.

"Hola, Isa. Listen, I need your help." Julia sounded rushed.

Isa was intrigued. It was a rarity for Julia to admit to needing help, much less from her. She probably wanted Isa to help convince Marco that Julia should have her own apartment instead of living in that boarding house with four other teachers. Isa knew how much Julia hated the "chicken coop," as she called it.

"I'm happy to help if I can," Isa said.

"I need to borrow your navy blue silk dress," Julia said.

"Well, that's easy enough." Isa headed toward her bedroom. "What's the occasion?"

"I think Eduardo's going to propose tonight," Julia half squealed, half whispered, her eyes glittery. Marco had played matchmaker between Eduardo, one of his fast-rising star employees, and his sister over a year ago, and a romance had blossomed.

"Really?" Isa said, grabbing Julia's forearm excitedly. Isa's delight at an impending proposal trumped her lack of affection toward Julia. "Tell me everything! Why do you think that?" Isa opened her closet door and rifled through her dresses.

"Well, he's been giving me not-so-subtle hints that it's a special night, a night I will never forget, and that I should wear something nice. It's got to be a proposal, right?" Julia sat down on the bed, twisting her hands together.

"It's been a year, so it's possible." Isa mused. "I mean, Marco proposed to me after just a few months, but that's Marco. Some men take longer than others."

"The other day, Eduardo pointed to a woman's ring and asked what I thought."

"Why didn't you mention that first? Oh, my God! He's proposing!" Isa turned to hug Julia, and the two of them jumped up and down, screeching like schoolgirls. Isa was genuinely excited. Julia had softened somewhat after meeting Eduardo, and maybe marriage and motherhood would sweeten her further. They'd have new things to bond over. Would she and Julia finally become friends? The idea pleased Isa tremendously. She'd always wanted a sister who was close to her own age.

"What time is he picking you up? Come over here. Let me do your hair!" Isa pulled Julia over to the vanity and sat her down. Julia nodded and examined herself in the mirror.

"Mami, Titi Julia, why are you shouting? What is 'prop-poniendo'?" asked Miguelito, who'd followed them into the bedroom.

"'Proponer matrimonio' is something you'll do one day when you want to get married to the woman you love," Isa said.

"But I'm marrying you, Mami. I do prop-poniendo." Miguelito's expression turned from serious to confused when the two women erupted in belly laughs.

As Isa brushed out Julia's hair, she remembered those heady days after Marco proposed. Julia's future was ripe with possibility, an exciting blank slate. Isa envied her because disappointment was yet to come. She also pitied her because Isa knew disappointment was inevitable.

CHAPTER 18

- Marco -
September to December 1941

Marco called out a goodbye to Sammy as he strode out of Banco Popular, looking dapper in his lightweight wool gabardine suit perfectly tailored to fit his tall frame, which had elegantly filled out since his gangly younger days. He was especially particular about the length of his jacket sleeves, which had to hit precisely at his wristbone to allow for a half-inch slice of shirt cuff to show.

Marco and Sammy's meeting with the bank had gone well. Solemar had grown exponentially, employed ten people plus a cadre of laborers, and had earned a reputation for quality, cost-effective construction. They had purchased five apartment buildings and now managed fifty rental units. Their next project, and the reason he'd finally left PRRA, was an urbanización—a four-block housing development in Hato Rey encompassing forty single-family homes. They were calling it Hato Rey Gardens.

Leaving PRRA had been bittersweet, he reminisced, as he got into his Chrysler and headed home. The Agency had created public housing and parks; built a cement factory, the first heavy industry on the island; established island-wide health clinics and parasite eradication programs; and constructed seven hydroelectric plants as part of a rural electrification program. He'd played a key role in this wave of progress, and though he'd moved to the private sector, his work still aimed to modernize Puerto Rico.

If only their own people would get out of the way of progress. He thought back to his argument with Isa last April after they'd taken Miguelito kite flying.

"Marco, you were so rude to those boys," Isa had admonished him that evening as they were getting ready for bed. "They're only children."

"I have no patience for the slum-dwellers, Isa. Half of them refuse to move out. Why would you willingly live under those circumstances?" Marco fluffed his pillow before getting into bed.

Isa addressed him from her vanity table, where she was brushing her hair. "Don't punish the children for their parents' actions. Besides, you know public housing costs money. Half the population is unemployed. How can they pay rent on an apartment?"

"They're unemployed because they're not lifting themselves up and using their smarts to get ahead. Look at me! If I can do it, anyone can!" Marco sat against the headboard, hands behind his head.

"You really are something else," Isa gave him a withering look. "If that were true, why are we called 'The Poorhouse of the Caribbean'? Even those who have work earn a little over a third of what workers make on the mainland. Our leaders should be writhing with embarrassment and looking for ways to fix the situation."

They'd gone around and around the argument that night and several times since. His work at PRRA had focused on improving life for the poor; he'd done his part to lift those left behind. But lately, he'd noticed a decrease in initiative among the needy. Many would rather live in the slums for free and get government handouts than help themselves. Isa didn't see that side of things. These people could get ahead! Wasn't he the perfect example?

Marco had toiled long hours these past five years. Spending such little time with Miguelito and now Luisito pained him, but they were in good hands with Isa. As his hard work began to pay off, he'd freed Isa from the tedium of laundry and household chores so she could focus on motherhood. He'd also purchased the home in Yabucoa for his mother and sent her a generous monthly allowance, ensuring she lacked for nothing. Mamá now sewed for her own enjoyment and had made extensive layettes for each of the boys—tiny, embroidered cotton smocks that Isa cooed over. She was also sewing Julia's wedding dress out of fine silk and lace. Julia, who'd complained all her life about having to wear homemade clothes, wouldn't hear of anyone else making her gown.

As he arrived home and parked beneath the building, he mentally tallied the projected expenses for Julia's November wedding. Yes, he could afford a wedding reception for his sister at the Casino, perhaps a small but elegant breakfast.

He turned off the car and sat back, suddenly feeling the full weight of his responsibilities: Isa's happiness, his family's safety, Julia's wedding, Mamá's welfare, Solemar and all the people he and Sammy employed. He fervently hoped he could keep all the balls in the air.

"Papi, I hate these pants. They're so scratchy," whined Miguelito, tugging fruitlessly at the black raw silk britches Julia had insisted he wear as her wedding page. They'd just arrived at the Casino after the morning wedding Mass. "Why is Titi Julia making me wear this?" This time, Miguelito pulled at the ruffles trailing down the front of his white silk shirt.

"I don't know, hijo. Don't tell anyone, but all brides are a little crazy." Marco whispered the last part.

Miguelito giggled. "Titi Julia, la loca."

"¡Shhhhh, nene! You'll get us both in trouble." Marco glanced around the Casino's foyer to make sure no one had heard. "Here comes Mami. Don't let her see you fussing. Just make it through breakfast, and then you can take it all off." Marco held his hand out, and Miguelito took it before dragging his feet up the wide entrance steps.

"Mami, we're going in," Marco called over his shoulder to his wife, who was carrying Luisito.

"Muy bien, amores." Isa waved them on and followed.

Although Marco had entered the Casino a slew of times, he was still impressed by its grandeur. He'd never been invited to grace its halls during his courtship with Isa. Don Gabriel hadn't deemed him worthy. Now he was a bona fide member of the venerable social institution, and today he was hosting his sister's wedding celebration here. His chest swelled. He belonged here now.

As Marco entered the salon where the breakfast would take place, he heard Isa gasp behind him. It did look impressive. Two long parallel tables, each set for thirty guests, took up most of the room. White roses, gardenias, camellias, and plumeria spilled from low crystal vases on the tables and scented the air with their mingled perfumes. Small packets of pale pink Jordan almonds wrapped in tulle and clinched with white ribbon marked each place setting. Cascading flower bouquets tied to white tulle swags adorned the large windows, which let in bright morning sunbeams to augment the gleam of the chandeliers, mirrors, fine china and silverware. A quartet dressed in white tuxedo jackets softly played guitars and scratched a güiro in the corner.

"Ay, Marco," Isa said with wonder. "Julia's going to love this! This room is fit for a princess."

"Gracias, mi amor," Marco said. He'd insisted on handling every facet of the wedding breakfast and refused to divulge any details. It was his gift to Julia, and he wanted it to be just right. He'd driven his secretary crazy because, in reality, Marco had the ideas, but she'd done all the work.

"Julia deserves a special day." Marco thought back on his own wedding festivities, so simple and small, at Don Gabriel's house. "I only wish I could have given you the same." He sighed and looked around the room ruefully.

"Stop that right now, Marco. Our wedding day was perfect, and this wedding day is perfect for Julia." Isa shifted the baby so she could take Marco's arm with her left hand. "Let's sit. The newlyweds will make their grand entrance soon." Marco felt a rush of love and gratitude and, for the thousandth time in his life, thanked God for his wife.

They found their seats near Mamá, Tío, Tía and his cousins just before the quartet welcomed the newlyweds into the room with Rafael Hernández's "Ahora Seremos Felices." Marco had selected this lovely bolero in which a groom tells his bride how happy they'll be in their new home with their soon-to-come progeny. Lord knew Julia wanted children, so the song was fitting. Marco watched as his sister took in her surroundings, and he could tell she was impressed with his efforts. Her eyes shone brighter than the room's gilt, and Marco knew every penny he'd spent on the event had been worth it.

When the song ended and Julia and Eduardo were seated, Marco signaled the waiters to fill everyone's champagne coupes and rose, holding his glass aloft.

"Welcome, family and friends, to Julia and Eduardo's wedding celebration. Normally, the bride's father gives a toast, but since Papá is looking down on us from heaven with great love and pride, this honor falls to me today." Marco shifted his attention to the newlyweds. "Beloved sister, from the moment I met Eduardo, I knew he'd be a good match for you. Not that I was constantly preoccupied with making sure you didn't end up jamona, but the thought of my sister as an old maid did somewhat motivate me to help you find love." Marco paused as the guests laughed. "And find it you did. You are radiant, my dear sister, and I see pure love in Eduardo's eyes. Yet this is only the beginning. I can tell you from experience that marriage only gets better as love matures and grows. May your love bring you lasting joy, and may God bestow many blessings on you both. ¡Salud!" Marco raised his glass high.

"¡Salud!" echoed the guests. Marco took a sip of his champagne and sat.

"Well done, hijo," Mamá said, seated to his right in a stunning silk lilac suit. "God willing, they'll be as happy as you and Isa."

"He's a good man with excellent prospects. I rely on him for all legal advice related to Solemar," Marco said. "He makes her happy, too. Maybe marriage will soften her toward Isa. They'll have more in common now."

Mamá looked at Marco intently and lowered her voice. "You know she never really recovered from your father's death. Some people, like you, take tragedy and use it as inspiration for moving forward, while others let it drag them down. Julia feels the world has done her a great wrong and envies those she thinks have had it easy."

"I know," Marco sighed. "Perhaps marriage will change all that."

Seated to his left, Isa had just tuned into the conversation and saltily commented, "Please, God, one can only hope!" She held up her champagne glass and, laughing, the three toasted to seal her plea.

A month later, when the Japanese attacked Pearl Harbor and the United States entered World War II, Marco was suddenly plagued with new worries. Tens of thousands of Puerto Rican men were called to serve in the National Guard or the 65th Infantry Regiment, the Borinqueneers. Two of his cousins, Tío's youngest sons, were in training and expected to be sent to protect the Panama Canal. Food, gasoline, and other goods were rationed, and San Juan's lights remained on blackout every evening.

Puerto Rico's location in the Caribbean rendered the island strategically crucial to U.S. defenses, and construction quickly began on several military bases, projects that consumed most of the cement manufactured on the island. Marco's business was forced to rely on imported materials, but with Nazi submarines targeting American ships in Caribbean waters, shipping volume had decreased significantly, with priority given to food. Construction supplies quickly became scarce, affecting the progress of several Solemar developments, most notably the Hato Rey Gardens urbanización.

On a Thursday in April, four months after Pearl Harbor, Marco visited the project's site. All the foundations had been excavated, and concrete poured into them to create a low outside wall from which tall steel stakes protruded in measured intervals, standing ready to help support the coming structure. He parked on the dirt road by one of the cement mixers and waved to his foreman, Ernesto.

"Ernesto, hombre. ¿Cómo van las cosas?" Marco asked, shaking the man's hand.

"Well, Señor Rios, with the cement shortage, progress is slow. The men are worried about their jobs." The foreman took a handkerchief out of his back pocket and wiped the sweat off his face, grimacing.

"I know, I know. I've been trying to use all my connections to get us a larger share, but construction on the military bases has priority." Marco looked around with a furrowed brow. Forty homes required a lot of cement.

"Ay, I don't know," Ernesto said, "But I think we could stretch the cement, make it go a little farther."

"How? Did you suddenly acquire Jesus-like powers? Going to multiply the loaves and fishes?" Marco chuckled.

"Bueno, no. But we could thin it out slightly and still ensure it holds strong," Ernesto said shrewdly. "I could run some tests to develop the optimum formula, make sure it's safe." He shrugged.

Marco was momentarily tempted by the idea. Could there be a way to safely stretch their cement supply? Of course not, because everyone would already be doing it. Marco's face tensed, his jaw jutted out, and the vein in his right temple started to pulse visibly.

"Ernesto, I think the optimum formula has already been developed. It's what's specified. Don't you remember San Felipe?" Marco's voice shook. "The homes we build must protect the families who live in them. I'd rather build ten safe homes than fifteen maybe-safe ones with weak concrete. Fine, upstanding people will make their homes here. We can't take chances with their lives."

"I know. I know, jefe. I wasn't suggesting we cut corners to the point of building dangerous structures. Just that we explore a way to make our resources stretch a bit more."

"It's not worth it," Marco said firmly. "My conscience wouldn't let me live with the decision." Both stood in silence for a few minutes, hands on hips, faces serious and eyes staring into the distance, considering their options.

Marco finally broke the silence. "What sort of company would we be, Ernesto? In the end, all we really have is our reputation."

"True. True. But what about the men?" Ernesto gestured toward the workers laboring under the punishing sun. "What should I tell them? They're worried they're going to lose their livelihoods. Half the island is already jobless."

"Tell them their jobs are safe. Solemar takes care of its own."

Amazing, thought Marco, how a war being fought an ocean away could impact his business so directly. He said a little prayer for his two Borinqueneer cousins as he got into his car and drove to the office to continue the workday.

CHAPTER 19

- Isabela -
May 1945

Isabela quickly settled the boys in the back of her teal Plymouth, jumped in the driver's seat, and headed to her father's house. It was only a fifteen-minute ride, but she was running late for her volunteer shift at the USO Club, and her hands were sweating under her beige leather driving gloves. She prided herself on punctuality precisely because she disliked the stressful feeling of not being on time. Leaving the boys home with Elena would have been much easier, but they'd been begging to see their aunts and grandmother.

Of course, if it were up to her husband, Isa would be the one staying home with the boys in the first place. Even though Marco was outwardly supportive of her work at the USO, even bragged about it to his friends, she knew he secretly wanted her to focus her full-time attention on their children. But after the war broke out, Isa felt a need to contribute beyond her work in El Fanguito. Puerto Ricans enthusiastically planted vegetable gardens, rolled bandages, and collected metal and rubber for recycling, but were these efforts impactful or simply a way for those not in the trenches to feel they mattered? Yet short of enlisting, which was obviously out of the question, she'd been at a loss for how to become more significantly involved in the war effort.

When the U.S. military took over the Casino de Puerto Rico to create a USO, much to Marco's and Papi's unspeakable horror, Isa saw her opportunity. How better to contribute to the war effort than by looking after the soldiers' wellbeing? Where better to do so than in her old Casino stomping grounds?

Volunteering at the USO was respectable enough to assuage Marco and even gave her a cover for her time at the slum, though Beatriz had been trying to get her to cut her hours there. Isa's friend had a first-hand appreciation for what USOs did for soldiers away from home. Bea's civil engineer husband, Emilio, was drafted and stationed in the Panama Canal. She kept insisting that she and others had El Fanguito covered and that Isa's work at the USO was of paramount importance.

Isa pulled into Papi's driveway to squeals from the back seat, "Abuelo's house! Abuelo's house!" Her boys loved coming here, where they were always the center of everyone's attention. During the next few hours, they'd be spoiled like two little sultans and wouldn't miss her for a second. She'd barely opened the car's back door when the rascals shoved past her and tumbled into the house. Isa laughed and followed, peeling off her gloves.

"Carmen, Connie! ¡Hola!" Isa entered the front hall. Her high heels clicked on the tile floor as she headed to the living room, past the stairs, and to the right.

"Abuela Connie! Abuela Connie!" The boys shouted when they spotted Connie sitting in the living room.

"Come here, mis guapos!" Connie answered. "Give Abuela Connie lots of kisses." The boys sprinted toward her, and Connie enveloped them in a hug.

When Isa leaned down to kiss Connie hello, her stepmother's eyes were swollen and weepy.

"Boys, go find Carmen," Isa said. She watched them run toward the kitchen. "Connie, what's wrong? What's happened?" Isa sat next to her stepmother and took her hand, concern forming a crevice between her eyebrows.

Connie sighed and cast her eyes upward. "It's nothing. Just, you know, your father can be difficult sometimes."

"Not so difficult that you should be crying. What did he do?" Isa's lips tightened into a severe line.

"He's like most Puerto Rican men, who think they're all Don Juans."

"What do you mean?" Isa hesitated to agree without knowing exactly what Connie was referring to. Did her stepmother know Papi was a philanderer?

"He's gotten particularly brazen with his latest puta."

Isa recoiled; she was shocked, but not at Connie's coarse language. "You know he cheats on you?" Isa's eyes were ready to pop out of her head.

"*You* know he cheats on me?" Connie seemed equally stunned.

"I guess the sinvergüenza is not very good at hiding it." Isa held Connie's hands. "I'm so sorry, Connie. I thought you were unaware and didn't want to hurt you by bringing it up."

"How could I not know when he's seen around town squiring this little putita from Cataño? He doesn't take her anywhere fancy, of course, but people still see them, and there's plenty of talk. It's humiliating." Connie's voice broke and tears formed rivulets down her cheeks.

Isa, comforter of many at the USO, didn't know what to say. She produced a handkerchief from her black patent leather purse and handed it to Connie. It was hard enough to compete with your husband's work for attention. How many nights had Isa spent watching dinner get cold? Explaining to her sons why their Papi wasn't there to kiss them goodnight? It made them all feel unimportant, dispensable. Those instances skewered her, but her heart would break if she caught Marco admiring another woman, much less squiring her. He wasn't perfect, but he was *her* husband and the father of her children. Why couldn't her shameless Papi at least be discreet? How could he allow the specter of his mistress to wound the family?

"I hate him for this," Isa said, fists clenched. "How can he hurt you this way?"

"He doesn't think it matters because he says I'm the one he loves. But if that's true, why does he need someone else? Why am I not enough?" Connie locked eyes with Isa, searching for an answer.

"Of course, you're enough. This isn't about you; it's about him and his inability to keep his pants on." Isa's hazel eyes went dark with anger. Connie and Papi had been married for thirteen years, and he'd been cheating on her for at least the last ten. Would this most recent affair be the catalyst that propelled Connie into action? Would she leave Papi? Her poor sisters. Oh, what a mess!

"Men are beasts," Isa said.

"Not Marco. You have one of the good ones." Connie twisted the sodden handkerchief in her hands.

Isa scoffed. "Only because work is Marco's mistress. He has no time for love affairs. But what about the girls? Do they know?"

"I'm not sure. You figured it out, so it stands to reason your sisters will, too." Connie wrung her hands. "I worry about them, especially Rosie. Her asthma has gotten much worse. The doctor says she needs to stay as calm as possible. Attacks come easily when she gets agitated." Connie's voice broke. "He also says the longer she's exposed to pollen, the worse off she'll be. But we live on a tropical island! How is she supposed to avoid pollen? And how can she stay calm in this tense house?" Tears streamed from Connie's eyes.

"Oh, Connie." Isa's eyes also spilled tears as the two women held onto each other.

Isa remembered the time. "Connie, amor, I need to go. I'm already late as it is. But you can count on me for support. Whatever you need. You've been a mother to me, and I can't bear to see you so despondent."

"Gracias, Isa." Connie squeezed Isa's hand. "Why don't you all come for dinner on Sunday? We haven't had a full family gathering in a while. It'll be good to remind your father what he's risking."

"We'll be here." Isa kissed Connie on the cheek and hurried out the door. She wished she could stay until Connie's mood improved, but duty called. She wondered whether today would also be tearful at the USO.

On the way to Papi's house the following Sunday, Isa worried about her father's philandering and its effect on her sisters. Connie could leave the marriage if she wanted; her father had left her a healthy inheritance. Maybe he'd smelled the cheater in Papi. People said girls married their fathers, and while Marco didn't sleep with other women, he did have a mistress: work. Isa was desperate to save her sisters from the same fate. They deserved to have choices. She'd wanted a career in the theater, but her father forbade it. She'd never even thought about going to college, which she now regretted, especially since Julia received her degree and seldom missed an opening to mention this fact in conversation. She hated being one-upped by her sister-in-law.

The world was very different from when she'd been eighteen. Women had more opportunities, and she felt strongly that her sisters should have a college education and take advantage of the new avenues open to them. She'd bring the subject up at dinner. Mati was already fourteen, a promising writer, and it was never too early to start with Papi. Might as well work on him now while Connie had some leverage, and he pretended to repent for his blatant cheating.

"Mati, are you still writing stories? I haven't read one in a while," Isa addressed her sister once the family assembled at the dining table for the Sunday meal of roast pork, rice with pigeon peas, and viandas, which silly Marco never ate, not even to be polite.

"I've been working on some poems. Maybe you'll read them?" Mati asked shyly.

"Of course, I'll read them! Papi, do you know how talented your daughter is? She'll be at the top of her class at La Upi."

"La Upi?" Papi barked. "What do girls need with La Upi?" He forcefully speared a chunk of roast pork with the serving fork and transferred it to his plate, making sure to get some of the crispy skin.

"An education, Papi," Isa said, her tone acerbic.

"Why? You turned out just fine."

Before Isa could respond, Marco interjected himself into the debate. "Women are doing all sorts of jobs these days, Don Gabriel. We employ several competent ones at Solemar. Three of my students are girls with razor-sharp minds. They'll make brilliant accountants."

Isa smiled wryly. Funny how her husband supported careers for women when it benefited him.

"Excuse me, but did I ask for your opinion?" Don Gabriel addressed Marco, his face turning crimson.

"The fact that you're in denial doesn't change reality."

¡Ay, Marco! Sometimes she wished Papi still intimidated her husband.

Papi ignored him and focused on eating.

"Gabriel, it's not like before when girls only got educations if their marriage prospects were poor," Connie said. "Women study and have careers now. I see no reason why our daughters shouldn't have this opportunity." Connie's tone meant business.

"They'll never need to earn a living. I give them everything they could possibly desire, and when they marry, their husbands will do the same." Papi was dismissive.

"Oh, really?" Connie said archly. "What if they don't marry? Or their husbands die young? How will they make a living then? What if they just want to use their brains for something more than rationalizing their husbands' wanton behavior?"

Papi glared at Connie, mouth open yet speechless, and Connie reciprocated with a fierce stare. Isa couldn't believe Connie had addressed him like that in front of the girls. Things must be worse than she'd realized.

"I want to go to La Upi and learn to be a writer," Mati said, her tone plaintive. "I don't want to be poor if my husband dies."

This shook Papi out of his catatonic state. He turned to Mati. "You think you're going to make money *writing*? You're worse than Isa, thinking she could be an actress."

Isa gasped and felt the blood rush to her head. "Papi!" she shouted. "I would have made a great actress. And if Mati wants to be a writer, she should, and Rosie a lawyer or an architect if she wants. The only thing standing in their way is you!" She banged her palm on the table. Papi's antiquated thinking would not get in the way of her sisters' dreams.

"Sí, Gabriel. Our girls will be educated." Connie's glare spoke volumes. Her pronouncement was final.

Clearly struggling to hold his tongue, Papi turned to Marco and said, "And how is your business doing, the one with all the *lady* employees?" Isa was relieved at the change of subject but knew the education discussion was far from over.

Marco chuckled. "We're almost finished building Hato Rey Gardens, and we've also gotten several projects at the Isla Grande and Roosevelt Roads military bases. Thank God for the U.S. Navy!"

"Good for you," Don Gabriel said, voice dripping with sarcasm. "The Americans have brought *me* nothing but trouble. First, people couldn't afford my imports during the Depression. Then just as I was inching myself out of *that* fiasco, we get into a situation where I have no goods *to* sell. Only necessities, like food and construction materials, are getting through."

"We're perfectly capable of growing our own food," Isa said, eyebrows raised. "There's no reason to be importing it, and there's certainly no need for anyone to go hungry." The people of El Fanguito were always on her mind.

"Let me worry about things like that, Isa," said Marco, patting her hand. "You have enough on your plate with the boys."

Isa bristled. It wasn't the first time Marco had dismissed her attempts to participate in a political discussion, and it infuriated her. She was already enraged about Papi's cheating and his attitude toward educating women. Now Marco was adding fuel to her fire by treating her like a child.

"What happens to our island affects all of us, including my boys." Isa looked Marco in the eyes, like a boa constrictor eyeing its prey. "That gives me every right to an opinion." She derived some pleasure from seeing Marco's jaw clench and was glad he kept silent.

Papi looked from her to Marco and back before continuing the conversation.

"Yes, Isa, we used to grow our own food before the Americans' decision to only grow sugarcane made us completely dependent on them," Papi said. "But food's not the only cause of my problems. The war's created a black market that's undercutting the prices of whatever inventory I manage to acquire. Los Yanquis and this devil Hitler will put me in the poorhouse." Papi used his napkin to dab at the sweat beading on his forehead.

"Calm down, viejo. You're going to upset everyone," Connie said with a warning glance. "We have a wonderful home, food on the table, and everything we need. We're alright, old man."

"Easy for you to say," Gabriel said.

"Papi, are we going to be poor?" Rosie asked, voice trembling. She sounded slightly wheezy.

"See?" Connie said, eyebrows raised and lips pursed. "Rosie, take slow, deep breaths. You don't want an asthma attack."

"Of course not, Rosario," Isa said, using her sister's full name. "You know how Papi exaggerates." She rolled her eyes at her sister across the dining room table, trying to make Papi's comments into a joke. What would her sisters think if they found out Papi resorted to bootlegging to keep his family in silk and lace during Prohibition? Papi would risk everything before he'd let them go hungry. Her heart skipped a beat, realizing her husband would do the same. Like it or not, she'd married her father.

"Mami, are *we* going to be poor?" Miguelito asked, distress etched on his face. "I don't want to live in the stinky slums."

"No, mijo. Don't listen to Abuelo." Isa gave Papi an exasperated look, and he shrugged back at her.

"Hijos, you'll always have everything you need and more," Marco said, patting Isa's hand again. "Don't you ever worry about that."

Isa slid her hand from under Marco's. As if money solved all problems. It wouldn't fix Papi's cheating and its effect on the family, would it?

CHAPTER 20

- Marco -
May to October 1945

Isa was quiet on the way home. They'd loaded their sons, asleep and floppy as ragdolls, into the back seat, and Marco checked on them periodically through the rearview mirror.

"Your father was in rare form today." Marco broke the silence.

"You know you're starting to sound like him, making me out to be some helpless damsel that needs your protection." Why was she challenging him with pursed lips and wide eyes? Of course, Isa and the boys needed his protection. He was responsible for their well-being. Marco reached over, took her hand, and brought it to his lips for a kiss.

"It's only because I love you," Marco said. Isa pulled her hand away. He returned both of his to the steering wheel and changed the subject. "How silly that Miguelito's worried about being poor."

"He doesn't understand what being poor means. I'm sure I'll be answering lots of questions tomorrow."

"My inquisitive boy," Marco said with a bittersweet smile. He was counting on Isa to ease Miguelito's mind. No son of his should be troubled about money.

"You realize I need to understand the world so I can explain it to him, right?" Isa's face was a mask of annoyance. She turned her head to look out the passenger window. For the love of God, what had he done now? Was she insulted because he wanted an anxiety-free life for his family?

"Don't be mad at me." Marco pleaded, even though he hadn't done anything wrong.

She sighed before responding in a wistful tone. "I miss our talks. We used to discuss politics, art, science, and all sorts of things. But now we only talk about the children. And if I try to introduce another subject, you tell me it's not for me to worry. Well, I worry. And I want to be able to talk to you about everything."

Marco took her hand in his again. "Of course, you can talk to me about anything, my love. I'm your husband. Tell me what's on your mind right now." He hoped his earnest expression would soften her shell.

After a few minutes, she looked back at him, serious, and said, "I'm concerned about everyone in Papi's house. My father's notions of women are archaic. He's also not behaving well toward Connie, and I'm sure the girls can feel the tension. Rosie's supposed to avoid stress. It's not a good situation."

Damn Don Gabriel's philandering. Didn't he realize the pain it caused Isa and her sisters, not to mention Connie? Isa was probably worried that Marco would cheat, too. Why did the man have to be such an indiscreet pig?

"Has Connie spoken to him about the cheating?"

"I don't know, and I don't feel right asking. I mean, it's their business. Except it's affecting my sisters. Ay, why is Papi such a hypocrite? He's infuriating." Isa balled her hands into tight fists and released a growl of frustration. At that moment, Marco detested Don Gabriel for causing his wife such despair.

"Well, you heard him tonight, and he's alluded to it before—his business is not what it used to be," Marco said. "I think he's trying to recapture the good old days, and the womanizing is a way to feel youthful and in control."

Isa didn't respond and continued to stare out the window.

Marco had a strong urge to protect her, to take her anger away. "You know I'd never cheat on you, right, my love? You never have to worry about that with me."

He knew because he'd declined many advances over the years. A successful man like himself drew loose women like hibiscus flowers attract bees. They didn't care if he was married. They only wanted a life of ease. Sammy had a woman on the side, most men of wealth did, but he had no desire to join their ranks. He had Isa. What more could he possibly need? He reached out for her hand and held it.

She slid closer to him in the car seat. "Sí, gracias a Dios. I don't know what I did to deserve you." Her eyes softened as she kissed his cheek. "You're one in a million."

"Thank you, my love." Marco smiled. He was glad Isa realized his life was dedicated to bringing her happiness.

They drove in silence for a few minutes until Isa asked, "You think Papi's really going broke?" Confusion wrinkled her brow.

How could this concept be surprising to her? "Surely you've entertained the idea before?"

"No... no... I really haven't." Isa shook her head, apparently starting to seriously consider the possibility.

"He should have diversified beyond luxury goods during the Depression when people couldn't afford them in the first place. I'll never understand how he survived those years. He must have had massive stores of resources."

Isa grinned mischievously. Marco was perplexed at his wife's reaction, and his confused expression made her burst into abandoned laughter. The woman could not stop, and soon tears of mirth streamed down her face. She was doubled over, her body shaking but silent. Marco grinned at Isa's debilitated state. Seeing her lose control was amusing, and he eagerly anticipated getting in on the joke.

When Isa wound down and could breathe, he asked her, "What in the world? Tell me!"

"Oh, my God! I can't believe I never told you." Isa started chuckling again.

"What? What?" Marco was getting impatient.

Isa grabbed Marco's right arm, which held on to the steering wheel, and whispered, "Papi was a bootlegger!" Laughter took hold of her again.

He couldn't have been more surprised if a stranger had walked up to him on the sidewalk and punched him in the face. The high and mighty Don Gabriel had been a goddamned bootlegger? He'd broken the law, put his family in danger, and then had the cojones to tell Marco he wasn't good enough for his daughter? What a piece of shit hypocrite.

"Can you believe it?" Isa said, holding onto her stomach.

Marco could only shake his head. He was scandalized, at a loss for words. Isa was doubled over again, crying with hilarity. He looked down at his wife, and a tickle of amusement began to rise from his stomach and up through his chest until it exploded out of his mouth in a roar of laughter. He started laughing so hard he could barely keep his eyes open and had to pull over on the side of the road. It was a miracle they didn't wake up the boys.

"Ay Dios mío," Marco tried to speak between bouts of cackles. His stomach muscles contracted painfully.

"I know! I know!" They fell onto each other, hooting. When they started to run out of steam, they wiped their eyes and took deep breaths, trying to recover their composure.

"¡Ay! My head hurts," gasped Marco, massaging his temple. "Why didn't you ever tell me?"

"At first, I was embarrassed, and Papi was making it so hard for you to like him. Then—I don't know—I guess I put it out of my mind. There was never any reason to bring it up."

"Jesus. He is some character." Marco shook his head.

"He's crazy! If bootlegging was still an option, he'd be doing it."

"Maybe that's why he's in trouble. No more bootlegging money." Marco steered the car onto the road and resumed the drive home. "But there are other things he could do. I don't understand why he's not taking advantage of the business opportunities the war offers. Maybe the old man's lost his edge."

"He's only fifty-five, querido. Hardly ready for the old age home."

"Ha! Can you imagine him retired?"

"I can imagine him complaining about retirement."

"Forget it. The man will work until his dying day."

"That better not be the case with you," Isa warned.

"Of course not! I look forward to rocking my days away with you on a porch." *A harmless white lie*, Marco mused. *Because what's a man without his work?*

The war officially ended the following September, and San Juan prepared to welcome home 65,000 returning troops eager to take advantage of their GI benefits. The need for housing was about to explode, and Marco and Sammy were poised to capitalize on the moment. Yet the number of balls they had up in the air was starting to keep him up at night. If one fell, would the others follow?

In the early days of the war, Marco had been afraid they'd go bankrupt. Thankfully, Puerto Rico's location was critical to defending the Caribbean, and the U.S. military had moved quickly to establish a strong presence on the island. Solemar had secured several contracts as construction began on four Navy bases. That kept their staff busy until they could get back to investment building. Now homes in Solemar's Hato Rey Gardens were selling quickly, solidifying the company's reputation for quality and dependability.

On this fine October day, Marco, eager to get to the office to discuss Solemar's next ventures with Sammy, drove to Old San Juan in record time. He parked on Calle San José and walked around the corner to 151 Calle Tetuán, a Spanish colonial building where Solemar had its offices on the second floor. There was that stinking beggar again. Why he chose this corner was beyond Marco's comprehension. It didn't get much pedestrian traffic. He took in the old man's torn black pants, one leg pinned up to fit his severed appendage, the filthy grey shirt that had once been white, the hat fashioned out of a wrinkled brown paper bag and looked away in disgust. He dismissed a slight pang of guilt, thinking the man was likely a Great War veteran. But God helps those who help themselves.

He entered the building through the tall wooden doors and quickly climbed the stairs to the second floor. The air smelled of fresh paint and old wood.

"Marta," he called out to his secretary. "That beggar is at it again. Call the police and have him moved. He's not good for our image."

"Sí, Señor Rios."

Marco headed behind his long wooden desk, dropped his cognac leather briefcase on the floor and swung open the tall, dark green wooden shutters that led onto a narrow wrought-iron balcony. He took in San Juan Harbor and the cobblestoned streets leading down to it and thanked God for the ocean breeze. He rarely had to use the oscillating metal fan he kept on his desk; several paperweights were usually on duty, protecting his work from the occasional gusts of wind. He picked up the fountain pen he'd left on the brown leather desk blotter last night—the Montblanc Isa had given him at graduation—blew a quick kiss at the framed photos of his wife and sons, and headed out to Sammy's office and its familiar smell of cherry tobacco.

Marco had never succumbed to the seductions of smoking. He'd had no money for such frivolities while young, and now that he could afford the finest cigars, he lacked the appetite for them. But he did like the fruity, smoky smell of Sammy's office. He sat down on Sammy's sturdy wooden visitor's chair, unlike the cushioned one Marco preferred to offer those who visited his office.

Sandra, his partner's secretary, brought them coffee pocillos, and they got down to business.

Sammy rolled open a blueprint that took up the entire surface of his desk. Both men stood up and leaned over it for a better view. "Bueno, here's the revised layout for the GI urbanización. By removing verandas from the design, we fit ten more houses on this stretch of land," Sammy pointed to a section on the top right. "I just wish we weren't building rows and rows of identical bunkers. And those metal jalousie windows are awful. They hardly let any light in."

Marco secretly agreed with Sammy. The Art Deco Falansterio

and stylish little Roosevelt homes he'd worked on while at PRRA had more panache than these houses could ever hope for. But this was a moment for maximizing profits, not creating beauty.

"They're patterned after the soldier housing on the military bases," Marco said. "We're not going to win any architectural awards, but we'll be able to build them quickly. They're practical and will meet a great need."

"Agreed. I think the plan is in excellent shape, good enough to take to the bank," Sammy said.

Marco sighed. "Yes, but I wish we could finance it ourselves. It's a lot of money we're asking for." Marco glanced at the wooden shelf unit across from Sammy's desk with its collection of accounting and business tomes, took in the manual adding machine and its almost-empty roll of paper, and knew Sammy had crunched the numbers repeatedly. As had Marco.

"Our capital is tied up in other projects," Sammy said. "But these houses are a sure thing, and the bank will recognize that."

"Yes. Let's do it." Marco made toward the door, ready to head back to his office.

"One more thing," Sammy said, raising an index finger. "Some of the apartment buildings we put on the back burner during the war, particularly El Comienzo, need work."

"What are we talking about?"

"Paint, new awnings..."

"That's all going to add up to an expense we can't afford right now. Can it go a bit longer?"

Sammy placed his elbows on the desk, tented his fingers, and considered Marco's question. "I don't know."

"It just feels like a low priority. Those aren't highly sophisticated people there, paying big rents. A few peeling walls won't matter." Like a butterfly, remorse briefly landed on his chest before fluttering away. Solemar's apartments were infinitely better than many of the alternatives.

Sammy looked at Marco, surprised. "What about offering the

middle class decent housing options? That's why we founded this company."

"We *are* offering options. But now the profit is in houses. Let's get this done, and then we'll spruce up the apartment buildings."

"Very well." Sammy wrinkled his nose. "We'll put apartment building maintenance on hold, but it better not bite us in the ass."

"Don't worry so much, hermano!" Marco said more gaily than he felt as he left Sammy's office. *The buildings are fine. It's not like I'm resorting to crime, like Don Gabriel.*

Back in his own fiefdom, he took inventory of the furnishings and décor. These offices were the ones looking tired. They'd need to upgrade to quarters befitting Solemar's progressive approach to land development and construction. Perhaps an office on Ponce de León Avenue in the tony Santurce area of San Juan. It would complement the house he'd started to envision, a permanent home for his family, something modern, with features never before seen in any of the island's houses. He'd read about architect Frank Lloyd Wright's masterpiece, Fallingwater, a house designed to look like a waterfall, and admired the idea of blurring the line between the indoors and the natural landscape.

He had his sights set on embedding a massive fish tank into one of the living room walls and was thinking of including an indoor rock pond with a swan couple—he'd read they mated for life, and what a metaphor for his union with Isa. Was that feasible, or would it be a mess? He needed to research that idea further. Isa would not take kindly to a living room full of swan feces. Marco chuckled to himself. His wife was flexible and shared his artistic sensibility, but she had limits.

If only Papá could have lived to see his success. The thought gave him pause. Papá would have been horrified to learn Marco was daydreaming about luxurious offices and homes when some of his tenants lived in dilapidated apartments. But the wise Roman playwright Plautus had been right: you must spend money to make money. Solemar's offices and his and Sammy's homes reflected the company's success and should be extravagant enough to attract the most profitable business deals. They would soon be in the black, and then, he promised himself, they'd invest lavishly in renovating the apartment buildings.

CHAPTER 21

- Isabela -
September to October 1946

After the war officially ended on May 7, 1945, the celebration continued for months as American soldiers mobilized to return to the mainland and Puerto Rican families prepared to welcome their Borinqueneers back to the island. The USO had been festive, although thoughts for the men who wouldn't come home always lay beneath the surface. Isa felt for their poor mothers and thanked God her sons had been too young for the draft. Meanwhile, Marco couldn't wait to sell new houses to the returning vets. His excitement was endearing, even if the home designs were not. And he'd been pleased Truman had finally appointed the first Puerto Rican governor, Piñero, a Muñoz ally. Isa liked to see Marco happy.

During the war, Isa had become adept at juggling her teaching, USO, and mothering duties. But with no USO and both boys in school now, she had too much time on her hands. She was proud of everything she'd accomplished in El Fanguito, but since the war ended, formally trained social workers, including Beatriz, had made great strides helping residents access jobs, education, medical care, and government nutrition programs. Bea had been one of the first to graduate from La Upi's Graduate School of Social Work, and with Emilio home from Panama, she was now pregnant with her first child. Isa had invited her friend to a celebratory lunch at the Condado Vanderbilt Hotel.

"Ay, Isa, I'm just doing my job," Bea said, blushing when Isa toasted her with a glass of iced tea. "I'm no one to admire or envy."

"You are the modern woman I've always longed to be. If only I'd set aside my silly aspirations to be an actress and gone to college," Isa said with a faraway look. "Ha! Who am I kidding? Papi wouldn't have approved of that either."

"What's stopping you now?" Bea sat back in her chair and crossed her arms.

"Are you seriously asking me that?" Isa counted on her fingers. "I'm too old. I have two children. My husband wants me at home. Marco doesn't even know I've been involved in El Fanguito. Nine years I've been lying to the man!"

"I don't understand that, Isa. Emilio and I tell each other everything. How can you have a marriage with secrets?"

"One secret." Isa held her index finger up and raised her eyebrows. One secret that Bea knew about, anyway.

"It's a doozy," Bea said. "I bet if you were honest with him, explained how fulfilling your work in El Fanguito was, he'd understand."

Isa shook her head with a sad smile, certain that would not be the case.

"Well, what about college, then?" Bea asked. "Marco knows the importance of education. He teaches at La Upi, for crying out loud."

"I'm thirty-two years old. That ship has sailed, Bea." Isa smiled at the approaching waiter and asked with a mischievous look, "Tell us, what do you have for decadent desserts?"

After lunch with Bea, faced with another afternoon of nothing important to do, Isa decided to stop by Papi's and return a hat she'd borrowed from Connie. She arrived around two and let herself in, but Papi's house was quiet. Just her luck that nobody was home. *Oh, well.* She set the hat on the foyer table and turned to go but was startled to hear Connie's shouting voice coming from the living room.

"I can smell her on you. I always can." Connie's every word dripped venom.

Oh my God! Was her stepmother finally standing up to Papi? Isa slid along the wall like a lizard, seeking the best vantage point to eavesdrop. Her heartbeat thundered inside her head. She wished she could see Connie's expression. And Papi's.

"You smell nothing, querida," Papi said, a bit too cavalierly to Isa's ears. "I would never do anything to hurt you."

Isa smirked. *Too late for that, Papi.*

"Every time you do this, a piece of me dies. I need to salvage what's left of my spirit." Connie's voice was softer now.

"Don't say that, mi amor." Isa imagined Papi's pleading eyes.

"No, Gabriel. I've had enough. This marriage is over."

Isa covered her gaping mouth with her hand.

Papi paused before answering. "Sure, okay. I'll stay in the guest room until you come to your senses."

"I *have* come to my senses. I'm moving the girls to New York," Connie said, rushing her words as if afraid she'd lose her nerve.

Papi must be fuming.

Gabriel snorted. "There's no money for that."

"I don't need your money. My father left me more than enough." Connie's tone turned firm and confident.

"But querida, it will break their hearts to go." Papi started to sound genuinely distraught.

"They'll be fine, especially Rosie. She'll have access to the latest asthma treatments."

"But when will I see them?" Papi's tone was plaintive.

Oh, no. The reality of the situation dawned on Isa. When would *she* see Connie and her sisters? Her shoulders slumped.

"Whenever you want. Flights go both ways."

"Bah. I've had enough of this. I'm going to take a nap." Papi tried to feign denial, but the undercurrent of defeat in his voice saddened Isa. Yet she lauded Connie's brave and bold decision. She wanted to step out of the shadows and hug them both but knew better. Papi would be mortified. Instead, she silently slithered into the kitchen and out the back door.

Isa returned home, anxious to discuss the conversation she'd heard with Marco. She fed the boys, put them to bed, and kept a plate of pork chops warm for her husband. She ran different scenarios through her head: Connie leaves Papi and takes the girls, Connie just leaves, Connie and her sisters move in with Isa's family, and on and on. What would happen? She could only predict that life was about to change.

Marco was still not home by ten, and Isa's anxiety had drained her energy. She was spent. Isa pictured Marco at his desk, so involved in his work that he'd forgotten to call her. She knew it was useless to phone his office at this hour. He wouldn't hear the phone and if he did, wouldn't answer. That was his secretary's job. Exhausted from her day and fed up with putting her needs second to Marco's, she went to bed and fell into a fitful slumber.

At breakfast the following day, Marco was as apologetic as always after standing his family up. He promised the boys an outing to Yabucoa for horseback riding and got on his knees to beg Isa's forgiveness, much to Miguelito's and Luisito's amusement. Marco knew she wouldn't show her anger in front of them. Making a mental note to address his manipulation later, she sent the boys off to grab their school bags. She still needed to fill Marco in on what she'd heard.

"Marco, I think Connie's really leaving," Isa said, leaning toward him as soon as the boys left the kitchen.

"How can she even think of doing such a thing?" Marco put his fork down, appalled. "It's disgraceful."

"You know what's disgraceful?" Isa pointed at Marco, lips taut. "Everything Papi's put her through." She ripped off a piece of toast with her teeth.

"What about the vows she made to your father?"

"Papi made those same vows and hasn't been too concerned about honoring them." Isa chomped on her scrambled eggs.

Marco shook his head. "He'll be so humiliated."

Isa nodded. "Thank goodness she has her own money because I don't think Papi can afford a household in New York."

"I doubt it, too," Marco said, pushing his plate away.

"Oh, what a mess!" Isa slouched in her chair.

"That it is, my love. That it is." Marco rose from the table just as the boys returned. After a flurry of kisses, they all got on with their day.

Connie mobilized quickly and was ready to leave for New York in a scant two weeks. Her stepmother and sisters were leaving Isa behind with all the men. *Ugh.* She'd miss them so much, but she also supported Connie's move; it was the right thing to do. Her sisters would live another, very different life, just as she had when she first came to San Juan. They'd attend American schools and become modern American girls, probably even college co-eds. Connie was in charge now and free from Papi's iron rule; the world was her sisters' to conquer.

When Connie's first letter arrived, Isa eagerly tore it open.

> *October 15, 1946*
>
> *Querida Isa,*
>
> *We arrived safe and sound, wearing wool skirts in eighty-degree weather. Apparently, it gets warm here in October, and they call it Indian Summer. And us with all our light clothes packed away. The Warwick Hotel is thirty-six stories high, the tallest building I've ever slept in, but not as tall as others here. Everything in New York is modern, shiny, and vertical. The buildings in Old San Juan are a hundred years older than the most ancient structures in this city.*
>
> *One step outside, and you're assaulted by the smells of exhaust, fine perfume, and steaming hot dogs, as well as*

the sounds of honking horns, men whistling for taxis, and police sirens. Everything—from the elegant wide avenues to the hordes of career women dressed in suits and pearls to the flora of Central Park—is so different from home.

We've rented an apartment at 55 East 72nd Street. It's a lovely, light-filled, three-bedroom on the fourth floor of a fifteen-story building. The neighborhood is cheerful and well-kept, with trees lining the sidewalk. The furnishings are plush and stylish, with a preponderance of light blue, which reminds me of the sea we left behind. It even has a fireplace in the living room! Best of all, Central Park is only a block away. The girls have already taken to calling it "the backyard." We move in next week, and I have a hunch we'll be happy there.

I miss you, as do the girls, who are each writing you letters. And not because I'm forcing them, either. They love their big sister and little cousins. Give those boys a big hug and kiss from Abuela Connie.

Con mucho cariño,
Connie

Isabela put the letter down and sighed. She was thrilled things were going well, but truthfully, she was also a little envious. After all, wasn't *she* the one who'd wanted to leave the island all those years ago? Maybe not for New York, but still. Isa shook her head, trying to disperse these unkind thoughts. Of course, she was thrilled for her sisters. She'd live vicariously through them, share their wonder and adventures.

At least the situation had one silver lining: Carmen had come to live with her! Carmen had declined Connie's invitation to go to New York, saying she was too old to learn new tricks. But she'd accepted Isa's offer to help Elena mind the boys and to cook for the family, much to Marco's delight. Isa smiled. Marco loved Carmen's cooking.

"Bueno, a la tarea," Isa said aloud. Today she planned to bring some of her sons' outgrown clothing to a family in El Fanguito. She found a parking space on Calle Estado and gave two boys sitting on a cement fence nearby a nickel each to "velarme el carro," basic insurance against theft or vandalism. She changed into her rubber boots, grabbed the bag of clothes, and headed toward the Quiñones' house. On the way, she passed a group of middle-aged women and heard one shyly call out to her.

"¡Señora! Excuse me, señora!" The woman waved an airmail envelope at Isa.

"Sí, buenos dias. How can I help you?" Isa approached the woman with a smile.

"Señora, you're the one who teaches reading, no?"

Isa nodded.

"My son's in New York with my sister's family. This is his first letter. Would you read it to me, please?" The woman's pleading expression melted Isa's heart. Oh, to not be able to read a letter from your son.

"Of course, I will! Can we go into your house?" Isa needed to put her bag down.

"God bless you, señora," the woman said, leading Isa and the other women into her hut. Isa sat in a rustic wooden chair and began to read the letter aloud. It had been addressed to "Familia Mendoza c/o Luli's Colmado."

> October 15, 1946
> Querida Familia,
> Saludos from New York! It's not very cold yet, but everyone says I'll be freezing my fundillo off soon. Titi Sandra and Tío Manolo's neighborhood is called East Harlem. The brick buildings are grimy, there's litter all over the streets, and piles of garbage in front of crumbling stoops. People dry their laundry everywhere, wherever there's space between buildings, just like back home.
> The apartment is huge, with three bedrooms! The floors

are made of wood, and the walls are shiny and bumpy from having been painted so many times. It smells like Pine-Sol because Titi is constantly cleaning. I think she's trying to get rid of the smell of mold and fried food that's stuck to the wallpaper in the building's hallways. It doesn't bother me, though. Anything smells better than El Fanguito! Our building is missing its front door, which Tío is trying to get fixed before the cold hits. The neighborhood kids play baseball with a stick in an empty lot full of rubble next door. There's no nature here, not a tree or a patch of grass.

This area used to be an Italian neighborhood, but as more and more of our compatriotas arrive, we've started to take over, and they don't like it. They call us names like "spic." I don't understand it. New York is so big, there should be space for all of us.

My job at the factory is boring, but the paycheck is nice. I'll send you money in my next letter because I've had to buy some clothes and other things first. I'm homesick for passion fruit juice, but Tío and Titi are homesick for everything. They keep talking about saving up to build a little house in the mountains of Aibonito so they can retire there. When their friends visit, they sit around singing sad songs and end up crying to "En mi Viejo San Juan."

I love and miss you all.

Your son and brother,

Pablo

Tears coursed down the mother's face. Isa smiled at her with empathy and gave her hand a little squeeze. She was aghast at how different Pablo's experience was from Connie's. His aunt's apartment had to be better than El Fanguito, but was living in New York an improvement? He'd left so much behind to perhaps gain little.

"Don't cry, Panchita," a woman Isa knew as Lourdes said. "He's making good money, eh?"

"But New York sounds so horrible. I *told* him not to go. I *told* him my sister just wants to come home."

"It can't be worse than this life," Lourdes said, handing Panchita a rag to wipe her tears.

"But didn't you listen? The Puerto Ricans all want to come back. They sit around singing, 'En mi Viejo San Juan,'" Panchita said, wringing her hands.

Isa loved the bittersweet song by Noel Estrada, a poignant ballad that spoke of a man who'd left his heart in Old San Juan, had always planned to return, but now faced death far from his island. It always pulled at her heartstrings.

"En mi viejo San Juan," rang out a melodious voice from the crowd of women, and one by one, they all joined in.

"En mi viejo San Juan,
Cuántos sueños forjé,
En mis noches de infancia.
Mi primera ilusión,
Y mis cuitas de amor,
Son recuerdos del alma.

Una tarde me fui,
Hacia extraña nación,
Pues lo quiso el destino.
Pero mi corazón,
Se quedó frente al mar,
En mi viejo San Juan.

Adiós,
Adiós, adiós
Borinquen querida,
Tierra de mi amor.

Adiós,
Adiós, adiós
Mi diosa del mar,
Mi reina del palmar.

Me voy,
Pero un día volveré,
A buscar mi querer,
A soñar otra vez,
En mi viejo San Juan.

Pero el tiempo pasó,
Y el destino burló,
Mi terrible nostalgia.
Y no pude volver,
Al San Juan que yo amé,
Pedacito de patria.

Mi cabello blanqueó,
Y mi vida se va,
Ya la muerte me llama.
Y no quiero morir,
Alejado de ti,
Puerto Rico del alma."

When they finished the final chorus of *"Adios, adios, adios, Borinquen querida,"* there wasn't a dry eye among them.

On the drive home, Isa fumed at the stark difference between Connie's and Pablo's letters. Connie could afford to live as comfortably as any middle-class American in New York. Most Puerto Ricans, however, endured sub-par living conditions, discrimination, and jobs in sweatshops. Where was "the land of opportunity" for her people? New York provided the opportunity to continue to live in poverty, suffer in the cold, and work at menial jobs nobody else wanted, all while being looked down upon, stuck on the lowest rung on the have-nots' ladder. It was ironic, really, that Italians harassed Puerto Ricans, who were American citizens. They had more of a right to be in New York than any Italian.

People like Pablo left the island with such high hopes. Sure, some prospered, but the majority did not. Why wasn't the myth debunked? Did those in New York paint too rosy a picture for their relatives back home? The truth needed to be told plainly so people could make decisions based on facts, not fairy tales. Isa thought of how the song "En mi Viejo San Juan" resonated with all Puerto Ricans. *We need more of that. The arts can help reach people and tell the real story.* Isa's pulse accelerated, and excitement fluttered in her stomach. A solution was staring her in the face. What about some sort of publication? Yes. A magazine! Her brain went into overdrive, rapidly firing thoughts and questions.

Many wrote about the New York experience—Julia de Burgos, Clemente Soto Velez, and Bernardo Vega. What if their work and that of island residents were assembled in one publication, a single literary magazine that published all viewpoints? She envisioned a collection of pieces about Puerto Rican culture, life in the mountains, life in the city, the push for autonomy, the pros and cons of American affiliation, and other vital issues. The magazine could educate Boricuas about their culture *and* about life on the island, as well as in New York. People would learn the facts before deciding to migrate. More and more people were learning to read in the slums, and she'd get them to host reading parties for those who still couldn't.

Isa grinned and banged her hand on the car's console. *This.* This would be her new purpose. She pressed against the car seat with an enormous grin on her face. Beatriz would love this idea. Almost immediately, her smile faded as she wondered how Marco would react. There was no doubt in her mind that she had a fight ahead of her. But Marco had never stopped her before, and he sure as hell wouldn't now.

CHAPTER 22

- Marco -
November 1946

Marco left the Solemar offices with a bounce in his step, thinking of his sons. He chuckled as he got into his car and headed toward his first destination. How he loved those rascals. Business was booming, and all his hard work, everything he'd sacrificed, was coming to fruition for his family—his boys and their future. Solemar had secured the financing for the GI housing development, and they'd sold every unit before construction was final. Two additional urbanizaciones were in the works, and those units were selling even more quickly. Much to Isa's disapproval, the houses were little cement boxes, but this didn't bother the buyers. On the contrary, they were desperate to own a piece of the American Dream.

Twenty minutes later, he slowed down by the construction site of his dream house on Cáceres Street in Hato Rey, a surprise for Isa and his sons. Designed by Henry Klumb, a Frank Lloyd Wright disciple, the modern residence would be worthy of the place he'd earned in the new Puerto Rican society. Klumb was skilled at adapting modernist architecture to the tropics, and the one-level structure featured clean lines, glass brick, and floor-to-ceiling glass jalousie windows opening to views of lush outdoor gardens.

One wall in the sunken living room housed the large built-in aquarium he'd envisioned and overlooked an indoor fishpond surrounded by a low stone wall. He'd decided against the swans. Klumb was even designing the modernist furniture, which would be made of bent wood, leather, rope, and fabric and have the same clean lines as the house. The extra touches had proved more costly than Marco had anticipated, but perfection was priceless. He'd invested all his personal capital in creating this homage to modernity, and it would be worth every cent. The house had come a long way in the past month. It was finally finished enough to show Isa, and he was eager to unveil his surprise.

Well, enough procrastinating, thought Marco. He turned the car around and backtracked toward Don Gabriel's house in Miramar. The old man had requested a meeting, and Marco expected Don Gabriel needed to vent about his business problems, as he'd done recently on multiple occasions. Frankly, Marco was tired of listening to his complaints. His efforts to convince the man to join current times had proved futile. Don Gabriel was entrenched in the old ways and insisted on continuing to import luxury Spanish goods, even though everyone wanted the latest American products. Most recently, he'd refused to let his employees unionize, and that was starting to cost him in defections to the more archaically named but union-friendly Porto Rico Shipping Company. Worst of all, Don Gabriel continued to blame the Americans for his troubles when most of them were due to his own reluctance to modernize. Marco couldn't see how he could help Don Gabriel if the man refused to help himself.

Okay, here we go, he thought as he pulled into Don Gabriel's driveway, the house and front garden to his right. *I must get in a sympathetic frame of mind.* He'd come to tolerate the stubborn old man, but his admiration for his business prowess had abated long ago. Successful men had to change with the times, and Don Gabriel was stuck in 1920. Marco took a bracing breath and entered the house.

Elegantly dressed in a light grey suit, Don Gabriel greeted Marco and offered him a glass of Don Q on ice. The two men made themselves comfortable in the living room.

"¿Cómo van las cosas, Don Gabriel?" Marco asked, trying to get comfortable on the wooden settee.

Don Gabriel sighed. "Bueno, las cosas están bastante mal. I won't lie. I'd say things are abysmal. I don't understand this new desire to unionize. If my employees have a problem, why don't they just come to me, like always? I've been to their weddings, christenings, and funerals. They're family. At least, I thought they were." Don Gabriel shook his head and raised both arms before letting them drop on his lap. Grief aged his face.

Marco nodded and took a sip of his drink. *Here we go again.*

"I don't know how to conduct business like this," Don Gabriel continued. "I haven't adapted well to the American ways, and I'm afraid I've led my company into bankruptcy. I'm embarrassed to ask, but I need your help." Don Gabriel's eyes were pools of anguish.

Don Gabriel defeated? And accepting part of the blame? At what cost to the old man's pride? But wait. Sweat broke out along Marco's hairline, and his heart raced as he considered a different thought. *Is he going to ask me for money?* No way would Marco invest in that sinking ship of a company. But how was he going to say *no* to Don Gabriel? He shifted his body slightly away from the man and crossed his legs.

"You know you can count on me to help in any way I can," Marco said, avoiding Don Gabriel's gaze.

"Don't look so frightened, mijo." Don Gabriel reached over to pat Marco on the knee. "I'm not asking for cash. But I need to declare bankruptcy, liquidate assets, pay debts, and close shop. Can you help me?"

"Of course, I'll help," Marco said, relaxing. "Sammy will, too. We'll assist you as much as we can."

Don Gabriel's left arm swung wide, gesturing around the room, "We'll sell this house, too."

"But you love this house," Marco protested. This entire conversation was surreal.

"This is a family home, and unless you and Isa want it, I need to sell it."

"Ay, Don Gabriel. Don't tell Isa, but I've been building us a house, and it's almost finished. Wait till you see it. It has all the latest conveniences." Marco couldn't hide his excitement.

"I'm sure Isa will be thrilled to have an up-to-the-minute home," Don Gabriel said with a forced grin. "We'll sell this place when we liquidate my assets. Let's move forward." Don Gabriel had adopted a flat affect. Marco hoped the man would continue to keep his emotions out of this miserable undertaking. He gave Don Gabriel a quick handshake, got back in his car, and headed home.

Marco fretted, wondering how Isa would take the news. She'd have a hard time seeing Don Gabriel in reduced circumstances. And what if Isa wanted to move into her father's house, preferred it to the one Marco had built? Surely Don Gabriel would come with it. No way could there be two heads of household, and Marco knew who would win *that* fight. Suddenly spent, he decided to keep the news from Isa, at least for tonight.

Marco sat down to a dinner of Carmen's piñón with great gusto. Everyone in the family loved the layered dish of sweet plantains and seasoned ground meat and made quick work of it. Isa and Marco lingered at the table after the boys asked to be excused to finish their homework. Marco, uncomfortably full, rued having eaten so much and contemplated a lie-down on the couch, but Isa had other ideas. She began to fill him in on the events of her day, highlighting the stark differences between Connie's and Pablo's letters.

"Marco, why are people moving to New York to work in factories? They can work in factories here." Isa reached over to take his empty plate, piled it on top of hers and set them to the side.

"Yes, for a much lower wage," Marco said. "At least they can earn more in New York, even if the living isn't any easier." He hated to see so many flee to the U.S. in search of jobs, but the exodus was inevitable, even necessary. At least until the island's economy improved.

"What about public housing? Plus, I thought your beloved Fomento was solving the employment problem," Isa said, referring to the government-created agency tasked with bringing U.S. industry, and thus jobs, to the island by offering reduced taxes and other incentives.

"Even Fomento won't be able to create enough jobs for everyone," Marco answered. "And the government can't keep pace with the need for public housing. Too many keep descending from the mountains and towns out on the island."

Isa sighed and grew quiet.

Marco put a hand on her knee and, for the hundredth time, wished his wife would focus on the boys and leave the political concerns to him. Fomento was such a brilliant concept that Senate leader Muñoz Marín stood staunchly behind it and even made a controversial about-face against the idea of Puerto Rican independence. Whereas Muñoz had advocated putting independence on the back burner until the island got back on its feet, he now renounced it altogether. Many had balked when the senator published a series of opinion pieces in the newspaper espousing this view, but not Marco. If the Puerto Rican economy was to improve and, God willing, even thrive, fostering free trade with the U.S. was imperative. If that meant forsaking independence, then so be it.

Later that evening, Marco made love to his wife with gusto. He never ceased to take deep pleasure in her silky skin and the many other delights of her body. Drained, he lay quietly on his back next to Isa until she turned on her side toward him and broke the silence.

"Now that Connie and the girls are settled in New York, I feel it's time for a new start for me, too," she said, running a finger down his naked arm. "I miss working at the USO and doing something useful. I want a job."

Marco shivered, unsure if the cause was her finger's caress or the topic she'd introduced. He'd considered Isa's work at the USO charitable and thus acceptable. But no self-respecting successful man had a wife with a career. Ridiculous. He trod carefully and appealed to her motherly instincts. "What about the boys?"

"They're both in school all day. Elena cleans, and Carmen cooks. What am I supposed to do? I can't spend all my time in dress fittings and luncheons with the Club Cívico de Damas. Besides, look how that turned out for Connie. She became a faded version of her old self until she finally left Papi."

Was that a threat? Marco's blood went cold.

Isa continued. "Besides, you don't even know what I want to do. I had a brilliant idea today." Isa clapped her hands with enthusiasm, her eyes dancing.

"What is it?" Marco was pleased to see a sparkle in her eyes, even if he disapproved of its source. Isa's parents' breakup had been hard on her, and now her father's bankruptcy would strike another blow.

"I'm going to start a magazine."

Marco groaned, and Isa held out her hand, palm up.

"Wait. Before you say anything, let me explain. I want to give voice to our people here and in New York. Offer a venue for differing opinions to be heard. Make sure our culture is celebrated and preserved."

Marco was taken aback at the scope of the venture Isa envisioned. He tried to tread carefully. "Querida, it's a wonderful idea. But do you know anything about running a publication?"

"Well, no! But just like you've done your whole life, I'll learn." Isa laughed. "I want you to set up a meeting for me with Ángel Ramos. He's a visionary when it comes to keeping the Puerto Rican culture alive. He'll get me started and guide me in the right direction."

It was Marco's turn to laugh, his attempt at wearing kid gloves abandoned. "The publisher of *El Mundo* doesn't have time to help dilettantes figure out how to run a magazine." The moment the words left his mouth, he knew he'd badly misspoken.

"Dilettante?" Isa raised herself on her elbow and looked down at him with hard eyes. "Dilettante? I don't think so, Marco. I'm more than serious about this. Get me a meeting with Ramos. I'll take it from there." Isa flopped on her back.

Marco was in trouble but couldn't help himself and asked, "But how will you finance this little venture?"

Isa faced him again, eyebrows arched, and meted out his punishment, "Oh, you will be funding my 'little venture,' mi amor. That's how I'll pay for it." She turned off her light, punched her pillow, and flipped on her side, away from him.

Marco recognized that she meant business. At least she wanted to do something artistic, even feminine. It wouldn't be a career, per se, but more of a dabbling. A magazine might even be something to brag about. *Hmmm.* Well, why not? She was a capable woman. She'd helped run the USO, so why not a magazine?

He spooned her from behind, kissed the back of her head, and said, "Your wish is my command." With all his personal money tied up in the new house, he'd worry about how to pay for this project of hers later. Let Isa be happy for a few more hours. He'd break the news of Don Gabriel's bankruptcy in the morning.

CHAPTER 23

- Isabela -
November 1946 to August 1947

Isa stared at Marco in stupefaction. He'd warned her Papi could go bankrupt, but it had always been a distant possibility. She turned inward, tuning out the rest of Marco's words while her mind struggled to process the information.

"Isa? Are you listening?" Marco waved a hand in front of her face, and she snapped back to attention.

"We'll buy Papi's house, of course," she said. She'd raise her boys there and create new memories in that beautiful home. And, best of all, Papi could stay. She immediately began planning which bedrooms would be whose.

Across the kitchen table, Marco's expression, already gloomy at having had to break the bankruptcy news to her, turned despondent. He avoided her eyes and, after a beat, answered, "We can't."

Isa shot him a confused look. "Why not? Are we broke?"

Marco sighed, stood up and grabbed his keys from the kitchen counter. "Let's go for a ride. I need to show you something, amor. Then you'll understand."

Increasingly perplexed, Isa followed him out the door. They drove in silence, Isa staring out the passenger window with a growing sense of impending doom. After a ten-minute drive that felt like hours, Marco pulled up in front of a newly built house. Isa examined it from the car. It resembled the cement cubes Marco planted all over the metropolitan area, except larger and more embellished. More designed. More ostentatious. Very showy. Suddenly she realized what was coming. Her stomach dropped, and her heart raced.

Marco exited the car, opened the door for her, and helped her out. He held her hand and jutted his chin toward the house.

"What do you think?"

Isa stared at the building, away from his eager and expectant expression. "This is your most modern yet," she said, experienced at uttering words that pleased him.

"I knew you'd like it!" Marco's relief was palpable. "I'm so happy, Isa, because this is our new home!" An elated Marco spread his arms wide.

Isa could only stand there, tears streaming down her cheeks. Marco grinned at her and, obviously mistaking her sorrow for joy, enveloped her in a bear hug, picked her up, and spun her around.

Back on solid ground, Isa wiped her face with her palms.

"But how did you do this? Why didn't you tell me?" She couldn't muster any enthusiasm, and her tone fell flat. Marco didn't appear to notice.

"It was *so* hard to keep it a surprise! But I knew you were going to love it." He pulled Isa by her arm up the walkway and into the house. "I thought of every detail you'd want. Come see!"

Isa's mind reeled. An indoor pond. A giant aquarium *inside* a wall. Modernistic angles and details. Five bedrooms. Why had Marco done this without consulting her? No. How *dare* Marco do this without consulting her? What about what *she* wanted? She wanted to be heard. She wanted to be included. Carajo, she wanted Papi's house!

But she couldn't tell Marco, couldn't break his heart. He was so proud of the thing. It was finished and ready for them to move in. Papi was finished, too. He'd live with them, then. Isa exhaled loudly. This had been, without question, the worst morning of her life.

Throughout the following months, Isa felt as if a piece of her emotional scaffolding had broken off. She walked off-balance, forgot what she'd said a moment ago, and was short-tempered with the boys. Meanwhile, Papi became diminished, shrunken. It tore her heart to shreds. True, he hadn't been the best husband, but he'd lost most of his family. Must he lose everything else?

Thanks to Marco's "surprise," it had been too late to save Papi's house. Their new house was ready, Marco loved it, and she'd resigned herself to living there. Thoughts of starting a magazine went on the back burner while she summoned the strength to pack and move her household into that soulless mausoleum. They were settled in by the end of February, after which Isa turned her focus to Papi's living situation. He'd refused to move in with them, even though they had room to spare. Men were so ridiculously proud. She fumed whenever she let herself dwell on the fact that strangers would live in Papi's gorgeous home while her family was stuck in a monument to Marco's ego.

Papi chose to live in a tiny apartment on Fernández Juncos Avenue near El Fanguito, not far from his old house but a world apart. The first time she'd seen the one-room efficiency, she questioned whether it could even be called an apartment. A small stove and refrigerator lined the back wall next to a tiny bathroom, while the rest of the narrow rectangular space was slated for living and sleeping. It was a far cry from 650 Calle La Paz but worlds better than a shack in the mud.

On the first of April, Isa stopped by to drop off a pot of Carmen's comforting sancocho.

"Careful, Papi. It's still hot." Isa handed the cauldron to her father, who took it and walked it and its savory aroma to the stove. "Sorry I'm late, but I was almost at La Paz Street by habit before I realized I'd gone too far." She peeled off her driving gloves and took in Papi's sad abode.

"God, I miss that house." As Isa uttered the words, her heart contracted, and her face darkened. She shook her head. "I'll never forgive the Americans for ruining you."

"I'm afraid I contributed to my own ruin." Papi shrugged his shoulders. "As Marco likes to point out, I never adapted to the new ways of doing business."

"Ways forced on us by los Yanquis. And we just keep getting in deeper and deeper with them," Isa said, hands on hips. "Look at Muñoz Marín saying we should abandon our quest for independence. His father dedicated his life to getting this island autonomy. He must be rolling in his grave. Meanwhile, we're going to lose our Puerto Ricaness."

"Our culture is beautiful and strong. It will survive the American influence."

"From your lips to God's ears," Isa said, glancing heavenward.

"Besides, your husband made a fortune thanks to the Americans. They take, but they also give." Papi shook his index finger at her.

Isa sighed. "Yes, it's not a black-and-white issue, is it? I worry about the boys' future."

"I hate to say it, but their future will be American." Papi shrugged again.

"It will if Marco has anything to do with it." Isa's smile did not reach her eyes. "I'm off." She gave Papi a peck on the cheek and headed home.

That evening Isa slumped hard on the bed beside Marco and shook her head.

"Ay, Marco, Papi's a shadow of his old self. It's tragic." What a relief to let her tears fall unrestrained.

"I know," Marco said, putting his arm around Isa. "I keep trying to unearth the powerful and vibrant man who tortured me all those years ago."

While she appreciated his effort to make her smile, her next words were encased in disdain. "Damned Americans."

She laid her head on Marco's chest and silently begged him not to launch into one of his long pro-Yanqui diatribes. She wasn't in the mood. Miraculously, he held her quietly and stroked her hair gently. Not that it helped Isa's pounding head. What had the Americans really done for Puerto Rico? Certainly, very little for the people of El Fanguito and other slums. When had everyone, including her own husband, forgotten about independence? They were making deals with the devil, and the more entwined they became with the U.S., the harder it would be to cut the cord.

Lately, she'd been increasingly drawn to the latest version of the Puerto Rico Independence Party, which, unlike the Nationalists, wanted to achieve independence peacefully. She'd chosen not to share this new political affinity with Marco and wouldn't bring it up now. That conversation would only worsen her headache. Isa pretended to fall asleep and pulled out of his arms to turn over. She wondered how many more secrets this marriage could handle.

With her family ensconced in their new house and Papi settled in his apartment, Isa regained the mental and emotional space needed to pursue her magazine project. Now more than ever, she felt that celebrating and disseminating Puerto Rican culture was of utmost importance. Something was needed to counteract the Americans' influence.

After much pestering, Marco finally smoothed the way for Isa to meet with Ángel Ramos, and today she sat outside the *El Mundo* editor's office waiting to be called in. She was anxious to get his reaction to her ideas and, hopefully, a bit of advice on getting started. Isa surreptitiously dried her palms on the skirt of her periwinkle straight skirt suit, determined to project self-assurance. And just in time. Ramos emerged from his office, shook her hand while leaning in for a cheek kiss, and led her to one of two chairs facing his imposing wooden desk. After getting the usual pleasantries out of the way and discussing their mutual concern for preserving the island's culture, Isa launched into her pitch.

"My magazine will give writers a platform for discussing their sense of national identity," she said, leaning forward. "We'll explore what being Puerto Rican means to a jíbaro who cuts cane, a policeman in Naguabo, a shopgirl in San Juan, a factory worker in New York, or a doctor in Ponce." She accentuated each example with a hand gesture.

"A bit like *Índice* in the 1930s?" Ramos sat back and tented his fingers under his chin.

"Yes and no." Isa had done her research and knew *Índice* had focused on defining the Puerto Rican persona without addressing politics. "I'll also present opposing views on important issues like independence, colonialism, migration, and religion."

Ángel nodded, and Isa continued, hands flying to emphasize her words. "And I'll publish great writing in all its forms, from poems to essays to book reviews."

Ángel leaned forward and asked, "What about society news, recipes, gardening tips, and things like that?"

Isa hid her annoyance at his assumption that a woman would only be interested in creating a women's magazine and responded, "Ah, but this magazine is for men *and* women, for anyone interested in our culture."

"Huh. I like your vision, Isabela. How often do you plan on publishing?"

"Bi-monthly to start." *He liked it!* Isa's body wanted to jump up and down, but she forced herself to stay seated.

"And do you have any experience in publishing?" His eyes were curious.

"Truthfully, that's why I'm here. I'm hoping you can offer some words of wisdom. I have a million ideas, and I'm blazing to get started." Her heart thundered inside her chest.

"Starting a magazine is a labor of love," Ramos said. "It's a lot of work, with little promise of monetary reward."

Isa waved away his concern. "Making a profit doesn't matter. Marco is a wonderful provider, as you know. And there's such a need for something like this. Every day we become more and more American and less and less Puerto Rican." Isa shook her head.

"True." Ramos squinted his eyes and nodded his head as if pondering an idea of his own. "You know... One of my top reporters writes brilliant poetry and, like us, is adamant about keeping our culture alive." He pressed the intercom button and asked his secretary to summon Antonio. "Perhaps he'd be willing to serve as a mentor and help you get started."

"That would be fantastic," Isa said, slightly disappointed that Ramos wasn't offering to help her himself.

A knock sounded on the door, and while Ramos made the introductions, Isa appraised this reporter, Antonio Badilla. His cream linen suit was so badly wrinkled, it looked slept in, his dark hair needed a barber, and he sported a distinct five-o'clock shadow, although it was just past lunchtime. This was one of *El Mundo*'s best reporters? Well, if Ramos said so... She ignored her skepticism, mustered back some excitement, and launched into her vision again.

As Badilla listened attentively and offered complementary ideas, Isa quickly warmed up to him. She'd been wrong to judge this man by his appearance. He was thoughtful, intelligent, and, she had to admit—charming. At one point, he leaned into her while making a point, and Isa swore she felt an electric charge.

"What do you think, Badilla?" Ramos asked.

"It's time for something like this." Antonio nodded and faced Isa with a twinkle in his eye. He spoke in a deep, seductive voice. "And with such an enthusiastic leader, the magazine is sure to succeed. Señora Rios, it would be my pleasure to help you realize this project."

A rush of warmth coursed through Isa's body, and much to her annoyance, she felt herself blush like a schoolgirl. Hand on her chest, she leaned toward Antonio and said, "I accept your kind offer. And, please, call me Isabela."

She quickly made plans to meet with Antonio the following week, thanked Ángel profusely, and left feeling both light and strangely discombobulated.

Despite the overhead fans, Isa sweat under her hat as she waited for Antonio at La Bombonera, a café convenient to *El Mundo*'s offices and where she'd told Marco the truth about her jíbara background. She felt pressure to ensure this first meeting excited Antonio as much as their initial conversation had. She could use a champion, especially since her husband considered her a dabbler. Isa still bristled when she thought back on how Marco had laughed at her magazine idea. She was certain he'd gotten her the meeting with Ramos without any expectation it would further her quest. But look at her now. Her vision had intrigued two professionals, Ángel Ramos and Antonio Badilla, who were willing to help her bring it to life.

She watched as Antonio took two steps inside the café and jovially greeted a group of men sitting at a front table. They stood to shake his hand and slap him on the back, seemingly in friendship and admiration, while Antonio flashed them a pleased grin and looked around for her. She waved to him from her table in the back, saw him see her, and waited while he inched toward her, stopping at almost every table along the way. Why he was practically a celebrity! Who would have guessed? Finally, he greeted Isa and sat across from her. The air crackled with his virility.

"You're like the mayor of San Juan," Isa said, laughing to hide her fluster. "It took you ten minutes to get through the throng of admirers."

Antonio's soulful brown eyes focused on Isa, making her feel like the center of his universe. "Reporters have many friends, of course," he said. "But don't be fooled. We also have many enemies. Not everyone likes the truth." He shook his head.

"I'm about to make some enemies then because the truth will be at the core of my magazine," Isa said. Without noticing, she'd leaned over the table toward Antonio. The man was magnetic. She quickly pulled back, pressing her spine against her chair. They ordered coffees and chatted more about the magazine, losing track of time until the newspaper sent one of its cub reporters to fetch Antonio so he could meet his afternoon deadline.

Antonio continued to volunteer his time and expertise in subsequent meetings, and before long, Isa found his input indispensable. She even enjoyed her secret attraction to the man and allowed herself a harmless flirt here and there. Working with him was enriching and exciting. When Isa invited him to be the magazine's managing editor, Antonio readily accepted. He'd fit the work around his job at *El Mundo*. Together they conceived of *Letras Boricuas*, a bi-monthly magazine highlighting the island's history and varied heritage and affirming Puerto Rican culture.

Marco funded the venture, although she suspected he was biding his time before it failed. Antonio, though, believed *Letras Boricuas* would fill a void. He had faith in her vision. The two collaborated well and made quick progress toward the first issue. Antonio paid attention to her opinions and respected her decisions. She'd never felt so appreciated for her talent and intelligence. It was heady, even a bit unnerving.

By August, she'd leased a small office in Miramar. Marco couldn't understand why she refused to work out of Solemar's perfectly good headquarters in Old San Juan. But she felt strongly that the two enterprises should be separate. She also didn't want Marco constantly sticking his nose in her business, trying to oversee how she spent his money. Hopefully, *Letras Boricuas* would pay for itself once it got off the ground through issue sales and maybe even advertising. As she'd told Ramos, she didn't care if it made a profit, but she did want it to at least break even so she wouldn't have to answer to Marco for every little expenditure.

The office was in a three-story walk-up, a one-room rectangular space. Isa squeezed in two metal desks against the longer walls, each furnished with a brass desk lamp, a mint green Underwood typewriter, and a telephone. An area rug between the facing desks added a hint of hominess. The space was tight and far from fancy, but it served its purpose. Her one luxury was a window air conditioner.

She hired a part-time typist, Luz, who came in the mornings to help with correspondence, contracts, and manuscripts. Isa knew how to type, had learned in high school, but the volume was too much for one person. Antonio often visited in the afternoons to discuss plans for the first issue or to edit work. His presence, though welcome, became so ubiquitous that she wondered when he wrote the articles for his job at *El Mundo* and hoped he didn't get fired. She wanted to pay her contributors well but couldn't afford to pay Antonio a reporter's salary. She also couldn't afford to lose him.

Besides, she loved having Antonio around. His bonhomie was contagious; she couldn't help but smile when he was in the office. She'd grown to appreciate his rough edges. His clothes were notoriously rumpled, and he wasn't handsome in the traditional sense, but his broad face, prominent nose, and fleshy lips somehow worked together to create a kind and attractive face. What really made him special, though, were his twinkly brown eyes and quick smile. She suspected he was a certified Casanova with a trail of broken hearts behind him. Those poor girls. She wondered whether the pain of losing him had been worth loving him. What was it like to capture this intriguing man's attention? Silly thoughts for a married woman.

Isa had found a great collaborator; that's what was important. Isa and Antonio bounced ideas off each other, played devil's advocate, and enjoyed a healthy repartee. On a stifling late August afternoon, they took refuge in her air-conditioned office and chatted about how Puerto Ricans were to finally vote for their own governor.

"It's a bone you throw a dog," Antonio said. "We're not animals. I won't rest until we're a self-sufficient, self-governing nation." Despite the cool air in the room, he wiped his brow with his handkerchief.

"To still be a colony. What a disgrace!" Isa scoffed from behind her desk. "I'm setting my hopes on the Independence Party."

Antonio snickered. "The PIP will be squashed, just like previous independence parties. I'm a Nationalist through and through. What we need is a revolution."

"But Albizu Campos is a murderer!" Isa didn't try to hide her shock. How could a man like Antonio support such a monster?

Antonio's eyes bored into hers. She could see him weighing whether to continue.

Quietly, he began, "Is a general fighting a war a murderer? Because make no mistake, Albizu Campos is fighting a war. He's tried to win at the polls, but the elections are rigged. Listen, both my parents worked all their lives. They still do. Papá reads all day to tobacco rollers, can barely speak, he's so hoarse by the time he gets home. Mamá sews at a factory, and her shoulders are permanently hunched over." Antonio mimicked his mother's stance. "During the Depression, their wages were cut in half to thirty-three cents for the same twelve-hour days. Starvation wages! Pedro Albizu Campos was the only one who cared. He led the workers, including my parents, and helped them negotiate a living wage of $1.50 per day."

"Yes, I remember that." Isa nodded. Antonio's story moved her.

"Los Yanquis didn't like that one bit. Albizu Campos threatened their colonial money-making machine, so they tried to stop him and declared war on everything he stands for. We're simply fighting back."

"But so many have died because of his tactics." Isa couldn't believe this kind man advocated murder.

"Yes, but mostly Nationalists. I count my own brother among the victims of the American oppression."

"He was killed?" Isa asked, hands clutched at her heart.

"Yes, and it could just as easily have been me," Antonio answered bluntly.

"Wha—what happened?" Isa's voice was shaky. She wasn't sure she wanted to hear the details but forced herself to listen.

"The Ponce Massacre happened. It's been ten years, but I remember it clearly," Antonio said, his voice steady. "It was supposed to be a peaceful parade in support of Albizu, who was in jail for no reason. It was also Palm Sunday and the anniversary of the Puerto Rican abolition of slavery. So much to celebrate, right? My brother and I were Nationalist Cadets of the Republic; I was twenty-one, and Pedro was only seventeen. We took a bus from Aguadilla to Mayagüez and then to Ponce with our parents and other supporters, everyone clowning around and singing. But when we arrived, there were policemen with machine guns everywhere. We were used to having police at our events, but this was something else."

Isabela nodded. She listened closely to Antonio and made no interruptions.

"Governor Winship had revoked our parade permit, and we couldn't appeal to anyone because Ponce's chief of police had conveniently disappeared. So, we decided we had a right to march, but the moment we stepped forward, completely unarmed and defenseless, the machine guns went off. People fell all around me." A vein throbbed in Antonio's forehead, and the cords in his neck strained. Isa tried to picture the horrific scene he described.

"It was pandemonium, and I couldn't see much. The tear gas burned my eyes. I remember frantically flinging my arms, trying to feel for Pedro. I screamed his name, but the gunfire drowned me out." Antonio's features were pinched with remembered pain. "I took cover in the doorway of a building, and that's when I saw him splayed on the ground. His black cadet shirt and white pants were soaked in blood." Antonio shook his head. "I rushed to him, but he was already dead."

Isa shivered, her eyes wet. "Ay, Antonio. What a horrible thing to witness. Your parents must have been inconsolable." A lump lodged in her throat. To lose one's child!

"I'll never forget my mother's wail when she saw him. Its anguish is embedded in my soul."

Isa shivered again. She'd known about the Massacre, had read about it, and even discussed it at the dinner table—but this first-hand account left her reeling. She couldn't fathom losing one of her sons so violently. And to think Antonio had been there, had lived it. How did one recover from such a trauma? Marco had experienced the Rio Piedras Massacre, but safely from inside a building. Poor, poor Antonio.

"They killed nineteen of us and injured one hundred and fifty more, even women and children," Antonio said, voice steely. "I carry the weight of my brother's death with me every day, but I'll make sure he didn't die in vain. I'll continue to fight for independence, and if that calls for violence, so be it." He nodded his head once.

"I can understand your desire to avenge Pedro's death, but I still think there are better ways," Isa spoke slowly. "Why kill more people?"

"It's the only way to get the Americans' attention." Antonio's eyes burrowed into hers. Seeing it was a losing battle, Isa decided to drop the subject. Sad as it was, the conversation had also perplexed her. This Antonio was hard to reconcile with the happy-go-lucky man she thought she knew.

"You live with a heavy heart, yet you always seem happy, joking and making people laugh. Is that an act? It must be exhausting," Isa said, musing aloud.

"No, I keep my spirits up. If I let hate take over, it will paralyze me, like it did during the first few months after Pedro's death," Antonio said. "Working toward bringing El Maestro's teachings to fruition fuels me. I know one day I'll see a free Puerto Rico."

"Please promise me you'll be careful," Isa entreated. God only knew what Antonio got up to.

"Don't worry about me. When it comes to one's mind, it's better to occupy than preoccupy." Antonio laughed and rose to get back to work. Why were the men in her life always telling her not to worry? She watched Antonio walk out of her office and attributed the flutter in her chest to annoyance.

CHAPTER 24

- Marco -
October to December 1947

The following October, on the way to work in the pouring autumn rain, the inside of Marco's car became a steamy swamp, and he could barely see out the windshield. He pulled out his handkerchief and wiped his face, then the fogged glass, before tossing it on the passenger seat. He'd need it again. *Coño, it's hot in this car.*

He resolved not to let the dismal weather bring him down. He thought about Papá and how he would have rejoiced that they could finally vote for governor next year. Not surprisingly, Muñoz Marín started campaigning immediately, and Marco expected him to win. In the meantime, Muñoz championed offering even better incentives to U.S. businesses for building plants and factories on the island. Fomento's Teodoro Moscoso had been courting takers with great success.

Despite the rolled-up windows, the stench of El Fanguito permeated the car as Marco drove by the slum. He held his breath and frowned at the wooden shacks built on stilts over water toxic with human waste. The government had offered these people perfectly good housing, but many wouldn't leave and acted as if they *liked* living there. Why wouldn't they help themselves? *It's disgusting.* That slum needed to disappear if Puerto Rico wanted to attract more shiny American companies. And especially if the plan to court tourism by legalizing gambling and building a Hilton Hotel came to fruition. Tourists did not like poverty. He made a mental note to find out the latest plans for El Fanguito; those people needed to relocate, whether they liked it or not.

Later that day, Marco was about to return a phone call when Sammy knocked on his office door, a folder in his hand.

"Do you have a minute? I need to review some figures with you."

Marco nodded, and Sammy closed the door. They sat at a round wooden table near the windows, where Marco liked to hold his small meetings, and Sammy opened the folder.

"I just spoke with Maldonado at Banco Popular. They're getting antsy about the project delays, and he wants assurances that we're good for the loan when it comes due."

Solemar had borrowed heavily to undertake simultaneous housing development projects. They'd broken ground on three locations in July, but a rainy hurricane season coupled with drainage challenges had significantly set back their progress, as well as that of several other projects in various stages of completion. All their capital was tied up, so they'd found ways to keep going by robbing Peter to pay Paul. It was imperative that they finish building these homes and sell them quickly.

Sammy, forearms on the table, leaned toward Marco. Worry creased his forehead. "We cannot pay this loan if the bank decides to call it in. We've got to generate some cash to have on hand."

"How? The houses won't be ready until early next year. That's our first influx of capital in the foreseeable future," Marco said, holding a pencil between his index and middle fingers and tapping it vigorously on the table.

"Can we cut any more project costs?" Sammy suggested, placing a hand over Marco's to stop the tapping.

"We've gone through the expenses. If we cut any more corners, we'll be building straw bohíos," Marco said, now chewing on the pencil.

"Then it's time to sell El Comienzo."

"Our first venture! We can't put it on the chopping block like a side of beef," Marco said, hand on heart. His first baby!

"You are ridiculous. Let's sell it while it's still worth something without us having to put any money into it. It's looking sad and neglected."

"I don't think we'll need to sell it," Marco said. "Maldonado knows us. He's not going to call in the loan." He dismissed Sammy's worrying with his hand.

Sammy bristled before responding, "I want to be prepared. We've spread ourselves too thin."

"We'll cross that bridge if we get to it. Now go away so I can get some work done." Marco got up from the table and shooed Sammy out the door.

Before stepping into the hall, Sammy pointed his index finger at Marco. "You're going to be the death of me, hombre. I'll keep a close eye on the situation, and we're selling if I say so." He walked away, shaking his head.

Marco closed the door behind his partner. Mind racing, he paced the floor. He was aware they were overextended but had not anticipated the possibility of their loans getting called in. This was exactly the kind of situation Don Gabriel had warned him about early on. Don Gabriel, who now lived in a one-room apartment with a two-burner stove. He'd preached moderation. But Marco and Sammy hadn't been greedy. They'd simply tried to keep up with the predicted need for new housing. Now all their projects were delayed, and like a row of dominoes, the entire enterprise could come tumbling down.

Marco tugged at his shirt collar, damp with sweat, and loosened his tie. He was roasting and took a moment to resent that his wife worked in an air-conditioned office while the ancient windows in his workplace couldn't accommodate a unit. It wasn't just the business that worried him. He had no personal reserves to weather a financial storm. Every cent he'd made, he'd spent. If Solemar failed, he'd be ruined personally and professionally. How could he have been so reckless? It was time to rein in his personal expenses. He must pare down. But how?

Isa mustn't know something was amiss with their finances. He didn't think she suspected anything, especially since she'd been busy with her magazine. The magazine. *Oh God!* Another thing he funded. How could he face Isa if he had to take the magazine away? But forget the magazine. Just the care and keeping of their new home cost a fortune. He could not lose his dream house, the one he'd lovingly built for his family. They were so happy there. Marco gulped, feeling his Adam's apple rise and fall. His stomach was sour. He sat at his desk and imagined scenarios of horrific ruin for the rest of the afternoon, each more terrifying than the previous one.

Home from the office, Marco entered his air-conditioned bedroom, and the contrast in temperature sent a chill up his spine. Why did Isa insist on keeping it so cold in here? He roasted at the office and froze at home.

Isa stood examining several piles of sorted clothing on the bed. She leaned her cheek toward him for a kiss.

Marco obliged and said, "Isa, amor. It's freezing in here."

"I know! Isn't it dee-vine?" She stretched out the word and flung her arms wide.

"More like alpine. Brrrr." He faked a shiver.

"Very funny." Isa threw him an annoyed look.

"What are you doing?" Marco shifted a pile of clothes to make room and sat on the edge of the bed, legs crossed.

"Going through this finery because some of it needs special cleaning." Isa held up a green silk gown. "Look, I spilled red wine on this one. I hope it can be salvaged."

"Why bother?" Marco shrugged. "Everyone who matters has already seen you in these clothes. You'll never wear them again."

Isa looked at him askance. "But others can, Marco. Plenty in San Juan have very little to wear."

Marco considered the small mounds of lush, colorful clothes.

How many of his hard-earned dollars were about to be discarded? Stomach acid singed his throat. Something had to be done.

"Why not sell them?" Marco asked.

"*Sell* them?" Isa laughed. "Wait, are you serious? Should I set up a stand on the corner like the children do to sell lemonade? Who's going to buy them? My friends?"

"I was just thinking of recouping the cost. That pile's probably worth a thousand dollars." Marco motioned to the clothes.

"What in the world has gotten into you, Marco?" Isa stared at him, frowning. "Since when are you such a tacaño?"

"I'm not a miser. I'm just trying to be smart about expenses." Marco's hands shook as he unbuttoned his shirt. So much for stealth when it came to Isa. He'd approached the topic as gently as a bull rushing toward a matador's red cape. But since he was in this deep, he decided to continue. "That includes *Letras Boricuas*, too."

"Tell me something, Marco." Isa lowered the blouse she was examining and looked at him, eyes narrowed. "Are we in trouble? Is Solemar doing alright?"

"Of course, we're not in trouble. What a question." Marco scoffed. "If there's one thing I excel at, it's making money."

"Well, that's good," she said. "Because Miguelito wants to learn to play the piano. He's going to need lessons and a piano for practicing."

"Jesus. Couldn't he have picked the guitar? How much does a piano cost?" Marco buttoned the casual cotton shirt he'd changed into and tried to temper his agitation.

"Shhh. Don't worry about it. He can practice at school, in the music room." Isa came toward him and placed a hand on his cheek. "No use buying a piano until we know whether he's really going to stick with it." She turned away from him and asked, "Have you seen the monstrosity of a house they're building on Calle Mariposa?"

Marco laughed. He knew Isa was trying to change the subject.

"It's the jíbaro version of the Taj Mahal," he said, going along.

"Money can't buy taste." Isa shook her head.

Marco nodded. He had plenty of taste. He just hoped he'd always have as much money.

Marco and Sammy closed the Solemar offices on Monday, December 15. Nationalist leader Pedro Albizu Campos, exiled for ten years in an Atlanta jail and later a New York hospital, was returning to Puerto Rico. Thousands were expected to meet his ship at the dock, and Old San Juan would be a circus. Getting work done would be impossible. And you never knew with Albizu. Bloodshed followed that man. It was safest for all Solemar employees to stay out of the fray altogether.

Marco spent the morning at home reviewing business ledgers on the living room couch. Just as his stomach was starting to growl for lunch, Isa walked into the room, turned the radio on, and leaned against the console to listen.

"Here at Sixto Escobar Stadium, we await the arrival of Pedro Albizu Campos, who is making his way from a Mass at San Juan Cathedral. I'm looking out at a boisterous crowd of at least 14,000 people," the radio announcer said. "It's standing room only here. Everyone's waving Puerto Rican flags with big smiles on their faces. The flags are everywhere, even on the trees. I'm told Albizu is almost at the stadium, so we're going to take a brief commercial break. Stay with WPRP."

It took Marco a few seconds to tune in. *Oh, for the love of God!*

"Turn that nonsense off," Marco said, surprised and displeased his wife wanted to listen to this drivel.

Isa shushed him with an index finger over her lips and sat on the other end of the couch. He sighed, and body temperature rising, got up to turn the volume down.

"Come on, Isa. I'm trying to work." He huffed back to the couch.

"Then go to the kitchen. As a publisher, I must hear all political views. It wouldn't hurt you to listen to someone other than Muñoz either," Isa said.

The damned magazine was putting ideas in her head.

"You know this guy's loco, right? You're about to listen to a crazy person. He's on his way from Mass, but if he's such a devout Catholic, how can he advocate murder?"

"Let's listen and find out. After all, Muñoz is no saint. What kind of man abandons his wife and children to have kids with another woman in front of the whole world? Nobody seems to think *that's* a scandal." Isa raised her eyebrows at Marco.

"Oh, please. Don Luis divorced Muna Lee and married Doña Inéz last year. It's all perfectly respectable," Marco said, though he didn't completely approve of El Vato's messy personal life.

"Ask Muna Lee if she agrees," Isa said archly.

Marco did not appreciate her tone and was about to answer when Isa held up her right hand, palm up and said, "Shush, the speech is starting. Are you going to listen or not?"

"Turn it up. Let's hear what the lunatic has to say."

I can't believe I'm listening to this.

"My name is Pedro Albizu Campos. You are my people, and this is our island," barked out Albizu in his raspy voice. The crowd roared for several minutes, and once it settled down, he continued, "It's not time for talk. It's time for action. The hour has arrived for the United States to withdraw its forces from Puerto Rico. Half a century of abuses is enough. Their technology is indeed more advanced. But it is also certain that, because of this, they are the semi-barbarians of humanity. They are like the perverse man with a pistol in his hands who faces a defenseless man. It is necessary to attack him to keep him from using the pistol."

"You see?" Marco asked, feeling redeemed. "He wants blood."

"You're right, and I don't agree with his methods, but he speaks the truth about our circumstances."

Marco rolled his eyes.

Albizu continued angrily, "Muñoz Marín has lost his mind if he says there is a democracy here. What supreme insolence to say that to our people. Let him stop being an instrument of destruction for the Puerto Rican nation. We shall stop him if necessary. Let him define himself. Is he a Yanqui or a Puerto Rican?" Again, the crowd cheered loudly.

If Marco listened to one more word, his head might explode.

"Okay, that's it. I can't take any more," he said, picking up his work and heading to the kitchen while Isa gave him a dirty look.

But strains of the speech reached Marco even in the next room; Albizu spoke for more than an hour, and Isa listened to every word. *Jesus*, thought Marco, *he's come to rile up the masses. He's come to kill. Even my wife is listening. God help us all.*

CHAPTER 25

- Isabela -
January to April 1948

Hot off the presses, the first issue of *Letras Boricuas*, January/
February 1948, arrived at Isa's office, and she looked upon it with
reverence, heart dancing in anticipation. She held the eight-by-ten-
inch publication, breathing deeply to take in the sweetly chemical
smell of freshly printed ink. It was real. It'd taken almost a year, but
she'd done it! Well, she and Antonio had done it. *Letras Boricuas*
now existed, and she knew it was good, maybe even great.

She opened the cover, which featured an illustration of the icon-
ic El Morro fortress, and turned the pages: table of contents, Editor's Letter explaining her vision for the magazine, and then all the
outstanding literary submissions and articles around the theme of
Puerto Rican culture. It fascinated Isa how, no matter their political
affiliation or race, Puerto Ricans were a nation strongly united by
culture. They were deeply proud of their shared heritage, customs,
language, folklore, food, and music. A roomful of people could be
loudly and passionately arguing their pro-independence, nationalist, or muñocista viewpoints but play a Rafael Hernández tune, and
they'd just as passionately stop mid-sentence and break out in song.

Isa and Antonio had chosen the broad theme of Puerto Rican
culture because they'd wanted to avoid divisiveness in the first issue,
a strategy to reel readers in gently. She leafed through the pages past
several short stories, two poems Julia de Burgos had sent from New
York (thanks to a friend of a friend), an essay by Ángel Ramos about
the importance of protecting the island's culture, a humorous piece
about how Spanish was once again the official teaching language in

public schools, and two poems by Antonio toward the back, because he'd refused better placement. Ángel had promoted the magazine in *El Mundo*, and it would hit newsstands in the morning. Cradling the issue in her hands, the fruit of her labor, was as thrilling as holding her newborn babies had been.

Isa and Antonio had started working on the second issue long before the first was finalized and had selected the more controversial theme of independence. The two sat in Isa's office late one January afternoon, discussing editorial options.

"We're skewing heavily toward pro-independence content. I'd like to be more balanced," Isa said, pressing her pen to her pursed lips. "What if we ask Muñoz Marín to write a piece for us? Let him explain why he wants to continue to work with the Americans? I, for one, would like a good explanation." Isa, proud of her gumption in assuming Muñoz would write for them, looked to Antonio for his reaction. Muñoz Marín wrote pieces for *El Mundo*, so why not for *Letras Boricuas*?

But Isa was taken aback by his instant outrage. "Absolutely not!" Antonio banged his hand on her desk, his face a cloud of dark fury. "Do not give that traitor a platform for his lies. Everyone bows at his feet, even though he's a common drug addict. It makes me sick."

"What are you talking about?" Isa smirked, amused at the thought of big old lumbering Muñoz Marín as a drug addict. She'd never heard anything so ridiculous.

"It's a well-known secret that Don Luis is very fond of the opium pipe, and when he's not smoking, he's pickling his brain in rum. Everyone knows it. They call him El Tecato de Isla Verde."

This was just too funny. "The Isla Verde junkie? Don't be ridiculous. How is that possible? The Americans wouldn't allow it."

"Maybe they like him that way. So they can control him."

Isa rolled her eyes. She disagreed with Muñoz and his cozy relationship with Washington, but that didn't make him a drug addict.

"Ay, Antonio. I don't know where you're getting your information, but you better check your sources. The things that come out of your mouth!" She shook her head. "We'll table Muñoz for now, but let's brainstorm who else we can ask."

Thanks to Ángel's promoting them in *El Mundo* and strong word-of-mouth buzz, the first issue sold out, and Isa hired a second part-time employee to deal with advertising sales. In the meantime, she'd begun to treasure her time with Antonio, particularly since she seldom saw Bea these days. Her friend continued to work full-time, despite having a toddler and another baby on the way. Their meetings were few and far between these days, and Isa missed her.

At least she had Antonio. Isa felt bright and alive when they bandied ideas around and discussed their pros and cons. He listened to her opinions instead of dismissing them like Marco. And when he challenged her, their debates awakened her and forced her to examine her beliefs and assumptions. Collaborating with Antonio was exhilarating.

And, truthfully, she enjoyed his physical presence, too. When he kissed her hello on the cheek, she'd always inhale for a pleasant whiff of his cedar aftershave with hints of bay rum. She felt a thrill when he touched her arm to make a point or looked at her a bit too intensely. Her heart did flips when they sat close together. Antonio never mentioned any women in his life, but surely, he didn't lack opportunities for female attention. He wasn't interested in a married woman and mother like her, and secure in this knowledge, she let herself flirt with him. Yet by the time they began work on the May/June issue, she'd allowed their flirtations and her fantasies to escalate. Was she being naughty? Maybe, but it was all very innocent.

One afternoon Isa and Antonio sat at her desk, side by side, reviewing proofs, Isa said, "I'm so glad we decided to place the motherhood essay near the front of the book," Isa said, pointing at the page. "Motherhood is revered in Puerto Rico, but mothers never admit that raising children can be mind-numbing at times."

"Is that how you feel?" Antonio asked.

"Not all the time," Isa said, leaning back into her chair and wondering how to explain motherhood to a bachelor. "But being at the mercy of a little person's needs can be exhausting. When they're babies, they take over your life."

"Yet I'm certain you're wonderful at it."

She appreciated Antonio's gallantry, but how would he know?

"I hope so. Sometimes I wonder." Isa mused. "I don't know what it's like to be raised by a mother. I had Abuela, and Connie later, but it can't be the same."

"What happened to your mother?"

Isa's usual response to this question was to say her mother died in childbirth and leave it at that. But Antonio's kind eyes showed genuine interest, and feeling the pull of his magnetism, she elaborated.

"She was a young servant at our house, María. She and my father supposedly fell in love, but when María got pregnant, she fled back to the mountains. She died in childbirth, and her mother dropped me off at Abuela's house, very dramatically, I hear. So now you know. I'm just a bastard who was almost a jíbara." Isa felt the blood rise to her face. The only other person she'd told this secret to was Marco.

"Don't tell me you're ashamed of your provenance." Antonio sounded surprised. For a second, he leaned forward to touch her, then seeming to catch himself, leaned back. "That has nothing to do with who you are."

Isa melted into his sympathetic eyes and craved his touch. The air between them sizzled. She wondered if he felt it, too.

"When your family avoids the subject, you grow up feeling shameful," Isa said, trying to keep her voice steady. "But what I really struggle with is that an accident of fate gave me a comfortable life. I could very well have been brought up in a wooden shack with very little. Why? Why did God decide that way?" Isa's puzzlement was genuine.

"God works in mysterious ways," Antonio said softly.

"A mystery it is," Isa said. "And one we can't solve today with all this work to do." She focused back on the proofs, trusting Antonio understood her need to diffuse the tension.

They continued to work in silence while Antonio rapidly bounced a pen off his left palm. The thudding annoyed her, and she was about to tell him to stop when he lost his grip on the pen, and it skittered across the proofs. Before she could move to retrieve it, Antonio leaned over to reach it, one arm behind her and one in front. Pen in hand, he turned toward her, eyes smoldering, lips parted, obviously ready for a kiss. *¡Dios mío!*

Titillated but horrified, face aflame, she abruptly rose and pretended to need something from the filing cabinet. When she sat back down, she edged her chair away from him, and neither of them acknowledged what had almost transpired. Isa called the meeting short, to Antonio's visible relief. After he left, her heart rate took ten minutes to slow back to normal.

She'd felt the sexual tension between them from the start, but there had also been a strict line separating them. She was a married woman! Did learning she was illegitimate embolden him to make a move? Perhaps, but the impetus didn't matter; his action propelled them into very different territory. She shivered. Antonio had wanted to kiss her. And why wouldn't he? She was still attractive and a woman with whom he could have intellectually rousing conversations. But she was also a married woman, the mother of two children, a good Catholic. Women of her class did not cheat on their husbands. Especially her, not after witnessing how years of Papi's infidelity destroyed his marriage and hurt her, her sisters, and Connie. She needed to get ahold of her emotions. She loved working with Antonio and did not want to give that up. Surely he'd gotten the message and wouldn't make any more romantic moves. In the future, she'd carefully avoid being in such close proximity to him.

But Isa couldn't control her mind. From that awkward moment on, Antonio dominated her thoughts and fantasies. What would it be like to come home to such a man, someone who considered her an intellectual equal? They'd have deep discussions that would lead to exciting and satisfying lovemaking. Isa imagined Antonio would be a thrilling lover. The thought of his warm skin on hers overwhelmed her with such desire she'd have to relieve herself, exploding in the strongest orgasms she'd ever experienced. She went through her days in a state of arousal, allowing herself to want him, even though having him was out of the question.

The sight of Antonio made her insides warm and quickened her breath. Her hands ached to feel the heat of his skin, and controlling herself in his presence was nearly impossible. She wanted him. There was no doubt about it. But how could she feel like this about Antonio and still love her husband? Marco no longer made her knees tremble with a kiss, and making love with him did not satisfy her physically, but she loved him. He was the father of her children and her partner in life.

Everyone thought she had the ideal husband—handsome, intelligent, successful, an excellent father to her sons. It was hard to believe, but she and Marco were wealthier than Papi had ever been. From the outside, her marriage appeared perfect. She hadn't even had to make money-stretching sacrifices for long, not beyond their second year of marriage. The road she'd expected would be fraught with financial worry had instead been awash with loneliness.

What little free time Marco had, he shared with the boys. She didn't begrudge them that; the boys needed their father more than she did. They were already seven and ten and worshiped Marco, became giddy and excitable when they saw him, craving his undivided attention. She felt a bit superfluous during those moments, a female outsider in their huddle of testosterone, so she'd leave them to read a magazine or take care of a pending chore.

Marco loved her. That wasn't the problem. He was as smitten as he'd been when they first met, always ready with a compliment about her style or beauty. He bought her extravagant gifts and proudly displayed her on his arm at social events, an adornment to round out his masculinity and success. But he'd never invited her to share in his work, as she'd first envisioned, relegated her to the role of dutiful wife and mother. And when he reached for her in the darkness of their bedroom, their lovemaking was always the same, as unsatisfying as the first time. Could you blame her for wanting more?

When the March/April issue turned a small profit, Isa called Antonio with the exciting news. That afternoon, after the two part-time employees had left for the day, he bounced into her office whooping, his smile threatening to split his face in two and twirled Isa around in a bear hug. Desire coursed through Isa's body, and her breath caught. Dizzy, she stumbled, and Antonio tightened his grip to keep her upright. He held her close, and this time Isa met his lips for a kiss. A cosmic explosion of ardor traveled through every nerve in her body, leaving her trembling and helpless. Like characters in a torrid romance novel, they tore each other's clothes off and finally, finally, bowed to their yearnings right there on the office rug.

Antonio's touch on her breasts sent electric shocks through her. She moaned in pleasure as his fingers found the special place between her legs and applied pressure in a steady circular motion. She felt for his penis, desperately needing to touch the rock-hard evidence of his yearning for her, and wrapped her hand around it. Antonio groaned as if the pleasure caused him pain. Isa stiffened under his hand, ready to orgasm when Antonio stopped stroking her. She gasped in momentary disappointment until he entered her and continued the steady rhythm, pressing his pelvis against hers, moving faster and faster until she exploded into a wave of such pleasure it was almost inconceivable.

Afterwards, spent and sweaty despite the air-conditioning, she was surprisingly unselfconscious. Nor did she feel guilt. Instead, she felt complete, joyful, calm. It was done. They'd opened Pandora's box. And she was certain they'd open it again.

PART
THREE

CHAPTER 26

- Marco -
April to July 1948

While Isa immersed herself in her magazine, Marco spent his days in a constant sweat about his finances. After their October meeting, he and Sammy agreed to forgo their salaries until the latest units were ready to market. Finding himself with no reserves, he figured he'd secure a short-term personal loan. When much to his shame and alarm he was denied, he realized how dire his financial circumstances had become. With no time to waste on self-pity, he'd put his ego aside and talked Sammy into asking Fomento's Teodoro Moscoso for help.

Officially the person working to bring industry to the island, everyone knew Moscoso was really in charge of Puerto Rico's overall economic development. Together with Muñoz, he was pushing to grant full tax exemption to any U.S. company that manufactured a product not previously produced on the island, an unprecedented enticement. Puerto Rico would boast twenty-four factories by the end of the year, and with the new incentive, that number was expected to double by the end of 1949. Best of all, workers needed housing, which Solemar provided, and since Moscoso couldn't afford to let one of San Juan's premier real estate development companies go under, he spoke with the Banco Popular executives on Sammy and Marco's behalf and bought them an extension on their loan until the new units could hit the market.

Marco's financial worries were compounded by Albizu Campos' continued rabble-rousing and his growing number of supporters.

He couldn't understand the man's appeal, and now Albizu threatened the peace at his beloved Upi, as if the Rio Piedras Massacre hadn't been enough. The student body and the administration were currently at odds over the students' desire to host an Albizu-run conference addressing the island's political status. Tonight, on the second day of April, Marco stood in front of his accounting class discussing the situation with his students.

"We've done everything by the book, Professor Soto," José Manuel Feliciano, one of his top students, said from his front row desk. His expression oozed earnestness.

"It's true," added another. "If it was Muñoz, they'd roll out a red carpet. But Albizu. Oh, no. Not welcome here." His voice dripped with resentment.

"And why should he be?" Marco countered, trying to keep his voice even. These young men's naiveté was astounding. "Albizu's constantly denigrating La Upi and calling for violence. His rhetoric dishonors the spirit and vision of this institution."

"Shouldn't he be allowed an opinion? Aren't universities supposed to respect free speech?" a latecomer asked as he entered the classroom and found a seat.

"But don't you think there's a difference between speech that peacefully communicates ideas and incendiary speech that provokes violence?" Marco stood tall and slid one hand into his jacket pocket to look professorial. He needed to dissuade them.

"Sometimes violence's the only way to achieve change," Feliciano said.

Marco was dumbfounded. If Feliciano could be brainwashed, there was no hope for the rest of them. He thought back to that bloody October day when he was still a student.

"As someone who hid in this very building during the Rio Piedras Massacre, I can assure you violence is no solution," Marco said. "Spilled blood just leads to more spilled blood."

"Albizu should still be welcome on campus," Feliciano said. "If Rector Benítez doesn't reverse his decision, we're calling a strike."

"Benítez should resign," a voice chimed in from the back. Marco bristled.

"Don't push him," Marco warned, wagging his finger at them. "Benítez won't hesitate to let you strike. He has before, and if it goes on for long, you could lose the work you've put in this term. Speaking of which, let's get started. Does anyone have questions about the assignment?" Marco had heard enough of their nonsense.

Marco thought of his students as he drove past a sad and empty UPR on the way to work the following month. The students, of course, had called a strike; they couldn't help themselves. But unlike past strikes, this one involved vicious confrontations and resulted in profound repercussions. Benítez had expelled more than four hundred, dissolved the Student Council, and closed the student newspaper. Now the university was locked down for the rest of the semester, just as Marco had warned his students might happen. What a pity.

Youth really was wasted on the young. The students had been so stubborn, and for what? To help canonize a murderer? Marco would teach his sons to know better as Papá had taught him. A bit later, as he circled the one-way streets in Old San Juan searching for a parking space close to the office, he passed the corner of Calle Cruz and Calle Sol. Albizu lived there above Bar Borinqueña, and his home served as the Nationalist Party headquarters. Their flag, black with a white potent cross, fluttered from the top of the two-story colonial building on the Calle Sol side. Marco watched as a young woman entered and shook his head. *Another fool jumps into the fray.* Thank goodness most of the populace supported Muñoz.

Papá would have admired Muñoz's respect for and rapport with the jíbaros, his push for a better life for them. The Popular Democratic Party slogan said it all: Bread, Land, and Liberty. Knowing he would have had Papá's blessing and because all facets of Muñoz Marín's policies spoke to Marco's ideological and financial interests, he'd donated time, knowledge, and what money he could spare to the man's campaign.

Muñoz had tapped Marco's expertise on several occasions as he crafted policies and strategies. This kept Marco abreast of any developments that could benefit Solemar. It was a win-win situation, and he'd struck a friendship with the man. The more Marco got to know Muñoz, the more supportive he became of the man and his politics.

It didn't hurt that Muñoz's policies also advanced Marco's agenda. Between returning GIs and new workers flocking to the city, Solemar began to enjoy brisk house sales, affording the company a much-needed cash influx. By the end of May, they were still not in the black, but at least they were making progress, and he could breathe a sigh of relief, albeit a small one.

In June, the well-regarded Dr. Francisco Susoni resigned as Speaker of the House and broke off with Muñoz and the PDP party, much to the shock of many, Marco included. Marco and Isa discussed the turn of events over breakfast the day after the announcement.

"Finally, someone stands up for the original ideals of this party," Isa said. "I agree with Susoni. We cannot forsake our quest for independence."

Isa's insistence on pursuing independence had become tiresome.

"There are plenty of PDP leaders who still support autonomy. The fight's not forgotten."

"But none of them are taking action, like Susoni," Isa said. "He's always said the only way to maintain our dignity as a people is by attaining independence, and now we can vote for that in November."

"Susoni's stuck in the old way of thinking. We need to move ahead under Muñoz's leadership."

"If Muñoz were a woman, you'd have married him." Isa rolled her eyes.

Marco briefly fantasized about a wife who agreed with him.

"By the way," Isa said. "I heard something very interesting about Don Luis. Did you know people say he's an opium addict?"

"That's a vicious lie, probably spread by Albizu and his Nationalist cronies to discredit the man," Marco said, feeling heat rise through his body. It was one thing for Isa to favor independence, quite another for her to spread lies about Muñoz. "Who's been putting these ideas in your head, anyway?" It was that writer Antonio and the *maldito* magazine. The one *he* paid for.

Isa sat back and crossed her legs. "I'm perfectly capable of forming my own opinions, Marco. I read the newspapers and listen to the radio, you know." Her tone was arch, as it had often been these past few months, ever since the magazine.

Isa forming her own opinions was exactly what Marco hoped to avoid. Wives should support their husband's politics and vote as their husbands did. Isa already leaned toward independence, and the last thing he needed was for her to become a Nationalist.

Marco watched his wife closely on July 25 while they listened to Albizu deliver a speech in Guánica over the radio.

"The U.S. needs to leave Puerto Rico. We want nothing to do with them," Albizu shouted over the airwaves. Was Isa actually nodding in agreement with this zealot? "If they don't, we have the right to sentence them to death. It's in the hands of the U.S. whether this will be resolved by peaceful means or by war."

"Ay, why does he always have to bring war into it?" Isa frowned. *Good.*

"The Yankee defenders say we are destined to always be a colony because we lack the natural resources of the U.S.," Albizu continued. "Yet the U.S. has exploited our natural resources with great success. If we are so poor, why deny us liberty?"

"See?" Isa asked, as if Albizu had stated the obvious and not a blatant distortion of the truth.

¡Carajo! The elections weren't until November 2. It was going to be a long three months.

That evening Marco reached for Isa in bed and pulled her toward him. His desire for her had never waned, even though her opinions were less than seductive these days. Whenever their connection felt tenuous, Marco initiated lovemaking to bridge the gap. It always made him feel better. He kissed Isa deeply and fondled her breasts over her nightgown. Isa kissed him back, fueling his yearning to become one with her, to completely possess her. Desperate for this communion, Marco gathered Isa's nightgown around her waist and pulled himself out of his pajama pants. Met with dryness, he pushed his way in and found his rhythm. Awash in pleasure, he quickly climaxed, and his body relaxed on top of hers. That was more like it.

Isa wiggled under him.

"Marco, please. I can't breathe." Isa tried to push him off.

"Sorry, amor. It's just I can't get enough of you." Marco kissed her, pulled out, and rolled over onto his back.

Isa's deep sigh was music to his ears, evidence she felt the same way. Marco drifted off into a contented slumber.

CHAPTER 27

- Isabela -
August 1948

Isabela, covered in a film of perspiration, arched her back and moaned at the pleasure of having Antonio's mouth between her legs. When she couldn't stand it for another minute, she pulled him up, guided him inside her, and bucked against each thrust, her mouth locked on his in a deep kiss. The motion was slow and steady, and soon, the tingle of sweet release began to course through her body. *Here it comes.* She groaned, eyes riveted on his. Seeing his face contort in pleasure always intensified her orgasm.

He lay on top of her, both too spent to move. Antonio's bedroom was sweltering, and the small fan by the window only moved the hot air around in circles, but she wished they could stay like this forever. Antonio made to move off her.

"Antonio, amor, no. Stay." She always called him by his proper name, even though most called him Toño, a moniker hardly suited for a writer, a poet of his caliber. Antonio was the name of a man who wove words into beautiful sentences that made readers weep. Antonio was the name of her lover.

"I need air, Isa. You've drained me, as usual," Antonio said, turning onto his back, eyes closed.

Isa raised herself on one elbow and studied him. She relished his toasted caramel skin, so rich compared to Marco's pale flesh. She admired his steely focus on attaining independence for his homeland, but after six months of being lovers, she knew little else about him. Antonio was a bit of an impenetrable wall. Every so often, he'd give her a glimpse of what lay beneath—his love of practical jokes, a weakness for his mother (like most Puerto Rican men), a crippling arachnophobia. Even his impersonal apartment offered few clues, functional save for the one framed photo taken of his family before his brother was killed.

What did Antonio do when he wasn't with her? Did he get together with friends to play dominoes? Probably not. The movement took up most of his time, and she suspected all his friendships were tied to it. Did he have a Nationalist girlfriend, then? Didn't he need more than what she could give him? He'd never asked, though, never pushed. Yes, he must have someone else.

Isa shook off a twinge of jealousy. She should be glad that Antonio was content with the status quo. He fed her intellect and spirit and only asked for a bit of time and attention in return. On the other hand, Marco expected her to give him every ounce of her being. But she and Marco had been through a lot together. They'd fought for their love, forged a life, and were raising two exceptional sons. She needed them both.

Isa grabbed the pack of Chesterfields on Antonio's night table, put a cigarette between her lips, and lit it. Another delicious thing she only did with her lover.

Antonio's eyes fluttered open. "Hello, beautiful," he said. "Give me one of those."

"Ah, I thought you were sleeping!" Isa handed him a cigarette and lighter.

"No, just resting." He sat up and smiled at her, tracing the side of her cheek with fingers that held the unlit cigarette. "God, you're beautiful." He paused for a beat and softly began to sing, *"Preciosa the llaman las olas del mar que the baña... Preciosa por ser un encanto, por ser un edén..."*

Isa blushed like a schoolgirl. "Ay, Antonio. That song is about the island, not me!"

Ignoring her protestations, Antonio continued to sing the beautiful Rafael Hernández bolero about Borinquen, its beauty; its Spanish, African, and Taíno heritage; and the unnamed tyrant who threatens it all with black malice. His deep voice grew stronger with each verse, melting Isa's heart like Gardel's crooning had so long ago. He ended with the lines, "*Preciosa, preciosa te llaman los hijos de la libertaa-aaa-aaaad,*" he flung his right arm out as he held the last note until his breath ran out.

Isa gave him a seductive look. "Your singing makes me sweat."

Antonio bowed his head, eyes twinkling. "Rafael Hernández taught me that song himself."

"Ha! Very funny," Isa said, refusing to fall for another of Antonio's jokes.

"No, really. I swear!" Antonio placed his hand over his heart. "My uncle went to school with him in Aguadilla before Hernández moved to San Juan to study music. They're still friends."

Isa's jaw hung open. "I can't believe you never told me that!" Another reminder of how little she knew this man.

Antonio shrugged. "I guess it never came up." He lit his cigarette and exhaled a long stream of smoke.

"What?! Have you lost your mind?" Isa gave him a playful slap on the chest. "He could write a piece for us, Antonio! I've told you about all the people *I* know!"

"Yes, but I despise most of them." Antonio wrinkled his nose, then turned pensive. "But you're right. Maybe Hernádez can write for us, expand on how the island is preciosa even sin bandera."

Isa knew Antonio referred to the Gag Law, the government's most recent effort to squash the independence movement. It banned the Puerto Rican flag, patriotic tunes, and even writing or talking about independence.

"At the very least, we can write a piece and refer to the song," Isa said. "I mean, how can they ban our flag? As U.S. citizens, shouldn't we enjoy freedom of speech?"

"The colonial master is a hypocrite." Antonio took a drag of his cigarette and blew it out forcefully before continuing. "You know what should be banned? That logo of a jíbaro Muñoz uses. What does he know about being a jíbaro?" The color on his face was rising.

"I know," sighed Isa. Antonio despised Muñoz as much as Marco admired him. All she ever heard from her men was Muñoz this and Muñoz that!

Antonio's face was getting redder by the second. "He sells them on labor laws and land reform and gets them to forget all about our political status. And that husband of yours. He's one of his biggest supporters, throwing money at him like it's candy."

Isa scowled. Antonio had tainted their time together by bringing up Marco.

"You know he has his reasons. I've told you about his childhood. And speaking of children," Isa rolled herself off the bed and stood. "I need to pick mine up at school." She dressed quickly, no longer bothering to hide the angry cesarean scar on her stomach, which Antonio said made her even more beautiful, and kissed him.

"Adios, belleza," he said, eyes fixed on the ceiling.

He was already lost to her, his mind on other matters. Isa closed the door to Antonio's second-floor apartment, just two blocks from the magazine offices on Ponce de León Avenue, and hurried to her car. It had rained while she'd been inside, one of those brief tropical afternoon downpours and the sidewalk smelled of steaming cement. The ride from Miramar to pick up her sons at Colegio San Antonio took long enough for Isabela to mentally transition from bohemian lover to respectable wife and mother.

Isa tried to compartmentalize her two existences. She became fully immersed when she played each role, keeping her other life at bay. It was simultaneously exhausting and exhilarating and the only way she could live with her actions. She'd followed in her father's footsteps but would not allow her deeds to tear her family apart. Discretion and care would keep her house of cards standing.

Isa pulled up to her son's three-story school on Barbosa Avenue. It was Miguelito's and Luisito's time now.

"Mami, Mami!" both her sons shouted as they got in the car, eight-year-old Luisito climbing over his older brother to sit next to her on the long front seat.

"Give me kisses, queridos," she said and gagged as she caught a whiff of the putrid stench that enveloped them. "¡Ave María, qué peste! You reek. Were you playing with those blasted gallitos again?"

The boys held gallito tournaments practically every day at recess. They collected carob seeds from the algarrobo tree, which looked like dates but were hard and not as sweet smelling. They'd carefully make a small hole in the seed, thread an arm's length of twine through the hole, and knot it securely. Then they'd draw a large circle in the dirt, their arena, and take turns trying to whack their opponent's gallito to death with theirs. The first one to destroy the other's gallito won. She had no problem with the game, but the seeds exuded a potent odor, a mix of cat urine and death.

"Sí, Mami. I beat Juan today, too!"

"Finally! Good for you. But next time, please wash your hands afterward, and don't bring the gallitos into the car. Don't you smell that? I'm suffocating from the stink. Throw them away *outside* when we get home." She wished she still carried Vicks in her purse as she used to during her El Fanguito days.

As soon as Isabela pulled into the driveway, the boys ran to throw their gallitos into the outdoor metal garbage barrel and hurried into the house, hungry for a snack. Isa lingered in the driver's seat and studied her house. Everyone admired "The House That Marco Built," as she thought of it. She understood this house was tangible evidence of Marco's radical leap upward. The man who'd grown up using an outhouse could now choose from three fully equipped bathrooms. He treasured living here more than she despised it; as sacrifices went, this one was bearable. At least he'd installed air conditioners in all the bedrooms. She couldn't complain about that.

Isa jumped at a loud honk behind her. A glance in the rearview mirror told her Julia was pulling into the driveway. Again. Lord knew how or why Eduardo, a sweet man, not only put up with Julia but doted on the woman. For a time after getting married, Julia had been almost bearable. The boys cherished their Titi Julia, who always brought treats and played with them tirelessly. But when she couldn't have children of her own, she'd reverted to her bitter ways and attempted to undermine her with Miguelito and Luisito. And she was always visiting. Always.

Isa rolled her eyes, took a long deep breath, plastered on a smile, and exited the car to greet her sister-in-law.

"Hola, Julia. What brings you around today?" The two women exchanged cheek pecks.

"Bueno, Isa, I spoke with Marco this morning, and he told me he was coming home at five, so I'm here because I haven't seen him in days."

"Well then, come in and say hi to the boys." Isa maintained her forced smile. Marco's pending early arrival was news to her and ignited the core of anxiety always lurking in her chest. With Julia visiting, she wouldn't have time for a quick shower. But she couldn't greet her husband with her lover's handprints still burning on her skin!

They entered through the yellow-tiled kitchen, where Miguelito and Luisito sat chomping on Vienna sausages and Sultana soda crackers, first and fourth grade homework papers spread around them on the Formica dinette table.

"Titi Julia! Titi Julia!" they exclaimed, bouncing on their padded chairs as if they hadn't just seen her three days ago. Julia gave them each a hug and a pilón from her purse.

"No candy before dinner!" Isabela said. Like their mother, the boys adored the cylindrical raspberry-flavored lollipops dotted with sesame seeds.

"Ay, Mami. Pleeeeease," Miguelito implored while Luisito gave her his adorable pleading eyes look. But Isa was immune.

"No. Give me those. You may have them after you eat." Isa held her hand out, and both boys obeyed her command.

"Ay Isa, there's nothing wrong with a little treat. Why are you so mean?" Julia said, pouting.

Isa tamped down the anger rising through her chest and replied, "There are rules because I know what's best for my children. *My* children, Julia."

"There's no need to get persnickety." Julia sneered at Isa before turning around to see what was simmering on the stove. "And what smells so good? Oh, Carmen's gandinga!"

"¡Ay, fó! Not gandinga," Luisito said, scrunching his face in disgust while Miguelito nodded in agreement. "Who would invent a liver stew? It's disgusting. And it tastes worse than gallitos smell. I don't want gandinga!" Luisito crossed his arms in front of his chest, earning a warning look from Isa.

"Gandinga for dinner!" Marco's voice cut through the tension as he entered the kitchen from outside. "You must stay for that, Julia."

"Papi! Papi!" Both boys flung themselves at Marco for hugs, their gandinga aversion forgotten. Isa's head started to pound. Great. Now Julia's visit would last all night. She opened one of the kitchen drawers and rummaged for the bottle of aspirin.

"You're home early, Marco," she said to her husband, trying to keep her distance until she had a chance to perform some quick ablutions. Isa wondered whether he could see her heart hammering in her chest.

"Even I need a break once in a while." He moved toward her, arms extended, saying, "Aren't you glad to see me?"

"Of course, amor." Isa grabbed two aspirin and scampered toward the kitchen door. "It's just my head is killing me. Let me splash some cold water on my face. I'll be right back."

In the bathroom, her hands shook violently as she tried to bring water up to her face, and what water made it that far mingled with her tears. *That was close!* If Marco had reached her, he would have smelled the sex on her, no question. How confused he'd be. He'd take a while to figure out she'd cuckolded him; the option was not remotely on his radar, not after all the times she'd made *him* promise not to cheat on *her*. She imagined the pain and hurt on his face, followed by fury and, eventually, sorrow. That dichosa Julia almost got her caught.

Isa dried her face and ran a wet washcloth over her body, paying particular attention to the area between her legs. She also needed to change her clothes, but would that seem suspicious? She had no choice. Quickly, she threw them in the hamper and donned a house-dress. She'd blame the need for comfort on her headache.

As she rejoined her family in the kitchen, Marco reached for a bottle of rum in the cupboard.

"¿Cuba Libre?" Marco asked.

"No, thank you. Not with this headache," Isa said.

"Julia?"

"Well, since you're offering," Julia coyly responded.

Oh, God. It would be a long evening.

CHAPTER 28

- Marco -
August 1948 to January 1949

Marco approached Solemar's offices, noting with satisfaction that he hadn't seen the corner beggar in months. He was anxious to get an update from Sammy on unit sales, which had been on an upswing in the last quarter. They were both hoping the trend indicated a permanent shift in their liquidity. Things were looking up. In a speech the previous month, Muñoz had lauded Fomento's work saying, "We are lifting ourselves by our own bootstraps." The message of hope and resilience had resonated, and Puerto Rico's ongoing turnaround was now known as Operation Bootstrap.

"Buenos días, Marisol," he greeted the receptionist. Marisol stood up to greet him and offered to get him some coffee, which he gladly accepted. He ran into Sammy in the hallway, who'd also just gotten himself a café.

"Buenos días, Sammy. Tell me, what is the definition of 'nothing'?" Marco didn't wait for a response. "An empty sausage with no skin on it. Ha!"

"Is that what you spend your brain power on when you're not here?"

"Just helping Miguelito with an assignment. You must admit it's brilliant." Marco cocked his head and spread his arms wide.

"If you say so," Sammy joked with a smile.

Marco rubbed his hands together. "What's going on today, compadre?"

"I'm glad to see you in a good mood because I'm about to make it even better."

"Well, don't just stand there. Let's go to my office." Marco led the way and sat at the small table near his desk. Marisol came in with the coffee, and he thanked her with a wink and a smile before taking a sip. "Ahhhh. Nectar of the gods. ¿Pues, qué pasa?"

"We are officially in the black, my brother." Sammy threw a report on the table and grinned.

"No! We did it. Did we do it?" Marco clapped his hands together and held them in prayer mode in front of his face for a few seconds before exuding a deep sigh of relief when Sammy nodded.

"With Fomento's help. And Moscoso says more factories are coming. We bet on a winning horse. Operation Bootstrap is just what the island needed!" Sammy rapped his knuckles on the desk and smiled broadly.

"And the bank is happy?"

"They are dying to lend us more money," Sammy laughed. "But I think we should divest some assets before taking out any new loans."

"The apartment buildings?"

"I know you're sentimental about El Comienzo and the others, but it's time. We're in the housing development business now, not the apartment rental business."

Marco sighed again. "I know. You're right. Let's get what we can for them and focus on the future. We're living in a time of opportunity, Sammy!"

His partner looked as relieved and excited as Marco felt. One thing was certain: Muñoz needed to win the election and become governor if prosperity was to continue. His biggest competition was the just-announced PIP candidate, Dr. Francisco Susoni, the former PDP bigwig and friend of Muñoz. He was a sober and well-regarded statesman, not a madman like Albizu, and the large PDP contingent who favored independence might vote for him, Isa included.

"P'alante, like Muñoz preaches," Sammy said, interrupting Marco's reverie.

"That's right, hermano. Forward we go!"

In early September, when Muñoz asked Marco to accompany him on a campaign visit to the mountains of Yabucoa, Marco readily agreed. The vast majority of jíbaros were still struggling and needed to hear a positive message. The motorcade headed out early Saturday morning, and Marco tried to hide his bruised ego at not being invited to ride with Muñoz.

After two quick pit stops in Caguas and Arroyo, they finally passed the sugarcane fields and refinery on the outskirts of Yabucoa and arrived in town mid-morning. Tío, his cousin Nando, who was now the town doctor, and other local leaders joined them as they headed up to the mountains to visit several barrios. Marco hadn't been to his hometown in months. He breathed deeply and swore the air tasted like grass, it was so fresh. He missed living in this lush landscape, so much beauty at his doorstep. But beauty had come with poverty, and he'd chosen to make his fortune in the city. Life was full of compromises.

In Barrio Calabazas, they abandoned their cars and set off on foot over dirt paths, the only way to reach the wooden shacks dotting the countryside. The jíbaros clamored to set eyes on Muñoz Marín and to shake his hand. He wasn't much to look at with his sad sea lion face, wrinkled white linen suit, and ever-present cigarette, but clearly, he connected with these country people.

Marco stood next to Tío as Muñoz Marín, atop a wooden crate, delivered an impromptu stump speech to a group of about thirty men and women who'd gathered around.

"Compatriotas, four years ago, I asked you to lend me your vote for senator instead of selling it to the opposition. I asked you to vote for justice because justice is worth much more than two dollars, and so is your dignity. And you listened. I also told you that if you were not satisfied with my work, you could simply take your vote away and give it to someone else next time. Well, I hope you don't do that. I hope you see the great strides we've made to push Puerto Rico's economy forward. But there is still much work to be done, and it supersedes the question of our political status. We need to improve the standard of living for all Puerto Ricans before we worry about independence. We need to make sure you're paid a fair wage so there is bread on every plate. We need to make sure you have an opportunity for better housing and access to doctors. And we must educate our children because they are our future. You already know that. Change takes time and effort, like climbing a mountain. But if we work together, we will do it. ¡Jalda Arriba! Up the hill!"

The audience clapped enthusiastically. One craggy-faced man with protruding ears offered Muñoz Marín a large bunch of green plantains; others gave him fruits and even a live chicken. Muñoz graciously accepted what these humble people offered; refusing the gifts would be insulting. Marco couldn't help tearing up and pretended to wipe sweat off his brow as he surreptitiously dabbed at his eyes. He wished Papá was standing next to him, experiencing this scene. Marco missed him viscerally just then as if he had a hole in his gut. Judging from Tío's rueful expression, his uncle was thinking about Papá too.

The contingent of politicians and townspeople moved on to the Aguacate and Guayabota Barrios. Marco proudly carried the PDP flag depicting the profile of a jíbaro wearing a pava hat in red against a white background. They sang the ¡Jalda Arriba! party anthem, a march with a peppy drum and trumpet introduction.

What a rewarding and emotional day. He wished Isa had been there, but she'd refused to come. Surely she would have been impressed with Muñoz Marín's rapport with the people. Marco was confident his candidate would win the jíbaro vote. A Muñoz win at the polls would benefit the people as well as his business. What could be better?

Although Marco hadn't been worried about Muñoz's chances, he still breathed a sigh of relief on November 2 when his candidate, with a whopping sixty-two percent of the vote, became the first elected governor in Puerto Rico's history. His election ensured that industry would continue to flock to the island, serve as the backbone of their new self-supporting economy, and push Puerto Rico further into modernity. The housing boom would continue. Muñoz would honor his campaign pledge to improve worker conditions and provide better health care and housing for the poor. Marco was thrilled to be invited to the January inauguration and to the many parties, picnics, and beach outings that followed.

He was even happier to give Isa carte blanche for a new wardrobe without feeling any financial angst. Marco had a pretty good idea that she hadn't voted for Muñoz; she'd been down since the election. Her joy at Muñoz's win felt forced, as if she was happy that Marco was delighted but not that Muñoz won. He hoped the inaugural speeches and celebrations would help change her point of view.

The invitation to the inauguration warned guests to arrive early. Huge crowds were expected to watch the parade and listen to the governor deliver his speech from a grandstand in front of the Capitol building. When Marco arrived with Isabela at eight in the morning, he was surprised to see hundreds of people already lined up along the parade route. He escorted Isa to their grandstand seats and said a little prayer to God that she would be in a pleasant mood throughout the heat of the day. He appreciated her effort to be one of the most stylish women present, stunning in her pale pink linen peplum suit with wide lapels and a gold and pearl brooch.

"Isa, mira, there's David Rockefeller and his wife," Marco discretely whispered, thrilled that his wife was dressed more fashionably than Mrs. Rockefeller.

Isa waited a few seconds before glancing where Marco indicated. "You're more impressive," she said, shrugging. Marco smiled. The woman could stroke his ego, but he could tell she was a bit dazzled by their company, as was he. The Catholic Bishop of San Juan, the head of Macy's in New York, and several leaders of the top mainland banks were all in attendance. He was a long, long way from the hills of Yabucoa.

The festivities began promptly at ten, a highly unusual occurrence in Puerto Rico and perhaps a harbinger of changes to come, hoped Marco. Chief Justice Ángel R. Jesus administered the oath of office, and flanked by his wife and daughter, the elected governor was sworn in. Muñoz then addressed the throngs of people filling every available space on Ponce de León Avenue, all dressed in their Sunday best. Most wore hats or hoisted umbrellas to protect themselves from the sun's heat on this splendidly tropical day.

Muñoz addressed the island's political status several times during his speech. "The colonial system will not only disappear in Puerto Rico," he said, "It will do so with vertiginous speed."

At these words, Isa expelled an audible breath through her nose as if scoffing at Muñoz.

A mortified Marco turned to his wife, eyes wide, and whispered, "Shhh." He looked around nervously, but nobody seemed to have noticed. To Marco's relief, Isa remained quiet until Muñoz finished, and they held hands during the parade that followed. An abundance of floats decorated in themes ranging from agriculture to nature to education passed by. Many celebrated the social programs already at work on the island. Beauty queens waved from convertibles. Military units marched, policemen rode motorcycles, equestrians trotted by on beautiful pasofino horses, dance troupes performed, and fire engines streamed along.

The crowd roared its appreciation and waved PDP flags for the six hours it took this showing of Puerto Rican pride to stream by. Marco thought back to the view of Yabucoa from the church tower after San Felipe, how his world had been destroyed that day. Now he was privileged to behold all that was great about his country, his Borinquen. The island's rich culture, natural beauty, and generous people were unparalleled. *We are ready. We are ready to show the world how exceptional we are.*

CHAPTER 29

- Isabela -
May 1949

On her way home from work, Isa motioned to the fruit vendor at a red light and bought a bag of guavas. Her head ached, and she needed a treat. Successfully editing a magazine, raising two active sons, running a household, and juggling two men who pulled her in opposite directions wore her thin.

Attending Muñoz's inauguration festivities with Marco in January had been particularly difficult. Her husband had been ecstatic, practically salivating at Muñoz's vision for the island. Isa suspected Marco's rapture was rooted in the money he was poised to make and less in the idea of creating a better life for his people.

She'd dressed up and stepped out on his arm, pretending to enjoy the parties, pretending to approve of the exultant throng so confident in the promise of Muñoz Marín's leadership. San Juan vibrated with energy and optimism. How could people be so blind? Couldn't they see that continuing to work with the Americans meant they'd remain a colony? Puerto Rico needed to take charge of its own destiny.

The January 24 issue of *Life* magazine had featured a multipage article gushing about the inauguration titled, "A New Puerto Rico Shows Off." It still graced their living room coffee table; she was surprised Marco hadn't had it gold-plated. The article made her all the more determined to ensure *Letras Boricuas* provided a counterpoint to the Yanqui propaganda.

Isa pulled into her driveway, and with a sigh, summoned the last of her energy to heave her body out of the car.

"Carmen, look at these guavas," Isa entered the kitchen, holding up the paper bag overflowing with the greenish-yellow fruit. "I bought them from that guy at the traffic light. Aren't they beautiful?"

"Las cosas te entran por un oído y salen por el otro. How many times have I told you to stop buying food on the street?" Carmen watched with disapproval as Isa rinsed a guava in the sink. "You don't know where those came from. They're probably full of worms. If you want guavas, I'll get you some en la plaza de colmado."

Isa bit into the fruit and closed her eyes with pleasure. She savored the sweet pulp while a trickle of juice traveled down her chin. Her bite revealed the fruit's coral meat, and she held it up to Carmen, "See? No worms."

"Fine, now get out of the kitchen," Carmen shooed her away. "But quietly. I think Marco's napping on the couch."

Isa nodded, finished the guava, and washed her hands. As she pushed the swinging door into the living room, the boys ran in from the side garden, loud as a herd of horses. Miguelito jumped on Marco, supine on the sofa, face covered with the March/April 1949 issue of *Letras Boricuas. Huh*, thought Isa. *He's actually reading it.*

Marco, jolted awake, grabbed Miguelito and tickled him into absolute helplessness.

"Boys, settle down. You woke your father up. Go do something quiet. Preferably outside." Isa pointed toward the garden.

"Sí, Mami," Luisito said, bolting back out of the house, Miguelito on his heels.

"Sorry, Marco. I just got home, or I'd have kept them outdoors," Isa said, perching herself on the sofa's edge.

Marco yawned and rubbed his eyes. "It's fine. I just closed my eyes for a minute."

Isa gave him a skeptical look. "Admit it, Marco. My magazine puts you to sleep."

"No, no, no! You know I love it," Marco scrambled to sit up and brushed his cowlick off his forehead. She cherished that cowlick. It let her imagine Marco as a boy.

Isa closed the magazine and placed it on the coffee table. "Don't torture yourself, querido. You don't have to read it. Plenty of others do." She teased him, eyes shining.

"I can't complain about that! Who knew you'd be turning an actual profit? My publishing tycoon wife." Marco grinned. Joking with him felt good, like the old days. She watched him lean over, pick up the issue, and flip through it. "But tell me, are your readers all independentistas?" He was serious now, piercing her with his eyes.

Isabela's neck muscles tensed. Of course, Isa hadn't told Marco she'd voted for the PIP's Susoni, but he probably suspected it. He hadn't asked her outright, probably didn't want to know for sure. To the world, they presented as a muñocista couple, and she did nothing to make people think otherwise.

"You know I publish many views," Isa said, matter-of-fact.

"Sure. Many independentista views," Marco said. "You may not see it, but Antonio's politics influence your content. Aren't you worried about the Gag Law?"

"The government doesn't enforce that stupid law. And if they arrest anyone, I doubt I'll be the first choice. Maybe someone named Albizu."

"Well, I wouldn't be surprised if you have a carpeta," Marco mused. "I'm sure Antonio does."

Rumor had it the FBI was amassing information and creating thick files about people suspected of favoring independence. Antonio had seen the FBI men at Nationalist events, wearing dark suits, roasting in the heat inside their black Fords, making a note if anyone so much as burped. Did they have a carpeta on her? How exciting! But her glee was fleeting as she realized her carpeta would include her relationship with Antonio. She'd ponder this quietly later. Time to get Marco off the subject. Let him think she was unconcerned.

"I hope I do! People brag about having them. Even Muñoz has one. Maybe you do, too, professor," Isa laughed. "Don't worry so much."

"Of course, I worry. You are the mother of my children. You can't go to jail. They don't have manicures there."

"Oh, whatever will I do, then?" Isa put one hand on her forehead and fell backward on the couch. Marco leaned in to kiss her as the boys sprinted back inside.

"Ewwwww," they said in perfect unison at seeing their parents kissing and made an about-face back out the door.

Isa lay awake in bed that night, anxieties spiraling in her head. She hadn't expected the Independence Party candidate to win the governorship, but to only get ten percent of the vote had been discouraging. She worried that the devastating loss would cement Antonio's belief that independence could only be won through revolution. Why did the Nationalists insist on playing with fire? Why couldn't they be more reasonable and team up with the PIP, generate power in numbers? Plus, Puerto Rico's history of gunning down Nationalists meant Antonio was always in danger. She couldn't bear to lose him the same way he'd lost his brother. Isa hadn't made much progress chipping away at Antonio's wall, had been unable to peel back his layers. Yet what he gave her was enough, necessary. But if the authorities were watching Antonio, was she also in danger? She probably did have a carpeta detailing her affair. Had she selfishly put her family in harm's way? Oh, God! Her mind reeled.

She finally drifted off to sleep, only to toss and turn all night.

The next day, Isa drove down Ponce de León Avenue to her office, intent on discussing her carpeta worries with Antonio. While stopped at a red light, she spotted her father standing frozen on the sidewalk, staring at nothing, eyes vacant. She'd seen him like this, wandering aimlessly in the streets on several occasions. It gutted her. Papi didn't know what to do with himself. Too old to start a new enterprise and too proud to work in someone else's, he'd become lost. Isa had ramped up her efforts to convince him to move in with them, but he staunchly refused. A man could go mad without a purpose, walking with no destination day after day. At least at her house, the boys would provide a distraction. She sighed in frustration and did not signal to him.

Alone at the *Letras Boricuas* offices that afternoon, Isa forced herself to concentrate on editing a short story about a jíbaro who makes a deal with the devil in exchange for a better life for his daughter. Art imitating life.

"Look at this. They love him," Antonio bellowed as he strode into her office, holding aloft the latest issue of *Time*, his face a contorted ball of anger. He flashed the magazine in Isa's face before throwing it on the floor. Startled, Isa jumped in her chair.

"Those pendejos put him on the cover and idolized him," Antonio said. "'Man of the People,' my ass. Not *my* people."

"What are you talking about? Let me see." Isa stretched her arm out and wiggled her fingers.

Antonio picked up the magazine and handed it to her. To Isa's surprise, an illustrated portrait of Muñoz graced the cover, complete with his cheerless, elongated face and messy hair. Isa leafed through the pages to find the article.

"I'll save you the time," Antonio said. "It's a love letter. He's making Puerto Rico a better place to live for the jíbaro. Sure, that's why people are moving to New York in droves." Antonio's tone was bitter. "Oh, and let's not forget his brilliant plan to bring industry here, where companies can pay our people less for the same work."

"A lot of what this says is true, though," Isa said as she scanned the article. "There *have* been improvements."

"It doesn't matter what he's done because he's a traitor," Antonio said roughly. "The ends don't justify the means. You know who belongs on this cover? Albizu. El Maestro should be the one applauded for staying true to his people. Albizu on the cover of *Time*. Ha! That'll be the day."

"Antonio, calm down," Isa rose from behind her desk and embraced her lover, softly stroking the back of his neck. "Shhh. Shhh. You're going to give yourself a heart attack." She tilted her head toward his and kissed him softly on the lips. Antonio pulled her in closer and kissed her back, gently at first and then deeply. Isa's desire was ignited, and God help her, they made love on the office rug like the first time, obliterating any thought of carpetas.

Afterward, Isa dozed off and woke to find Antonio standing over her holding a paper cup that emitted the sweet earthy aroma of well-made Puerto Rican coffee. "I went to get you un cafecito, mi bella Isabela," he said.

Isa smiled broadly, reached for the cup, and resolved not to ruin the afternoon with more talk of politics. "How did you know that's exactly what I need?" she asked. "You read my mind like the genie in *Thief of Baghdad*. Did you see that movie? He was a trickster."

Antonio waved her comparison away and sat down on the floor by her, his face a mask of seriousness. "Isa, there's something I need to tell you."

"Oh, that does not sound like good news." Isa braced herself for a discussion about their carpetas.

"I'm afraid it isn't. Look, I'm working on a story for the paper about the living conditions in some of the apartment buildings in San Juan and Rio Piedras. Your husband's El Comienzo is on the list. The tenants say it's infested with roaches and mice, and by the looks of it from the outside, I believe it."

Isa's body relaxed, glad the issue wasn't political and certain Antonio's information was incorrect. She shook her head. "No, that can't be true. Marco only renovated it ten years ago. It was his first baby. He takes care of it."

"Drive by on your way home."

"No, Antonio," Isa said. "Marco does right by his people."

Antonio laughed. "Do you really believe those little cement bunkers he calls homes are right for the people?"

"They're better than wooden shacks."

"Go spend a day in one of those cubes. You'll flee in horror at the lack of air circulation."

"They're decent homes." Isabela put her underthings and stockings back on. She didn't want to continue this conversation.

Antonio went to her and kissed her on the cheek. "Take a look at the building, Isa."

Frowning, Isa batted him away. "Ay, Antonio. You're like a dog with a bone."

"I know what I know," he said as he walked out the door.

Just what she needed, a new worry. Damn Antonio. But he'd planted a seed, and now she'd have to see if what he said was true. She fumed at her desk for several minutes before deciding to abandon her work, grab her purse, and leave. During the ride to Rio Piedras, she worked herself into a frenzy, alternating between being furious at Antonio for inventing lies about Marco and wanting to kill Marco for betraying their dream of improving the lives of Puerto Ricans. Her thoughts went back and forth until she rounded the corner of Calle Parque and faced El Comienzo.

Well, it didn't look that bad. It certainly wasn't falling apart like Antonio made it sound. Isa pulled over across the street from the building. It wasn't in great shape, though, either. The off-white paint was dingy, and a spray of black mold burst from above the entrance to the roof. The once bright white paint on the wrought-iron balcony grills had peeled off in strips, leaving behind rusted pieces that bled burnt orange rivulets down the building's facade. She imagined the indoor areas were no fresher. The entrance door hung loose, and a rather large pile of garbage sat in front of it. No wonder they had roaches. Where were the garbage cans for the tenants?

A young woman ushered two boys out of the building. They looked to be about three and five years old. The mother took their hands and led them around the garbage, admonishing them not to step on it. That could have been her with Miguelito and Luisito. It would have broken her heart to bring up her boys in a building like this. So dirty and probably unhealthy. What if one of those boys had asthma like Rosie? This building was a disgrace. Isa clenched her hands on the steering wheel. How could Marco allow this? So much for making life better for his compatriots. What a hypocrite.

Isa's stomach twisted itself into a knot, and her head pounded.

She'd wondered about Marco's motives, but she'd never had reason to question his integrity, had always been centered on the belief that her husband was a good man doing work that improved life for others. The houses he built were no palaces, but at least they were new and clean. People seemed to love them, and they sold so quickly that Solemar couldn't keep up with the demand. But what if he was cutting corners with those homes, too? Were those houses destined to crumble? Could they survive a hurricane? He, of all people, should know the dangers of poorly built homes.

Isa started her car and pulled into the road, the drive home a blur. She told Carmen she wasn't feeling well, took two aspirin, and lay down on her bed to wait for Marco. She'd find out what was going on, and she'd find out today.

CHAPTER 30

- Marco -
May to December 1949

Marco glowed with optimism on his drive home from work. Since deciding to focus on the construction side of their business, he'd put aside his nostalgia and sold El Comienzo and the other apartment buildings. They'd exchanged final papers the week prior, and to his and Sammy's surprise, had even made a small profit.

On a whim, he decided to take the family out for dinner, maybe to that new restaurant down the street from the house, La Cueva del Chicken Inn. Such a funny name. The boys loved the low ceiling, replete with white stalactites that made it feel like a cave, and couldn't get enough of their new favorite food, pizza. Marco imagined other restaurants would start making it soon since it had become a huge sensation. A simple food, yet so delicious. Maybe he should invest in a pizza restaurant, he thought, pulling into his driveway. Just what he needed—another venture. He shook his head. *Stick to real estate, Marco.*

He burst into the kitchen where Carmen was preparing dinner and the boys were doing homework and exclaimed, "Carmen, put those pork chops away. We're going out to dinner!"

"Pizza, pizza!" shouted Luisito, while his brother chimed in, "Papi, can we get pizza?"

"Yes, pizza for everyone! Where's your mother?"

"She's lying down," Carmen answered. "She came home with a splitting headache."

"Let me see if I can cure her," Marco said, moving toward the bedroom.

As he left, Carmen mumbled under her breath, "Ave María, pero que Dios aprieta pero no ahoga."

"I heard that, Carmen!" Marco said. "God is rewarding, not testing you. Just think of all the work you've already done for tomorrow night's dinner."

Marco quietly opened the bedroom door, not wanting to disturb Isa if she'd fallen asleep. He found her wide awake, sitting on top of the light blue satin bed cover, her back against the padded headboard, legs stretched out and crossed at the ankles, puffing on a cigarette. Acrid smoke invaded his nostrils.

"Are you *smoking*?" Marco couldn't hide his shock.

Isa glanced down at the hand holding her cigarette and calmly answered, "Yes, it looks like it."

"Since when do you smoke, querida?" Marco let out a nervous laugh.

"What do you care? Anyway, it helps when I have a headache." She flicked the ashes into the heavy, cut glass ashtray she'd grabbed from the living room. It already held several extinguished cigarette butts.

"Carmen said you're not feeling well." Marco chose to ignore the first part of her statement.

"I've certainly been better." Isa raised one eyebrow, took a long drag on her cigarette, and blew the smoke out audibly. He racked his brain to figure out what he'd done to displease her. Isa did not get mad often, but when she did, it could be epic. She still had a bit of the old actress in her. He approached the bed, intent on fixing a pillow behind her back that was sliding downwards. Anything to soften her up.

"Don't you come near me, you miserable liar." Marco recoiled from Isa's aggressive hostility, her words like venom in his ears.

"Isa, amor, what's the matter? Why are you so upset?" He stood by the bed, truly at a loss.

"I drove by El Comienzo today." Isa stared him down the same way she stared down their sons when they misbehaved. So she'd seen the building's condition and wanted to reprimand him. A pang of shame quickly turned into resentment. She had a nerve; Marco already had a mother. He was willing to put up with a lot from Isa, but he was still the man of the house, and he would not be scolded like a child. He went on the offensive.

"What were you doing in Rio Piedras?"

"What difference does that make?" Isa took a drag and blew it out. "The point is those tenants are living in a slum. How can you allow that?"

"Isa, we sold El Comienzo last year." What was a little white lie when it came to the timing? "We've sold all our rental buildings to focus solely on new construction."

Isa squinted her eyes at him and pursed her lips. "What condition were they in when you sold them?"

"They were fine, just as always." Marco prayed that his saintly expression would lend his words credibility.

"I don't believe you." Isa crushed the end of her cigarette in the ashtray.

"I admit some of the buildings were a bit tired, but they certainly weren't slums."

"I don't know, Marco. You've been building little cement bunkers and calling them houses. It stands to reason you also stopped caring about your tenants."

The audacity! He was seething inside but played it cool. Marco raised his right palm, "I swear it. And I'm hurt that you'd think I'd let my tenants live in squalor. Do you really see me as that kind of man?" Marco cast his eyes down and shook his head.

He could feel Isa's eyes on him as she weighed whether to accept his explanation. Silence hung in the air for several beats until she finally said, "Maybe not completely, but don't pretend you haven't changed. You're not as sympathetic to the poor as you used to be."

"What are you talking about? I've dedicated my career to making this a better island for everyone." Marco allowed his frustration to tinge his words. Why was Isa being so unreasonable?

She looked at him, still clearly skeptical. "You swear you treated those tenants well?"

"I swear it." Marco sat down on the bed, held out his arms, and said, "Come here."

Isa acquiesced to the hug, but she stank of cigarettes, and he pulled away. "What's with the smoking?"

"It's nothing. I don't even know why I lit up. I won't do it again." She seemed abashed.

"Well, then. Let's air this room out. It smells like an ashtray." Marco started cranking the glass jalousie windows open. "And, for your information, people love the little houses we build. It's the first time most buyers can own a home, and I'm happy to give them that opportunity. Not everyone can live in a palace." Marco turned to face Isa again. "I'm proud of Solemar's work. It's fed and clothed you and the boys and even paid to launch your magazine."

"Of course, Marco," Isa's tone was conciliatory. "You provide an important service. Absolutely."

Appeased, Marco said, "Let's get out of this room. I told the boys we'd go out for pizza."

"Pizza and a drink. Sounds heavenly." Isa flashed her incandescent smile at him as they exited the room, hand in hand. *Guess her headache's gone*, thought Marco, glad he'd dodged a bullet. The conversation was over, and she'd never find out the buildings had only sold the previous week. *Phew.*

The following Tuesday, Marco ate breakfast at the kitchen table, suit jacket draped over the chair back, and scanned the newspaper's front-page headline: "Three Injured in Apartment Fire." He stared in shock at a photo of El Comienzo with flames shooting out of its top floor widows. His eyes jumped over the story, trying to take it in as quickly as possible. Faulty wiring was suspected, faulty wiring by the previous owners, Solemar Enterprises, which had just sold the building two weeks ago. His pulse pounded in his temples, and his hands shook. Carmen had served him a breakfast of toast and coffee and was now outside, sweeping the patio. She'd brought him the paper, but had she looked at it?

At the sound of approaching heels, Marco scanned the kitchen, desperately looking for a place to hide the newspaper. Without thinking, he leaped backward and shoved it into the yellow enameled garbage can, all in one motion, just as Isa swung the kitchen door open from the living room.

"Good morning, querido," Isa said. She greeted him with a kiss by the garbage can. "Are you leaving? You barely touched your breakfast."

"I'm in a rush this morning." Marco struggled to sound calm.

Carmen, finished with her sweeping, entered the kitchen, and addressed Isa, who was pouring herself coffee at the counter. "Can I make you some breakfast?"

"Thank you, Carmen. Just toast, please. I'll drink my coffee while I read the paper."

Marco's head was sweating. "There wasn't a paper today," he said, putting on his suit jacket.

Carmen frowned. "Yes, there was. I put it on the table for you, next to your coffee. Don't you remember?"

"Oh, well. I'm not sure what I did with it then," Marco said, feigning confusion.

"Did you throw it out accidentally?" Isa asked, making her way to the garbage can with her coffee. She pulled the paper out. "Here it is, you fool!"

Marco was pinned to the ground, unable to respond. He watched as Isa shook the paper out and scanned the front page. She walked toward the kitchen table, sat heavily, and banged her cup, spilling coffee on herself and the paper. Carmen took one look at Isa's face and made herself scarce.

"Isa," Marco said, grasping for words. "Isa, I'm so sorry. I swear to you, Sammy and I didn't know the buildings were in such disrepair before we decided to sell them. One of our employees was putting repair costs in the books but pocketing the money." Marco walked toward Isa as he spoke yet another lie and sat facing her. "You've got to believe me, my love."

"Why should I believe anything you say?" Isa's voice was arctic, her arms crossed. "You're a proven liar. And a sneak."

"No, amor, no. I just didn't want to worry you." Marco held a hand out to Isa, but she ignored it. Coffee churned bitterly in his stomach.

"Just go, Marco. Please get out of my sight." Isa would not look at him. How disgusted she must be. Marco nodded once and stood. He gathered his briefcase and left for work, his insides in knots.

Later that morning, Sammy and Marco breathed a sigh of relief; the new owners and their insurance were liable for damages related to the fire. It was a shame people were injured, but it wasn't Solemar's responsibility. Thank God. His relief was fleeting as his thoughts turned to Isa. He'd never seen her that angry. Perhaps because he'd never betrayed her. His mind spun. She wouldn't leave him, would she? Surely, she'd forgive him, right? He was glad he'd scheduled lunch with Julia at La Bombonera because he needed to get his mind off the situation for a bit.

Julia was already at the table when he arrived, and Marco leaned over to kiss her before sitting. He shook out his napkin, smiling, but his grin shriveled when he noticed her sour face. She looked like she'd just gargled with vinegar.

She wasted no time digging into him. "How could you let El Comienzo get so run down?" Julia was close to shouting, and Marco fanned his right hand down to quiet her. "¡Sinvergüenza!"

"Not you, too!" Marco was tired of being on the defensive. "I'd be ashamed if it was my fault, but it isn't. It *officially* isn't my fault."

"You let those buildings go to pot, and you know it." Julia's words were acerbic.

Their waiter appeared, and Marco ordered bistec encebollao with tostones while Julia curtly asked for asopao de pollo.

Marco launched into myriad explanations and excuses. When their food arrived, he forcefully cut into his steak and caramelized

onions and continued to argue his points and insist on his innocence. Satisfied he'd done the job, he asked her, "You understand,
right?"

"No. I don't," she spat. "You've soiled Papá's memory. If he were
alive, he'd be devastated." She dunked her spoon into her chicken
and rice stew, causing some of the liquid to splash over the edge of
her bowl.

"I have always honored Papá's memory. How dare you insin-
uate otherwise?" A wave of heat enveloped Marco, but he knew it
was due to shame and not to the indignation he was faking. He *had*
dishonored his father's memory. *Papá, I am so sorry. I will never do
anything so sordid again.* He couldn't change the past, but he could
control what he did in the future.

Marco cut the remainder of his steak into small bites while Julia
quietly stared at him. "You're a real piece of work, hermano," she
said, shaking her head with a wry smile. "No wonder Isa spends so
much time with that man she works with."

"Who? Antonio?" Marco dismissed her comment with a wave
of his hand and tried to portray a carefree visage while intensely
disliking this new topic. "What are you talking about? They work
together."

"And maybe more," Julia looked at him suggestively.

"You've always been a chismosa." Marco chided his sister. He
wished she'd just spill whatever beans she thought she had.

"This is not gossip." She huffed and scrunched her nose before
continuing. "I was shopping at Gonzalez Padín the other day and
saw them across the street. They'd had lunch, I think, and looked
pretty cozy walking out of the restaurant. He had his hand on her
back in a too familiar way." Julia raised her eyebrows and shook her
head in disapproval. "You should watch that man, Marquito."

"Don't be ridiculous," Marco said. She was overreacting and
trying to give him a heart attack for the millionth time.

"How am I being ridiculous?"

"First, Isa would never cheat on me. Never. Never. No way." Marco
shook his head emphatically. "She bears deep scars from her own

father's philandering. When we got married, I had to swear never to stray. Second, Antonio is a Nationalist. We're Muñoz people. She likes that Antonio has a differing viewpoint because it helps her magazine's content stay balanced, although I do think it's been increasingly leaning toward independentista rhetoric because of his influence. But she'd never support violence as a means to an end. Isa can barely kill a fly."

"Well, I'm just telling you what I saw." Julia wiped her mouth with her napkin.

God, Julia could be such a bitch. And how she loved to stir the pot. Why was she hell-bent on making everyone around her miserable? She'd been a sweet girl but had turned out so bitter. He'd had enough of her for today.

"Are you finished?" he asked while signaling for the check. He paid quickly and gave her a dismissive goodbye peck on the cheek. Son-of a-bitch. He was in a bad mood again. Nothing was going on between Isa and Antonio. Isa wouldn't cheat. It was inconceivable. But what if Antonio had made moves on his wife? What if he'd worn down her reserves and made her feel like she had no choice? No. There's always a choice.

He huffed the three cobblestoned blocks from the restaurant to his office and wiped the sweat off his face before climbing the stairs.

Coño. What a hell of a day.

Six months later, Isa still hadn't fully forgiven Marco. After apologizing every way he knew how, he'd been on his best behavior, a model husband, and she'd slowly started to thaw. He'd also kept an eye on her these past few months. Not because he thought there was any truth to Julia's suspicions that Isa and Antonio had gotten too chummy, but just to be on the safe side. He'd detected nothing out of the ordinary. Of course she wasn't sleeping with Antonio.

Sometimes she smelled like cigarettes when she got home, so

maybe they smoked together at work, but he was confident that was the extent of her rebellion. He'd been pleased when Isa made a concerted effort to tone down independence-focused rhetoric in *Letras Boricuas*. Not that he'd influenced that decision. She'd ignored his requests and only restored balanced content when readers complained. He was glad to see the changes, even if it irked him that his opinion had had no sway.

Regardless, tonight was a night for celebration, and he was looking forward to having his stunning wife grace his arm dressed in a spectacular turquoise satin strapless gown. She looked like a mermaid fresh from the sea, perfect for attending the opening of the Caribe Hilton Hotel, Fomento's shining effort to foster American tourism. Another win for Muñoz's Operation Bootstrap.

Located on a little inlet on the road to Old San Juan, near the Escambrón Club, The Hilton was a ten-story triumph of modernity. All three hundred rooms had balconies overlooking the ocean, as well as air-conditioning. This detail had cost his friend, Henry Klumb, the commission because he'd insisted air-conditioning had no place in a tropical building. You had to admire the man's principles, but Moscoso wanted cool rooms and wasn't satisfied with natural breezes. Ultimately Klumb lost out, Fomento spent more than $2.5 million to build the hotel, and Moscoso convinced Conrad Hilton to run it to his company's high standards.

Marco pulled into the hotel's curved driveway, replete with waving palms, lush yellow hibiscus bushes, and fanning klieg lights, just like at a Hollywood movie premiere. A small combo greeted guests with mambo melodies. He turned his car over to the valet and helped Isa out. A refreshing breeze welcomed them into the airy lobby.

"¡Caballero, bienvenido! ¿Como estás, Marco?" Teodoro Moscoso, positioned at the lobby entrance to greet all arrivals, welcomed him with a firm handshake.

"I'm feeling fantastic. Who wouldn't, standing inside this phenomenal structure?" Marco said, admiring a twenty-five-foot mural of a typical Puerto Rican feast.

"And how is the beautiful Isabela Rios?" Moscoso said, turning to Isa and taking her hand.

"I am well. Congratulations on this monumental achievement. It's truly a marvel," Isabela said wide-eyed while bestowing a sweet smile on Moscoso.

"Wait until you see the rest. Go! Enjoy yourselves." Moscoso waved them off and turned to his next guests. Marco led Isa into the spacious lobby and admired the mid-century rattan furnishings, floating staircase to the second floor, and tropical bar overlooking a brightly lit swimming pool surrounded by yellow and white striped cabanas. Banquet tables laden with delicacies, both Puerto Rican and American, abounded throughout the space. The display was impressive. Pride swelled in his chest, and he thought of Papá. How awed he would have been at all this splendor.

They accepted two champagne coupes from a tuxedoed waiter and toured the gambling casino, the first on the island. They tried their hand at roulette but lost and turned away from the table, where they ran into Antonio.

"Antonio! What are you doing here?" Isabela seemed surprised. *See? If they were having an affair, she'd have known he'd be here.*

"Buenas noches, Isabela," Antonio greeted her with a quick kiss on the cheek. *Nothing unusual about that. It would be strange if he hadn't.* He then extended his hand to shake Marco's. "Marco, a pleasure, as always. I'm reporting tonight. Just interviewed Conrad Hilton. He's very pleased with himself."

"He should be. The place is gorgeous," Isabela said.

Marco was glad she'd ignored Antonio's sarcastic tone and added, "It certainly is. Can you believe this exists on our little island?"

"As long as it creates jobs for people, I have no objection. Although this party is really an obscene display of excess, don't you think?" He looked around distastefully.

Marco scowled at him. "No, I don't. I think it's exactly right for celebrating our accomplishments."

"This spread could feed an entire town for several days," Antonio said.

Isa looked around and said, "Yes, that's true."

Marco had had enough of this talk. "Lovely to see you, Antonio. We're in search of Muñoz. Have you seen him?"

"I saw him in the lobby garden chatting with Doña Inéz and Gloria Swanson."

"Very well, we'll head that way." Marco placed his hand on Isabela's back and led her in the garden's direction, where they greeted the governor, his wife, the movie star, and David Rockefeller. Marco didn't want to act like a jíbaro in the face of such greatness and tried to take it all in stride. Isa, of course, was charming and graceful, but at that moment, he felt oafish and clumsy. He was once again a shoeless fourteen-year-old boy trying to sneak into the cinema. What was wrong with him? He'd sat with American titans of industry at Muñoz's inauguration. This was no different. He belonged here because he'd built half the housing developments in the metropolitan area. He, too, was an industry leader. He, too, was raising the standard of living for Puerto Ricans.

He snapped his cuffs, grabbed another glass of champagne, and led Isabela to one of the food displays, where they loaded their plates with paella, morcillas, and pernil. They spent the rest of the evening eating, drinking, and hobnobbing with the crème de la crème of Puerto Rico's society. He had one of the best times of his life, even after Isa became strangely subdued. She claimed another headache. Marco blamed Antonio for putting ideas in her head, for making her feel guilty she was at a glittering party while others starved. Antonio always managed to leave a grey cloud in his wake.

CHAPTER 31

- Isabela -
May to August 1950

After dropping the boys at school, Isa sat on the garden patio by the kitchen entrance savoring a cup of café con leche on a cloudy May morning. She hoped the rain would hold off so she could enjoy the newspaper outside and listen to the birds singing. After catching Marco in his colossal lie about El Comienzo, she'd been so disappointed that she couldn't bring herself to speak to him for weeks and had taken refuge in Antonio's arms as often as possible. Knowing her husband had lied to her so blatantly had assuaged any guilt she felt at being with Antonio. She eventually forged an uneasy peace with Marco for the boys' sake. But the betrayal still smarted.

Isa shook the newspaper open and turned to a feature about Elizabeth Taylor and Conrad Hilton Jr., newlyweds spending part of their honeymoon at the Caribe Hilton. Isa had always admired Taylor's talent and beauty, had enjoyed many of her films. To think the actress was just a short car ride away. She let her mind wander. Someone as famous as Elizabeth Taylor could call attention to the plight of Puerto Rico's poor. Isa imagined photos of Taylor visiting a slum and listening to how fellow Americans were going hungry and working in factories for slave wages. The actress could use her fame to pressure the government into action. Isa grunted. *Yeah, that would be the day!*

She slapped the newspaper closed, ripping it in the process, and flung it away from her. The tourists, especially the famous ones, hardly ever left their hotel to visit Old San Juan, much less a slum. She pictured herself going to the Hilton, finding the newlyweds, and convincing them to take a tour of the real Puerto Rico. Imagine if Marco got a whiff of that plan. He'd club her on the head like a caveman and drag her home by the hair. Wouldn't that be a sight?

Letras Boricuas had a solid readership and made a moderate profit, but it hadn't been the catalyst for change she'd envisioned. Muñoz was a sorcerer. He'd convinced the populace that the U.S. would help Puerto Rico escape poverty. Few paid attention to the independence party, much less to Albizu, when either tried to explain that the U.S. *was* the cause of their poverty. It made her blood boil.

Worst of all, she was married to a man complicit in the conspiracy. She'd been disgusted with his posturing at the ridiculously lavish Caribe Hilton opening. He was exceedingly proud of being part of the muñocista business machine running the island. Everything they did was aimed at either attracting more American industry or supporting its interests upon arrival. All to benefit themselves because little trickled down to the poor. Isa took a swallow of her coffee and wished for a cigarette. Hiding her disappointment and anger from Marco was becoming impossible. Her husband supported everything she stood against, had forsaken his vow to improve life for Puerto Ricans. All he cared about was having the right to brag about his part in bringing the island into the twentieth century. That, and money. And keeping it meant continuing to pal around with the Americans.

Her face contorted in distaste. Not even the golondrina flitting around the red hibiscus bushes lightened her mood. It was time to go to work, and good thing, because she needed a healthy dose of Antonio. She'd make arrangements to meet him in the afternoon. Anticipation, finally, put a smile on her face.

The day moved more slowly than her sons after being commanded to brush their teeth at bedtime. She stared at the clock and counted the minutes until she'd see Antonio. When it was finally time, Isa drove recklessly and was already unzipping her dress before she barged into his apartment. She was desperate for the sweet release of his lovemaking. Antonio was amused at her urgency but humored her, and they made love aggressively. Lying on their backs next to each other afterward, they both lit cigarettes and smoked pensively.

Isa liked the silence and was annoyed when Antonio asked, "What's on your mind, mamita?"

"Absolutely nothing," Isa lied. "I was simply enjoying a moment of perfect contentment."

Antonio traced the outline of her breasts with his index finger, sending a shiver up her spine. She covered herself with the white sheet and turned to face him.

"What's new with you? I didn't have time to ask earlier." Isa gave him a coquettish look.

"You had more urgent things on your mind." Antonio smiled back.

"Have you been to see El Maestro? He must be fuming over the status issue Muñoz is pushing so hard."

"Fuming like his head's going to explode. It's the only topic of conversation at Nationalist headquarters. It's becoming clear that there aren't enough of us to make a difference anymore. Albizu thinks we need to make a big statement to focus the world's attention on how the U.S. treats this colony."

"Ah, no!" Isabela cried out. "No more bloodshed!"

"We've never set out to be violent, Isa. The police just like to shoot at us, and what are we to do? Just let them?" Antonio shrugged. "If they'd let us protest peacefully, there would be no injuries."

"If the plan is peaceful, I'd like to help," Isa said earnestly. "I can't attend an event, but perhaps I can publish something." Her face lit up. "Oh, my God! Why haven't we thought about it before? Let's publish a piece by Albizu. An opinion piece about the island's status!" Isa sat up, ready to get going on her idea.

"I don't know, Isa." Antonio frowned. "That could get you in trouble. Don't forget the Gag Law." Isa was surprised. It wasn't like Antonio to put a damper on any enthusiasm directed toward Albizu.

"Why would they start enforcing it with me?" She lit another cigarette.

"No. It's too risky. Publishing independentista content is one thing, but publishing a piece by Albizu is perilous. But... I do think there's another way you can help." She could see the wheels of Antonio's mind turning.

"How? Tell me!"

"There's been talk about staging a demonstration at the governor's mansion in the fall, having a march that starts at the Capitol and ends at La Fortaleza."

"And what would I do? I can't march," Isa said.

"Haven't you been to parties at La Fortaleza?"

"A few times, yes, especially during Muñoz's inauguration."

"Could you draw a map of the rooms?" Antonio said.

"What for? People won't be able to get inside. There are guards, you know."

"We won't be armed, and they won't dare shoot at a peaceful crowd again," Antonio said. "The police don't want a repeat of the Ponce Massacre. Our plan is to peacefully take over the governor's office and declare Puerto Rico an independent country."

"It's a terrible idea. Horrible. No." Isa shook her head with force. Did he really think the guards would give up La Fortaleza without a fight? "I won't be a party to this insanity."

"We need a map, Isa. Without one, we'll be in more danger. We can't go in blind."

"God help and protect you," Isa said. She knew she'd never be able to talk Antonio out of this lunacy. She also highly doubted force wasn't part of the plan. She wasn't stupid. What to do? She didn't want Antonio to get hurt. Perhaps helping him stay safe by showing him where to go was the wisest move. "I'm not sure I remember the rooms well enough. I wasn't scanning the premises for invasion during my visits."

"Will you try?" Antonio intertwined his fingers in hers and lifted their hands to his lips for a kiss.

Isabela paused, then made up her mind. "I can do better," she said. "This summer, there will be a slew of parties to celebrate the success of Operation Bootstrap and to continue to court American companies. I'm sure some will be held at La Fortaleza."

"Isa! That's wonderful! Will you do it?"

"Just call me Mata Hari." She struck a glamorous pose, even as unease crept up her back.

Isa left Antonio's apartment thinking about her undercover mission. Her desire to keep Antonio safe overshadowed her qualms. It really could be like starring in a spy movie. Could she wear a fedora? Ha! But her stomach caved, and her grin melted when she spotted Julia chatting with another woman diagonally across Ponce de León Avenue. *Dammit!*

Julia taught at Central High School, about five blocks down, so Isa was usually very careful entering and leaving Antonio's place. Enthusiasm with her new mission had made her careless today. Did Julia see her emerge from the building? Thank God Antonio lived near the office. At least she could easily explain her presence in the area. But what was her excuse for being in that building? Isa turned, sped away, her back to Julia, and prayed with all her might that her busybody sister-in-law had been too distracted spreading gossip to spot her.

Puerto Rico's most elegant facade was on display at the governor's party in August, all to impress the group of American industrialists Fomento currently courted. The night sky was clear, and a full moon shone down on the mansion's flowering gardens, where the guests enjoyed cocktails. Isa needed to get to the second-floor rooms and planned to explore them during the cocktail hour when the party guests, especially Marco, would be farthest from her target. After that, the party would move to the building's courtyard for dinner and dancing, and she'd be too easy to spot trying to sneak upstairs.

She'd selected her outfit carefully. Ability to move was of paramount importance, and her tea-length chartreuse sleeveless silk dress with the not-too-full skirt was perfect. Long black gloves, black patent leather pumps, and a matching clutch completed the look. After greeting the usual suspects and getting a drink, Isa excused herself to use the restroom and left Marco talking to a group of American pharmaceutical executives.

She nonchalantly sauntered past the catering station and reached the front of the executive mansion. They didn't call it La Fortaleza for nothing. The place was built to be a fortress and had been housing the island's governors—Spanish, American, and now Puerto Rican—since 1544. The amount of history in the building awed her, and she wished its thick walls could talk. Outwardly calm, though her heart beat a rapid Bomba rhythm in her chest, she strolled through the front archway and turned left to access the main entrance. She silently tiptoed up the narrow marble staircase, its walls replete with plaster reliefs of old kings or perhaps saints. The governor's office, marked with a plaque, was situated to the left at the top of the stairs. Well, that would be easy for the marchers to find. The five windows with white plantation shutters that lined the building's front must belong to the office, so the protesters would have a window on the world, so to speak, when they stormed the building. She didn't risk jiggling the handles on the tall, dark wooden doors to see if they were unlocked and peek inside. Someone could be in there. Better safe than sorry.

Staying left, Isa continued to tiptoe into a room with a black and white checkered marble floor and soft blue furnishings. Queen Isabela II watched her majestically from a life-size painting hanging on the wall. Isa ignored her, tiptoed through a long room bedecked with golden mirrors, and stifled a scream upon seeing her reflection. She took a moment to gather her wits, hand on heart, and took several deep breaths before continuing past a grand piano and the library, with its glass paneled doors. Each room led into the next, and she focused on imprinting the sequence in her mind.

Conscious that she didn't have much time, she quickly headed toward a cozy-looking room sporting Spanish wooden furnishings and lavish coral drapes.

A man cleared his throat behind her, the sound as jolting as a police siren. Isa jumped and gasped, almost succumbing to her flight instinct, but instead stood her ground.

"Can I help you, señora?" asked the tuxedo-clad man who carried a case of wine, probably to serve at dinner.

"Oh, forgive me. I came up to peek at my favorite painting, the one of Queen Isabela, my namesake, and I'm afraid I got carried away by the building's grandeur and kept going." Isa conjured a charming smile and ignited a twinkle in her eye. "There's just so much history here. But I better get back to the party." Her dress was damp under her armpits. Ugh. She hated armpit stains.

"Yes. Please follow me," the man answered curtly. He led the way down, and Isa followed, her mission partly accomplished. The information she'd managed to gather would have to do. She couldn't get caught again snooping where she didn't belong. How did people do this for a living? She took her Spanish fan out of her purse and attempted to cool herself before rejoining Marco and the party.

CHAPTER 32

- Marco -
August 1950

On his way to order a second scotch, Marco hummed along to the string quartet's version of "Campanitas de Crystal" and looked around for Isa. She wasn't back from the restroom yet, and he hoped nothing was wrong. It would be a shame to leave the party if she wasn't feeling well because this was no mere soiree; it was a celebration of Puerto Rico's exceptional progress since Muñoz and Moscoso launched Operation Bootstrap. Two years ago, a scant twenty-four manufacturing plants operated on the island. As of today, the count had doubled, with eighty in total expected by the end of 1951. And the Caribe Hilton shone like a jewel on the island's shore, attracting tourists like hummingbirds to nectar.

"Scotch en las rocas, por favor," he said to the bartender.

He thought about the conversation he'd just had with the heads of two American pharmaceutical companies. He'd assured them quality housing was available for their employees in Puerto Rico, housing built by his company. What would his teenage self, shoeless and eternally hungry, think if he could see himself now, clad in a tuxedo and hobnobbing with captains of industry at the governor's mansion? Papá was surely beaming down at him.

"Señor," the bartender said, handing him the drink.

"Muchas gracias." Marco took the glass and finally spotted Isa. She was coming from the main house, headed toward the restrooms. *That's strange.* Marco's brow furrowed. She hadn't even gone yet. What had she been doing?

"Compay, why the frown? Aren't you enjoying this wonderful

party?" Sammy put his arm around Marco's shoulders. "I saw you talking to the pharmaceutical people. Is Moscoso any closer to reeling them in?"

Marco grinned and took a sip of his drink. "They are chomping at the bit. Can't wait to profit from all the tax incentives."

"Ah, here comes your enchanting wife." Sammy greeted Isa with a kiss on the cheek.

"About time, too. Where have you been?" Marco asked.

"After I went to the bathroom, I peeked at the dinner tables in the courtyard. They're always set so beautifully with gorgeous flower arrangements. Then the sound of crashing waves lured me to the fortress wall, and I think I became mesmerized. A nice waiter found me and thought I was lost." Isa laughed.

Marco smiled at his wife and wondered why she'd lied. She'd gone to the bathroom *after* coming back from the main house. He was sure of it. Had she had some sort of tryst? He glanced around nervously. Was Antonio at the party?

The next day the question of Isa and Antonio's relationship kept nagging at him. Julia had called the previous week to make insinuations once again about Isa and Antonio. She told him she'd spotted Isa several times in the vicinity of an apartment building near Julia's workplace at Central High School. She'd thought nothing of it until last week when she said Antonio emerged from the same building shortly after Isa. He had to admit he didn't like the sound of that, but surely it was either a coincidence, or they'd been meeting with one of their writers together. But still. Questions lingered.

"Have a great day, boys! You, too, Isa!" Marco called out as he left the house, same as always. But instead of heading toward the office, he drove to Colegio San Antonio, parked the car on a cross street where he could glimpse the school's entrance, and waited for Isa to drop the boys off. It was time for some answers.

He followed her all day like a lovesick puppy, feeling like a louse for not trusting his wife. But he couldn't help himself. Isa went straight to her office after dropping off the boys. Marco scouted the building's entrance and saw Luz and the other employee, whose name he couldn't remember, arrive. An hour later, Antonio made an appearance. He looked rushed, held a sheaf of papers in his hand, ran into the building and left almost immediately. Everything about his body language indicated he was a man on a mission. At noon, Luz went out and returned with a bag of what had to be lunch for everyone. Promptly at one, everyone but Isa left for the day. Would Antonio reappear? He didn't, and when Isa exited the building at three, Marco followed her to her seamstress's house, where she left after twenty minutes to pick up the boys.

Marco watched Isa pull into their driveway and lamented his wasted day. She'd done nothing out of the ordinary, and while this didn't prove there wasn't an affair, it didn't indicate there was one. She'd spent a total of ten minutes with Antonio, in the company of the others in the office, and when she'd been alone for two hours, Antonio hadn't returned. Marco felt like a fool, a complete idiot. He'd squandered his day, and with so much work at the office. He really needed to stop listening to Julia's bochinches. Whatever was making Isa so prickly these days was not an affair.

Marco turned his car around and headed to La Upi to teach his evening class. He wanted to chat with Benítez, now Upi's chancellor, about creating opportunities for students to gain work experience at local companies. Luckily, Benítez was in his office and delighted to see him.

"Marco!" Benítez shook his hand. "Come in! Come in! You're not going to believe what I just learned." Benítez looked amused.

"Good news?"

"Funny news!" His grin was wide. "Jorge Rodríguez, one of Muñoz's assistants, called to tell me I have a carpeta. They just got a list from the FBI."

"A carpeta? What could an FBI file on you possibly contain?"

"What color socks I wear," Benítez laughed. "That I tell terrible jokes. Maybe that I didn't learn to tie my shoes until I was five. Who knows? Even Muñoz has a file. These people are clowns." He leaned back in his padded desk chair, shaking his head.

"What a waste of time and resources," Marco said, disgusted. "Why don't they focus on the Nationalists? They're the ones who need carpetas."

"Rodríguez says they've cast a wide net. It includes the Nationalists and anyone with an iota of influence on this island. We knew Muñoz had a carpeta, but apparently, there are thousands of files. Can you imagine?"

"I wonder if I have one," Marco said. Wouldn't he, an influential businessman, warrant vetting? It sounded as if having a carpeta was a badge of honor. Well, as long as you weren't a Nationalist. They *were* real criminals.

"Let's find out!" Benítez called out to his secretary, "Milly, please get me Rodríguez at La Fortaleza on the phone."

Milly placed the call, and Benítez was jocular when he spoke into the receiver, "Mira, Rodríguez! I've got Marco Rios in my office. He wants to know if he's got a carpeta, too. Can you look him up?" Benítez nodded to Marco. Rodríguez had agreed to the request.

"Really? That's interesting." Benítez paused. "Bueno, muchísimas gracias. Nos vemos." He hung up and looked at Marco, eyes mirthful. "*You* don't have one, but get this: your wife does!" Benítez laughed.

"Goddamit! It's that magazine of hers. I warned her she'd get in trouble." Marco tried to hide his crushed ego. There was a carpeta on Isa, but not him? Wasn't he a significant citizen?

Benítez flapped his hand. "Ay, hombre. Don't worry about it. She's in as much danger of arrest as I am."

"She does publish independentista pieces."

Benítez grinned. "Maybe we'll both go to jail, along with Muñoz and everyone on his staff. We'll call you to bail us out."

Marco forced a laugh, "Maybe I'd leave you all in there. Or maybe they'd come to get me too." Maybe they would. Surely he was prominent enough to be arrested. More than his wife, for God's sake. Why didn't he have a carpeta? He felt like a petulant child, but the slight needled him during the rest of his conversation with Benítez and throughout the class he taught that night. He was also concerned about Isa's carpeta, given that she wielded little, if any, political influence. Did the FBI think she was dangerous?

He broached the subject as soon as he joined Isa in bed that evening. "I met with Benítez today and found out he has a carpeta. Can you believe it?"

Isa looked up from the book she was reading. "I've heard most people do. That there are more with carpetas than without."

Marco stiffened, again unsure of why he'd been ignored. "You have one, too," he said. "But apparently, I'm not important enough to warrant surveillance."

Isa rolled her eyes. "Are you serious? You're the only person I know who'd get upset that the FBI's not watching him."

"I'm concerned that *you* have one."

"Well, of course, I have one. I publish viewpoints they don't like. Don't worry about it." Her laugh sounded hollow to his ears. Was she hiding her worry from him? He wondered what information Isa's carpeta contained and whether her actions could destroy everything he'd worked for.

CHAPTER 33

- Isabela -
October 1950

Two months later, on an otherwise ordinary Saturday, rioting prisoners at El Oso Blanco, the massive penitentiary in Rio Piedras, killed two guards and injured another four. More than one hundred convicts were on the loose, spread over the San Juan area and beyond, like fleeing vermin, each desperately scurrying to safety. The authorities suspected the Nationalists had orchestrated the escape to monopolize police resources and divert attention from a different, more significant event they'd planned. Police raided the home of the head of the Party's Ponce chapter and confiscated an arsenal of weapons, from machine guns to grenades. The island sat on pins and needles, not knowing what to expect and fearing mayhem from the escaped prisoners and the Nationalists.

Isa was beside herself. None of these events had anything to do with the peaceful calling of attention to the Nationalist cause Antonio had promised. Chaos was imminent. She felt it in her bones and asked Papi to stay with them.

On Sunday, J. Edgar Hoover flew down sixty FBI agents to help manage the upheaval. Police raided another Nationalist house, this time in Peñuelas, finding an additional cache of weapons, but not before a shootout during which three Nationalists were killed and six policemen injured. The governor refused to declare martial law, but most of the citizenry was erring on the side of caution and staying safely indoors.

By Monday, October 30, her family remained hunkered down at home, all outside doors closed and locked. Had Isa put her family in peril? If Antonio was caught, they'd come for her, too. Isa and Antonio had been careful to hide their love affair, but they worked together and would be in each other's carpetas. Perhaps the FBI had even listened in on their conversations.

Marco, Papi, and Isa were glued to the radio, and she worried about how much the boys were absorbing. They were frightened enough without having to hear a continuous play-by-play of the situation.

"Mami, is a pillo going to break in and rob us?" Luisito, just ten, was failing to put on a brave face. Miguelito rolled his savvy, twelve-year-old eyes at his brother.

"Of course not. We're absolutely, positively super safe here. Come boys, it's lunchtime. Let's go see Carmen." Isa led them into the kitchen, where Carmen was also listening to the news. Isa signaled for Carmen to turn off the radio. "How about we fry up some Spam? And for dessert, we have quenepas, Carmen, don't we?"

"Quenepas! Yay!" Luisito said.

Miguelito smiled, rubbed his tummy, and moved his eyebrows up and down. Her sons loved the fruit. Carmen served them fried Spam slices with left-over rice and beans, and they eagerly dug in.

"Are you excited about Halloween?" Isa asked. Miguelito, who'd just read *Treasure Island*, had chosen to be a pirate, while Luisito was fascinated with all things cowboy. They were supposed to wear their costumes to school the next day. If there was school. She hoped so. She needed this to be over.

"Sí, Mami. I need to practice my shooting," Luisito said, holding up his plastic silver toy gun. "Pew, pew, pew!"

"But who are you shooting at?" Isa asked.

"The Indians, of course."

"What have they done to *you*? Indians lived on this island once, you know. Way before us. We all have some Taíno blood in us. Do you want to kill your ancestors?"

"Maybe I should be an Indian and shoot at the cowboys."

"You know that gun is fake, right?" Miguelito enjoyed bringing his younger brother down to earth.

"It shoots." Luis made a mocking face at Miguel.

"If you say so." Miguelito rolled his eyes again. Isa smiled. Already such a man of the world.

"Shooting at people is never the best solution, mijo," Isa said. Damn those American cowboy movies for promoting killing. And damn the Nationalists for doing the same.

The boys cleared their plates in silence and pounced on the quenepas. Each picked one of the grape-sized fruits from the bunch Carmen had washed, bit down with his front teeth to split the leathery green skin, and sucked on the sweet and sour apricot-hued pulp inside. Isa took one as well.

"Delicious," Isa said, immediately taking another. Quenepas reminded her of Abuela, who'd had a tree in the backyard. Tree climbing had not been a señorita-approved activity, so she'd secretly scale the branches to pick quenepas. She fell once, badly scraping her knee, but Carmen bandaged her so Abuela wouldn't find out.

"Isa! Come!" Marco's agitated voice interrupted her nostalgic reverie.

"Boys, finish your quenepas and go play. Put on your costumes if you want." Isa left them with Carmen and entered the living room. It was just past noon.

Papi covered his mouth with his hand, and Marco's eyes bulged as they stood by the radio.

"What is it?" she asked them.

"¡Dios mío! More bloodshed. Listen," Marco said, making a quieting motion with his hand.

Isa tuned into the announcer's voice. "...in Arecibo this morning. Four police and one Nationalist are dead after the attack. We'll continue to bring you the news after this commercial break."

"I didn't catch what happened." Isa frowned.

"A group of Nationalists attacked the police station in Arecibo," Papi said, lips in a tight line. "They've gone crazy."

"My God!" She wrung her hands, deeply apprehensive about the escalating situation.

Marco shook his head. "Your father's right. The whole island's gone insane." A laundry soap jingle played.

Isa struggled to hold back tears. If this was Albizu's big move, Antonio was involved. *Please, Antonio, stay safe!*

Clanking typewriter keys indicated the news was coming back on. The announcer's voice carried urgency, and the three listened with dread, muscles tense. "I have breaking news, ladies and gentlemen. There has been a shooting at La Fortaleza. I repeat, there has been a shooting at La Fortaleza. Five men in a blue Plymouth barreled onto the grounds of the governor's mansion. The guards shot the driver and stopped the car, but one of the passengers emerged, shooting a machine gun at the second floor where the governor's office is. The men are assumed to be Nationalists."

Isa felt the blood drain from her face, and her limbs grow cold. Were the attackers using information she'd given Antonio about La Fortaleza's layout? Had she had a part in this travesty?

"Oh my God!" she said in a shaky voice.

Papi and Marco remained silent, and Marco shushed her as the announcer continued. "We don't know whether Muñoz was hit. One moment... I've just been told four of the attackers are dead. A fifth is wounded and has taken cover under the car. He continues to trade shots with the guards." Isa went numb. Five people were dead, maybe more.

"What if they shot Muñoz?" Marco, face pale, covered his nose and mouth with his shaking hands. He looked like *he'd* burst into tears at any moment. Papi sat on the sofa, stunned.

Luisito and Miguelito, who'd changed into their costumes, attached themselves to each side of their mother and cried silently.

The announcer continued. "We have received reports of additional Nationalist uprisings in Utuado and Jayuya. Pedro Albizu Campos and his followers are waging war. We now go to Paco Rivera, who is live at La Fortaleza. What are you seeing, Paco?"

"I'm around the corner from the entrance to La Fortaleza, but I can see it's a bloody scene, with several bodies on the ground," Rivera said, then quickly added, "A guard just confirmed that Muñoz is safe. I repeat, Muñoz is safe."

"Thank God!" Isa said and stumbled toward the couch. Marco relaxed visibly and hugged his wife hard, almost knocking her over. Even Papi, no fan of Muñoz, breathed a sigh of profound relief.

The three continued to listen to the reports and were reassured that, while the Muñoz family had been in the family quarters and suffered a serious fright, they were all unharmed. As the afternoon progressed, more details came in from Utuado and Jayuya, and uprisings were reported in Mayaguez, Naranjito, and Ponce. Meanwhile, the police had surrounded Albizu's home in Old San Juan, where the Nationalist leader had barricaded himself.

The scope of the revolt shocked Isa. This was a far cry from the peaceful march to La Fortaleza Antonio had described. They'd tried to assassinate Muñoz, for God's sake! While his wife and young daughters were in the building. What if the shooters had gotten inside? She'd given them a map to guide them! She'd have been complicit in an assassination. Mother of God! This was a grave situation. How could Antonio have put her in such danger? Not just her, but her children!

She was overwhelmed with emotions. Thankfully, concern and fear were normal reactions to the events being reported in the news. But she had to hide how her choice to believe Antonio's lies weighed her down physically, that shame had her innards in knots, and that she anticipated angry knocking on the door at any moment. What had she wrought on her family? She was a vile, disgusting person. And so was Antonio. Tears flowed, but she felt unworthy of Marco's attempts to embrace and comfort her.

The aggression and its news coverage continued through the evening, and she listened until the boys' bedtime. Miguelito and Luisito begged to sleep with their parents, so Isabela read to them in her bed until the three fell into an exhausted slumber. While Marco and Papi stayed glued to the news, fierce nightmares plagued Isa's fitful sleep.

In the morning, the newspaper counted twenty-eight dead and twenty-three injured in ten towns across the island. The radio reported that Muñoz Marín had finally declared martial law and mobilized 3,500 National Guardsmen to maintain order. He'd declared the rebellion an attack against democracy and accused the communists of lending the Nationalists a hand. With school still closed, her boys wouldn't be celebrating Halloween, and nerves shot, she struggled to keep them occupied and away from the radio. Eventually, she sent them to their rooms to play with their Lincoln Logs. She desperately wanted a cigarette but gnawed on her thumb instead.

Radio reports continued as more than forty police and National Guardsmen opened fire on a barbershop in Santurce where a group of Nationalists had hidden. For three hours, the radio reported live from the scene. Back and forth went the bullets, each pop making Isa jump out of her skin. Any loud noise sounded like police banging on the door. At least she hoped they'd knock and not shoot. When the gunfight ended, the police discovered they'd been shooting at a lone man, Albizu's barber. Much to Papi's amusement, he'd held off the National Guard by himself for hours.

Somehow, Isa got through that day and the next when Albizu, who'd been under siege in his apartment, was finally captured. Martial law remained in place, and with each passing moment, Isa wavered between hope that she wouldn't be arrested and certainty that they'd come for her as the net widened. On the fourth day after the revolts, with Albizu captured, the violence ended. Isa allowed the boys to play outside, and they were busy expending all their pent-up energy when the radio reported breaking news. Two Puerto Rican Nationalists had attempted to shoot President Truman at Blair House, where he was living during ongoing White House renovations. One Nationalist was killed, and the other captured. Would this nightmare end?

"¡Carajo!" Marco said. "They're crazier than we thought."

"I can't believe it," Isa said, shocked. "What were they thinking? How does killing Truman help their cause?"

"They wanted the world's attention," Papi rasped in anger. "Now they have it—the world's negative attention. This is not the right way to oust los Yanquis."

"The Americans will never support our independence now." Isa was despondent.

Marco responded. "Well, they never did, amor, but if the Nationalists wanted support from other countries, they've made a severe tactical mistake. We've fought world wars to end this kind of hate."

"All this death for nothing." Isa shook her head and walked out of the room. She needed to lie down. Her head was pounding.

On the fifth day, November 4, the newspapers reported that Muñoz had apologized to the United States for the misguided Nationalist attempt on the president's life during a coast-to-coast radio broadcast the previous evening. Isa thought he'd eloquently expressed the Puerto Rican population's horror at the assassination attempt and the events leading up to it. She was also reassured when Muñoz addressed the Puerto Rican people later that day, firmly stating that "the recent attempt against the peace and your democratic rights has ended."

"I finally like something the man says," Papi smiled for the first time in days. Isa and Marco nodded in agreement.

Muñoz continued. "Know once and for all, so we don't lose any more lives to this kind of madness, that a government based on the votes of the people cannot be destroyed, or even derailed, by the bullets of the perverse or misinformed."

Muñoz was right. Independence needed to be won by votes, not force. Frustrated that the Independence Party had been so blatantly defeated in the election, Isa had let herself lose sight of this. The moment she'd given Antonio the map of La Fortaleza's rooms, she'd become a Nationalist. She'd known that, let it happen, and was paying the price. The authorities would come for her; it was only a matter of time. Acid shot up her esophagus into her mouth. It tasted of her future.

Then Muñoz's words pierced her heart. "And for you, woman," he said. "Puerto Rican mother who is listening to me—who has a son and is praying to God that no one will ever poison his sincerity and good faith to the point where he is willing to destroy his body and life—defending democracy is especially important."

Isa held praying hands before her lips, feeling the full weight of Muñoz's words. What if Miguelito or Luisito grew up to listen to a crazed man like Albizu? What if they misguidedly put their lives on the line for his cause? Causes should be championed peacefully. She couldn't fathom losing one of her sons because a madman poisoned his mind and turned him into a killer. Antonio had been brainwashed to believe violence was the only solution and to pursue independence at any cost, even if it meant betraying people who cared about him. *I will spend the rest of my life righting this wrong. If I avoid prison, I'll make it my life's mission to teach my children to contribute to society in the best ways possible. They will be great men and make an enduring positive impact.*

The bang of the modernist metal doorknocker exploded in the room. Jolting upright on the edge of the couch, Isa froze, her heart beating a discordance of dread. Her mind went blank as she stared at the door. *No.*

"Who could that be?" Marco said, getting up to answer the knock.

The banging continued insistently.

"I'm coming! Con calma," Marco muttered under his breath. Isa's adrenaline kicked in and her body staring quaking. She stood slowly, and scanned the room for an escape route, even though she knew she was trapped. Papi looked at her with wrinkled eyebrows and questioning eyes.

"Yes, gentlemen, what can I do for you," Marcos's voice sounded strained. The murmur of a deep male voice answered, but she couldn't make the words out.

"There's some mistake. You have the wrong Isabela Rios."

"No, sir. We have the correct address." A uniformed policeman pushed past Marco into the house, followed by three National Guardsmen. Papi bolted to standing, threw a protective arm around Isa, and hugged her hard to his side. Isa hoped he couldn't feel her trembling.

The policeman addressed her. "Are you Isabela Rios?"

Isa, unable to answer audibly, nodded.

"Mami, look outside! There's an army Jeep!" She heard the boys before she saw them run into the living room and come to a stunned stop upon seeing the uniformed men.

"What's happening?" asked Luisito, eyes wide.

"Nothing, hijos. Please go to your rooms," Marco said.

"But Papi! Why are these men here?" asked Miguelito.

"Go to your rooms!" Marco shouted, and the boys scurried away.

The policeman continued addressing Isa. "Isabela Rios, you are under arrest for suspicion of supporting the Nationalist insurgency. Please turn around."

"Over my dead body, will you take this woman." Papi's hold on her was going to leave a mark. "I don't know what you think she did, but I assure you she is innocent."

"Let me go, Papi." Isa extricated herself from his grip and averted her eyes as she turned around to be handcuffed.

A panicked Marco shouted and flailed his arms. "Stop this right now. What are you doing? This is a respectable household with law-abiding citizens. I will call Muñoz himself and stop this madness." He tried to intercept the policeman leading Isa out of the house, but the National Guardsmen pushed him back. She heard the boys sobbing, and her heart shattered.

"Isa, don't worry. I'm sure this is a misunderstanding. I'll come to get you immediately," Marco called, as the men forced her into the Jeep. She looked back at him, helpless to prevent him from learning the truth.

CHAPTER 34

- Marco -
November 1950

I knew that maldito magazine was going to get her in trouble, thought Marco as he rushed back into the house. He almost ran into Carmen, standing staunchly in the living room, clutching the boys to her sides.

"Papi, where are those men taking Mami?" Luisito asked.

"It's all a mistake, boys. There's no need to worry. I'm going to go get her now."

"I'm coming with you." Don Gabriel sprang into action, looking and sounding a lot like his pre-bankruptcy self.

Marco nodded, then signaled Carmen to take the boys into the kitchen. She'd know to keep them occupied.

"Where do you think they took her?" Don Gabriel, all business, grabbed his hat.

"I'll find out." Marco grabbed the phone. Without divulging why he needed to know, it only took two calls to learn all persons arrested in San Juan were being taken to the National Guard headquarters in Puerta de Tierra. Marco sprinted to the car, Don Gabriel in tow.

Marco clutched the steering wheel hard. "How could they treat her like a common criminal?" Fury colored his face. "Someone's going to pay for this."

"Calm down, mijo," Don Gabriel said, gently touching his arm. "Anger won't solve this problem. Let's keep our wits about us. We may need them."

Why wasn't his father-in-law more riled up? The man lived for Isa's happiness.

But Don Gabriel was right. Marco needed to diffuse his rage and keep a clear head before dealing with the authorities. Arrogance and bluster wouldn't help Isa's cause.

Myriad cars and military vehicles crowded the front of the National Guard headquarters, and he had to park blocks away. He ran with Don Gabriel toward the two-story building, stunned to see rows of men and women pressed against the concrete walls while soldiers stood guard across from them, pointing rifles at their heads. Several men wore pajamas, obviously having been taken from their beds. The scene was eerily quiet. He didn't care how the Nationalists were treated. They deserved to be terrorized. But his wife was another story. He scanned the prisoners' faces for Isa's and, unable to spot her, entered the headquarters with Don Gabriel.

For two hours, they waited in the crowded airless room, fanning themselves with newspapers, their shirts sweat-soaked. Marco's anger festered. Finally, the sergeant in charge called them to the counter.

"Sargento, there's been a serious mistake. My wife, Isabela Rios, has been wrongly arrested. I'm here to take her home," Marco said, trying for his most reasonable and even tone. Don Gabriel remained quiet, but his presence was comforting.

The sergeant gave them the once over, seemed to assess they were men of means and opted for civility. "Señor, let me see," the sergeant flipped through a ream of papers, "Ah, yes. Isabela Rios." He frowned and looked at a loss for his next words. "It says here your wife is suspected of conspiring to overthrow the island's government by force."

Marco couldn't help but guffaw in disbelief.

"This is not a laughing matter," the sergeant responded curtly.

"Please excuse my son-in-law." Don Gabriel intercepted. "It's simply that the accusation is ludicrous. My daughter is not a revolutionary."

"We're friends with Muñoz Marín, for God's sake." Marco was losing patience.

"Friends or not, she must be interrogated." The man shuffled his papers officially.

"No. I demand that you release my wife immediately." Marco leaned into the counter. "Call the governor's office. They'll vouch for her."

The sergeant looked at Marco with pity and whispered, "I don't think you want to do that, sir. There are certain facts you might not want widely circulated."

"I don't understand. What are you saying?" Marco wished the sergeant would listen to him already.

The officer glanced at Don Gabriel, as if reluctant to continue in front of the accused's father.

"Out with it, hombre," Don Gabriel barked.

"Your daughter." The officer looked from one to the other. "Your wife. Her file states she's in a romantic relationship with Antonio Badilla, a known Nationalist who actively participated in the uprising. She's been under surveillance for more than a year. I'm sorry, señores, but she stays here until further notice."

Marco's blood froze. He shook his head at the sergeant, sure he hadn't heard correctly. But one glance at Don Gabriel's dumbfounded face and he realized his ears worked fine.

"Sí, señores. Es verdad. I need you to step aside. Next!"

Marco staggered from the counter and out the door, pulling Don Gabriel along. Isa and Antonio? No. Hadn't he debunked that theory when he's spied on her? Or had the lovers simply not gotten together that day, leading him to favor a truth he preferred? Could Isa have a carpeta because she had a Nationalist lover and not because of the magazine? Why else would they detain her? Julia had been right. The force of Isa's betrayal knocked the air out of him. He stopped in his tracks and looked at Don Gabriel, whose face mirrored Marco's bewilderment.

"That bastard Antonio put her in danger," Marco said, trying to save face in front of his father-in-law. "He must have lied or framed her."

"We'll get to the bottom of this, Marco." But Don Gabriel didn't look him in the eye. Did *he* think Isa had had an affair? A cheater would know another.

Marco nodded and, feeling like he'd stepped outside his body, led the way to the car, surprised his feet knew what to do. He continued to process the unfathomable news. Was Isa somehow complicit in the uprising? What had she been up to that night at La Fortaleza when she'd lied to him about going to the restroom? *How dare she?* He was temporarily blinded by a white flash of anger. How dare she put their family in danger by associating with the Nationalists? What if the boys had been hurt? What kind of mother puts her children at risk? And what kind of wife makes you promise never to cheat on her but turns around and cheats on you? What an idiot he'd been. He imagined Antonio and Isa in bed, laughing at how they'd fooled him, and his vision clouded with tears of hurt and rage.

He couldn't face the boys in this condition, and his skin crawled at the thought of spending another minute in Don Gabriel's company. A fine example he'd set for his daughter. Marco dropped the old man at his apartment and told him he'd try to reach Muñoz personally. Instead, he headed to Julia's house, hoping Eduardo would be at work. She might not be the warmest person, but Julia was family, and he needed familial support.

"I knew it!" His sister screeched when he was done telling the story in her living room. "I knew it, and I wish you'd listened to me." She banged the sofa cushion with her hand.

What deranged part of him had expected empathy?

"Saying 'I told you so' is less than helpful right now," Marco said. "What am I going to tell the boys? That she's taken after that pig, their grandfather?" He cradled his head in his hands.

Julia sprung up and started pacing the room. "You'll tell them their mother is ill and had to go to the hospital. You're not sure how long she'll be there, but she can't have visitors until she gets well. That will cover you for a while."

"Oh, God!" Why was this happening to him?

"You need to file for divorce and get custody of those boys. She's obviously an unfit mother. *I'll* help you raise them." Julia's satisfied expression reiterated her disdain toward Isa.

"Are you crazy? I can't file for *divorce*." Marco was aghast. "I can't leave my boys motherless. What kind of failure would that make me? What would happen to my business if word got out I can't even control my wife?"

"Marco, everyone knows she's always been a comemierda," Julia said with disgust.

"You've never liked her."

"She'll always be a spoiled debutante, despite her efforts at being a regular person. I knew she was trouble the moment I met her," Julia said, arms crossed in front of her chest.

"The boys will be heartbroken without their mother. They love her so much."

"Fuerza, Marco. You must be strong for them like you were for Mamá and me after Papá died."

"Mamá must never know. It'll break her heart," Marco said with urgency.

Julia waved that worry away before adding a new one. "Do you think Isa's guilty of anything other than screwing Antonio?"

Marco flinched at her crudeness. "Who knows? I don't recognize this person as Isa anymore."

"I guess we'll know after she's questioned. What are you going to do to get her out?" Julia asked.

"Nothing." Marco fought tears. "She can rot in there for all I care. It's one thing to use my contacts when she's innocent, but she's not. I don't need everyone in San Juan knowing I'm a cuckold."

"Oh, my poor, poor brother," Julia said, sitting down next to Marco and finally showing compassion by rubbing his shoulder.

For the seventh consecutive day since Isa's arrest, Luisito and Miguelito begged to visit her in the hospital. Marco had told his sons

Isa's wrongful arrest had been so traumatic she needed a few days in the hospital to recover. He'd told Carmen Isa was being held for questioning related to *Letras Boricuas*, a version of the truth, but Carmen couldn't understand why he wasn't moving heaven and earth to get her out. Marco wasn't sure what was worse—seeing his sons so dejected, deflecting Carmen's accusatory glances, or having to take Don Gabriel's constant phone calls asking for updates and sharing theories and ideas for rescuing his daughter.

"I miss her, Papi," Miguelito said.

"I know, mijo, but the doctors said she needs complete rest. She'll be all better and back before you know it." Marco needed to protect the boys from the truth, but he hated lying to them. And what if Isa wasn't released? Or what if she was? She'd want to come home for the boys, but could he bear that? He didn't think so.

In the week following the Nationalist revolts, more than 1,000 people were arrested on suspicion of supporting the insurgency, including forty-one women, Isa among them. Marco knew she was at La Princesa Jail awaiting questioning. It was difficult to imagine perfect Isa in those decrepit, vermin-infested surroundings. He checked twice daily to see if there'd been any progress, but interrogating 1,000 people takes time, the police told him repeatedly.

Marco vacillated from anger to sadness and back. He'd come to grasp that his wife had taken a lover and, in his more rational moments, tried to understand why. He'd been a good husband, hadn't he? Or had work taken up too much of his time and attention? But without his hard work, they wouldn't have their comfortable lifestyle. Isa would still be sweating in their little apartment kitchen, getting her fingers stuck in the washing machine, fed-up and miserable.

Maybe he'd given her too much. Without the magazine, none of this would have happened. He should have kept her at home where she belonged, but she'd wanted more out of life. They'd talked about working together to bring Puerto Rico into modernity while courting, so why hadn't he included her in his work? Because her work had been motherhood. And she was a great mother, despite this recent lapse in judgment. What would his boys do without her? They'd already taken to sleeping together, finding comfort in proximity.

That evening as Marco tucked his sons in bed, Luisito looked at him with molten chocolate eyes and asked, "Papi, is Mami coming home tomorrow?"

When Marco did not respond, Luis continued, "I'm going to dream that she's coming home, and then my dream will come true, and she'll be here in the morning."

Miguelito, old enough to know better, let himself get carried away by his brother's fantasy, and chimed in, "I'm going to give her the biggest hug ever!"

"No, I am!"

"Mami's coming home! Mami's coming home!" The two chanted in unison, giant smiles plastered on their faces.

"We'll see, hijos," Marco said. His heart couldn't take much more of this, and he knew there was only one choice. "We'll see. Settle down now. Good night." Marco turned the light off and left the room.

"Bendición, Papi."

"May God bless you and keep you safe."

His boys were suffering. He had to bring Isa home.

CHAPTER 35

- Isabela -
November 1950

The itching, relentless and excruciating, woke Isabela up. She rose from her grimy cot and inspected her body, willing herself not to scratch and claw at her scabby skin. The bed bugs thrived in the dank and windowless cell, co-existing with a colony of enormous shiny black roaches that kept her in a constant state of vigilant panic. Isa struggled to breathe in the fetid air, nearly impenetrable with the stench of feces, urine, and the funk of unwashed bodies. And she'd thought El Fanguito was foul.

The rightly dreaded La Princesa Jail. There was nothing royal about this ancient Spanish fortress. After being arrested and held at gunpoint by National Guardsmen for more than fifteen hours, Isa was brought to this vile place with seventeen other women. Ten days later, they remained crammed into a warren of tiny rooms, and the warden had yet to summon any of them for questioning. At least she had the comfort of company and of praying with others. She'd heard they put the most dangerous prisoners in solitary confinement, Pedro Albizu Campos now among them.

Isa's dress, rank and moldy, was starting to hang on her starving limbs. She was surviving on a diet of bread, water, and the occasional rice and chicken broth served lukewarm with slicks of yellow grease floating on its surface. Two days ago, some of the women succumbed to eating lice they picked out of each other's matted hair. Yesterday a cellmate had swallowed a roach. Isa shivered violently, bile rising in her throat at that inconceivable thought. But who knew what she'd be capable of after a few more days of this living hell.

At night she tried not to add to the cries, screams, and sobs that kept her awake, but it was impossible. Her body was suffering, yes. But these inhumane conditions couldn't compete with the agony that suffused her soul at having betrayed her husband and family.

She'd had plenty of time to contemplate how she'd arrived at this juncture, that she'd risked it all for stolen moments of tawdry sex with a man who was likely using her. She'd known what Antonio was up to, yet she'd turned a blind eye. No, she'd done more, God help her. By giving him the floor plan to La Fortaleza, she'd abetted his efforts to assassinate the governor. Antonio could have gotten the Fortaleza room layout from any number of sources. The information she'd provided was hardly classified. But he'd gotten it from her. If Muñoz had died, she would have been an accomplice to murder. She'd let herself be seduced mind, body, and soul by a killer.

But they'd had such an electric connection. With Antonio, she had created the kind of partnership she'd always envisioned she'd have with Marco. She hadn't given up on her dream of becoming an actress to solely be a wife and mother. Marco had known that, had encouraged her growth as a person with opinions and a desire to make a difference in the world. And then he left her in his wake. Marco forged two lives: work and family. She was an integral part of one but ached to be involved in both. Somehow she'd convinced herself this was enough justification to vilify their love. She'd been so blind, so selfish.

Her body cringed with the excruciating heat of embarrassment whenever she wondered how much Marco knew by now. Did Papi also know what she'd done? Carmen? The boys? Surely Marco would protect the boys from the truth. As much as she needed to get out of this jail, she dreaded facing her family. She would have to, of course. Her sons needed their mother. But could Marco forgive her? She, who'd made him swear to never cheat on her like Papi had on Connie? The irony made her gag, but her empty stomach had nothing to offer.

On the eleventh day, while eating the measly piece of bread and watery coffee that comprised breakfast, Isa finally, finally heard the warden call her name for questioning. She followed him to a small room with paint peeling off the walls and sat at a table facing two men in dark suits. The younger one flinched and covered his nose with his handkerchief, clearly offended by her odor. A hot flush crawled up her face, and she fought back tears.

The older man addressed her in a gentle tone. "Señora Rios, I'm District Attorney Ángel Viera Martínez and this is my assistant, Jorge Guzmán. Do you know why you're here?"

Relieved at being spoken to kindly, Isa broke down in sobs, releasing a torrent of anger, humiliation, and exhaustion. When neither man offered her a handkerchief, she used her trembling hands to wipe the tears and mucus off her face.

"Señor Martínez, I'm a respectable woman from a good family," she said in a shuddery voice.

"Hmmm," responded Martínez with pursed lips. He picked up the top sheet from the stack of papers in front of him and scanned it before addressing her. "Do you publish a magazine called *Letras Boricuas*?"

"Yes, I do." She sounded so meek and beaten, her pride in the magazine now turned to regret.

"I understand it's a vehicle for Nationalist propaganda," Martínez stated matter-of-factly.

The blatant fabrication shocked Isa and began to awaken her fighting spirit.

"That's absolutely untrue," Isa said with more strength, secure in her knowledge of the facts. If she just told the truth, they'd have to let her go. "We've run some pro-independence pieces, but certainly nothing advocating violence. I'm not a Nationalist. You must know that." She pressed her hands together. "This is all a terrible mistake. Please. Let me go home."

"You are in no position to ask for anything," Guzmán said. Martínez raised his palm at him, signaling for quiet.

"And tell me, Señora Rios, which home would that be?" Martínez looked down at his papers again. "The one where you live with your husband and sons or the one where you sleep with your Nationalist lover?"

She shrank from the man's disdainful smile. Her stomach sank. Of course, they knew Antonio was her lover. She hadn't really expected otherwise. But how dare this man speak to her so crudely? She deserved more respect. *Any* of the women in the jail deserved more respect. Voice shaky, Isa lifted her chin and said, "The answer is none of your business."

Martínez narrowed his eyes, and she immediately regretted her show of hubris.

"It is my business, Señora Rios," Martínez said slowly, voice rising, "because we can't have women of your standing having sexual trysts with murderous revolutionaries."

Isabela nodded in submission. Now was not the time to challenge this man's power.

Seemingly satisfied that he'd made his point, Martínez continued. "Tell me, how much money did you give him for 'the cause'?"

"None!" Isa said, aghast. Why did they think that? Had Antonio lied about her involvement? Would this nightmare ever end? She decided to come clean about the affair.

"It's true we had an affair," she rushed the words. "But Antonio never asked me for money or anything that would help the Nationalists. I swear it. He knew I strongly disapproved of their violent tactics." Her entire body quaked. If they knew about her Fortaleza reconnaissance, she was doomed to spend her remaining years in a cell, forever separated from her sons.

Isa summoned the last of her remaining strength to speak calmly and credibly. "I was horrified at the events of October 30. I didn't know of the revolts in advance. I had nothing to do with any of it. You must believe me."

"And why should we believe a woman who has lied about who she is all her life?" Guzmán spoke up again.

"What do you mean?" Isa was genuinely confused.

"Aren't you the bastard child of Gabriel Soto and María Cárdenas? You're just a jíbara pretending to be a society lady," Guzmán said.

Isabela gasped. Her mind reeled as Guzmán continued his brutal attack.

"Does your husband know who you really are?" Guzmán sneered at her. He was practically salivating. "I bet he doesn't."

What a despicable, wicked little man, thinking he could ruin her life with this information. As if her entire existence wasn't already in shambles. Being illegitimate was the least of her worries right now. She'd developed a deep respect for society's powerless people, for the endurance of the jíbaro who suffered a life of hardship with little hope for betterment. Drawing on the strength of her jíbaro stock had provided solace during her incarceration.

"You would lose that bet, Señor Guzmán," Isa said, eyebrows raised. "I'm not ashamed of my roots. In fact, I celebrate them."

Guzmán attempted to stammer out another question, but a look from Martínez silenced the assistant.

The interrogation continued for two more hours, during which Isa focused on one goal: freedom. She had to get out for Luisito and Miguelito. She collected her emotions and kept cool while repeatedly answering the same questions.

For the fifth time, Martínez asked, "What did you know about the events planned for October 30?"

"I knew nothing." Isa tried to hide her fatigue.

"No whispered pillow talk?"

"No. I tell you. I swear on my sons' lives!"

Martínez sighed. "Yes, that's what Badilla says, too. He insists you are clean and innocent."

Isabela took a moment to digest this information. Antonio cleared her. A piece of her hoped he wasn't suffering. But what was she thinking? Antonio had gotten her into this mess in the first place.

What she really hoped for was his eternal damnation.

"So Antonio's in custody," Isabela said.

"Badilla's going to jail for a long, long time. He was one of the insurgents who set fire to the police station in Jayuya." Martínez shook his head.

Isabela couldn't speak. She was appalled at what her lover had done and the danger he'd put her in. She'd loved him, had spied for him. But clearly, all he'd cared about was the cause. What a great actor he was to fool her into thinking he loved her. Her heart ached, and she wanted to double over in pain, a pain intensified by rising fury. The animal! He deserved a long jail sentence with the cockroaches, bed bugs, and rats. Isa tried to imagine endless days of the dreadful indignities she'd just endured. It would serve him right. How could she have been so blinded by lust to give herself to such a villainous man? Choking on her disgust, she launched into a coughing attack. Martínez handed her a glass of water, which she drank gratefully.

"Badilla is a dangerous man, Señora Rios. I don't think you really knew to what extent," Martínez said, suddenly conciliatory.

Isa's heart quickened. She held her breath, not daring to hope.

"We've checked your financial records, and nothing indicates you helped fund the Nationalist agenda. You've been dutifully followed by FBI agents, but without raising suspicion. I believe you're guilty of cheating on your husband but innocent of being a Nationalist. You're free to go. The warden will contact your husband to come get you."

Isabela burst into sobs of relief, her body shuddering violently. She nodded at Martínez but couldn't voice any words of thanks through her gasps for air. She was free! She was free! She stared at Martínez's back as he and his cohort exited the room. Her degradation and sorrow were all-encompassing, almost palpable on her skin. Slowly, her cries abated, and she gathered herself together. She'd jumped through one hurdle, but the worst was yet to come.

Isa sat outside the warden's office on a hard wooden chair, head bowed, waiting for Marco. Would he come? He had to know about the affair. Did her betrayal obliterate his love and concern for her? She was mortified to be seen in such a diminished state, but she needed him to get her home. *Please come, Marco.*

"Isa." Marco's voice was gruff. She couldn't bring herself to look at him. "Isa, come. Let's go." A surreptitious glance at his face told her all she needed to know. The man was destroyed, his heart shattered. His features were hard and angry, devoid of affection or compassion. His eyes wavered when Isa stood; he seemed shocked at her condition but made no move to touch her. He simply walked out of the station, expecting her to follow.

"The boys are at school, so you'll have time to clean yourself up," he said on their way home. "They can't see you like this." Isa felt a stab in her chest. His concern was for their sons, not for her.

"I'll hide my bruises and bites as best I can," she said quietly. "I don't want to spark nightmares."

"You should have thought of that before you got yourself into this sickening mess," Marco hissed at her. "They've been inconsolable. I told them you were in the hospital and couldn't have visitors until your mental state was better."

"So, they think I went insane?"

"Didn't you?" His voice was steely.

"Marco, please," Isa's eyes implored his attention. "I never meant to hurt you or the boys. I don't know what came over me. Maybe I did go a little crazy. I'm so, so sorry."

"Don't tell me you're sorry," Marco said, clearly repulsed. "You had your fun. You got your kicks. I never want to hear the words *Letras Boricuas* or the name Antonio again. You're in this car only because of our sons. If not for them, you'd be dead to me."

Isa stared out the passenger window, exhausted and drained, unable to relieve her shame and anguish through tears.

Isa showered and made herself as presentable as possible with Carmen's help, unsure of how much of the truth her beloved maid knew. The woman's concern and tenderness moved her. At least one person still loved her. Exhausted, she opted to greet the boys while tucked in bed to confirm the illness story. She never realized how luxurious clean sheets and a cozy bed in an air-conditioned room could feel. She reveled in her cleanliness and fresh nightgown. Swathed in this newly appreciated comfort, weariness got the best of her, and she drifted off to sleep.

"Mami, Mami," a hushed voice whispered in her ear while little fingers lifted her right eyelid open. "Are you awake?" Isa's other eye fluttered open, her entire field of vision taken up by Luisito's face, his nose resting on hers.

"Move over! I want to see her!" Miguelito protested and, for the first time since her arrest, Isa's face broke into a grin. Her sons!

"Come here, my beautiful boys!" Isa grabbed them both in a tight hug. "There's room for everyone."

"How are you feeling, Mami?" Luisito asked, examining her with concerned eyes. "Are you home for good?"

"You bet! I'm a little tired, that's all. The doctors took good care of me. How about you both get a book and read here in my bed while I nap some more?"

They both sprinted to get their books.

"But you've got to be quiet, right?" She called as her eyes followed them out the door. She was thrilled to be with her boys again. Never again would she put them in jeopardy. Never.

"Sí, Mami!" They both called back. If only adults were as simple to please as children, she thought, detecting Marco's shadow across the doorway.

When Papi visited Isa that evening, he looked like he'd aged ten years. She'd put him through so much! She assured him she was fine, albeit slightly battered, and they sat side by side on the patio.

"Papi, I've ruined my life. I don't know what to do." Isa covered her face with her hands.

Papi gently placed a hand on her back. "I won't pretend the situation isn't dire, mija," he said, face solemn. "Whatever possessed you to have an affair? It's unbecoming of a lady of your standing."

"Oh, but affairs are fine for gentlemen of your standing, right?" Isa shot back, stung by his judgment.

"Don't be ugly. It's different for men. We have needs."

"Sure, Papi. Whatever excuse makes you feel better. I knew cheating hurts the ones you love, yet I did it anyway. What kind of person does that make me?"

"It makes you human." Papi's eyes were kind.

"Marco can't even look at me." Isa glanced away.

"Give him time. He just discovered the love of his life loved someone else."

"Antonio put a spell on me," Isa said, her words bitter. "I never stopped loving Marco. I belong with him, but he doesn't want me back." She wiped away the tears rolling down her cheeks with the back of her hand.

"He still loves you, but he's wounded, mija," Papi said tenderly. "Give him space, and when he starts to thaw, fight for your marriage. Be strong. I let Connie go too easily, and that's *my* regret." Papi stared into the distance.

"The girls say Connie's really happy now, even dating an American who owns a clothing factory."

"I know," Papi nodded his head, resigned to the truth. "Your sisters are thriving, as well."

"See? Maybe Marco and the boys are better off without me."

"Nonsense!" he said. "The boys need their mother, and Marco loves you. Win him back."

"I'll try, but it's not going to be easy."

"I didn't say it would be." Papi kissed Isa on the forehead. "Get some rest."

The days passed slowly. Isa felt a sense of normalcy only when she was with the boys, Carmen, or Papi. She ferried her sons to school and back, helped with their homework, played with them, ate with them, and put them to bed. She was still the same old Mami to them, and she took comfort in that. Carmen had had a few choice words for Isa. It turned out she'd known of the affair; she did the laundry, after all. But Carmen's love prevailed.

Papi remained surprisingly caring and continued to offer helpful advice. But Marco gave her the silent treatment; he slept in one of the extra rooms and avoided her as much as possible. When they crossed paths around the boys, she felt his judging eyes on her, but she remained upbeat, trying to showcase her mothering skills as much as possible. There had to be a way to break through to him.

After a month of this status quo, Isa decided she'd given Marco enough breathing room. She couldn't go on like this. If there was any way to save her marriage, she had to try. She and Marco needed to talk, clear the air. With nothing to lose, she dared to take the first step.

CHAPTER 36

- Marco -
December 1950

Marco lay in the guestroom bed, staring at the ceiling in the dark. He preferred the current hollow feeling to the blinding rage and disgust that consumed him during the first weeks following Isa's arrest. His fury had slowly abated enough for him to tolerate being in her presence for short periods. They'd told the boys that Isa was still recuperating and was more comfortable sleeping alone, even though they knew that explanation wouldn't satisfy them forever.

Few people knew of Isa's arrest, and those who did believed it was due to the content she'd published in *Letras Boricuas*. Blessedly, there were no rumblings about an affair. Moving through life was difficult enough without also being publicly cuckolded. Every day he rose and went to work, trudged through the hours like a somnambulant, mustered enough presence to interact with his sons at dinner, and escaped to the guestroom for the solace of solitude. This existence was all he could muster.

He'd tried to get some work done tonight to no avail. It was late, but sleep eluded him even though the house was silent. A light knock on his door startled him.

"Marco, may I come in?" Isa entered before he could respond. She'd recovered from her physical injuries, but her haggard face bore her trauma. He felt no pity for her, and certainly did not want her in this room.

"What do you need?" Marco spat out the words.

"We need to talk." Isa turned on the bedside lamp and sat beside him. She flinched when Marco instinctively shrank from her.

"There's nothing to discuss. What's done is done."

Isa met his eyes and held his gaze. Marco looked away and willed her to leave.

"I wish I could go back in time and make different decisions, erase my actions, but I can't," she said. "I can only try to get you to believe how incredibly sorry I am to have hurt you this way. I'm asking you for forgiveness, although I'll never forgive myself."

"Even if I could forgive you, how can I ever trust you again?" Marco grimaced and shook his head.

"I'll earn your trust, Marco. Just like you earned mine again after lying to me about El Comienzo, remember? Neither of us is a saint in this marriage," Isa said.

The nerve! Marco pulled at his pajama shirt collar.

"Some sins are worse than others," he shot back, crossing his arms in front of his chest.

Isa continued softly. "Look, Marco, I will account for every second of my days moving forward if that helps. I want the boys to have their family back, their mother and father on good terms."

Marco's heart fluttered. The boys. She knew they were his soft spot. And everything aside, Isa had always been an excellent mother. After all, the boys had been the reason he'd brought her back home.

"Were the boys on your mind when you slept with that cabrón?" Though his words were gruff, Marco detected a tiny crack in his protective shell.

Isa ignored his question. "Please, let's give our sons the happy family they deserve." She leaned over, hands in prayer position.

"If we were so happy, why did you need another man's arms around you? You did exactly what you made me promise never to do to you."

"I don't know. Maybe I felt a void. Antonio and I had a common goal in the magazine. We worked together to create something meaningful, and the relationship got out of control."

"Our children are meaningful. Our marriage was meaningful. Or so I thought."

"Yes, of course! But don't you remember how you and I were going to change the world? We were supposed to work side by side for a better Puerto Rico. I gave up my dream of becoming an actress to marry you. But while you built an empire, I wilted as a housewife, just like Connie."

Marco sighed. "You had everything, Isa. I'm not going to feel sorry for you because you got a little bored. As Carmen would say, 'You made your bed. Now lie in it.' I'm tired. Goodnight."

Marco turned away from her and heard her leave, closing the door behind her. He punched his pillow. God, he had to get over his anger and resentment. For his sons.

Marco began to exchange pleasantries with Isa during the following days: how are you, good morning, thank you. This softening had an immediate effect on the boys. He hadn't realized how stressed Luisito and Miguelito had been until he saw them start to relax. Of course, they'd sensed the tension between their parents. How silly of Marco and Isa to think they could hide it from them. Encouraged by the change in his boys, Marco continued to make an effort to heal his family.

He joined Isa as she read in the living room after the boys had gone to bed one evening, testing his comfort level at being alone with her. The air didn't crackle, but the atmosphere was still far from normal.

Immediately, she began to plead with him. "Marco, is there anything I can do to turn things around?"

"I wish," he said, avoiding her gaze. "If only we could wave a magic wand and return to the way it was. I know you're sorry, but that doesn't make the hurt disappear."

Isa paused. "Tell me something, Marco. Do you still love me?"

He met her stare and spoke the truth. "Yes, God help me. I will always love you."

"And I love you," she said. "Isn't that enough? Let's grow and nurture our love."

"It might be too late for that." Marco almost gasped at realizing he needed the opposite to be true. With every cell in his body, he wanted his life back.

"No. No, it's not," Isa shook her head. "Give me a chance. No, give me twenty chances! Give me twenty dates to prove that our love is still strong, that it can survive this storm. It's only fair. I gave *you* the same opportunity."

"Ay, Isa. I don't know."

"Please, Marco. Please. For the boys."

Marco wavered. He had little hope that life could go back to how it'd been, but perhaps they could forge a new normal. He owed it to his sons to try.

"Very well, twenty chances. Make them count," he said.

Isa beamed at him. For the first time since her arrest, Marco went to bed feeling hopeful.

Marco had considered divorce, like Julia had suggested, but he couldn't reconcile throwing away the past fourteen years. Isa was woven into the fabric of his being. Would it be possible to extricate himself? And was that what he wanted, for the world to know he'd failed at marriage? Whatever reason they gave for divorce, the truth would eventually come out. They'd be the talk of the town.

Besides, as much as he tried, he couldn't imagine life without her. And the boys needed Isa. He must set aside his anguish for them. Something or someone needed to give. Sure, he'd go along with Isa's courting idea. Maybe it would help him put his feelings into perspective, help him make the right decision.

On their first date, Isa took Marco kite flying, just like he'd taken her all those years ago. He was amused that she'd even made the kite herself. He couldn't help but smile as she ran around like a lunatic trying to get it to fly, finally succeeding, but not before sweat stained her blouse. They carefully avoided serious conversation and talked only about their sons. The outing hadn't moved his forgiveness needle, but it had been civil, bordering on enjoyable. On the second date, she opted for a more high-end experience with dinner and a show at the Caribe Hilton. She took him to Ponce to tour the city of her birth, to El Yunque for lunch, to Isla Verde for a dip in the ocean, and to a tiny restaurant in Hato Rey that made the best alcapurrias in the San Juan area.

With each outing, being together felt more and more natural. They reminisced, laughed, and enjoyed each other's company like in the early days of their relationship. Marco ached to touch her, to be physically affectionate, but he restrained himself. He didn't want her to know she was winning him over.

With their renewed ease came the ability to talk about subjects weightier than how Luisito was faring in math class. Out for a drink after seeing a movie one evening, Isa brought up a topic they'd yet to discuss as they sat across from each other at a small candle-lit table by the front window of a neighborhood restaurant.

"Marco, you know *Letras Boricuas* was never a platform for Nationalists, right?" Isa said in a tentative tone. Had she forgotten he never wanted to hear the name of that magazine again? He gave her an inquisitive look and let her continue. "I published all points of view, but the truth is I am pro-independence." She looked relieved at having spoken the words.

Did she think this was news to him? At least she was being honest. Marco waited before responding. A bolero played in the background, the male singer pining for lost love.

"I figured as much, although I appreciate the confession. If we're not truthful with each other, this marriage won't survive."

"While I'm at it..." Isa let her words linger. Marco didn't want to hear the rest. How much more did she expect him to handle?

"Jesus, Isa. What?"

"Remember how I wanted to teach people to read in El Fanguito when we were first married, and you wouldn't let me? I think you actually forbade it," Isa chuckled.

Marco felt his defenses go up. He nodded, wary.

"Well, I did it anyway. I helped out in that slum pretty much until the war began."

"What? When?" Marco couldn't believe his ears.

"Three mornings a week. I taught eighteen adults to read. Some were able to move out with their families." Isa's pride in her accomplishments was evident in her tone.

Marco struggled to process the information.

"Isa! I don't know what to say. You could have brought all sorts of diseases home."

"But I didn't." She shook her head with a smile. "What I brought home was a sense of satisfaction and fulfillment beyond that of being a wife and mother. I became a better woman."

Marco pondered their early years, how she'd still be washing clothes some days when he got home. Huh. Laundry hadn't taken her all day. She was just fitting it into her schedule. He felt duped yet impressed by her resourcefulness.

"I really wanted to tell you, Marco, to share my experiences there. But I knew you wouldn't understand."

"I guess not. No, I wouldn't have wanted you to continue." He would have forced her to stop, true.

"And I needed to go there. Very much."

Marco sighed. "What else don't I know?"

"That's it. No more lies, Marco. I swear it." Her voice was true.

"No more lies." Marco nodded. Relief washed over his body as he realized he believed her.

They sat in silence for a minute until Marco spoke again. "So, my little social worker independentista, promise me you'll stay on the peaceful side of the fight."

"Of course." She took a sip of her gin and tonic. "But you must admit the conditions here are forcing hordes to move to the states, and for what? Puerto Ricans don't have it any better in New York.

We're U.S. citizens with the duty to fight in wars but without the ability to vote for president. We're in limbo. I's not acceptable."

"It's a temporary situation." Marco swirled his glass of scotch. "Muñoz is working on forging a new, better-defined status. We'll be an almost-state while continuing to give American corporations the tax cuts that have helped industrialize the island."

Isa propped her elbows on the table and leaned toward him. "I like Muñoz, I really do. I think he's a good man who means well, but I don't think his 'Free Associated State' is the right solution for us."

Marco took her hand between his, caressing her for the first time since the arrest. Her skin was warm, soft as velvet, and touching her made his heart soar. "I promise you our new status will be a step in the right direction." He squeezed her hand gently to emphasize his point.

"We'll see. In the meantime, I'll vote my conscience at the polls." Isa leaned back but didn't remove her hand from his.

"It's a secret ballot, Isa. You should vote as you wish." Marco smiled at her, secure in the low numbers of PIP supporters. It wasn't likely they'd see the Independence Party win any time soon.

"No more secrets!" Isa laughed. She looked at him, head tilted and mused. "This new status will continue to increase the demand for housing, won't it?"

Marco nodded. "Solemar will be very busy and profitable in the coming years."

"At what cost, Marco?"

"What do you mean?" *Now, what's the problem?*

"I've watched you lose your respect for the poor." Isa's eyes bored into his. Marco swallowed hard. How did he explain to Isa that some deserved help more than others?

"Not at all, my love," Marco shook his head. "But there are those who try and pull themselves up and those who wallow in the mire expecting handouts. Nothing is free in life."

"Not everyone has your smarts." Isa looked at him pointedly. "Or your luck."

"Luck?" Taken aback, he released her hand.

"You have to admit you were in the right place at the right time to build your real estate empire." Isa raised her eyebrows as if challenging him to contradict her.

Marco had to agree that luck had played a part in his success, but her words still smarted. "Maybe. But I worked hard to get where I am."

"The jíbaros and the good people of El Fanguito work their fingers to the bone but can't feed their families," Isa countered.

"But that's exactly what Muñoz is trying to remedy. Our new status will provide a better life for those who work hard. You'll see, Isa. Why can't you just be patient? The world doesn't change all at once."

"Okay, then. Speaking of changing things one at a time, would it cut too much into profits to design nicer homes? I don't know how people live in those airless cement cubes you build. It's criminal."

This was the old Isa, asking to fix a simple and specific thing to improve people's lives. It was a wish he could fulfill. "None of them are complaining, but if it makes you happy, I'll see what I can do," Marco smiled, took her hand again and kissed it.

When they got home, Isa gave Marco a questioning look before checking on the boys. He knew what she was asking, and God help him, he nodded. When Isa came to him in a sexy silk negligee, he held the bedcovers up, and she slid in beside him. Blood pounded through his veins, engorging his penis, and inciting a level of desire he didn't know was possible. When she took his hand and placed it between her legs, he almost recoiled. Was this something she'd learned with Antonio? But as she gently, and then more urgently, moved his hand on her mound, he became mesmerized by the ecstasy on her face. After that, he was helpless in her arms as she took full charge of the seduction, straddling him so he could enter her and then moving to a slow and steady rhythm. His head spun at the pleasure, obliterating all thoughts of where Isa had learned to make love in this abandoned and wondrous manner. What did it matter, if nobody knew and she was his again?

The next day, Marco moved back into the master bedroom. They never officially finished the twenty dates. Instead, they entered a frenzy of lovemaking rivaling their newlywed days. Marco was mortified to learn he hadn't pleased Isa all these years. He wished she'd shown him the way sooner. If she had, maybe she wouldn't have allowed Antonio to intrude on their marriage. Isa never mentioned the man, acted as if he hadn't existed, which was fine with Marco. Through his contacts, Marco had investigated Antonio's fate and was gratified to learn he'd been sentenced to life imprisonment with hard labor. Let the cabrón rot in jail. He was out of their lives forever. Marco had his wife and family back.

CHAPTER 37

- Isabela -
May 1951

Isabela signed her finished application to La Upi with a flourish. She'd begin her undergraduate studies in the fall and aimed to attend La Upi's Graduate School of Social Work upon graduation. She was thirty-seven years old, but Beatriz had finally convinced her she still had plenty of life left in her to make meaningful contributions to society. Isa had advocated for her sisters, supporting Connie's insistence they be college educated. Now Mati was about to enter law school at New York University, while Rosie majored in education at City College. It was time for Isa to practice what she preached.

Marco ended up being surprisingly supportive of her new direction. Their newly minted policy of honesty allowed him to express his continued discomfort with having a working wife. But after lengthy discussion, they decided her need to help people was greater than any reservations he had. Women were making their mark in social work, journalism, law, and even politics. Why the mayor of San Juan, Doña Felisa Rincón de Gautier, was a woman, albeit a muñocista, but female nonetheless.

Isa marveled at the amount of heartache Marco and she could have avoided had they been open and truthful from the start. Her need to be more than a wife and mother, her sexual dissatisfaction, their diverging political views, the house, Solemar's money troubles, his disturbing turn from those he set out to help—all these issues had silently plagued their marriage. In hindsight, it was hard to say why neither brought up the tough topics. Perhaps to not hurt the other, yet causing untold grief instead.

Isa had recounted her incarceration to Marco in great detail, appalled at how she and the other prisoners had been treated. Rumors abounded that Albizu, still held at La Princesa, was being tortured with radiation that left burns all over his body and caused severe swelling in his hands and legs. Nobody knew for sure; he was still awaiting trial. The man was a murderer, but he didn't deserve that kind of horrifying mistreatment. Antonio, she knew, would spend the rest of his life in jail. Did he deserve such a harsh sentence? Maybe, maybe not. She'd tried to forgive herself for allowing him to seduce her, had opened herself to accepting more of the blame for the affair. But that was still a work in progress. She preferred not to think about Antonio at all. Why dwell in the past when the future promised fulfillment and possibly joy?

Isa gathered her application materials and placed them in a manila folder. She'd personally drop everything off at the admissions office that afternoon. She imagined herself studying alongside her sons while they did their homework come September and smiled. But before that scene could become a reality, she had another important mission to complete.

María Cárdenas. Isa had seen her mother's name on her birth certificate, but when Jorge Guzmán said it with such disdain during her interrogation, it was the first time she'd heard the name spoken. It was a melodic name given to a woman who'd made a mistake and who didn't deserve derision from anyone, much less that miserable man. Thankfully, Guzmán's scorn had awakened Isa's spirit, given her enough strength to endure the subsequent hours of questioning. It had also given her plenty of food for thought.

A young and careless Papi had seduced her mother, who'd fallen hard for his charm. Now more than ever, Isa understood how easily a woman can lose sight of what's right. Like mother, like daughter.

Isa understood why María's mother, her grandmother, had brought her to the Soto house as a newborn. The woman must have been crazed with grief at the loss of her daughter and, likely too poor to feed a new child, did the best she could by giving her to the Sotos to raise. With that one action, she'd afforded Isa every advantage yet deprived her of knowing her true self. But not forever.

According to Carmen, María had come from Barrio Guaraguao in the Ponce mountains. It was a starting place, and with any luck, she'd find relatives still living there or at least people who knew where they'd gone. Marco had been up for the adventure, partly to please her and partly, she suspected, to check on his wife's origins. She'd pictured him praying they wouldn't find anything too untoward or inheritable, like a history of insanity.

Marco and Isa set off on a bright summer Saturday morning, driving first to Ponce and then north to Guaraguao. As Marco slowly navigated the curves of Route 123, the old farm-to-market road the Spanish built, Isa took in the lush scenery. The higher they climbed, the more mountains appeared in the distance, emerald green and majestic. The narrow kelly green leaves of the Guaraguao trees, which gave the barrio its name, shaded the landscape. The air smelled of sweet fruit and rich earth. Every so often, she could hear water streaming underneath the foliage, a brook intent on serving flora and fauna alike.

Marco pulled over at a cluster of wooden houses, shacks really, to inquire about the Cárdenas family. There, they learned from a toothless old man that Doña Cárdenas, presumably Isa's grandmother, still lived just a few kilometers up the road. Like a child who'd found the prize in a scavenger hunt, Isa was elated. Then, almost immediately, her flight instinct kicked in. Adrenaline coursed through her body, making her shake. She felt light-headed, unmoored, and tripped over her feet, walking back to the car.

"Whoa," said Marco, grabbing her by the upper arm to prevent her from falling. He took a close look at her and said, "Are you alright? You look whiter than tembleque."

"What if she doesn't want to see me? She never tried to find me.

Maybe I should let sleeping dogs lie." Isa picked at her fingers and tried to calm her breath.

Marco helped her into the car.

"Amor, please don't worry. We've come this far, and if you leave empty-handed, you are no less blessed than you were this morning." He turned the key in the ignition. "Let's find your roots."

Marco's hand felt comforting on her leg as they drove toward her past. They followed a dirt road off the main drag, like the old man had instructed, and maneuvered around potholes and ditches until they reached a one-room clapboard house elevated off the ground by wooden stilts with a thatch, not even tin, roof. It sat beneath a wide flamboyán tree in full bloom, ablaze with red and orange flowers. An ancient woman, a lifetime of hardship and disappointment visible in her gnarled hands and craggy face, stared into the distance from a rocking chair on the balcony. She turned her head at the sound of their car.

Isa's heart beat a crescendo inside her chest. Slowly, as if her body had a will of its own, she got out of the car and took several steps toward the old woman before stopping. The woman reached toward her cane with shaking hands and leaned on it to stand up. She was tall and angular, with thinning grey hair gathered in a long braid. She squinted her rheumy eyes at Isa and took an unsteady step forward. She opened her mouth and closed it before opening it again and letting out a hoarse croak.

"María?" She reached out to Isa with one hand, simultaneously smiling and frowning.

Isabela broke into sobs.

"María?" The woman cocked her head in confusion.

"No, Doña," Isa caught her breath long enough to say. "Soy Isabela. La hija de María."

"¡Ay, ay, ay! ¡Virgen Santa! ¡Dios mío!" Tears coursed down the woman's face. "Pues ven acá, mija." Isa's grandmother opened her arms wide, and Isa ran toward her embrace.

CHAPTER 38

- Marco -
August 1952

Almost two years after Isa's arrest, Marco's wounds had scarred, the pain a dull memory. His relationship with Isa had never been better. Their communication was open, and when their opinions differed, they agreed to disagree. Her studies and her newfound roots fed her soul on a deeper level than Marco could ever understand, and he was in full support of it all. She'd even influenced his approach to housing, resulting in improved design and functionality.

Even Julia had moved on from her venomous anger toward Isa as soon as she and Eduardo adopted a newborn baby girl. They named her Susana after her grandmother, who made her exquisite little dresses. Motherhood had softened and humbled Julia; she even sought baby advice from Isa these days. Marco prayed that from now on, she'd mind her own business and stay out of his marriage.

Isa had finally persuaded Don Gabriel to move in with them by arguing that he'd have more money to send Connie and the girls if he wasn't paying rent. To Marco's complete amazement, he liked having the old man around. Part of him suspected that Don Gabriel moved in so he could keep a close eye on Isa. Every night when Marco got home from work, Don Gabriel gave him a curt nod as if to indicate all was well. Marco had come to trust that Isa wouldn't stray again, but to be frank, he welcomed Don Gabriel's extra assurances.

The Nationalists had been suppressed, most of them arrested and serving long jail sentences, like Antonio. Shortly before the uprisings, Muñoz had gotten Truman to approve the Federal Relations Act, which would make Puerto Rico a "Free Associated State" and allow it to have its own constitution. Marco agreed with those who thought this policy had instigated the violent events of 1950. Blood spilled needlessly because Puerto Ricans had just voted in a referendum to approve the Act, so its widespread support was clear, and its implementation assured as soon as Congress ratified it.

Out for pizza at La Cueva del Chicken Inn, Marco and Isa tried to explain the new political status to their sons, who sat across from them in one of the restaurant's booths.

"What does 'Free Associated State' mean, Papi?" Luisito's forehead was a wrinkled map of confusion.

"Yeah, the Americans say we're going to be a 'commonwealth?' What's the difference?" asked Miguelito. At age fourteen, he followed the news but was confused.

"They're two terms for the same thing. We're part of the United States, but with our own government and constitution. We have a lot more autonomy than before," Marco said, grabbing a piece of garlic bread from the center of the table. "Oh, my God! This is so delicious!"

Isa passed the basket of bread to one boy, then the other. "Don't be fooled, hijos," she said. "We're only a U.S. territory. In fact, we're more officially under their thumb. Call it what you want, but this status is just another link in the chain of colonialism." She flopped her hands on the table.

"How can you say that?" Marco protested, giving her a playful side nudge. "This is the most independent we've been since our Spanish days."

"How are we independent? The president and Congress still have ultimate control, yet we don't have a voice in electing them." Isa was having none of his lightheartedness.

"But Mami. Puerto Ricans vote." Luisito looked at his mother as if he was stating the obvious.

"We vote for our own governor and for representatives in our Puerto Rican Congress," Isa answered her son. "We don't vote for president, and we don't have a voting representative in the U.S. Congress. No one with any power is looking out for our interests in Washington."

"Didn't the American founding fathers fight against taxation without representation? We learned that in school," Luisito said. "Wasn't that the whole reason for their revolution?"

"We don't pay federal taxes, so it's a trade-off, boys. There's no taxation *nor* representation," Marco said with a chuckle, trying again to inject some levity into the conversation.

"So that makes it okay? And what about our culture?" asked Isa, decidedly not in a playful mood. She leaned toward the boys, her expression resolute. "You boys must always remember your roots, everything that makes you Puerto Rican. Don't ever lose the stain of the plantain."

"There's no way to lose that!" Marco was again met with a solid wall of seriousness. He put an arm around Isa; it was time to appease her. "Our culture is strong, Isa. Boricuas are Boricuas through and through."

"¡Yo soy Boricua!" Miguelito exclaimed.

"Me, too!" added his brother, pointing at his chest.

"That's right, hijos," Marco said.

"Time will tell whether our culture will live on, and I, for one, will remain very vigilant," Isa said.

Marco changed the subject. "And boys, with the new status, the industrial incentives remain in place, so many more American companies will set up factories and other facilities en la isla del encanto," Marco said.

"That means we'll need more houses, right Papi?" Luisito asked.

"That's right! More business for Solemar. We're going to build a high-rise with fancy apartments next. Just like in New York, except with a beautiful ocean view."

"As long as it doesn't look like an ugly cube. Please promise me it will be attractive, Marco." Isa looked at him beseechingly.

"My darling wife, haven't our housing designs improved significantly?" Marco said, laughing. "We're trying. I promised to factor
in form and function, and I admit you were right. The results are
stupendous."

"Yes, I've been pleased. Our people deserve the best, right boys?"

"Puerto Rico *is* the best!" Miguelito affirmed as the waiter placed
a steaming sausage pizza in the middle of their table. He grabbed
a piece with a long string of mozzarella cheese still connecting it to
the rest of the pie and took a bite before his mother could stop him.

"¡Ay, ay, ay!" he shouted, fanning his mouth, eyes watering. "It
burned my tongue. Too hot!"

"That's what you get for being greedy," Isa said, handing him a
glass of ice water. "Drink this. And then wait a while. God rewards
those who wait, as Carmen would say."

"How many dichos does Carmen know?" Luisito asked.

"All of them," Isa said rolling her eyes mischievously, much to
her sons' delight. They laughed so hard that Marco hoped Carmen
couldn't hear them back at the house. After all, she was as much a
part of his family as his wife and sons, and nothing would ever hurt
his family again.

They'd come far, he and Isa, Marco thought as he chewed his
pizza. He remembered when she held no political beliefs, and now
here she was, a full-fledged independentista. He disagreed with her
viewpoint but respected it. Anyway, she was an intelligent person,
so he fully expected her to eventually come around to seeing things
his way again. A politically unified household would be much better
for the boys.

In the meantime, everything he'd told his sons was true. American manufacturers were flocking to the island, and the need for
housing continued to explode. Solemar had grown to such an extent
that he and Sammy had delegated the day-to-day running of the
business to several managers and only focused on big-picture decisions. This gave him more time with Isa and his remarkable boys.
It felt good to reap the fruits of one's labor. A modern Puerto Rico

had arrived, one he'd helped craft. With continued support from the U.S., the possibilities for his island were unlimited. Marco looked around at his family, smiled contentedly, and helped himself to another slice of pizza.

EPILOGUE

The Hurricane 2017

Luis Rios flicked the light switch as he'd done every morning since María had pounded his island seven days ago. Still no electricity. He held his breath as he relieved himself in the large jug he'd been using for that purpose, but the acrid stench of stale urine still hit his nostrils with prickly force. His seventy-nine-year-old bones ached, and his mind reeled at facing another day of no communication with the outside world. He'd been stuck in this tenth-floor apartment because he knew he could make it down the stairs, but no way could he climb back up. And where would he go? WKJB's reports—the only station he could get—were clear: the island was devastated.

He sat on the spacious balcony and turned on the radio. Thank God he had an ample supply of batteries. His parents had taught him how to prepare for a hurricane, and he'd weathered a few. But none like this. He'd filled the bathtubs and any available vessel with water, had stocked up on canned foods, and gotten diesel gas for the generator, which he used sparingly and only in the evenings. Despite entreaties from his children to evacuate, he'd insisted on weathering the storm in his apartment, where he could see the ocean from every window. They were all in the States, his three kids, surely worried sick about him, but phone lines were down, as were cell phone towers. He was completely incommunicado. *Evacuate. Ha!* What was he going to do? Sleep in a cot in the Roberto Clemente Coliseum? *No, thank you.*

He turned the radio up, girding himself to listen to the desperate souls calling in from the States and from pockets on the island with cell service. They begged for news about missing relatives, for rescue, for water, for food. Their helplessness and his inability to come to their aid ate at his core.

He'd been lucky. He'd stayed in his apartment, knowing the building would protect him. His father had constructed it—Solemar's first high rise in Condado—and named it "Solemar" after the company he'd founded. Luis had forged a career at Solemar alongside his brother Miguel, but none of their children had been interested in continuing the legacy. They'd studied in American colleges and scattered to the winds. They'd left the company in the hands of Sammy's son, who embezzled it into bankruptcy. Thank God Papi hadn't lived to see *that*.

Miguel had died a decade ago, and sometimes Luis wished he had as well. Pain pierced his soul when he let himself think about his island's financial, and now physical, destruction.

Papi had been so excited when Puerto Rico became a Commonwealth of the United States. Mami, not so much, but the two grew to tolerate each other's opinions. Muñoz's Operation Bootstrap brought hundreds of American companies to the island through the 1970s, much to his father's delight. Luis was glad Papi had lived to see modernization and prosperity reign during those decades and thankful he'd died in the late 1980s without witnessing the aftermath. Because when the incentives ran out, the Americans packed up with zero remorse, creating an unemployment crisis and a significant tax shortfall. Seeing that would have killed Papi, all his dreams turned to rubble.

The government's brilliant idea, instead of adjusting the budget, had been to issue bonds. They borrowed money from Wall Street, and when they couldn't pay it back, the banks allowed them to borrow more. María had hit an island with a debt of $74 billion and an infrastructure in ruins. The Americans, in whom Papi had held such faith, had abandoned them decades ago. According to the news, they weren't stepping in to help now either.

Luis wondered whether Puerto Rico would have fared better if the independence movement had ever gathered real steam. But much to his mother's chagrin, PIP party support percentages remained in the single digits throughout her lifetime and the real political fight was always between statehood and the status quo.

Luis stood up and sighed. He checked on the towels he'd draped around the apartment to dry. Even with the storm shutters in place, leaving him in the dark during María's lashing, water managed to leak in. He'd sopped it up, but the towels refused to dry in the relentless humidity. A few showed signs of mold. He thought about aiming a fan at them, but his diesel supply was too precious. According to the radio, people were waiting in line for entire days to get gas. In any case, hospitals should have priority, in his opinion. The sick would die without electricity; he was simply inconvenienced.

At least he lived in the city. There was destruction, but not obliteration, as reports from out on the island indicated. The beautiful mountain towns hadn't fared well. So many homes destroyed, so many lives lost. Thank God for the Puerto Rican spirit. His only neighbor on this floor had fled to Florida before the storm, but he'd had visits from several friends on other floors, making sure he was okay. They'd also enjoyed a few community meals, pooling their resources for the benefit of all. None had heard from the outside world except by radio broadcast. One had trekked to SuperMax only to find empty shelves.

He peered out the balcony toward Washington Street, which was no longer flooded. The road was still a minefield of debris, yet every so often, a car would venture down. Likely relatives checking on loved ones. All the trees, bushes, and palms were bare. Where had the seagulls and coquís gone? Nature was silent. Everything stood still.

Luis opened a can of Campbell's Chunky Beef soup and ate it cold. It was preferable to lighting his tiny propane stove. It reminded him too much of the bitter smell of diesel that permeated the evening air, his own generator included. But at least he had some power. Most suffered in complete darkness.

He and his neighbors wondered when the Americans would

arrive. Where was the help? The delay wouldn't have surprised Mami, but Papi would have been beside himself. Would any state be in such dire straits an entire week after a natural disaster? Weren't they United States citizens? Surely it was only a matter of time. He needed, now, for Papi to have been right. So he sat on his balcony and waited.

AUTHOR'S NOTE

Historical fiction authors create stories based on actual events. Isa and Marco's story is fiction, but the events they live through and some of the characters in their story are very real. All speeches attributed to Luis Muñoz Marín and Pedro Albizu Campus are direct quotes. Carlos Chardón, Ángel Ramos, Jaime Benítez, Teodoro Moscoso, and Ángel Viera Martínez were important players in the Puerto Rico of the last century. However, I've imagined all their dialogue.

While researching this book, I amassed quite a library of books on Puerto Rican history and culture. If you're interested in reading more about the island's history, I recommend any book by Fernando Picó. *History of Puerto Rico: A Panorama of its People* is excellent for starters. I also recommend *War Against All Puerto Ricans* by Nelson A. Denis and *Tiempos Revueltos* by Vionette G. Negretti. Puerto Ricans love their dichos, and I thank Pablo Rodríguez Rosado for amassing them all in *De Boca en Boca*.

Isa and Marco's courtship was inspired by the story of my grandparents, Margarita Gutiérrez Feliciano and José Manuel Feliciano. He was poor, she was a debutante, and her father disapproved of their love. My great-grandfather tried hard to sabotage the lovers, but they prevailed. They honeymooned in El Yunque, he banned viandas, they had a modernist home, and later lived in the Solemar building, where I grew up.

Carlos Gardel indeed rode around San Juan in my great-grandfather's car, and so my grandmother met the singer several times. She always spoke of him with great reverence. See margaritabarresi. com for photos of them together. Like Isa, my grandmother went on a fake hunger strike, but her cousin kept her well-fed. She'd wanted to be an actress and loved declaiming poetry. However, Abuela was not an independentista, revolutionary or adulterer.

My Abuelo hails from Yabucoa, and I give the town a big shout-out. I have fond memories of playing in the countryside there as a child. Abuelo attended UPR, taught there, and served as comptroller. He counted Jaime Benítez as one of his best friends; Benítez wrote Abuelo's eulogy.

Muñoz and his wife, Doña Inéz, were also family friends. In the 1940s, Abuelo answered Muñoz's call to civil service and worked for the Puerto Rico Land Authority, Metropolitan Authority of Autobuses (AMA), and the Aqueducts and Sewers Authority. He subsequently salvaged several companies from bankruptcy—including Cerveceria India and Indulac Dairy, both still going strong today—and founded the Caguas Federal Savings Bank in the 1960s.

My research uncovered a slew of interesting facts and stories that did not make it into this book. I expand on several of them on my website, margaritabarresi.com.

ACKNOWLEDGMENTS

It takes a village to write a book, and I now understand why author acknowledgments are always so long. So, to my village:

Thank you, Grub Street in Boston, for offering classes and programs that enabled me to hone my craft. My deepest gratitude to the second cohort of the Novel Generator Program, where this novel got its start and where I found the best writing group I could have hoped for, "The Novel Gener-Laters": Raquel Pidal, Rose Himber Howse, Lauren Clarke-Mason, Susan Larkin, and Kate Burcak—all stellar wordsmiths.

Many, many, many thanks to Lisa Borders, instructor extraordinaire and even better editor, for all her developmental help and consistent encouragement. Who knows, I could still get that Oprah seal she envisioned on my cover. Thank you, Ainslie Campbell and Anne Gao, who took my manuscript on as students in Raquel Pidal's graduate-level novel editing class at Emerson College. You helped me get to the next level. Feedback from Barbara Rosenberg and Ciara Duggan got me further, and Asata Radcliffe propelled me to the final level. You are all highly skilled editors and a pleasure to work with.

Thank you, first readers, Marta López Moerson, Veronica De-Greiff, Nina Barresi, Leah Barresi, Andrew Barresi and all the Gener-Laters. Your insights were invaluable. Katherine Mariaca-Sullivan, you opened my eyes to a new direction for Isa, and I am beyond grateful for the result.

Aida Guzmán, what would I have done without your research help when I couldn't be in Puerto Rico? The details in this novel would be half as rich. Huge thanks to Harvard's Widener Library, the University of Connecticut's Thomas J. Dodd Research Center, the Center for Puerto Rican Studies at Hunter College, the University of Puerto Rico Library, and the Archivo General de Puerto Rico. I thank

Cruz M. Ortiz Cuadra for answering all my food questions and archaeologist Raymond Feliciano of the National Forest Service for all the historic El Yunque information. Also, my appreciation to Libros 787 for always having exactly the book I needed for my research.

Although they are no longer with us, my grandparents inspired this story. Gracias, Abuela y Abuelo.

So many friends put up with my whining about writing, pushed me to get my butt in the chair, and never stopped believing I could do it. Thank you, Tricia Desrocher, Jeanne Attaya, Mary Lou Splaine, Pam Veerman, Sue Mansfield, RaeAnn York, Michele Penta and Anne Danehy. A special shout out to Tricia for finding that fabulous thirty-minute sand timer!

Barresi clan, you are the best support group imaginable, and I can finally answer you when you ask, "When can I read your book?" I adore you all to pieces. And all my love to the most ardent cheerleaders of all: my daughters Leah and Nina, and my husband, Andrew. I told Andrew I wanted to write a book when we were on our first date more than thirty-four years ago. That's a dream with real lasting power, but I could never have realized it without his love, unwavering support, and blind belief in me. Thank you, Andrew. As I said in the dedication, this book is for you, for everything you are to me and everything you do.

A huge thank you to everyone at Atmosphere Press for your tremendous support, for making the publishing process so enjoyable, and for giving me the cover of my dreams. So glad I found you!

And, finally, thank you, reader. I hope this novel brought to life a little piece of Puerto Rico for you. And if you're Boricua, ¡Wepa!

ABOUT ATMOSPHERE PRESS

Atmosphere Press is an independent, full-service publisher for excellent books in all genres and for all audiences. Learn more about what we do at atmospherepress.com.

We encourage you to check out some of Atmosphere's latest releases, which are available at Amazon.com and via order from your local bookstore:

Icarus Never Flew 'Round Here, by Matt Edwards

COMFREY, WYOMING: Maiden Voyage, by Daphne Birkmeyer

The Chimera Wolf, by P.A. Power

Umbilical, by Jane Kay

The Two-Blood Lion, by Nick Westfield

Shogun of the Heavens: The Fall of Immortals, by I.D.G. Curry

Hot Air Rising, by Matthew Taylor

30 Summers, by A.S. Randall

Delilah Recovered, by Amelia Estelle Dellos

A Prophecy in Ash, by Julie Zantopoulos

The Killer Half, by JB Blake

Ocean Lessons, by Karen Lethlean

Unrealized Fantasies, by Marilyn Whitehorse

The Mayari Chronicles: Initium, by Karen McClain

Squeeze Plays, by Jeffrey Marshall

JADA: Just Another Dead Animal, by James Morris

Hart Street and Main: Metamorphosis, by Tabitha Sprunger

Karma One, by Colleen Hollis

Ndalla's World, by Beth Franz

Adonai, by Arman Isaya

ABOUT THE AUTHOR

Raised in Puerto Rico by her grandparents, **MARGARITA BARRESI** grew up hearing stories about the "good old days"—the genesis for this, her first novel. She studied public relations at Boston University, and after a successful career in marketing communications, now devotes her time to writing. Her essays have been published in several literary magazines and compilations. Margarita lives in the suburbs north of Boston with her husband and two Puerto Rican cats, Luna and Rico.

Printed in the USA
CPSIA information can be obtained
at www.ICGtesting.com
CBHW031747201123
1999CB00003B/8